ACROSS DECADES OF TURBULENCE . . . WOMEN WHO DARED TO BELIEVE IN LOVE

RACHEL DA SILVA—She sailed from a Portuguese convent to a life of brutal bondage as a Brazilian planter's wife . . . shamed by his brutal lust . . . doomed to endure the tyrant's bed . . . until a renegade's love set her free.

RENATA AVELAR—She was a child given by fate into the hands of a grotesque leper, who was also Brazil's most famous sculptor. She would become a women driven by destiny into the arms of a bandit, to risk a life of danger for the rewards of love.

CATERINA DOS SANTOS—She was born an outcast with only her incomparable beauty to help her survive . . . and the daring to use it to acquire a fortune. Her money would build a business empire, but her desires would become an obsession that could break her heart.

MARILIA DOS SANTOS—She was the daughter of a mother she loved for her tenderness but hated for the betrayal that drove her to a man who promised her only the passion of the night . . . when she needed him forever.

Other Avon Books by
Jeanne Williams

THE CAVE DREAMERS
THE HEAVEN SWORD

Avon Books are available at special quantity discounts for bulk purchases for sales promotions, premiums, fund raising or educational use. Special books, or book excerpts, can also be created to fit specific needs.

For details write or telephone the office of the Director of Special Markets, Avon Books, Dept. FP, 1790 Broadway, New York, New York 10019, 212-399-1357.

So Many Kingdoms

Jeanne Williams

AVON
PUBLISHERS OF BARD, CAMELOT, DISCUS AND FLARE BOOKS

With love, admiration, and gratitude, this book is dedicated to Barbara and Don Worcester, who have not only enriched the narratives, but in many ways and for many years have enriched my life.

AVON BOOKS
A division of
The Hearst Corporation
1790 Broadway
New York, New York 10019

Copyright © 1986 by Jeanne Williams
Published by arrangement with the author
Library of Congress Catalog Card Number: 85-91537
ISBN: 0-380-75091-0

First Avon Printing: July 1986

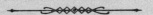

BOOK I
To Make a Killing

"The sun, the moon and the stars would have disappeared long ago, had they been within the reach of predatory humans."

—Havelock Ellis

Marilia held the dead child. She knew it was a dream, but she could not wake up or look away from the thin, heart-shaped face, shriveled like wind-blasted fruit. The great staring eyes were green. Strangely, in the dream, the child seemed to be a young Caterina, Marilia's own mother, though Caterina dos Santos, darling of some of Brazil's richest and most influential men, had most certainly neither died nor stayed in the drought-starved backlands where she'd been born.

Green eyes showed that somewhere in this little girl's family a red mother had quickened with a white man's seed. She was *cabocla,* that mix of Indian with Portuguese or other white fortune-seekers, with often a strain from Africans brought to replace Indian slaves who died too easily on the vast sugar plantations of the sixteenth and seventeenth centuries, the gold and diamond mines of the eighteenth and nineteenth.

Of the families whose forebears had come to Brazil over four hundred years ago, even the palest and most aristocratic were sure to have, from far back, Indian or African blood, often both. But that gave them no feeling of kinship with children like the one into whom Marilia, now in her dream as in life three years before, vainly tried to breathe life. Janos, Marilia's husband, wrenched the pitiful huddle away from her and tossed it on an offal pile, which took on distorted, broken shapes of women, men and children whose mouths, eyes and desperate fingers were full of dust from seared croplands and cattle ranges.

Some were not quite dead. They stretched out pleading hands. *Flagelados:* scourged ones. For centuries these folk of the parched northeastern backlands had flocked to any crazed mystic who promised a better life, yearned for a messiah to ease their burdens, gone anywhere in hope of work—to Amazon rubber hells, the golden slime of cacao

3

plantations, the slums of cities. They starved by the thousands. Countless *nordestino* babies died in their first year, and many survivors were stunted in body and brain.

Janos, the handsome masterful husband Marilia had worshiped since he'd begun courting her when she was sixteen and whom she'd married at eighteen, frowned at the stains on her clothes. "Take a shower and change your clothes, darling. You can't go mucking around these garbage heaps."

He tried to drag her away from the baby girl. Struggling away from him, Marilia woke, a splintering pain vibrating through her head. She was bathed in icy sweat.

During her four years of marriage, mostly spent in Janos' elegant São Paulo mansion or his townhouse facing Copacabana Beach in Rio de Janeiro, she had been insulated, whisked around by limousine to go visiting or shopping. But on her first trip to Janos' vast holdings in the *sertão* or backlands of Bahia, she asked for a horse and went exploring, stopped at a vaqueiro's hut, found the starved child.

She recalled grimly how she had carried the little girl to Janos, sure that if he saw, if he understood, he couldn't go ahead with what he'd come to do—evict twenty of these families from their small tenant ranches so he could put in foreign-financed irrigation to raise luxury crops for export to Europe.

He had forcibly taken the child from her, handed the corpse to a servant to dispose of, and thrust a stiff drink at her. "Sweetheart, I'd give anything if you hadn't seen that. But you've got to realize that these people are breeding a race of subhumans—wretched creatures who get worse with each generation. There's no land or food or work for them. If they all lived, well . . ."

She couldn't believe the man who loved her so tenderly, who was so lavish with her, could say these things. "Janos, that baby—" She fought for control and gazed imploringly into crystalline eyes, which for the first time since she'd known him, were hard as diamonds. "Don't make these people leave! You're rich enough without driving them off their land."

"My land. I don't need them."

"But you can't trash people like worn-out tools."

He shrugged and his mouth hardened. "Marilia, I won't have you interfering with my business affairs. Stick to your charity benefits. I'll give these tenants train tickets to the Trans-Amazon. They can take up homesteads there. There's nothing for them here."

Her husband had changed into a stranger. Or she had never known him. Marilia put down the unfinished drink. "Janos, my own family was like these people. Leave them in their homes. It's so little to you and so much to them."

He would not. They quarreled. Her eyes were opened. Food stuck in her throat. Luxury was hateful. When the exiled *caboclos* were piled into open trucks like so many cattle, she gave them all the food, clothing and cash she could scavenge, then packed a small bag, leaving her jewelry and everything Janos had given her. She used her credit card to fly to Belo Horizonte. Caterina met her there and took her home to Ouro Prêto, the beautiful old colonial silver town nestled in the hills of central Brazil.

Bitter as she was at her mother, Marilia had to credit Caterina with not trying to persuade her to go back to Janos.

Dressing inside the mosquito netting, Marilia grimaced to remember: Caterina had paid for her divorce and fended Janos off when he tried to see Marilia. Caterina had paid for Marilia's agronomy studies at the University of North Carolina's special arid lands agriculture program. Marilia knew she owed her mother everything, but that very debt added to her devastating anger at Caterina.

Not because of what Janos had flung at her during their divorce—that Marilia's father wasn't dead but unknown, one of the men who had helped build Brasilia, the new capital deep in the backlands.

Juscelino Kubitschek had rushed to finish that astounding feat before the end of his presidency, since no administration completed the projects of the last one. It had drawn workers from the whole country, but especially from the starved *sertão*. It had lured women like Marilia's mother, who was long bereft of her kindly foster mother and determined to do more with her beauty than continue yielding it to the fat old rancher who'd had her virginity, or let it fade in a vaqueiro's hut.

Men of every color paid high to feel a woman's softness for a few minutes, find comfort in the frantic illusional place where white buildings sprouted almost overnight from the red mud. One of those nameless men, one of those *candangos*, was Marilia's father.

By the time she could no longer take customers without endangering the fetus, Caterina had saved enough to buy a house in Ouro Prêto. She caught the eye of a wealthy, aging man who helped her make shrewd investments. She loved him tenderly, the wise, kind father she'd never had, and mourned him when he died. He left her so comfortably situated that she need never have taken another man, but she had a lusty hunger for life.

She was discreet. Marilia never suspected that Janos had been her mother's lover, but he hurled the fact at her along with the taunt that the indulgent old man Marilia remembered vaguely hadn't been her father.

Marilia had never blamed Caterina for escaping the bleak *sertão* in the only way she could. And after the first shock, she took a certain defiant pride in having an unknown father, in being so perfectly a child of Brazil. What she could not forgive her mother was fostering Janos' courtship, handing Marilia over to a former lover. Oh, Marilia understood why. Having known Janos since his university days at the School of Mines, Caterina knew he would guard his wife, provide her with everything, give her a glittering life. And he was a skillful, ardent lover. Marilia wondered how much weight Caterina had assigned to that. Furious because he'd been her mother's lover, Marilia felt as if he'd bedded them at the same time.

She hadn't seen Janos since the divorce. On her return from North Carolina six months ago, Marilia had taken a job with the government bureau that was trying to alleviate the Northeast's chronic problems. But she'd quit when she saw that all the money, including aid from the United States, went to enriching men like Janos.

She'd been offered a job with a private foundation that was helping *flagelados* homestead in the newly opened Amazon basin or on the high central plains. The job was just right for her. The foundation had sent her to this remote two-year-old settlement on a tributary of the Amazon. Ordinarily, families and neighbors tried to migrate as a body, taking up adjoining homesteads, but these villagers were mostly from other failed colonies and were strangers, united by a need to survive and a desperate resolve not to be driven on again, losing what they had claimed from the jungle so painfully.

It was like watching people sliding down a cliff, clutching at a ledge before it crumbled, slipping to the next ledge before that, too, gave way.

Having gotten into loose white cotton trousers and shirt, Marilia sank down on the hammock till her dizziness subsided. Of all days to get sick, why did she have to do it today when she was going to confront Janos? She'd have believed her illness was plain dread except that she had an unmistakable fever.

She couldn't avoid the meeting. The villagers were just beginning to trust her a little. She had to stand with them today. One of the men, Sinho Tavas, was an uncle of that dead child who haunted her dreams.

Janos was Brazilian partner and front man for Grandeza, a giant consortium of foreign investors that had been given the right to exploit this region and build a dam to flood out not only the village but also the traditional hunting grounds of the Zarina tribe. The Zarinas' principal chief, Takara, had been educated by priests in Belém, and he trusted Paul Radford, a priest who headed the Land Committee, which was doing all it could to protect settlers from being forced off their homesteads.

Paul had arranged this meeting between Janos, the Zarinas, the villagers, and the National Indian Foundation, or FUNAI, in the greasy person of one Victor Soltas. Victor was in charge of the agency office a few miles from the village. Entrusted with protecting the remnants of tribes that had once peopled the Amazon, FUNAI more often than not protected construction of highways, dams and power lines from the Indians.

Marilia tried not to speculate on what loathsome ailment she might be getting. With her emergency medical training, she was the closest thing to a doctor in a hundred miles, so she took a broad-spectrum antibiotic, put coffee water on the bottled-gas hot plate and nibbled a small papaya.

Too faint to keep on her feet, she sat down to brush her teeth and comb her hair. The mirror above the washstand gave back dark-hollowed gray-green eyes that looked too large and brilliant in her thin face. Her angular cheekbones were hectic with fever. Janos would hate the way her curly auburn hair was cut short. He had loved to twine his hands in it, bend back her head. . . .

The coffee made her sweat, so she left most of it and was putting on sunscreen when a jeep stopped in front. The villagers must have assembled already, she thought as she heard them greeting Paul's arrival.

If only she weren't sick. If only Janos would send someone else to represent Grandeza. She fought down a surge of nausea and passed through her quarters, connected to the foundation office, and on out to the long, thatched porch. The building housed showers as well as the treated water supply, and served as school and dispensary. Next to it was Chiquino Domingos' store, the center of village social life.

Unlike the uniform boxes of planned government *agrovilas,* settlements, most of which were abandoned within a few years because of poor soil, the palm-thatched, half-open dwellings stood on raised platforms among plantings of sugarcane, manioc and bananas. Behind these, stretching to the fields and forest, were oranges, limes, jackfruit, pineapple, cashew, mango, tamarinds and big patches of squash and yams.

Women and children watched from porches. No women were in the group piling into Paul's jeep or Chiquino Domingos' truck. The men who took off their straw hats to Marilia were wiry and seemed carved from the various barks of forest trees—some as fair as Marilia, others nearly black, most coppery brown.

Paul helped her into the front seat of his jeep. A tall, stooping man with a big nose and lopsided grin, Paul came from a wealthy plantation family but had spent considerable time in jail for counseling settlers to resist seizure of their farms. His clear hazel eyes swept her face.

"You don't look well, Marilia."

"I'm taking my own medicine," she joked. "I haven't heard a plane, so maybe—"

"Oh, Senhor Janos will be there." Paul smiled grimly. "He called before I left Belém, offering all kinds of inducements if the Land Committee would stay out of this."

Marilia spoke to the men in back. Sinho Tavas, pockmarked and wizened, a former vaqueiro; his sons; and Adrien Vaz. Adrien was one of the few villagers who had always lived in the region. His family had long been friendly with the Zarina, often marrying into the tribe. That was why there had been none of the usual bloody clashes between Indians and *civilizados*. Too, each side respected the river boundary. With wavy black hair, smooth honey-brown skin and chiseled features, Adrien was beautiful. He and his flower-like child-wife had just had their first baby.

The jeep rumbled across the bridge above the thundering waterfall, and as they jounced toward the concrete-block FUNAI agency, shaded by one straggly palm, the whir of a small plane increased and reverberated through the air. Marilia shrank. Janos. In minutes, she'd have to face him.

Suddenly it was as if their battle had been waged only yesterday, not three years ago. She was frightened, desperate.

Takara and his head men were already at the FUNAI building. All except Takara wore disks in their lower lips. Takara was otherwise as savagely elegant as the others. Toucan-fluff earrings slanted through his earlobes, and he wore a coronet of red and yellow feathers. A black butterfly decorated his broad chest, and its wings were repeated around his eyes. A scarlet wrestler's clout was his only covering. His iron-muscled midriff and muscular long legs and thighs were bare.

Together, villagers and Indians stood on the porch, watching the small plane circle like a bird of prey before it swooped down.

Unable to stand, Marilia went into the office and sat in the corner across from Victor Soltas' desk. The settlers and Zarinas followed, so that, mercifully, she wasn't alone when Janos strode in, dominating the gathering in the way Janos dominated just by being there.

When she'd last seen him, he'd still had some black streaks in his thick hair, but now it was pure silver, startling against his tanned skin. His white, tucked, pocketed shirt jacket was immaculate, his trousers creased. Emerald fire flashed from his engineer's ring and dazzling rainbows from the huge diamond on the next finger. His watch was simple, platinum or white gold.

His eyes were the same, silver, outlined by black lashes, centered by fathomless pupils. Those eyes were on her, making her vulnerable to that down-curving, sensuous mouth that every part of her body remembered with sudden jagged pain. A neatly seamed forgotten wound tore open, spilling its poison through her bloodstream.

"It's wonderful to see you, Marilia." Behind his university accent sounded Janos' other voice, the rough Paulista who'd made his fortune, like some of their mutual ancestors, by finding gold in the backlands. He bowed, mocking her. "I'll be fascinated to hear all you learned in your Yankee college, dear. But for now we must deal with practicalities." He shook hands with Paul. "I hope we'll have a reasonable discussion, Father."

Their eyes locked. "That depends on you." Janos broke the moment by turning to the tall black-haired man just entering the building.

"Marilia, allow me to present Trace Kendall of the World Preservation Society and National Institute of Amazonian Studies. He's trying to determine how large a piece of forest must be left for most species to survive. Trace, this is Marilia Valente dos Santos, an expert on governmental inefficiency." His smile taunted. "Which branch of governmental inefficiency are you working for these days?"

"I had enough of government agencies in the Northeast," she said, her voice light and dry. "I work for a small private foundation."

The stranger, Kendall, looked *norteamericano*. She had encountered numbers of them in Brazil, studying crops, the soil, plants, birth and death rates, folklore, and of course the Amazon. Her hand clasped Kendall's only briefly but his smoke-gray eyes held hers so that it took effort to look away. "Do you include human beings among the species you'd like to see survive, Mr. Kendall?"

A dark eyebrow rose. "That's someone else's problem, Dona Marilia." He turned more of his back to her than was necessary as Janos introduced him to Paul.

"Radford?" he asked. "Are you connected with the Anjo do Guarda family?"

Paul studied strong cheekbones, cleft chin and straight nose. Then he smiled and altered his handshake to an *abraço*. "You must be one of the Kendalls who started marrying into the family several generations ago. We share a set of great-grandparents. Let's just be cousins."

"For that matter," said Janos, "I think all of us, including Marilia, descend from a famous old *bandeirante* called Sertão. The tradition is that I resemble a remote forebear, Dário Ferraz. One of his numerous bastards married a descendant of one of Sertão's even more numerous bastards." He chuckled and dropped a hand on Marilia's shoulder. "So here we all are—one big family."

Wonderful to know Paul was a relative, however distant! But disconcerting that this *norteamericano* was also kin. Marilia moved away from Janos' hand, her face expressionless.

Sweat and wood smoke permeated the air. There seemed to be no oxygen. "I appreciate your meeting with us, Senhor Janos," Paul said.

Janos' tone went cool as his eyes. "I like to be accommodating. But the dam will be built."

"Will you listen to why we think it shouldn't be?"

"Certainly. And then I'll explain Grandeza's position."

He sat on Soltas' desk, waiting for Paul to begin speaking, but it was Takara who stepped forward. As always, it was startling to hear educated Portuguese coming from the fiercely painted warrior.

"This land has been my people's since the spirit of Woman Who Taught Us brought us away from the River Sea where we were being enslaved by whites. She led us here. She lives in the waterfall your dam would destroy. All our children who die young go to live with her there. We can hear them laughing and playing."

Janos crossed his arms. "You speak the white man's

language too well not to know that superstitions can't get in the way of progress. Grandeza will give your people presents and food if you leave peacefully. There's plenty of open land. You don't have to stay here. You know that as well as I do.''

"This land is ours, and not by superstition. It is a reserve, guaranteed us by the government.''

"And the government has given us the land on the other side of the river," Sinho Tavas said. "You have forgotten, senhor, but you yourself forced me off the little ranch where my people had always lived. A pulpwood planter drove me off my first homestead.'' He cradled the old shotgun against his skinny chest. "We'll fight for these homes.''

Swinging off the desk, Janos ignored the *caboclo* and confronted Paul. "Grandeza has acquired two million acres, including what these people claim. This is the optimum place to build a dam to supply power for our mining and smelting operations. It will be built.''

A murmur ran through the settlers. Takara's face tightened. "There's no need for us to be enemies," Janos added, dividing a good-natured smile between settlers and Indians. "Grandeza will mine iron, bauxite, nickel, copper, whatever we find. But there will also be cattle ranches, rice plantations and *gmelina* trees planted for pulp. Lots of jobs for you.''

The sullen expression of a few of the farmers changed. Most of them had known of old-time *patrãos* who worked their people, true, but gave them a feast on Saint John's Day, stood godparent to their children, allowed them to sleep out their days once they were past usefulness. Now before them stood this potent, strong *patrão,* handsome as some dream of King Sebastian. If he would tell them what to do and feed them for doing it . . .

Glancing around at them, Marilia understood. Janos had that effect on people. They surrendered their wills in order to be protected.

She held her breath as Sinho glanced at his fellows. None of them spoke. Sinho's pockmarks gave his skin the look of pitted earth, scarred and baked by the seasons. "Rice isn't a good single crop here, senhor. On my last farm I grew rice because that was the only crop the bank would

loan me money for. I went in debt for fertilizer and pesti-
cides. Then it rained before harvest. All that rice rotted in
the fields. If I had planted manioc I could have fed my
family and sold some, too.''

"If you farm for Grandeza and lose a crop, you can have
credit for more seed and food.''

Sinho laughed bitterly. "Credit. I would rather plant
what I choose on my own land, senhor, than run up a debt
that would make me Grandeza's slave. Whether we work
in cacao or rubber, coffee or sugar or jute, it ends the same
way. The work of our whole lives never pays us what we
need to feed and clothe ourselves.''

"Perhaps you don't work hard enough.''

"I will work my own fields, senhor.''

Silence. Then Janos said, "I wish you luck. But your
fields cannot be here.'' He studied each farmer in turn, and
the eyes of many dropped beneath that hard gaze. "If
you go without trouble, Grandeza will pay you the cost of
relocating—even truck you to new homesteads. If you
stay . . .'' He turned his hand over.

There was fear, but beneath that a stubborn fatalism.
Sinho, looking like a work-deformed little brown gnome
next to the white man, spoke again. "I will be buried in
this earth before I will leave it.''

Keeping a tight rein on himself, Janos turned to the
priest. "Cousin, if you care about these people, you'd better change their minds.''

"It's their decision. But the Land Committee is behind
them. If you bring in gunmen, as some developers have,
the whole world will hear about it.''

"Small wonder you Land Committee people spend a lot
of time in jail.'' Cool eyes traveled to Marilia. "I hope
you're more concerned about these people than our cousin
is.''

"I'm concerned,'' she said, forcing herself erect though
the room kept whirling. "The foundation I work for has
good contacts in the capital.''

His mouth quirked. "Do you know how many senators
and government officials Grandeza owns?''

"It doesn't own them all. Besides, even the bribed ones
know something has to be done about drought areas. They

see Amazon development as the answer. But projects like the one you're promoting could turn the whole Amazon into a Sahara.''

"Please, my dear,'' he interrupted. He nodded toward Trace Kendall, who had been listening through all of it without any change in expression. An aloof American scientist who probably cared a lot more about butterfly species than people, Marilia thought bitterly. "Trace is looking into consequences.''

"For macaws and orchids?''

It was as if a switch had tripped inside Kendall and brought him to life. He laughed, and gray-blue eyes touched her, but with the shock of lightning, not the warmth of the sun. She knew he was seeing her as a woman. There was nothing pleasant in his look, and nothing of kindness. It was elemental seeking.

She had thought herself slashed and burned over like cleared forest, nothing left to ignite or nourish a flame. She'd been wrong. Sick in heart and body though she was, a single direct glance from this man stirred her as she had not been stirred by any of the lovers she'd taken to try to rid herself of Janos' ownership.

"If you'd care to see what I do, Dona Marilia, I'd be happy to show you,'' Kendall said with mocking courtesy. "And I'd be interested in learning how you propose to keep forest land productive for more than two or three years.''

"That's beside the point,'' cut in Janos. "The dam will flood at least three hundred square miles. We start clearing forest in two weeks.''

"Clearing?'' Paul frowned.

"We've learned some lessons from rain-forest dams,'' Janos explained patronizingly. "Decomposing trees make such a stink that workers have to wear gas masks for years, and rotting vegetation makes the water so acidic it corrodes cooling systems and ruins steel casings. We don't want that kind of mess.''

"You're going to log three hundred square miles?'' Marilia asked in disbelief.

"Logging's too slow. We'll use defoliants.''

Kendall's head jerked up. "Defoliants?''

"Tordon 101 and Tordon 155. They've been pretty effective in clearing water hyacinth."

Kendall said slowly, "Tordon 101 contains the main components of Agent Orange. It's linked to birth defects."

Janos shrugged. "You can't do anything this big without running a few risks." Then he wheeled on the short, fat, slick-haired Indian agent who was eyeing Marilia. "Senhor Victor, these Indians are your responsibility. I rely on you to see that they cause no trouble."

"I'll do my best," said Soltas unhappily. "But—"

"Brazil says we're wards of the government," broke in Takara. "We say we are men. To flood our sacred waterfall, you will have to kill us."

Janos ignored him. "It is your responsibility," he repeated to Victor Soltas. Then he turned and looked at Marilia as if they were the only people in the room. "You must be bursting with complaints you intend to make to every agency you can think of. May I offer you a ride to Manaus?"

It was hard to meet those molten eyes, but she forced herself. "No, thank you."

She would go to Brasilia, sick as she was. Maybe the foundation could do something about this. And she had to see a doctor.

Janos inclined his silver head. "I'll see you in a few weeks, then, Marilia. It's good you've come back to your own country—even if you haven't learned where you really belong."

He gave Paul a perfunctory nod, ignored the Indians and settlers, and strode out of the sweltering room without another word.

On the way back to the village, Adrien Vaz said, "Please, Dona Marilia, will you be our son's godmother?"

Startled, she turned to stare at him. When he smiled steadily, she knew he meant it. She nodded and tears filled her eyes.

The Minister of the Environment had surely been bought or threatened, for he refused to do anything about the defoliation, refused even to listen seriously to her arguments.

He escorted her firmly to the door, then halted, eyes

widening with surprised delight, as he saw the tall woman whose lush body wasn't at all disguised by her tailored white suit. Her tawny hair was caught back in a chignon, emphasizing the strong planes of a face beautiful in spite of its angularity. Topaz eyes lit at the sight of her daughter. Caterina Valente dos Santos kissed Marilia on the cheek and smiled graciously at the minister, extending her hand.

Bowing over the hand, he said, "Dona Caterina! A joy to see you! There are so many dos Santoses that it never occurred to me this young lady could be your daughter." He glanced inquiringly at the black-haired man lounging on a seat near the door, a man whose presence Marilia greeted with amazement and alarm.

Trace Kendall rose, towering over the minister as he acknowledged the introduction made by Caterina. "I've already spoken with your aide, senhor, on the dangers of defoliation. He has my address in Manaus if you need my testimony or my professional opinion."

"I'm well aware of the problems." The minister spoke tartly. "Thank you for your interest. I'll let you know if you're needed." His tone warmed as he turned back to Caterina. "Are you in town for a while, dear lady? It would be a pleasure to arrange a small function."

"Thanks, my good friend, but I've come to seduce my hard-working daughter into visiting me for a few days." She flashed a smile at Kendall. It was almost a caressing smile. "Senhor Trace and I met only this afternoon, quite by chance, as we were both waiting for Marilia. Since it develops that he's a relation of ours, though born in the United States, I've prevailed on him to visit Ouro Prêto."

"Fortunate man!" sighed the minister.

Caterina kissed his plump cheek. "You know you're always invited." She slipped her arm through Marilia's. "We mustn't take up more of the minister's time."

Marilia thanked the man mechanically, scarcely hearing his flowery response. He wouldn't help. All that dashed hope made her want to crawl away and hide, at least until she got over whatever was winning over the antibiotics. She was faint and dizzy all the time.

The ambiguous sensations Trace Kendall aroused warred

with the equally ambiguous feelings her mother always inspired.

"How did either of you know where I was?" she asked as they got into the elevator.

"As a biologist assessing the rain forest, I had every reason to report to the Ministry," Trace said blandly. But he let his eyes touch her mouth and throat and then he laughed. "Fact is, I dropped by the Land Committee office. Paul told me where you'd gone, and when I got to Brasilia and called your foundation, the lady thought I might find you importuning the minister. I bet you didn't get very far."

Caterina's full-bellied laughter made people turn around. "I also tracked you through the foundation, dearest. Shall we have something to eat before we leave? I chartered a plane at Belo Horizonte. My car's at the airport there."

"I haven't said I'm going." It sounded churlish, even to her own self, but she so often behaved churlishly around her mother.

"But I haven't seen you since you came back from North Carolina," Caterina begged.

With one part of her mind, Marilia knew her mother loved her more than anyone, and that, of all the people on earth, she alone had the power to wound this splendid woman, sensual, self-assured, rich and influential.

Will I always feel raw and awkward around her? Marilia wondered. Hard to believe this extraordinary woman was nearly fifty. Marilia leaned against the wall. "The truth is, Mother, I—I don't feel very good. Some fever—"

"Marilia!"

Caterina's arms closed around her as Marilia's knees dissolved. She quit fighting, slipped into welcome darkness.

A man's strong arms, her mother's frightened face, nurses, doctors . . . Everything was a blur till Marilia woke in the room where she'd grown up. She hadn't spent a night there since her wedding seven years ago.

Gilt roses on white furniture. A canopied bed with rose-embroidered white satin coverlet. The comfortable big chair by the bookcase had been reupholstered in the same rich rose velvet. Stuffed animals, treasured from baby days, her dolls, some bedraggled, others exquisite, all gathered on the window seat, facing Marilia.

Marilia's bones ached, but the debilitating nausea and cramps had left. How long had she been sick? She started to get up and pain exploded in her head. She fell back, panting and sweating.

Caterina came in. "What's the matter, darling?"

"I—I tried to get up."

"But you mustn't."

"I have to get back to the village!"

"And die? You're staying here till Dr. Varghas says you're all right."

The brief argument exhausted Marilia and her eyes closed. "What's wrong with me?"

Caterina hesitated. "At least it isn't schistosomiasis, that awful snail-spread stuff. Dr. Varghas can't pin your trouble down, but your fever's under control and he thinks rest and good food will fix you up."

"How much rest?"

"As much as you need."

Caterina always won arguments like that.

"What will people in the village think?" Marilia asked herself, forgetting she was speaking aloud.

"Trace is getting a message to them. But I wish you were out of there for good. When you're well, why don't you go back to Fortaleza and work with the farmers there?"

"When I'm with Sinho Tavas and the *nordestinos*, I feel they're my family. You remember that little girl—? I'll stay with them to the last ditch."

"That last ditch may be a grave."

Marilia didn't answer. She'd hoped Caterina, who'd escaped the drought country, would understand.

She believes I've forgotten, Caterina thought. And that family history which she thinks I did out of pride, can't she understand how important it was to me—who had no parents—to know where I came from? To have that to give to her, since I can't name her father?

I suppose if she knew I underwrite the foundation, she'd quit working for it. Caterina sighed. Why was it easier to let Marilia think the worst of her than admit her generosities?

Because I want her to love me, Caterina told herself with amused bitterness. I want her to love me because I love her. Because when she was little she thought I was wonderful. She used to kiss me and say, "A kiss means love." She used to hug me and sigh with contentment and say, "I love the sweetness of the breath of you." *Oh, Marilia, Marilia! I have loved you better than I ever loved a man. I, who had no mother, love you so.*

And you wish you had no mother—not me, anyway, a whore grown rich, with friends and ways you don't approve of. My God, you could as well be a *crente*, a convert to one of those dour U.S. sects.

Caterina straightened, ordering her emotions to heel. She wouldn't explain herself or plead for her daughter's tolerance. Knowing all too painfully a woman's vulnerability in Brazil, she had thought she was protecting Marilia in nurturing her acquaintance with Janos.

She hasn't forgiven me because she's still not free of him, Caterina thought. Blessed Mother, let her love someone else then—maybe this American.

Frowning as she considered Janos and Grandeza, Caterina began a mental list of ministers, deputies and senators to call about the defoliation. She swallowed a wicked chuckle. *My dear child, if Grandeza is stopped from flooding out your colonists and Indians, it won't be because of the Land Committee or you but because of my ass—and a little delicate blackmail.*

"Listen, dear," she said carefully. "You're going to have a long convalescence. Paul Radford sent a book about our family. Between it and what geneaologists have tracked down I know a lot about some of the women in our line." She laughed. "You can be proud of them, even if you aren't of me." She held up her hand before Marilia could differ. Why go through that?

"Let's not. Let me take care of you the way I did when you were little. I'll tell you stories."

Marilia reached for Caterina's hand and tucked it under her cheek. "All right, Mother, tell me a story."

Caterina smoothed Marilia's auburn hair back from her

burning forehead. "We don't know much about Raya the Inca, the first of our women who came to Brazil. She was a Sun Virgin who was abducted by the first Spanish expedition to travel the Amazon all the way from Peru to where it empties into the ocean. But she escaped them and lived for a time with Caramuru's family."

Every Brazilian schoolchild knew who Caramuru was. He was Diogo Alvares, a shipwrecked Portuguese nobleman who had so many children by his Indian wife that his descendants were legion. "Was Raya one of Caramuru's women?" asked Marilia.

"I don't think so. The tradition is that she loved a handsome French dyewood trader named Drouet. He took their son back to France with him, and that branch rejoins ours later. Raya kept their daughter, who married a son of Caramuru's. Raya died while nursing in one of those smallpox epidemics that took such a toll of the Indians."

"Do you think Raya is the one Takara calls She Who Taught Us?"

"It may be, but I don't know. Now, rest. Close your eyes, love, and let me tell you what we do know."

BOOK II
The Sinhá-dona

With this paper is sold . . .
Cosmé, Zulu, twenty, sound, well-favored, branded on one cheek.
Efigenia, Congo, upstanding breasts, pretty figure,
very black; twelve years old, and virgin.
Irene, Fulah, Mohammedan, along with infant son;
thirty, big buttocks, good milk and plentiful.

Cosmé to die of sadness for his country;
Efigenia to purge master's pox in virgin flower
and birth a womb-blind yellow baby.
Irene to suckle the young master, chew meat for him
and cuddle him to dreams;
Her son, Bento, to be young master's plaything,
pull his cart, play horsey and always be the horse;
See his master use the girl he worships—
sold for his rage. Eight years in the mines.
That's all the best do, eight years in the mines.

With this paper . . .

If You were resolved to give these same lands to the pirates of
Holland, why did You not do so when they were still wild and
uncultivated, instead of now? . . .
    Must heretics and enemies of the Faith thus enjoy the fruits of
the work of Portuguese and the sweat of Catholic brows? . . .
Burn, destroy, consume us all, but it may chance one day that
You will need Spaniards and Portuguese . . . Holland, in short,
will serve You and venerate You as religiously as they do daily
in Amsterdam, Middleburg and Flushing, and in all the other
colonies of that cold and watery hell!

—from a sermon preached in Bahia in 1641
by Padre Antonio Vieira

I

The Orphan

Except for Elena, the other orphan, who gripped her rosary and murmured prayers, as soon as the lighthouse and harbor of Bahia had been sighted that dawn, the other women in the fetid cabin had begun to primp. Those who had perfume used it to mask the odor of ten weeks without washing while cramped with twenty other women in space meant for ten. Some had been violently ill much of the time, and those who weren't had endured disorders caused by water and food that grew fouler by the day.

Only such conditions could make Rachel glad to reach Brazil and the unknown man who would be her husband. No Portuguese maiden of good family would be allowed to journey to these remote colonies beset by savages and Dutch, so the King sent orphans as wives for the colonists. When there were not enough of them, prostitutes were rounded up and forcibly given this chance at a reformed life.

These unwilling recruits had ignored Rachel and Elena except to now and then tell stories that made Elena clap her hands over her ears and pray at the top of her thin, reedy voice. As they finished their toilets, the slatterns hurried from the cabin. Some had broken the monotony of the voyage by sneaking out to the seamen, but the most hardened had voiced dreams of a good husband—think of it! Just one man!—and a home, and had wistfully hoped that past abortions and disease wouldn't prevent their having children.

From all Rachel heard, they weren't being foisted onto upright models of pious rectitude. Of the thousand settlers Tomé de Sousa, the first governor of Brazil, brought with him to the Bay of All Saints almost ninety years ago in 1549, four hundred had been *degredados*, exiled convicts.

In addition to royal officials and six Jesuits, the other colonists had been soldiers and New Christians—Jews converted to Catholicism, often by force.

Rachel herself was New Christian. In 1496 the king of Portugal had ordered all Jews to convert or leave the country. Rachel's great-grandparents had fled to Holland, but children under fourteen could not be taken from the country, so their young son was baptized and placed in a foster home. He was already counted a man of the Hebrews and practiced his faith in secret, instructing his family in it, so Rachel's parents had been secret worshipers of Jehovah. They died of pestilence while she was about four years old, but sometimes she dreamed of the Sabbath dinner or the Seder when a place was set for Elijah.

Brought up in an orphanage by strict nuns, longing to escape days of sewing, prayers and scant food, she had pleaded to work in the garden, carry in wood and water, dump the slops—anything to get outside the cold stone walls and feel the sun and breeze.

Live like this her whole life? That might mean another meager, boring fifty or more years, since she was only sixteen. When the government's envoys had asked for orphans of marriageable age, she would have been glad to go anywhere, even to Brazil, which the nuns said was full of cannibals and godless men who lived in concubinage with slaves of every hue, peopling the land with heathen bastards.

It still sounded better than the convent. When she had combed her waving auburn hair or caught a glimpse in the water basin of a wistful face with a broad forehead, clefted small chin and black-lashed green eyes, she had wondered if she might be pretty but had thought disconsolately that it couldn't matter if there was no man to tell her so.

Still, she feared to go ashore to this new land. As she picked up her bundle, her stomach knotted. She hoped it would be a while before her husband claimed her.

Giving Elena a shake, she pulled the dark, fragile girl to her feet and made her take her bundle. "Come on, Elena! I should think you'd want to get off this stinking old wreck."

Elena's eyes spilled over. "I—I never wanted to come. I would rather have stayed with the sisters."

"Then your convent was a better place than mine," Rachel said bracingly. She tried to fluff the other girl's dank locks, frowned and advised, "Bite your lips a little and get some color in them. You don't want wife-seekers to think you're puny."

"But I *am* puny," Elena wailed. "I'm afraid of men! They're big and loud and hairy and—"

Rachel took her by the shoulder and firmly steered her on deck, where they stood at the back of the mass of women who were crowding into the small boats that would take them to shore. Other ships were anchored in the immense harbor, but it was to this one that the crowds had flocked. As the boat carrying Rachel and Elena was pulled onto the sand a huzzah went up from a throng of men as the women climbed out, some rolling their hips and displaying their bosoms.

"Skimmings to the scum," Rachel heard an officer remark. "It's said malaria can burn out syphilis. For the health of future Brazilians, I hope that's so." Flushing, Rachel glanced back at the ship.

Cattle were being driven up from the hold, stained to the hocks by manure. *Stock for the plantations—as we are,* Rachel thought. *And here on shore are our future owners, come to inspect the new brood females.*

Black-robed Jesuits had come to meet the women, but respect for them didn't keep jostling, eager men of every age and manner of apparel, all armed with rapiers slung from broad sword-belts, or baldrics, from commenting on Falita's ample breasts, which bounced with each step, and on the physical charms and shortcomings of the newcomers, or ridiculing the facial tic of one raddled whore who tried to smile and thereby revealed her rotted teeth.

One burly young wag held his nose. "Are these the sweet flowers we've been pining for? God's wounds, their smell would knock a buzzard off a gut wagon!"

"A bath will do wonders," philosophized a white-haired, red-cheeked man whose gaze wandered over Rachel before it began to strip her.

Beside him, a broad-shouldered pallid man in maroon velvet, handsome except for softness around the jaw and pouchy eyes, flicked cold black eyes past the praying Elena and the parade in front of her to examine Rachel. "If this is how the king finds us brides, he needn't marvel that we prefer our concubines," he drawled without lowering his voice. "Whey-face babes or the dregs of Lisbon's brothels!" He rubbed his chin, staring at Rachel till she felt handled and shamed. "The redhead's the best of the lot. Clear skin, and though she's not got much up front or behind, a few babies should change that."

Trembling with humiliated fury, Rachel kept her head high and stalked past him. Maybe these were just gawkers, not serious prospects, but she was beginning to wish herself back in the nunnery. The offensive dark man was talking to one of the Jesuits, and as she came abreast, the Jesuit beckoned to her, long face cracking in what might have been intended as a reassuring smile.

"Daughter, you are indeed well come to Brazil. This gentleman, the Senhor Duarte Álvares, is a member of the municipal council, knight commander of the Habit of São Bento de Aviz, a member of the Board of Guardians, the Misericordia, and the owner of a sugar plantation and mill. He desires you for his wife." As Rachel stared, thunderstruck, the priest added soothingly, "The senhor has a chaplain living on his estates. You can be properly married there."

"But I don't know this gentleman."

The narrow-faced man looked at her in surprise. "When was that a condition for marriage? You need a home or you would not be here. What is your name?"

"Rachel da Silva."

Finding it on his list, the Jesuit scrawled a few words and made a check. Álvares reached under his doublet and placed a clinking pouch in the priest's hand.

"Bless you for your charity, my son," intoned the priest. "This will go to help in the instruction of the natives in our mission." His black robes swished as he hurried to assist in the reception of the other women.

The ruddy-faced white-haired man was speaking softly to Elena. The terror on her face was echoed in Rachel's heart as Duarte Álvares laughed and slipped a broad hand beneath her arm, squeezing her flesh.

"Come, girl. If we are to make Seraphim by nightfall, we must be on our way."

He drew her toward where black slaves, clad only in loincloths, waited with two litters draped with dark green velvet. Rachel stumbled and glanced down. The beach was littered with all manner of refuse, including human waste. But what her foot had caught on was a human arm, protruding from the sand.

Her horrified gaze fixed on a bent dark knee. Álvares jerked her forward. "That was a man!" she cried.

"A slave," he said indifferently. His accent was very different from that of Lisbon, softened and slurred, with no trilling of the r's. "They're often buried along the shore or tied to a board and cast out to sea. All Bahia's garbage is supposed to be dumped only on the beach."

He grasped her hand and thrust her into one of the covered litters as the carriers lowered it. "You can rest on the way." His eyes ran over her and he gave a rumbling laugh. "I advise you do. The chaplain will marry us this evening and I don't want a fagged bride."

Could even as coarse a man as he mean to force himself on a woman who didn't know him, who had just disembarked from a grueling journey? She protested urgently, "Senhor, the banns—"

"My chaplain does as I say. Such things count for little here. Why, priests have baptized hundreds of Indians at a crack and married them the next minute."

He closed the curtains. She felt herself being lifted. Bright though the sun was, it couldn't reach through the silk-lined draperies, but when her eyes grew accustomed to the dim light, she saw the litter was heaped with cushions of stained silk, velvet and damask, redolent of dried sweat and stale perfume.

It was stifling. She parted the curtains slightly, peering out at the long waterfront packed with warehouses, shops, hovels and a big shipbuilding yard. The people were every color from ebony to white, many apparently mixtures. Tall black women in striped robes and turbans hawked trays of food and confections. Children pelted through the alleys. Fights were going on with no one paying any heed, and seamen who joked or quarreled in a dozen languages swaggered along the street or stood in grog shop doors. Garbage was heaped outside doors and scattered in the thoroughfares.

Narrow streets wound tortuously between this bustling commercial section, fortified against attack from the sea, and the city on the heights, where handsome stone buildings rose among luxuriant trees and gardens. The slaves panted as they toiled up the hill. They passed other richly draped litters and a stream of pack mules, horses and slaves carrying burdens to or from the lower town, but no wagons or carriages. The steep ascent was too hazardous for wheeled vehicles.

As they gained the upper city and came out on a fine broad cobblestoned street, they passed churches, mansions that could be called palaces, and tile-roofed balconied houses of two and three stories shaded by trees and softened by flowers and vines. Fine public buildings reminded Rachel that Cidade do Salvador, commonly known as Bahia, was the seat of the governor-general of all Brazil, a bishop and a High Court, and was said to be possessed of at least a hundred thousand inhabitants.

Tropical flowers scented the air near shady public squares where people walked or sat to watch the busy scene. Piles of offal and other waste were dumped at some street corners, showing that many householders disobeyed the law Duarte had mentioned.

As they passed out of the city, Rachel had a wild impulse to spring from the litter and run to the nearest house, begging for refuge, offering to be the lowliest servant if the owners would shield her from this stranger. But even if she should reach a dwelling, Duarte Álvares was obviously a man of wealth and influence. It wasn't likely that anyone would risk his anger for the sake of an orphan— who, in any case, had been expressly sent to become a colonist's wife.

She had no hope that Duarte would be shamed by her unwillingness into letting her escape him. What *fidalgo* would give in to a fractious mare or slave?

As the slaves moved past fields of what she supposed was sugarcane, she drew the curtains as far apart as she could, but there was no breeze and her garments stuck to her. She would much rather walk than be cooped up in this hot, stuffy conveyance, but she was sure that Duarte's wife would do what was expected of her station, not what was comfortable.

This certainty and the menace of the man in the litter ahead of her made her wish that she were back with the nuns. Duarte Álvares was not the husband she had shyly dreamed of; even had he been, she would have needed time to know him.

She shivered in spite of the heat, but she was weary and the rhythmic sway of the litter began to lull her. Cradling her face against her arm to protect it from the soiled cushions, she drifted into a torpid half-sleep.

She was jarred from this respite by the halting of the litter. They had stopped before the entrance of a great two-storied house. Rachel shrank as Álvares came back to her and hauled her out of the litter, tossing her bundle to one of the slaves.

"This is the *casa grande,* the big house of Seraphim," he said. "I trust you can bring some order to it. The slaves have grown lazy since my last wife died."

"Your *last* wife—"

"Three women, but not one gave me a child!" His charcoal-black eyes moved over her. "I hope you'll do better once we get some meat on your bones."

As she stared at his callousness, he grasped her elbow and drew her forward. "If you want to be mistress of Seraphim, don't look like a scared ninny! You must run the slaves or they'll run you."

Somber portraits hung on the whitewashed walls of the reception room, but the big room was furnished only with a few high-backed chairs, benches and small tables. The tiled floors were dirty, the walls above the fireplace smoky, and a splendid silver candelabrum was tarnished black.

Duarte gave a vigorous pull on a bell rope and led her up the stairs. By the time they reached the top, a dozen women crowded there. Some were crones, while others had just the hint of breasts. Their colors ran from the rich blackness of fertile earth to creamy gold. There were several boys and an immense yellow-skinned man.

"This is your new sinhá-dona," the master said.

He turned to a statuesque woman with mahogany skin who wore a blue-and-white-striped garment pinned with a gold brooch at the shoulder, gold bracelets, charms and large hoop earrings.

"Felicia, your mistress requires a bath. If she has nothing suitable for a wedding, see what you can find in the chest." Felicia bowed, but she looked like a queen, not a slave.

All the household watched Rachel, some with barely masked hostility, others with shy smiles, but it was a tawny stare from an oval face that glowed a delicate rose-gold amber that made Rachel stiffen.

Fury radiated from the slender young woman, whose thick yellow-brown hair was caught back with orange flowers matching the loose embroidered smock she wore. The emeralds that flashed at throat and ears were incongruous on a servant.

Both this woman and Felicia had commanding strength of personality, far more than Rachel, and the younger didn't bother to conceal her hatred. As Duarte gave the golden-eyed slave a careless smile, the answering look on the girl's face told Rachel she was confronted with a rival—and for a man she didn't even want.

To the big yellow man with crimped reddish hair who wore what looked like a woman's lace-trimmed, beribboned smock, Duarte grinned. "Fix us a good wedding dinner, Damião—something to strengthen this pale little bride. Let them have meat tonight in the *senzala* and double rations of rum."

Male gratification made fleshy red lips fuller as he glanced amusedly at the bejeweled mulatta. "Lay out my best clothes, Luzia, and fetch me a bowl of fruit."

Deliberately he took Rachel in his arms and brought her against him, kissing her mouth with ruthless avidity. "Felicia will bring you to the chapel," he said huskily and strode off down the hall, followed by Luzia and a red-haired, copper-skinned man of about his own age.

Rachel stood helplessly at the top of the landing, ready to drop with fatigue, numbly trying to comprehend that this was not a shipboard nightmare but reality, that she was in a house where she might spend the rest of her days among the people she'd spend that night with. Most especially she could not believe that before morning Duarte Álvares would make her his wife.

Something—was it sympathy?—flickered in Felicia's eyes. Ordering two of the lads to fetch hot water and taking Rachel's belongings, she motioned Rachel to precede her in the direction opposite to the way Duarte had gone, and mur-

mured softly, "Come, sinhá. A nice bath and you'll feel
better."

She softened Portuguese even more than Duarte, but her
rich, deep voice made it sound caressing, not slovenly. Rachel gave that only partial notice, however. When the black
woman opened her mouth, half her front teeth were missing.

The others were strong and white, but the gaps turned
Felicia's expression into a travesty of what it must have
been. This was an age when many women's teeth went
early, especially after having children, but how could Felicia have lost that many when the ones beside them were
sound and beautiful? Rachel tried not to gape, but surprise
must have shown on her face, for the other woman's mouth
tightened. She gestured down the hall and Rachel moved
slowly ahead.

A great bed seemed to fill the chamber. Attached to the
canopy was a white netting which Felicia explained was to
keep out mosquitoes and other flying pests. Heaps of satin
pillows covered a crimson satin counterpane. A silver and
ivory crucifix with startling ruby blood drops hung above
the bed, and a wall niche held an exquisitely carved Madonna dressed in real blue and white robes, golden crown,
glittering jewels and ornaments of gold and silver.

Woven rush mats covered most of the tiled floor. Above
a stand holding a tarnished silver ewer and basin hung a
mirror in a silver frame. Pegs for clothing were driven in
the wall by the big carved chest, and a stool completed the
furniture except for a copper tub.

The iron grille fitted over the single window increased
Rachel's sense of imprisonment, though there was no place
to which she could flee. Glancing at the tub, she said,
"The senhor evidently expected to bring home a bride."

"He went to Bahia two weeks ago, at the earliest time
your ship might arrive, in order to have first choice." Felicia
looked straight at her, not attempting to hide her ruined mouth
by facing to the side. "He was bound to have a wife from
Portugal, since the ones from here have borne him no heirs."

"Perhaps it wasn't his wives' fault," Rachel ventured.

Felicia's laughter was as deeply sonorous as the sound-
ing of a heavy bronze bell. "Sinhá, it was not *his* fault."

She caught herself, crossed to the chest and began holding up garments, some of dimity, linen and calico, others of satin, velvet and silk. Studying Rachel, she tossed some garments on the stool and deftly folded the others back into the chest. She added slippers and silk stockings to her selections, then began to hold up gowns for Rachel's inspection, though, muttering to herself, she discarded most of them before Rachel could comment.

"Not black for a wedding, or the green, though it becomes you. But this pale blue satin—or the white silk and lace?"

"Didn't they belong to the senhor's dead wives?"

"Yes, but you need not fear, sinhá. None of the ladies died of illness that could taint the clothing."

"I would still rather wear my own things."

Shrugging, Felicia undid the bundle, a mantle of holland serge wrapped about the linen petticoat and pale gray dimity gown the nuns had helped her to sew. "The senhor doesn't like plain things." The black woman frowned.

"Then he should have picked a fancier wife."

A smile glimmered at the edges of Felicia's mouth. "Well, perhaps with this silver lace mantilla and these slippers . . . You can't wear those shoes, sinhá. They are like to drop from your feet."

The boys came in bearing large buckets that they poured into the tub, stealing curious glances at Rachel before they retreated. Felicia hung the gray dimity from a peg and, disregarding Rachel's blushing protests, helped her undress.

"Get into the tub and soak," commanded this imperious slave. "I'll wash your hair when I come back, and there'll be more water to rinse off with."

In spite of Rachel's anxiety, the warm water relaxed her, gradually seemed to draw out and dissolve the grime and weariness of the voyage. She was almost drowsing when the door creaked open.

Dismissing the water bearers to carry in the buckets herself, Felicia set them near the tub and returned with a silver flagon and a wooden bowl. "Coconut milk with rum," she said, giving Rachel the flagon. "It'll make you feel better."

Between sips, she spooned pudding into Rachel's mouth, good-tasting though full of small transparent balls that were rather chewy. "Tapioca," the woman explained. "It comes from manioc, like much Brazilian food. You'll have manioc three times a day, cooked in a dozen ways, and you'll get tired of it, but some nice tapioca's just what you need right now.''

By the time she had finished the drink and pudding, Rachel felt light-headed but considerably less troubled, as if she were floating above the young woman who languorously permitted the older one to lather her hair and rinse it. When Felicia began to soap her back and shoulders, though, Rachel tried to fend her off.

''Sinhá,'' chided the servant, ''this is not a nunnery.''

That struck Rachel as tremendously witty. She giggled till her attendant made her stand for a final rinsing and then helped her to the mat, where she was dried gently with linen towels and her hair rubbed to a tumbling mass of moist curls. Unsteady on her feet, she gripped Felicia's arms.

''I—I—maybe I shouldn't have drunk that rum.''

''You should,'' said the ebony woman. ''And whatever I give you to drink at dinner, swallow it all.''

A cold chill shot down Rachel's spine. Staring into the dark, masklike face, she blurted, ''The senhor's other wives—did they drink what you gave them?''

''The last one did. Poor little Dona Caterina, just past her twelfth birthday at her wedding, dead with the babe she was too small to deliver before she was thirteen, may they both rest in Mary's arms!'' Felicia crossed herself before her expression hardened. ''The other two, I gave them nothing.'' Gaze boring into Rachel, she said sternly, ''You mean, did I give them poison? No. Though another might have. A word that may save your life, sinhá: do not take food or drink from anyone's hand here at Seraphim till you are sure you can trust them.''

Sobered, though strangely it no longer mattered that she was naked before this woman, Rachel watched her. Something strong and sure ran between them. ''I trust you,'' Rachel said. ''I don't know why you have decided to help me, but I am grateful.''

''That is wild talk from a sinhá-dona,'' Felicia said with a bitter laugh. ''You could have me flogged or blinded or burned with hot irons. It is to my benefit to have a soft-hearted mistress.''

She helped Rachel dress, exclaiming that she needed no

stays and hoping that the master wouldn't mind the lack of a farthingale to stylishly hold out the skirts. It took a time for her to carefully comb out the fall of auburn hair and arrange the silvery cobweb of a mantilla. Stockings and brocade slippers that slightly pinched her toes completed Rachel's attire. She hung back as Felicia moved to the door.

"I—Felicia, I can't!"

"Must, sinhá."

Rachel only stared her paralyzed fright. Moving to her, Felicia grasped her hand. "You'll live through it. He needs you for children. Give them and he won't bother you much."

"But—is that what my life is going to be? Having babies and hoping my husband will leave me alone?"

"That's how most ladies live." Felicia smiled sardonically. "Maybe you'd rather be a slave?" Slipping her hand beneath Rachel's elbow, she led her into the hall.

A stair led to a gallery that opened into a chapel. Duarte waited before a flower-decked altar, but the fragrance of blossoms and incense could not blot out a faint but unmistakable odor of decaying flesh that came from the raised family tomb. The last wife?

Emeralds, rubies, diamonds and other precious stones hung from images of saints and Virgins to whose robes were pinned ornaments of gold. Rachel, forced by Felicia's relentless grip, moved forward and knelt at the priest's command.

Now she was the wife of Duarte Álvares, more surely his than any slave, for she could not be sold away. He had seated her beside him at the head of the hand-hewn plank table, which itself was dwarfed in the huge dining room which had no other stick of furniture apart from a dozen chairs. Only seven of these were occupied, but the others were in place as if occupied by uninvited, invisible guests.

Thinking of the three women who had preceded her, Rachel could not repress a shiver. The father of the last one, young Caterina, who was Duarte's brother-in-law as well as his former father-in-law, had staggered drunkenly when he took the chair his servant held for him. A gross, pink-faced balding man, he had attended the wedding and bowed over Rachel's hand when it was over, but now kept up a running lament to the skeletal priest on his right. Rachel could not help overhearing.

". . . finest plantation in Pernambuco. Eight thousand arrobas of sugar a year! If those heretic Dutch hadn't seized it, my poor wife wouldn't be dead. I wouldn't be refuging under my brother-in-law's roof. And my little Caterina— she'd still be playing with her dolls, for I never intended for her to wed till she was fourteen. Twelve is too young, my good wife always said. Too young to bear children and nurture them." He sighed and drained his goblet. "It's all the fault of those heretics. And those thrice-damned New Christians! Traitors all!"

Across the table from him, seated next to Bento, Duarte's red-haired foster brother, the slender, dark young man who had been introduced to Rachel as Manoel Vargas, the plantation manager, flushed and leaned forward.

"Senhor! Do you call me a traitor?"

"You?" Tomé Vilhena blinked. "Curse me if I don't forget you're a New Christian! Of course I didn't mean the ones who've really turned to the true faith. But you'll have to admit that a lot of Judaizers wasted no time in moving to Recife and Olinda, where they can openly practice the religion they hid while living here as Catholics."

So Manoel was of her race! Rachel studied him, hoping that here might be someone she could talk with. He had a thin face with a long straight nose, deep-set brown eyes, dark brown hair and a neat beard. Turning up his hands, Manoel smiled slightly.

"The senhor will also agree that a great many Catholic planters, offered religious freedom by the Dutch, have vowed allegiance to Netherlands Brazil, and are flourishing."

"Their day of reckoning will come!" sputtered Tomé. "We drove the Dutch out of Bahia twelve years ago and we'll get them out of Pernambuco and the north as soon as the Crown sends another Armada."

Manoel's smile deepened. "Philip IV, king of Spain, has more on his mind than a Portuguese colony. His wars with the Low Countries and the French have drained the treasury. Nor has he forgotten that Portugal contributed only five of the twenty-one warships sent to relieve the colonies in 1631."

Banging down his goblet so hard that wine sloshed out, Tomé bellowed, "Are you saying the heretics will keep Pernambuco, the richest captaincy in Brazil?"

"No," said Manoel pacifically. "Only that if the Dutch are expelled, Brazilians must do it."

"Brazilians? You mean the Indians?" Tomé's jaw dropped. "The Tupi couldn't stand up to hard work. They've died off except for those in the Jesuit missions and the ones who fled inland. The Caeté were wiped out, which served them right for eating the first Bishop of Brazil. As for the Tapuyas, they've sided with the Dutch—"

Duarte finished gnawing on a chicken bone taken from a dressing of rice, cashews and spices. Like his brother-in-law, he had emptied his goblet several times. Now he belched and patted the arm of the immense black woman in violet calico who sat on his left.

This was Irene, presented to Rachel as Duarte's *mãe preta*, black mother, who had been his wet nurse. "She fed me my first rusty gravy and manioc paste with meat," he had said affectionately as she beamed at him. "She rocked my cradle and taught me my first 'Hail Mary,' for my mother died birthing a second child while I was a babe. My stepmothers were a poor lot, always miscarrying or stuffing themselves with sweets while their slave girls fanned them."

Now, grinning, he said to the blue-turbaned black woman, "My milk-brother, Bento, and I are both good Brazilians, if that means having mixed blood. I suspect that my father's will freed you and Bento for more than your being my *mãe preta*. As for me, I'm proud to be descended from old Caramuru and his Tupi princess. Is that what you mean by Brazilians, Manoel?"

The young man said deliberately, "A Brazilian is surely anyone born here." His gaze touched Rachel briefly, but she felt that in that instant he had made a shrewd appraisal. "Or those who come to live here so that their loyalty is to Brazil, not Europe."

Father Paulo coughed. "It is to be hoped that all good Christians of Brazil, Portugal and Spain will unite in routing the heretics." His tone changed to one of mild reproof. "In fairness to your great-grandmother, my son, one must point out that Catherina Alvares spent her last years most piously in Bahia and built a chapel to the Virgin.''

"I'll show it to you when we go to Bahia for Corpus Christi," Duarte promised Rachel. For the first time he noticed that she had barely touched the food he'd heaped on her plate. "You must eat more heartily than that, little bride." He winked at the others and pressed some baked fish into her mouth. "You'll need your strength tonight."

The succulent fish tasted of onions and red peppers, flavors Rachel usually relished, but her mouth was so dry that she had difficulty in chewing. When Duarte grew absorbed in wrangling with his brother-in-law over whose fault it was that the Dutch were still in Pernambuco, Felicia unobtrusively removed Rachel's heaped plate and put in its stead a bowl of rice cooked with milk, which proved to be light and delicious.

She also kept Rachel's goblet refilled from a graceful pitcher, silver like all the rest of the table service, a strange contrast to the scarred wood table. A silver candelabrum lit either end of the board, and besides spoons and knives, there were three-tined instruments Duarte had called forks. "These come from Italy," he'd boasted almost as soon as they'd taken their places at table. "Even in France, only a few noble houses have them." Noticing her surprise at the silver, he'd shrugged. "Most planters of any account have such services. We get the metal in plenty from Spanish ships bringing it from Peru." He chuckled. "They aren't supposed to stop in Brazil unless forced by weather, but it's amazing how troublous the seas get when it's more profitable to exchange silver in our ports for provisions and slaves."

His voice, directed at Tomé, sounded in her ears now, but she could no longer distinguish his words. Candle flames flickered on the faces at the long table, black, copper and white, first illuminating, then obscuring. Rachel felt as if a drugged warmth spread from her vitals through arms and legs, turning even fingers and feet pleasantly heavy. Felicia filled the goblet again, and in response to her admonishing glance, Rachel sipped it.

Candles and faces blurred now. She blinked, managed to reorganize shifting yellow features into those of Damião, the cook, who was graciously bowing to the compliments of his artistry. Rachel tried to smile as she followed Duarte's example in drinking a toast.

And then candles, staring eyes and her husband's face swirled into soft darkness. She heard Duarte laughing, felt broad arms lifting her, and then knew nothing.

Almost nothing.

Flashes. Like the sudden veer of the candles. Fingers digging into her shoulders. The panting of some great beast. Bright wounding pain that brought a cry she didn't know for her own. Savage hurt, a heavy weight collapsing. Moaning, she wrenched her head sideways.

She could breathe now. Down she sank, deeper and deeper. She scarcely knew when the weight rolled off her, but dimly realized that she was free to turn on her side. She hid her face against her arm and slept.

She didn't wake so kindly, but to moist hands that moved over her like rooting blind animals. Stiffening, she reached for cover, but Duarte captured her wrists and held them above her head, laughing as she tried to writhe free.

"A shy little nun, is it? But pretty. Much prettier than in those prim clothes." Bending his tousled head, he nipped her breasts, her belly, her flanks.

"Senhor!" she pleaded. "This—this is sinful!"

If she must, she could endure the pain that had left its raw memory between her legs, but to be mauled like this, preyed on by eyes as greedy as his hands . . .

He brought her under him. "Did you think I would do it through a hole in the counterpane, like some prissy fools?" he gibed. "I saw Felicia serving you wine and no doubt there was a drug in it, but I let it pass. I don't enjoy deflowering virgins or hearing their wails. But now you're a woman. Spare me your tears and prate of sin."

Watching her face, he lunged into her. The big silver scapular hung about his bull-like neck struck her lip. It brought blood, but the sting was lost in pain and terror. She realized something of what Felicia had saved her, also, with a detached part of her mind, knew that if this hadn't killed her last night, it wouldn't kill her now. A primitive instinct to survive burned out the horror.

He was her husband. It was for this, the production of children to people the colonies that the Crown had sent her to Brazil. But she was more than a body, more than a womb.

She was herself, with her own mind and will. She had no home or family; even her religion was not the one graved deep in her first childish memories, mingled with the closeness of loving parents, who now seemed to her like saints or angels. But through her years in the orphanage, some desperate citadel had formed within her. Duarte Alvares could not command it or take it by storm.

As he rolled off her, she felt bitter triumph. He was disarmed. He would always be after what could only be a longer or shorter time of that fevered thrusting.

In spite of this comforting realization, it was oppressive to lie in the thick spill of his seed, pinned by his leg and outflung hairy arm. It was all very well to laud spirit and mind, but not too practical when her body was weighted down by a larger, stronger one.

When he was snoring, she disengaged herself, placing a silk pillow beneath his arm and leg as she slid free. She longed to wash but feared to wake him. Felicia would find her a place to bathe.

Stealthily slipping into the gray dimity, Rachel gathered up petticoat, slippers and stockings and held her breath as the massive door groaned. Duarte muttered something but didn't wake. She crept out the door.

Blessedly, Felicia was waiting. Without being told, she knew what Rachel needed. Signaling to the boys loitering at the end of the hall whence floated appetizing odors, the woman relieved Rachel of her things and brought her past stairs and dining room to a small bed chamber where tub and towels waited.

"You are all right," she said after a close scanning of Rachel's face. "You know what he can do. You can endure it." She frowned at the petticoat and stockings, dropped them to a bench. "Such things are too hot for this weather. Except for going out in public, even sinhá-donas wear only smocks or a chemise and petticoat."

"But—"

"Indians went naked year-round except for paint," said Felicia. "The first Portuguese women of Bahia lost most of their babies because they swaddled the poor little things against the 'bad air' and dressed them as they would have in Portugal. It was only when they stopped smothering babies that they survived.'' She nodded toward several loose embroidered cotton smocks folded on the bench. "After your bath, you must put on one of these.''

The boys came in to fill the tub. When they were gone, Rachel gratefully lowered herself in the breast-deep water. A pretty young cinnamon-colored girl brought in a silver tray with a bowl of fruit, a napkin-covered basket and a mug of some steaming brew.

As some of the tenderness soaked out of her plundered body, she sipped the spicy herbal drink and ate pieces of the fruits Felicia prepared for her as she named them. "Have you tasted bananas? These are the big kind from Africa, much better than the small native ones. This is pineapple. Do you like the mango?''

When Rachel was refreshed, Felicia drew her out of the tub, toweled her with gentle thoroughness and slipped one of the light cotton smocks over her head.

Indicating that Rachel should sit on a reed mat, Felicia tucked on her slippers. "That's all you need, and more than you'll want before the day's over. Now eat your *curada* and I'll take you around the house.''

The napkin-covered basket contained a thick warm cake of what Felicia explained was tapioca dough baked with cashew nuts. It was tasty, but after weeks of weevily ship biscuit, Rachel hungered for some good wheat bread.

Felicia shook her head at a query. "Manioc is what all Brazil eats, in pastes, breads and cakes, porridges, in dozens of ways. Even the governors-general have preferred it to wheat.''

Compared to being Duarte Álvares' unwilling bride, the lack of her accustomed bread was a small thing, but Rachel sighed as Felicia stood over her till she dutifully finished the tapioca cake.

The chapel she had already seen. Felicia explained that the chaplain's room was above the sacristy. Across the gallery on the second floor was a library. "The senhor's father loved to read.'' Felicia gestured at a shelf of books and a chair with a footstool located between two windows. A big table was covered by neatly arranged papers and ledgers. A candlestick stood near writing quills and an ink bottle. "It is here that Senhor Vargas keeps the records."

The overworked nun who kept the convent's accounts had noticed an aptitude in Rachel and taught her to read, write and cipher so that she could be of use. Eagerly Rachel eyed the volumes. There should be something there besides the pious works and sermons her teacher had loaned her.

"I can come here?"

Felicia bowed. "It is your house." She hesitated delicately. "Of course, if Senhor Vargas is here, it would be best to retire to one of the parlors." There were three of these adjoining the library and across from the dining room and two small bedrooms. The parlors were furnished with a few chairs, benches, tables and big reed mats. The only touches of luxury were silver candelabra. Beyond the staircase were more bedrooms, including Rachel's. The right wing began with a laundry room and dispensary, wine closet, and a pantry with an inscription on the door.

Praise Saint Benedict, 'tis a sin
That ants should come here to enter in.

In the big kitchen, three boys darted about at Damião's orders, and two girls were making round flat cakes out of what Rachel was sure was manioc. Glancing up with a broad smile from finely chopped peppers he was dicing with a formidable broad-bladed cleaver, the saffron-hued cook ducked his head to Rachel and asked how she had liked her *curada*.

When she assured him that it was delicious, nothing would do but that she should sample honey rice cakes and coconut pastry sprinkled with cinnamon. Damião's ribbon-trimmed smock worn over cotton trousers made Rachel's lips twitch, but she managed to hide her amusement till they were safely out of the mulatto's domain.

"Best never let Damião know you laugh at him," Felicia advised as they started downstairs and a muffled giggle escaped her mistress. "You don't want too much pepper in your food for the rest of your life."

Guest chambers were on one side of the reception hall.
Beds canopied with satin or damask were spread with silk
counterpanes. Each room had a chest, a stool, clothing
pegs, a washstand, and chamber pots showing from beneath the bedclothes.

Shouting laughter came from the room between reception hall and chapel. "That's the children's playroom,"
Felicia said hurriedly. "Now, if the sinhá wishes to see
the gardens—"

A Negro boy of seven or eight crawled past on hands
and knees. The long ends of the cord in his mouth were
held by a small black-haired boy on his back who switched
him with a reed.

"Giddap, horse!" commanded the rider, kicking thin
dark ribs.

"Little master!" begged the older child.

"Shut your mouth, beast!" The rider slashed at him with
the reed and dug in his bare heels, cream-colored flesh
against dusky plum. "Giddap, I tell you!"

Children were an unknown element to Rachel. She supposed rough play was common, but this seemed entirely
too one-sided. She commanded sharply, "Get off your
playmate! He's not big enough to carry you."

The small tyrant, perhaps four or five years old, stared
up at her, yellow eyes ablaze. She realized whose child he
was even before Luzia glided from the chapel.

She wore no emeralds today, but tied to a sash at her
slender waist was a golden frame from which hung dozens
of golden charms, bells, animals, birds, religious medallions, suns, moons and stars. Their mellow clinking music
was like an echo of Luzia's assured tone.

"The sinhá does not understand. Chico is Gilberto's *muleque*. Such a lad is always given to a young master, as
was Bento to the senhor."

"I did not know," said Rachel, holding the tawny-haired
woman's eyes, "that this house had a young master."

An insolent smile curved Luzia's red mouth. "Gilberto
is the senhor's child. It is not unknown, sinhá, for such a
lad to be his father's heir or inherit with legitimate sons."

Felicia made a hissing sound. Luzia gave her a mocking
glance. Rachel drew herself up.

"However that may be, I am mistress here. Tell your son to get off Chico's back and not to abuse him unless he himself wants a good spanking."

Rachel's eyes contested with furious golden ones, held them steadily. After a long moment, Luzia turned to the boys and muttered something to Gilberto, whose small jaw dropped. He scowled ferociously at Rachel, but most reluctantly he slid off his companion, giving him a last disguised kick.

"I want some candy!" he yelled, grasping his mother's skirts.

"Come, then, we'll find you some," the woman soothed.

Taking Gilberto by the hand, she moved toward the stairs in her undulating walk. Chico trotted behind, keeping a distance sagaciously estimated to be out of range of cuffs or pinches. Felicia moved her turbaned head in misgiving.

"That one, she hate you for sure now."

"She would anyway. She wants her son to be heir of Seraphim."

"Don't go drinking anything she gives you, or eating any little treats she offers."

"She'd use poison?"

Felicia shrugged. "Maybe. Maybe magic. She keeps the senhor by putting her menstrual blood in his wine." Felicia's gap-toothed smile flashed with singular coldness. "She knows I have magic, too, *mandingas* stronger than hers. But you had better watch her."

From the garden in front of the house, Felicia pointed out the complex of buildings and sheds that processed cane into sugar, molasses and rum. Mill, refinery, distillery, cane trash shed and stables. Close by were the quarters of slaves who worked in the fields or mill.

"House slaves live in this *senzala*," Felicia said, leading the way around the Big House. Joined to it at the back was an L of stone dwellings that formed a courtyard where children played.

Servants passed in and out through the entrance that led through the wine cellar up to the kitchen. Felicia escorted Rachel through the cellar and out a passage opening into an interior garden fragrant with brilliant flowers. A fountain sparkled under several big trees that sheltered stone benches.

The court was neglected and overgrown with vines, but Rachel immediately loved it, the old sundial, the stone pots of herbs and marigolds. Gazing at frondy palms beyond the wall, she thought how different life could be if her husband had been another sort than Duarte. So far the only thing she'd seen to commend him was his affection for Irene, his allowing her and Bento, his milk-brother, to sit at the family table.

Perhaps any man would be like him in bed? Rachel ached as she walked and she blushed with humiliation to remember that morning. Would he always inflict such pain? Felicia opened an iron gate. The wing with the kitchen extended beyond the garden and a chicken pen was attached to the wall. As Rachel watched, a bucket of peels and other kitchen scraps were tossed out the window. The rest of the big fenced enclosure was taken up by an orchard, a kitchen garden and, in one corner, a pigsty.

"There used to be another palisade that ran around all the plantation buildings, including the mill," said Felicia. "After the danger of Indian attack was over, the fortifications were taken down. We'll wish we still had them if the Dutch come."

"Do you think they will?"

"Who knows? The Portuguese won't win this country easily. They drove the French out of Rio de Janeiro over seventy years ago, but the English have settlements on the Amazon." Felicia gave a bitter laugh. "It would seem that Africans are the only foreigners who don't want to come here—and us, the Portuguese want!"

"Were you born in Africa?"

"No, I was born in Seraphim's *senzala,* but my parents were from Dahomey, part of what you call the Gold Coast."

"Then you have family here?"

Felicia's face looked like carved ebony. "My parents died of smallpox when I was little."

"No brothers or sisters?"

"The old master had the French pox. It's said that by taking a black virgin just as she is becoming a woman, the disease can be passed to her. I don't know if the master was cured, but my sister was riddled with sores. She was lucky to die giving birth to a deformed baby who died before it breathed.''

''Felicia—''

The tall woman seemed not to hear. ''My brother ran off to the *sertão,* the backlands, when the Dutch took Bahia. So many slaves escaped that they have villages in the wilderness. I hope my brother is alive in one of them.''

''You must hate us.''

Somberly regarding her mistress, Felicia said, ''I do not hate you, though it's said that you're a New Christian and New Christians have much to do with both the slave trade and marketing the sugar that makes black slaves necessary. Indians died like flies at the work. Africans may last for eight or ten years.''

When Rachel cried out at that, Felicia added, ''It's different with house servants if they have a kind master and mistress.''

''Is the senhor kind?''

Felicia hesitated. ''He is not cruel.'' She turned toward the house, stopped abruptly. ''Do you want his child?''

Rachel blinked. It had never occurred to her that there was any choice. Since that was what Duarte had imported her for, she grasped something of the risk Felicia ran in suggesting such a thing.

It was, in all her life, the only time another person had dared danger for her sake. Deeply touched, Rachel would have liked to take the woman's hand, but something in her face forbade demonstration.

''I don't know,'' Rachel said slowly.

A baby would give her something to love, a reason to live. But she didn't think she could love it if it were like Duarte. Deep down, she still hoped for a miracle of deliverance. Meeting Felicia's eyes, she half whispered, ''If there is a way—''

''There is, but don't go confessing it to the priest.'' Felicia's tone was unexpectedly humorous. ''After all, what do you know about the herbs I put in your drinks?''

She opened the gate. Rachel passed through to confront the Big House and her first full day as its sinhá-dona, but she was much heartened by knowing that she had a friend.

* * *

She also had an enemy.

Wanting some time to herself to sort out her impressions of Seraphim, she was grateful that Duarte was nowhere to be seen. Avoiding the bedroom in case he might still be there, Rachel dismissed Felicia and went through the big vacant parlors to the library. The room was empty. Sighing with relief, Rachel perched on the stool by the table and stared out the window at palm trees and the deep blue sky. She hadn't wanted to be Duarte Alvares' wife, but since she was, she intended to put meaning into her days by becoming Seraphim's mistress inasmuch as Duarte would allow. He was, she suspected, indolent and careless. Probably, so long as she didn't annoy him, he would care little about what she did.

Except— Reasonable plans scurried to the far corners of her mind and she trembled to remember that morning. He could feed on her at will. Her body was his banquet.

With all her strength, the hard-won endurance of a child orphaned too young to expect love and kindness, she fought down the panic that made her want to scream, cry out that she could not bear this. The only way to keep him from consuming her, soul along with body, was to build a life of her own, be something besides a female to make Seraphim heirs.

The discipline of a plan would help, something to impose order and recall her to her aim when she might be in no condition to think.

Finding a piece of blank paper, she glanced guiltily about. Then, reminding herself that she was the sinhá-dona and would have to do things more daring than appropriating a piece of the manager's paper if she hoped to establish her authority, she selected a quill, took the plug from the mixed ink and began to make a list.

Indians. Were any left on the plantation?

Slaves. Was food and shelter sufficient? Care for the sick? The aged and disabled?

Call house servants together. Find out who is responsible for what and then check to be sure chores are done.

Helping the old nun with convent records had given Rachel some idea of the problems encountered when many people lived together. On a plantation worked by slaves, there were sure to be different concerns, but she felt better from having laid out a course.

She was plugging the ink when the door opened. Manoel Vargas' thin cheeks colored as he saw her. "Your pardon, senhora," he muttered, and turned to go.

"I must beg your pardon, senhor, for I have filched a sheet of your paper." His shyness, emboldened Rachel, along with the knowledge that he was, like her, a New Christian. "I am leaving, but since I'd like to read the books and sit here sometimes, perhaps you'd tell me the hours you need the room."

"You can read?" His dark eyes went to the paper in her hand. "And write?"

"A nun taught me so I could help with the accounts." Rachel smiled at his doubt. "I think she was a bit vexed when I enjoyed it so much."

His voice was even more astonished. "Numbers, too?"

"I made up games with them. When I was scrubbing floors or laundry, I worked problems in my head."

Amazement overcame diffidence. "I have never known a woman who could do sums above what was needed for cozening her husband to believe it cheaper to buy material for a new gown than refurbish an old one!"

Stung, she challenged, "If the senhor will give me an example?"

He blushed again. In spite of his beard, he wasn't much older than she was, surely not even twenty. "The senhora will pardon me. I was surprised—"

"For favor, senhor, a problem!"

"Very well." He bowed. "If we produce eight thousand arrobas of sugar this year, how many quintals is that?"

"That would depend on whether you figure two or four arrobas to a quintal, but if you call if four, that would make two thousand quintals."

"Can you turn that into English pounds?"

For her own amusement she had learned foreign measures, but she had to pucker her brow to remember the rarely used formula. *Thirty-two pounds equals one arroba.* "Two hundred and fifty-six thousand pounds," she said as if she worked such sums every day. "And if you want it in *onças*—"

He held up a hand, laughing. "The senhora is formidable! I could wish for your aid when it's time to figure taxes."

"I should be glad to help," she said quickly, then remembered and bit her lip. ". . . if my husband permits."

"You might like to see what Seraphim produced last year." Manoel flipped an open ledger back about halfway to a neatly detailed summary. "Of our eight thousand arrobas, over two thousand were *muscavada,* sugar with molasses still in it, and *panela,* from drainings, made up a thousand. Besides Seraphim's own crop, the mill crushes cane and makes sugar for many small planters in return for half the yield." He flipped a page. "Here, you see, are the leased sections with the number of cartloads of cane each brought to the mill, reckoned in *tarefas.*" He grinned at her. "I'll wager *that's* a new measure for you."

She laughed too. "What is it?"

"The 'task' or amount of cane the mill can grind in twenty-four hours. Seraphim's mill does about thirty cartloads."

"It'd do thirty-five if you'd move the oxen at a faster pace," came Duarte's voice from the door.

They whirled. Duarte chuckled, arching up a heavy black eyebrow. *"Tarefas* of sugarcane! What a thing to be discussing with a woman." He drew Rachel to him possessively. "What a polite little girl it is! Listening as if she were interested."

"Indeed, the senhor's lady has a good comprehension of mathematics," defended Manoel.

Duarte frowned down at her. "How can that be?"

When she explained about the convent records, he put back his head and roared with laughter. "It must be in the blood of you Jews—pardon me, New Christians. God knows I can't make heads or tails of all that scribbling. That's why I need a clever manager." Pleased by a sudden thought, he showed his teeth at Manoel. "By Our Lady, it may not be an ill thing to have a wife who can decipher your hen tracks. And read those letters from your friends in Amsterdam."

Manoel's tone was stiff. "If the senhor believes I have cheated him, he should employ another manager."

"Of course I don't think that," Duarte said hastily. "Your merchandising connections turn me a nice profit, and I'm grateful. But it vexes a man not to understand his business affairs."

"As I have told the senhor, I will be delighted to have him concern himself more with the balances. Any time he would choose to examine the records, I am at his disposal."

"No, no." Duarte looked alarmed as he fended off the offer. "But if my wife understands such things, it might not be amiss if she occasionally went over the accounts with you?"

Manoel bowed. "The senhora is equally welcome."

"Fine," beamed Duarte. "But don't start your figures now, Manoel. Damião has made his special *vatapá*. He'll be angry if we aren't all sitting down when he's ready to serve it."

As Duarte swung out of the room with Rachel on his arm, she glimpsed Luzia watching from the second parlor. The startled look in the golden eyes gave way to fury in the flash before the woman spun on her bare heel and vanished.

Chatting with Manoel, Duarte hadn't seen her, but Rachel, chilled at the malevolence of that stare, was sure he had been sent to the library by Luzia, and that Luzia had hoped to cause trouble. That a lonely young man and woman might find pleasure in simply conversing would be unbelievable to the voluptuous favorite.

This time, if never again, Rachel found herself blessing her husband's dislike of financial matters and his evident satisfaction in deputing her to represent him.

She would have to be careful, very careful. But, laughably, Luzia's scheming had led to Duarte himself authorizing her closer acquaintance with this young man.

Yes, Rachel had an enemy. But she believed now that she had two friends.

The *vatapá* was fish in a spiced batter of manioc and oil. Rachel didn't have to lie when she complimented Damião, but as she ate a flat cake of moist tapioca flour, she wondered if she'd ever stop missing wheat bread. Tomé didn't appear for lunch.

"My brother-in-law stays in his hammock most of the day," Duarte said contemptuously. "His mulatto wench brings him food and drink, fans him and hunts his lice."

The master of Seraphim snorted. "You've heard him lament his wife, but the poor woman might be living still if her health hadn't been broken as she struggled here on foot while he carried his Valeria pillion on his horse."

Father Paulo's eyes widened. "My son," he rebuked, "your brother-in-law has suffered greatly."

"Not he," retorted Duarte. "He has his mistress and a soft living. If he ever gets his plantation back, it'll be because braver men have fought for it."

The meal ended with sponge cake drenched in pineapple syrup and coconut. Used to vegetables from the convent garden, Rachel missed them and determined to find out if there were some in that big garden adjoining the orchard.

Rising, Duarte yawned. "I'm fatigued," he said with a roguish look at Rachel. "But I shall be in my hammock in the room next to ours, little bride, so if you wish to nap, you may do so undisturbed." He winked broadly. "I should suggest a good rest. You must still be tired from—your journey."

A tide of blood rose to the roots of her hair. With a gratified laugh at her confusion, he strutted out. Loathing turned her almost sick, and for a moment hot blackness weaved between her and the others at the table.

How could she go about her tasks, dress and eat and do the ordinary things, when that night, and many of those to come, had in store what she'd suffered that morning? *That* was the reality of her position here.

It dwarfed the defenses she had started, her lists, the grace of the library, a use for her accounting skills. The friendship of Manoel and Felicia could not help her in Duarte's grasp.

She wanted to run. Run from that night, all the nights. But she was in a strange land on an isolated plantation. In a strange world, for that matter. She had never thought of it before, but on the whole earth she had not a close relative or friend.

Except Felicia?

Somehow this very aloneness steadied Rachel. She had no place, not even that of an orphan, for she was grown up. No loving family to sigh for, no friends to regret.

Out of herself, she must make a place. Duarte—well,

she would think of him no more than she must. Rising, she excused herself.

"Will the sinhá rest?" asked Felicia, who was waiting outside the dining room.

Rachel wanted to get outside the house, away from her mental picture of Duarte lounging in his hammock, perhaps with Luzia attending him. She was tired, though, and knew it must be hot in the gardens.

As if reading Rachel's mind, Felicia said coaxingly, "Has the sinhá ever slept in a hammock? No? Then let's go to one of the guest rooms and sling one for you. It would be much cooler for napping than the big bed." And would have no memories of Duarte.

"I might lie down for a little while. Then I'd like to see the mill and visit the *senzalas.*"

"Why would the sinhá do that?"

"I want to understand how the sugar's made, the work people have to do. I want to be sure they have decent homes and good food."

"The sinhá needn't bother her head about that. Before Senhor Vargas came, too many were jammed in small rooms and the food was bad. Now each family has a garden patch for growing okra and other fresh vegetables we had in Africa. Senhor Vargas himself visits the quarters daily to be sure everything's all right. He's dismissed two overseers for keeping *senzala* beef and selling it."

"I'm glad to know Senhor Vargas looks after the workers. All the same, there may be things a woman can see to better than a man."

"Yes, sinhá." Felicia's tone was indulgent. "But first have a little rest."

It took Felicia only a moment to string a hammock from pegs already fixed in the wall for guests who preferred a hammock to the pomp and heat of the silken bed. "You get into it like this," Felicia demonstrated, sitting down and agilely swinging up her legs, setting them and her shoulders at angles to balance comfortably in the expanded cotton mesh.

Dubiously Rachel followed her example, expecting to feel snared in a big net. Instead, she sank into a flexible buoyant support that accommodated each motion. She

exclaimed with delight, "This must be how babies feel
when their mothers put them in shawls tied to their
backs."

"Yes." Felicia smiled. "And what of this?"

Gently, she moved the hammock back and forth. It
brought back to Rachel a memory so deeply buried that she
wasn't sure it was true, the safe, comforting rocking of a
cradle, a sweet voice singing.

> "This little girl of mine
>   Does not sleep in a bed
>   She sleeps in the blessed lap
>   Of the good Saint Anne instead."

"That's a song for children, Felicia!" Rachel protested
laughingly.

"Sometimes it's good to be a child. Just for a bit, sinhá.
Sometimes it's good to pretend one has a child."

"You have none?"

Felicia shook her head. "Close your eyes, sinhá. Be a
child again." She crooned, moving the hammock,

> "See the old black man up on top the roof;
>   He says that he's a-wanting roast child on the hoof!"

That was a lullaby? Rachel giggled. But then Felicia
sang in a tongue Rachel didn't know, softly murmurous
as the wind soughing through the palms, and Rachel,
feeling cared for and protected, lapsed into a deep, healing slumber.

She woke to an intermittent breeze, an almost impercep-
tible lulling motion. Opening her eyes, still half asleep,
she was prepared to see her parents, their consciously forgotten features remembered in her dreams. Her smile froze
as she saw a long, austere black face. Then she remembered where she was and why she had felt in her sleep like
a young, well-loved child.

"Felicia!" Sitting up too abruptly, she almost spilled out
of the hammock. "I hope you haven't been fanning me all
this time. You need a nap more than I do."

"I'm not a bride. But, sinhá, if you want to walk before supper, we had better start."

After supper came the big bed. Rachel shivered involuntarily. Felicia touched her shoulder. "I can drug your wine again tonight, but I can't do anything against the mornings. It wouldn't be good to get used to having the draught each evening. Soon you need it in the day, and always oftener, till you move like a zombi, a dead body without a soul or mind."

One part of Rachel could despair of life under Duarte's rule, use anything that cushioned the humiliation and ugliness. Another part warned that she couldn't maintain her integrity by numbing herself with potions. She wasn't brave enough, though, to face in a few hours what she'd found such shameful pain that morning.

"Let me have the help tonight," she said under her breath. "but, Felicia, for favor don't let me have it after this unless there's a time when you think I might go mad without it."

Felicia nodded. Positioning Rachel on a stool, she combed her hair and then held the door for Rachel to precede her.

Passing the great cross that rose as high as the second story in the garden outside the chapel, they followed a path to the sugar works, deserted now, for the harvest that began in September had finished in mid-April, and the grueling labor was over till what would have been autumn in Portugal but was summer here.

"I'm glad to see the works while no one's around," Rachel said. "It's a lot less confusing."

During the next half hour Felicia showed her how oxen turned the wheel that powered huge vertical rollers through which cane passed as the juice ran in troughs to great copper caldrons in the boiling house.

"Slaves skim off the impurities," Felicia explained. "Then the juice is ladled into these smaller caldrons and cools off. After that, it's poured into these cone-shaped tile forms. When the sugar crystallizes, it's taken to the purging house."

Leading the way to that building, she showed the fine clay that was placed on each cone. "The clay's wet and water from it trickles very slowly down through the cone, washing out the molasses. Finer, whiter sugar is treated several times before it's put to dry in the sun, and molasses-filled sugar goes in another heap. Then the sugar tithe contractor comes, and he and Senhor Manoel argue about how much sugar the government gets.''

"Those big rollers and the boiling juice," said Rachel. "Are there many accidents?''

"Not as many as before Senhor Manoel. The mill runs all day and night during harvest, but Senhor Manoel hires enough Indians from the mission so that no one has to work more than eight hours at a stretch.''

Behind the main buildings were a distillery for making potent rum from cane juice, and a shed for the cane trash, which was dried and used as fuel. Beyond the stables was a fenced pasture. Aloof from the oxen, two splendid horses stood on a slope, the head of one resting on the back of the other.

"The senhor will have his blooded mounts," Felicia said.

As they passed the *senzala*, a long, low rock building with a thatched roof and several doors, Felicia said that unmarried field hands lived here. Women from the compound near the house cooked for them and did the laundry. They were out now weeding cane and doing other work that had been let slide during the frenetic harvest and milling time.

Rachel took a quick look inside the building. A few men had chests or boxes shoved against the wall beneath one end of their hammocks and extra garments hung from pegs. The long row of hammocks was suspended from stout ceiling beams, a passage left along one side. On some chests lay a flute or a stringed instrument. These and the pegged garments were the only hints that the dozens of men living here were individuals, people who liked certain colors and had favorite songs.

The packed-earth floor was clean. The room was in perfect order. And Rachel found it appalling. Her tiny shared cell in the convent had been just as sterile, but she'd had the hope of escaping it. This—this was how intelligently cared-for beasts would be lodged.

"It's a place to sleep," she said aloud. "It's not a home."

Felicia's mouth twisted. "Slaves have quarters, not homes.''

They passed out through a dining hall with long plank tables and benches. "Surely the married ones don't live like this," said Rachel as they walked toward the upper *senzala*.

"Each family has its small room," allowed Felicia. "But when you know that someone owns you—well, you don't have a home, sinhá. You have a stall or a manger."

All the same, there was laughter in the married quarters, laughing children chasing about, and good smells of cooking. There was life. Felicia explained that these families shared several big kitchens with tables for eating. The children of women who worked in the Big House were looked after by older women who also did most of *senzala* chores and tended the garden patches.

Greeted by a wrinkled old woman who was trying to soothe a wailing baby, Rachel glanced swiftly about the room. Here, the hammocks were draped from holds on one side, leaving the space free. A big chest of woven palm leaves was the only furniture, but two little girls sat playing with rag dolls on a big rush mat that covered most of the floor. They wore no clothes, but each had a knot of red ribbon tied among tight black ringlets. A shelf on the wall held a black saint dressed in a scrap of red satin and, surrounded by flowers, a Virgin with a gold halo that resembled a hoop earring. Both images were crudely carved but had strength and dignity.

Felicia's bitter comment was probably true, but from what Rachel had seen of Lisbon and Bahia, she knew that plenty of free people lived in much worse places. The family of this room possessed little more than an unmarried man would, but there was a great though intangible difference.

The children? The shrine? Whatever it was, a stranger could tell that the people who lived here shared more than the big matrimonial hammock.

"Sweet little girls," said Rachel to the old woman. The baby was still crying, tiny fists squeezed tight as his eyes. "Is the little one sick?"

"It's the umbilical cord," said Felicia.

Rachel had never seen a navel cord, so she didn't know how one should look, but she didn't think the puffily inflamed stub projecting could possibly be healthy.

To her glance of alarm, Felicia said, "Mothers often rub

the cord with red pepper. They think that helps it heal, but this can happen.''

"Is there anyone at Seraphim who serves as a doctor?"

"I do more than anyone. The old master, for all his venery, knew many cures and had a big chest of remedies. He wrote some of his medicines down, but I don't think Senhor Duarte has ever looked at the book. Certainly he doesn't trouble himself over sick slaves."

"There's no hospital? No separate place for a sick person to stay so that disease doesn't spread?"

"I've heard Senhor Manoel argue the need for such a place, but the master says by the time illness breaks out in the *senzala* it's too late to check it."

It always would be so long as he thought like that. "Where's the baby's mother?"

"Working in the kitchen."

"From now on, mothers with babies under six months old will be excused from other work." Rachel nodded good-bye to the old woman and started for the Big House. "Show me the medicine chest. Maybe we can find an ointment for the baby."

By the time the bell rang for supper, Rachel had inspected the drawered chest that sat in a small room off the stairwell amid a jumble of parasols, cleaning equipment, and other odds and ends. Felicia had refilled some bottles and pouches and added some tested herbs of her own. On top of the chest was a thin ledger, and while Felicia took some ointment to the *senzala,* Rachel acquainted herself with the medicines.

Buds of the embaiba tree for healing wounds and sores; tobacco for afflicted sexual organs; *pau cardoso* for coughing; cashew gum for mixing poultices and a number of other remedies, including several jars labeled Raya's Cure for Sore Eyes, Raya's Fever Medicine and Raya's Mixture to Purify the Blood.

Who was Raya? Rachel wondered as she scanned the pages. The book had probably been started by Duarte's grandfather, to judge from the dates going back to 1570. Along with medical advice, there were instructions for curing gourds and making dyes and ways to use various native plants.

"Have you read this?" Rachel asked Felicia when she returned.

"I can read Arabic but not Portuguese."

Rachel started to ask if the woman was Moslem before she decided that was none of her business. Touching one of the jars, she asked if Felicia knew the identity of Raya.

"I've heard stories about her. She was a wife of the Sun in Peru and came all the way across the country to Bahia when the senhor's great-grandfather, Caramuru, was living among the Indians. Later, after Caramuru died, Raya lived in Bahia with his widow, the one who built the chapel. It is said Raya had healing skills learned in Peru. When a great plague of smallpox swept the city, she nursed the sick and died herself."

Rachel felt a pang for this woman who had died so far from home. "Did this Raya have children by Caramuru?"

"No. The daughter she had by a Frenchman married a son of Caramuru, though, and they have descendants scattered all over the settled parts of Brazil."

"It sounds as if families who've been here from the start of colonization must have intermarried a lot."

"If people aren't cousins, they're godparents or godchildren," Felicia agreed.

Rachel put the ledger back on top of the chest, resolving to study it more fully and bring the medicine chest up to date.

As she shut the door, cobwebs and lint wisped over the floor. "The *senzalas* are cleaner than the Big House except for the kitchen," she said. "Why is that?"

A faint smile curved Felicia's lips. "Senhor Manoel has charge of the *senzala*. Damião runs the kitchen." The smile faded. "Don' Caterina was a child."

Rachel thought of a twelve-year-old trapped in Duarte's embrace, then trapped even deeper in pregnancy. No, poor little Caterina would have no thoughts to spare for the house. For a moment Rachel hated Tomé for delivering his daughter to such a fate. What a blind country! Lacking women, it used them hard and buried them young.

She vowed that Duarte wouldn't bury her.

* * *

That night, drugged again, she felt little of Duarte's lust, but in the light of morning his ruthless sensuality shocked as much as it brutalized her.

A bath and Felicia's ministrations partially restored her and she spent most of that day inspecting the house except for the kitchen and occupied bedrooms. She certainly had no desire to intrude on Duarte or Tomé, whether they snored in their hammocks or dallied with slaves.

Before dinner, she refused a fresh smock and asked for her gray dress. "I'll wear cool things in the day," she said, "but in the evening I want to dress properly."

"The sinhá may change her mind when the hot season begins," warned Felicia. She helped Rachel into the dimity and frowned. "If you must wear so much, let me make you some gowns of thinner material that will fit loose and let air reach your skin."

Rachel agreed that that seemed a good idea. Now that it was dinnertime, the courage engendered by the busy day with all its new sights and discoveries began to ebb. She raised frightened eyes to Felicia. "You—you will put something in my wine?"

The black woman nodded. "Yes, and something to keep you from getting a baby. But if you take the draft long enough, you may not be able to conceive."

Rachel couldn't imagine ever wanting Duarte's child. When she was silent, Felicia spoke slowly. "Perhaps there is something I can give the sinhá to help when you decide to do without the drug that deadens what you feel."

Her voice grew softer, breaking on some of the words. "When my teeth were pulled, I said to myself what my mother told me she said when she was whipped—and she was whipped often, for she never forgot she was a prince's daughter. I said, 'There is pain, but I am not the pain.' I said it and said it and somehow, though Don' Thereza laughed to see me bleed, I did not cry out."

What? Shocked into a silence that it took her moments to break, Rachel hated to ask yet felt she must know. "Your teeth, they were not pulled because they were rotten?"

Felicia's harsh laughter revealed the gaps in her otherwise beautiful white teeth. "It was Don' Thereza with rotted teeth. She was jealous of mine even before the master began to notice me. When that happened, she waited till the master was gone for the day and—'' Long dark fingers touched the disfigured mouth.

Sickened, Rachel reached out to Felicia and bowed her head. ''This was the old master?'' she said at last.

''No. Senhor Duarte. Ten years ago.''

''What did he do?''

''I think he beat Don' Thereza. There were bruises on her. She didn't care. He didn't want me for love anymore.'' Staring past Rachel, Felicia muttered, ''By the time my gums had healed, Don' Thereza was dead. She had a weak stomach.''

Rachel thought it best not to ask if there had been another reason for her predecessor's early demise. That Felicia had told her the horrible truth in order to help her gave her the strength of sudden but firm resolve.

Taking Felicia's hands, seeing in her face the beauty ravaged by an envious woman, Rachel said, ''You have given me something better than the drug, Felicia. Don't put it in my wine tonight, only the potion to stop a baby.''

Felicia smiled, not trying to hide her mutilation. This time, instead of grotesquerie, Rachel saw unconquerable spirit.

II

The Sinhá-Dona

When Felicia brought her breakfast the next morning, Rachel asked to have all the household servants, except Damião and his helpers, assemble in the bigger parlor in half an hour.

Entering the parlor with her list, Rachel was astonished at the number of black, brown and yellow women, boys and girls. Counting quickly, she noted a dozen women in young maturity and ten boys and eight girls ranging from perhaps twelve to almost full-grown. She was exceedingly surprised to see Luzia lounging near a window.

Munching on a bonbon, Luzia watched Rachel with lazy curiosity, as if she were the mistress and Rachel an inept but entertaining new slave.

Rachel sat down on the reed matting and motioned to the others to do the same. Felicia looked around and said severely, "The sinhá-dona has seen that the *senzalas* are cleaner than the Big House. She wishes to speak to you about it."

"And other things," said Rachel, trying to sound firm but gracious. "First, I would like to know your names." She smiled at the gangly black child who'd brought her orange juice. "You're Floria. Next to you?"

A handsome lad of coppery hue with reddish hair averted hazel eyes. "I Gaspar, sinhá."

"Rosa, sinhá." That was the plum-colored strongly built young woman who served at table. She put a protective hand on the shoulder of a boy who reached to her chin and had an eager, childish smile. "This my Joaquim. He no talk but work good."

"He is stupid," said Luzia. "He should be sold away."

59

Tensing, though she tried to seem confident and relaxed, Rachel looked directly into slanting golden eyes. "It is not for you to say who will be sold. Nor, since your services do nothing to improve this house's cleanliness, is there any use in your being here. You may go."

Luzia's eyes flamed, but Rachel dominated them. She had some sympathy for the woman. It must be hard to know that a newcomer to the household where she had queened it could order her flogged or worse. Probably Luzia had come hoping to provoke Rachel into commanding her to do demeaning tasks from which Duarte would excuse her, thereby invalidating Rachel's authority. Rachel had no intention of permitting that, nor did she see any reason to pretend blindness of Luzia's function.

It was hard to flounce out in petticoat and chemise, but Luzia almost succeeded. Someone laughed, and as the servants continued giving names, most of the women looked gratified. Luzia was not loved.

"It will take me a while to learn your names," Rachel said, "but I want to know you. If you are sick or have problems, come to me and I'll try to help."

She let her eyes rest on each person, trying to fit a name and impression to each. Some of the boys and girls smiled at her, but most expressions were guarded. "How many of you have babies under six months old?"

Four women stepped forward. Three others were advanced in pregnancy, including one with peach-colored skin who seemed little more than a child. "If you could stay home with your babies for their first half-year and be excused from work in your seventh month of pregnancy, would you be willing to work harder the rest of the time?"

The slaves exchanged surprised glances. Rosa said, "Sinhá, that would leave only eight women and the *mucamas* and *muleques.*"

"That's why I'm asking. If the tasks are properly apportioned, eight women with the lads and girls should manage the work."

Eva, tall and very black but with straight hair and a long nose that betokened Indian or Portuguese blood, said in a voice of deep velvet, "We all have babies this year, next year. To have time then, I glad work hard now."

Rosa said, "Maybe I have no more childs, but is good for my Izabel." She looked fondly at the youngest of the pregnant, whose breasts scarcely curved beneath her loose smock and whose light color indicated a white or mulatto father.

There was a murmur of general assent. "Fine," said Rachel, relieved that her strategy was working. "After this meeting, those in their seventh month or with young babies may finish their day's tasks and go home." She studied her list, wondering how to conduct the next part of her campaign. She had never given orders, only taken them.

"I have made an inspection of the house. It's dirty. In three days I shall go around again and expect it to be clean. No stained chamber pots, mold in the corners, dust under the furniture or on it."

Squirming, shuffling, downcast eyes. Beginning mumbles: "Eva, she won't—"; "Gaspar's supposed to—"

"I don't care whose fault it has been," cut in Rachel. "What we're going to settle now is whose fault it will be when a certain room or task is neglected. I'll make sure that everyone has enough to do but no one has too much. Let's begin with the dining room."

In less than an hour, the chores and responsibilities were assigned to everyone's reasonable satisfaction. Rosa would oversee the state of the first floor, Eva the second, and Felicia was in general command. A schedule for serving at meals was worked out. Rachel did not give the girls tasks in the men's rooms, not even Father Paulo's, though she would have trusted Manoel Vargas.

When Rosa's brow grooved at the end of the session, Rachel asked, "Have we forgotten something?"

"Sinhá, if masters stay all day in hammock, how we clean?"

Rachel stared. The woman was serious. Choking back laughter, Rachel said, "Mop under the hammock, then. Once things are tidy, a clean every three or four days should be enough. Surely no one will stay in a hammock that long."

Eva's well-shaped lips turned down. "Senhor Tomé, he have food brought. Even have *muleque* bring gourd for *pipi*."

Sniggering made Rachel realize what was meant. Except for the coarse talk of the prostitutes on the ship, it was the first time she'd ever heard bodily functions mentioned, and her cheeks grew hot.

"Do the best you can. I think the masters will be glad to have their chambers clean so long as it's no trouble to them."

Rising from the reed mat, she ached where Duarte had hurt her, but, in her feeling of accomplishment, she could almost ignore it. She was not the pain.

Brooms, mops, scrub brushes and cleaning cloths were used fervently in the next days, particularly, Rachel suspected, when she or Felicia happened by, though it was apparent that Rosa and Eva took their positions seriously and were vying to determine which would be most resplendent, the lower or upper floor.

"All this dust flying about," complained Tomé peevishly. "I was trying to sleep when Eva took my pillows off to be aired." When he thrust out his lower lip, pink face and bald head made him resemble an aged pouting baby. "And, senhora, my pretty little Izabel had duties elsewhere and couldn't fan me."

Duarte laughed. "From the swell of the wench's belly, I'd say she did more than fan you, brother-in-law."

Searching his armpit with his tremendously long scratching fingernail, a loathsome attribute Duarte also cultivated, though not to such exaggeration, the gross elderly man chuckled. "I hope I'm dead before my thing fails to stiffen at the whiff of a pretty *mucama.*"

"Senhor!" cried Rachel.

Father Paulo protested weakly, "My sons, this is sinful talk."

"And worse doings," rapped Manoel. He addressed himself to Duarte. "I leave the morals of it to Father Paulo, but the senhor should be aware that the strong, intelligent stock of Seraphim is being tainted with disease. I would appreciate time to discuss this more thoroughly."

"Managing the slaves is your business," growled Duarte.

"Senhor, I cannot manage blind and crippled slaves into

operating the mill." Manoel's tone was icy. "I respectfully request a few hours of the senhor's time immediately after lunch."

Startled, Duarte frowned and then burst into laughter. He pinched Rachel's cheek. "It seems your passion for setting things to order has become infectious, my dear. Very well, Manoel. Allow me two hours to rest and then come to my room."

"It would be helpful for the senhor to see the records."

Grimacing, Duarte let his hand trail along Rachel's neck and bare arm. "This is the one to show your records to. If I can't listen to your lecture from the comfort of my hammock, Manoel, I must decline to hear it."

Grimly Manoel inclined his head. "I will present myself to the senhor in two hours precisely."

"Precisely! Did I hire you to manage me or the plantation?"

Manoel's ascetic face softened in a grin. "Sometimes the tasks become the same, senhor." He bowed as he rose to excuse himself, and though the nod was directed to Duarte, the young man's eyes touched Rachel's. His were full of surprised admiration that sent a glow through her, but that froze when, as soon as Manoel was gone, Duarte gripped her hand and drew her up with him.

"If I must talk figures with our earnest New Christian, you will understand that I must first console myself with a figure of a different kind."

Tomé roared. Bento sniggered. Irene's immense girth heaved. Only the faces of Felicia and Luzia reflected dismay that echoed Rachel's as she kept her head high with an effort and tried to match her step to Duarte's rather than be half dragged down the hall.

In contrast to his elegant public attire, Duarte, like Tomé, lounged about the house barefoot in long white drawers and a garish calico dressing gown. He divested himself of these. Rachel averted her face. The jagged sound of his excited breathing turned her faint. She had not expected this, had lacked time to prepare—

"Blushes, wife?" Greedy hands that were, like his feet, remarkably small, caught the skirt of her smock and snatched it over her shoulders. "Since you're so enterprising in other fields, you should devote some of that energy in pleasing your husband!"

"Senhor—"

"God, you have beautiful breasts, those pale blue veins and rosy little buds! Can I squeeze something from them?" Dropping to his knees, he sucked and bit till she winced in spite of herself. He rose, laughing huskily and threw her on the bed.

No long ordeal like those she had previously endured. Seconds only, minutes at most. As the master of Seraphim rolled off her, its sinhá-dona could almost smile.

The limp thing that had been so arrogant now lay like a shriveled pouch against her hip. When he began to snore, she slipped out. Felicia had another bath ready.

"It was bad?"

Sighing as she leaned against the back of the high tub, Rachel said, "Not as bad as—as before. I'll never like it, but I'm not so afraid."

Felicia's laugh was bitterly amused. "Sometimes you'd think that's all masters are, their *bimbinhas*. They use them enough." After a few moments of kneading Rachel's shoulders, she asked, "Will the sinhá have a nap in one of the empty bedrooms?"

Rachel would have liked to go to the library, but Manoel might be there, and though Duarte had suggested she examine the records, she had no heart to face the shy young man this briefly from her husband's embrace.

"I'll pray in the chapel for a time."

She had the need. Certainly she was in rebellion against the order of things that had brought her here: the King's will, her husband's will, the rules of the Church that allowed her grace only as she was in subjection to imperative male dominion.

In spite of this revolt, prayer had been part of her daily life in the convent. She missed the quiet time of worship. Long ago the Madonna's sweet face had merged with her mother's; when she had been sent to bed without supper or punished, it had comforted her to sob out her childish woes to Mary.

"Will you come with me?" she asked Felicia.

"If the sinhá will excuse me, I must find needles and thread for all the mending that's piling up in the small parlor. I don't think anyone's taken a stitch since the days of Don' Thereza, who, whatever can be said about her, ran a clean, thrifty house."

As she passed the library and turned down the stair, Rachel hoped that Duarte would haul himself from their bed and into the hammock in his private room. Her cheeks burned to think of Manoel having to speak to him while he lolled on the counterpane where he'd taken her.

The family tomb exuded a faint but ghastly odor. Rachel shivered and hurried to the front of the chapel, as far from it as possible. Poor little Dona Caterina! Dead so young and sharing a crypt with vengeful Dona Thereza.

Had any mistresses of Seraphim been happy? It was hard to see how they could have been unless one or two had been fortunate enough to love and be loved by their husbands. Otherwise, in what amounted to a harem, with the master's word absolute, and few outside contacts, it was no wonder that a woman who survived her task of producing offspring might grow hysterically jealous or avenge her humiliation by tormenting the servants in her power.

Rachel sank to her knees.

"It is good, daughter, that you show yourself devout." She glanced up at the reedy voice, bowed her head for a moment and got slowly to her feet. Father Paulo's left eyelid twitched spasmodically. "Perhaps you might persuade the senhor to follow the practice of his father, who gathered the slaves for prayer each morning and lashed those who came late to mass on Sunday."

"A pious usage." Rachel's tone was dry as she remembered a young black virgin in whom that patriarch had tried to purge himself of disease. "I fear that you exaggerate my influence."

No doubt the priest meant his smile to be paternally encouraging, but to Rachel it seemed a leer. "Come, daughter, there's scarce a limit to what a pretty young wife can wheedle from her husband."

If I could wheedle anything, it would be that he leave me alone. "Perhaps you should ask Luzia to intercede,"

Rachel said with pleasant distinctness. As the priest gaped at her, she genuflected and left the chapel.

Twice each week the members of Bahia's municipal council were supposed to assemble in the city, though most of them, like Duarte, were *senhores de engenho,* masters of sugar mills, and planters, the majority of both classes living in the Reconcavo, a strip of land perhaps thirty miles wide stretching about sixty miles along the Bay of All Saints.

"Though God knows what good it does us to meet when we lack money to keep up the streets, parks and bridges and pay employees like the sanitation inspectors," Duarte grumbled at lunch.

"The council was given much property by the first governor-general," said Manoel. "Even without taxes on food and the sale of licenses to vendors, the rents on council lands should be enough to finance expenses."

"That shows how much you know about it," retorted Duarte, obviously pleased at finding a gap in his manager's knowledge. "The council's records were destroyed while Bahia was occupied by those heretic Dutch. After that some tenants claimed the land as their own and the council couldn't prove otherwise. In any case, the rents are low."

Manoel looked sympathetic, but Rachel wondered if he were as innocent as he sounded when he remarked, "I've heard that another problem is the exemption from tax claimed by members of the three military orders of Christ, Santiago and Aviz, and by some who claim to be Familiars of the Holy Office."

"The knights should be exempted!" cried Duarte, flushing. "It's the religious orders that refuse to pay their lawful obligation! It's a scandal, the plantations and properties owned by Franciscans, Carmelites and Jesuits, who reap fortunes but won't pay their taxes! Anyway," he added righteously, "the planters whose cane I grind pay plenty of tax."

"So do the poor of the city," said Manoel. "For all of their necessities are taxed."

Duarte dismissed that with a wave of his shapely hand. "All they do is bleat, wanting an easy life and protection from the Dutch, while we of the council must wrack our brains and funds to keep the city and captaincy afloat.'' He pushed back his chair. "I'll be gone one night, maybe two," he said to Rachel with a possessive grin. "Keep busy and you may not miss me too much."

Rachel could think of no answer. He didn't notice. In a moment, accompanied by Bento, he was gone.

The prospect of Duarte's being away several days of the week filled Rachel with a relief approaching joy. She intended to use this first respite to visit the *aldeia,* the mission, from which Indian workers were hired during the grinding season. When she confided her plan to Felicia, the woman frowned.

"The master may not like for you to leave the house unless he's with you. Many sinhá-donas never leave their plantations from the time they enter as brides till they are buried in the chapels."

"And they're buried alive all the time between." Rachel shuddered. "Felicia, I won't go crazy-mean like Dona Thereza or let the master maul me to death as he did Dona Caterina. If I can't get out from under his shadow sometimes, I'd rather die before he wrecks me."

Felicia tucked in her chin. "The sinhá better speak to Senhor Manoel. He's in the library."

Manoel thought Rachel had come to see the accounts and explained them so thoroughly that she finally pressed her hand to her head and laughed. "Pardon, senhor, but I really came to beg your advice to visit the *aldeia.*"

Manoel's brows drew together. "Why?"

"I want to know something of the people who were here before the Portuguese."

His sensitive lips curved down. "You will learn no more of Indians by visiting the mission than you would know of the perfume and color of a jungle flower after it's been trampled in the dust."

"Perhaps that itself is something I should know."

His scowl gave way to musing. "The mission is on Seraphim territory. Since the senhor wishes you to oversee the records, it's reasonable that you be acquainted with the plantation." He gave an abrupt nod. "Very well, Dona Rachel. If you'll be ready after breakfast, I'll escort you around some of the fields, and we'll stop at the mission for refreshment.''

"I wouldn't want you to incur the senhor's displeasure.''

"You'll bring your woman. The senhor trusts her. And I'll bring along one of the overseers whose grandmother lives in the *aldeia*.''

"You're very kind.''

"Cautious, too.'' When he laughed, he seemed little more than a boy.

Rachel twinkled back. "If it can be arranged, I should prefer to ride a mule or horse or ride in a cart rather than in a litter.''

"It will be arranged.'' She grasped suddenly how lonely he must be here, understood that he might be vulnerable to coaxing, and resolved not to put him in any truly embarrassing position.

He bowed her out. She went to the parlor and with Felicia attacked the big reed hamper that overflowed with mending.

Felicia said with grim amusement, "Senhor Manoel is smart to bring Diniz, the overseer. He and the master have the same grandfather. They played together when they were little.''

"You mean the Indian grandmother at the mission was a concubine of Duarte's grandfather?''

"She was very beautiful. Old ones say that the master loved her better than any woman he ever had, much more than his wife. She bore him four sons. Except for Diniz's father, they lived in the *sertão*, the wilderness. They were the most successful slavers in the country because, being half Indian, they could convince inland tribes to come live with the white people, who would give them fine gifts. Over the years they sold hundreds of savages to Seraphim for a *cruzado* each, the price of a sheep.''

Even in an age of slavery Rachel found such valuing of human life appalling. It must have shown on her face, for Felicia raised a shoulder.

"A healthy slave from Africa cost twelve or fourteen times as much, but planters found out they were cheaper in the long run, especially if they made more slaves for the plantation. *Caboclos* like Diniz, with well-mixed blood, are a tough people.''

"Diniz is free?"

"To be sure." Felicia's tone held a note of envy. "His grandfather's will freed his Indian woman and all her children. She didn't dare stay at Seraphim, though. The mistress had had one concubine's eyes served to the master in a sauce of blood, and Diniz's grandmother, she didn't want anything like that to happen to her."

In spite of his heritage, there was nothing flamboyant about Diniz. Rachel thought his white ancestor might be closer than his grandfather, for he had greenish eyes and pale skin, though his lips and nose were broad and he had kinky black hair.

The four of them rode mules. Rachel found her sideways perch uncomfortable, but Manoel told her a cart would rattle her teeth loose. As they followed the rutted track used by the cane wagons, he told her something of how Portugal, only fifty years ago the center of a vast trading empire and dominant in both spice and slave trades, had become only a clearinghouse for European merchants, its main resource now being Brazil, which it had neglected in favor of Africa, Asia and India.

The spice trade had once supplied nearly half of Portugal's revenues, more than the total of all other overseas trade, more than taxes collected in the country. By seizing ports on the Indian Ocean and establishing trading stations at strategic points, the Portuguese had cut off overland merchant traffic from its sources, while they were able to buy directly from the growers.

Ginger, cloves, cinnamon, spice and nutmeg were luxuries, but all Europeans needed pepper. Within a few years of Vasco da Gama's 1498 voyage to India around the Cape of Good Hope, most of Europe's pepper traveled that route on Portuguese ships.

"If you can believe it," said Manoel, "between 1522 and 1543 the Crown spent more on royal marriages and dowries than on the garrisons in Morocco and fleets of the Indian Ocean, Africa and Brazil. The Crown borrowed with the spice trade for collateral, but capital grew so scarce that

Portugal stopped carrying trade goods to Antwerp, where it got the things traded for spices and slaves—silver, cloth, copper and hardware. Meanwhile, the overland spice trade with the Mediterranean had reopened and captured half the pepper trade. In 1586 the Crown leased a German trading house the right to buy pepper in India. Now with the Netherlands competing for Asian ports, more and more of the trade between Europe and Asia skips Portugal entirely.'' Manoel shook his head. ''So Portugal depends on Brazil to enrich it.''

''But Portugal has been ruled by Spanish kings since a few years after King Sebastião died on crusade against the Moslems in 1578.''

''Yes, but it's not governed by Spanish officials and has remained a separate kingdom. Brazil has never become a Spanish viceroyalty but is managed by Portuguese councils and tribunals.'' He chuckled. ''As you must know, the King has had a hard time getting Portugal to contribute ships to defend Brazil, while the Portuguese blame their poverty on the King's wars in Europe.''

''Too bad countries that haven't learned to live peacefully in Europe should bring their wars to new lands.''

''All the more reason.'' Manoel shrugged. ''They're afraid their neighbors will find El Dorado.''

Slaves were chopping weeds from between the cane rows, but though there were overseers, Rachel saw no use of the bamboo rod each carried. When she mentioned this, Manoel said, ''Each slave has a reasonable number of rows to work. If he finishes early, he has free time. If he lags, he's late in the fields. At first the master didn't think the system would work, but it does and we've had fewer runaways.''

''Do many run off?''

''Enough so that there are men who make their living hunting runaways and bringing them back. Diniz's brother is a *capitão do mato,* a bush-captain.''

Leaving the vast expanse of fields, they followed a track cut through a forest spangled with bright-flowered growths sprouting from the trees and interwoven with vines. Parrots flashed green and red and gold and monkeys chattered as they traveled overhead or alongside.

"The dyewood trees near the coasts have all been taken out," Manoel said. "These forests used to be thirty miles or so wide, but they've been cleared for planting or fuel or building. This strip serves as a barrier between the cane fields and the cattle range that surrounds the *aldeia.*"

"Seraphim cattle?"

"Yes. They're tended by vaqueiros, some Indian but most of mixed blood who live in huts scattered about the land. It really is the beginning of the *sertão.*"

"Are the vaqueiros free?"

"Some are, but it makes little real difference. They live out here because they like it. They're not likely to go to some other place. So long as they supply Seraphim with beef and trail a herd to Bahia now and then, no one molests them."

Very different from the life of a field or mill hand. Rachel wondered if such men, though nominally slaves, would be able to accept the rules and goads of plantation existence.

As the little group emerged from the forest, Rachel could see the *aldeia* in the distance. The white-plastered church with its red-tiled roof and towers was flanked by a number of handsome plastered buildings facing on a large square. Huts of mud and wattle formed neat streets on three sides of the plaza.

Rachel had heard so much about painted naked Indians adorned with feathers that it was a shock to her, as they approached, to discover that the people in long white cotton robes were Indian. Except for the smallest children, all wore this costume. They gathered in the plaza as Rachel's party approached. The black robes and four-cornered black caps of the two Jesuits contrasted starkly with their flock.

They came forward to greet the visitors with a sign of blessing. One tiny old woman, face withered as an ancient apple, ran forward to embrace Diniz, who slid down from his mule to hold her. Rachel saw no trace of the beauty that had made her the preferred woman of Duarte's grandfather, but Diniz swung her off her feet in an adoring hug. She and Diniz went off, eagerly asking each other questions, while Manoel introduced Rachel to the priests.

Gaunt Father Adolpho said he must get back to his pupils, but after the senhora had refreshed herself, perhaps she would visit the classrooms.

"I would like to," she said.

He hurried to a building near the church. Father Bartholomeu, square-built and square-faced with piercing black eyes, escorted them to his quarters and had a portly, middle-aged Indian woman bring porridge and manioc cakes.

"Our choir sings as sweetly as any in Portugal," he said. "And many of the boys have learned Christian doctrine so well that they teach it at home to their parents."

"The parents weren't brought up at the *aldeia?*" Rachel asked.

"Only a few." He sighed. "The truth is, my daughter, that diseases that only make a Portuguese sick will often kill an Indian. This mission has been here almost since the founding of Bahia, but I doubt if there is an Indian living here descended from those first converts."

Rachel stared. "Then from where—"

"Most of these adults were persuaded to come in from the wilderness."

"How?"

"They hungered for the mysteries of the Faith. And they knew we would protect them from planters who'd enslave them."

"Don't many work at Seraphim in the harvest and milling?"

"Yes, for a wage. What would you have them do, daughter? They must learn to work in a civilized way." He added proudly, "Instead of living hand to mouth as they did in the wilds, they grow crops enough to feed themselves, even though most of the game has been hunted out."

Manoel said, "I've heard they used to move their villages every few years when the earth lost its fertility and hunting got poor."

Father Bartholomeu sniffed. "Yes, and when those long huts indecently shared by many families grew so infested with lice and insects that even Indians couldn't stand it! We have taught them to manure the earth so they can stay in one place. Each family has a house, and they are decently clothed now instead of prancing about with feathers on their ankles and arms and nothing where it matters."

Rachel returned his earlier astonishing revelation. "I've heard there used to be thousands of Indians along the coast. Do you mean there are none left?"

"Like your honored husband, my daughter, many esteemed families have Indian blood. That is true also in Pernambuco, where Jerónimo de Albuquerque, brother-in-law of the first donatory, had so many children by his Indian princess that he was called the Adam of the captaincy. In the South the Paulistas mostly descend from the many half-breed children of João Ramalho, a shipwrecked Portuguese. Like Caramuru, he had been living for years with his heathen family when the first settlers came to the São Paulo region."

"But there are no"—Rachel struggled for a word—"pure Indians left?"

"Pure?" gasped Father Bartholomeu. "How could deluded flesh-eating savages be pure?"

"I meant those with no African or European blood."

Father Bartholomeu pursed his lips. "It is almost impossible that there are any such survivors. Shortly after the missions were established, disease carried off most of the converts, and when more Indians were brought in, within a few years these died by the thousands of fevers, hemorrhaging and coughing in an epidemic that did not kill Portuguese. It seemed God's mercy to call his new-won children to him before they could lapse into apostasy and merit hell. For their hearts were so hard that even after receiving the faith, when plague and famine struck they tried to flee the missions and formed cults, horrible perversions of Christianity, that said a savior would come to save them from the white men."

"And the Santidade leaders told them not to plant manioc because the deliverer was coming," Manoel put in. "That added to the famine. Many sold themselves into slavery for something to eat."

"So were they punished for their blasphemies. Next came plague and smallpox. Even though Governor Mem de Sá's successful campaigns against the Caeté and other heathen filled the *aldeias* to overflowing, thirty thousand died in the first few months of the epidemic and two-thirds of the survivors perished in a second outbreak.''

Rachel remembered that smallpox and plague had killed forty thousand in Lisbon in 1561, but that was a great city. ''The wonder must be that any Indians are left at all. Surely the fathers must have seen that crowding many groups into close quarters where they'd be exposed to strange diseases was the same as killing them.''

Father Bartholomeu's eyes flashed. ''You forget that thus their souls were saved! Better dead and safe in heaven than living like beasts in their sinful delusion!''

''Or like bright birds of the forest?''

''Would you think it good, daughter, if Caeté and Tupi were still braining each other and eating captives?''

''No, but—''

''When I came to this *aldeia* twenty years ago, an old Tupi woman was dying. I went to ask if she would relish some delicacy, perhaps a lump of sugar. The poor old wretch said, 'Thank you, grandson, if someone brought me my favorite food, the tender hand of a young Caeté lad, I think I could pick the meat from the little bones.' '' With a triumphant glance at Rachel, the Jesuit arose. ''Come. You must see the school. That will convince you that we have given these poor creatures things much better than those we took away.''

The visit did nothing of the sort, though Rachel thrilled to the beauty of the clear young voices chanting their choir responses: ''Praised be the most holy name of Jesus,'' sang one group of bronze-skinned boys. ''And of the most holy Virgin Mary his mother,'' returned the sweet, piercing voices of another mass of black-haired lads.

In another room, boys practiced on flutes and two oboes.

''Savages are alike in one thing,'' said Father Bartholomeu. ''They all love music. When the bell for mass rings in the morning, all the people gather in the chapel and two choirs of boys, on their knees, sing till mass begins. When the bell rings for the evening services, they form a procession in front of the church and then proceed through the streets singing canticles in their own tongue.''

The boys in the next room were practicing their penmanship. Another class read from pious books, and the last group was doing simple arithmetic.

"Girls aren't instructed?" Rachel asked.

"After morning mass, girls and women receive religious instruction. That's all they need."

"Do any of the boys ever become priests?"

"There were a few ordainings, but these proved so disastrous that Indians are educated now only within the limits of their capabilities—that is, they learn to carry out their religious duties and how to clothe and feed themselves."

"But they fed themselves before, Father."

"Only by vagabonding from place to place." Annoyed by her dubious look, he said quellingly, "Our young converts are so devout that they beat up old witch doctors who formerly terrorized everyone. Some have even reported their parents for adhering to heathenish ways."

Neither activity commended itself to Rachel, but a New Christian dared not be critical of anything pertaining to the church. She and Manoel thanked the priest for his hospitality. He had their mules fetched. Diniz joined them after having to break away from his grandmother, who embraced him and patted his cheeks as she clung to him, resembling a wizened monkey garbed in white.

An eerie chill fingered Rachel's spine as they rode past the ranks of copper-tan faces. *They wear their shrouds. The priests have dressed them for their burial.*

"Well?" asked Manoel at last.

She turned a stricken face to him. "They can sing and make processions, but they aren't learning how to hold their own against the Portuguese."

"They aren't supposed to. It's fortunate for them that they're baptized and have a place in heaven. There's no room for them here."

Rachel had thought the *senzala* of the single men a sad place, but the *aldeia* was worse. She wished she had not gone, and yet, she'd had to.

"The Jesuits deserve more credit than the other orders," Manoel admitted. "They've condemned enslaving the Indians and they don't use the women as concubines, which many other priests do. During the epidemics, they nursed sick Indians with no thought for themselves; some died of illness and exhaustion. They're devoted to saving the natives, but to them, that means souls."

This life was not supposed to count against eternity, the pangs of hell and the bliss of heaven. Still, as Rachel rode through what was left of the forest, she could almost see brown bodies painted to blend with vines and flowers and shadows and wondered if the Indians' souls might not be like that, too, indistinguishably mixed with their homeland. What sort of pale, frightened wraiths belonged to the white-robed converts, who seemed not so much to be living as, uprooted from their natural ways, to be awaiting death?

Immediately after breakfast next morning, she heard the reports of Eva and Rosa and went to inspect the house. As the servants hovered anxiously, Rachel praised clean tile floors, polished furniture, gleaming washbasins and chamber pots, corners where no wisp of fuzz lingered.

"You've done wonders!" she said at last. "We could entertain the governor-general himself." It was easy to punish a slave, but how was one rewarded? "So long as you keep the house like this, you may each have a day of your own in addition to Sundays. Fix it with Rosa or Eva so that you aren't all off at the same time."

Apparently she had picked a thing important to them, time, free time, since their hours as well as their bodies belonged to Seraphim. She was applauded with clapping and smiles while Joaquim, who couldn't speak, showed his pleasure by turning wonderful loose-armed, loose-legged cartwheels across the resplendent reception hall.

Then, Rachel seated on a mat in their midst, in the largest parlor, both upstairs and downstairs servants went to work on the accumulated mending.

Luzia came in, glanced around in scornful disbelief, then bobbed her head in mock servility. "The sinhá had an interesting ride yesterday?"

"Very."

"No other sinhá-dona ever went to the *aldeias*."

"Nor has one recently managed the household," Rachel said lightly. "If you wish to work with us, you are welcome, Luzia."

The shapely red lips curled. "I don't work."

"Then run along and don't work someplace else."

A furious blaze of the golden eyes and the ripe-breasted woman was gone, moving with cat grace, but like a cat that's had its tail twitched.

Muted chuckles greeted her departure, and many ill-concealed smiles, though several of the older women looked uneasy. Rosa gave a muffled cough. "Does the sinhá know the story of how one *senhor de engenho* stabbed his wife and daughters because a wicked slave convinced him that they were having lovers when he was away?"

A chill shot up Rachel's spine, but she spoke with casual interest. "That sounds exciting. Why don't we take turns telling stories or singing? It would pass the time and I'd like to hear the legends of the country."

Rosa told her bloody tale. It was followed by romances, tragedies, ghost and monster stories that involved terrifying creatures from Portugal, Africa and Indian Brazil.

"Whose house is this, here by the way?
    Do I eat a child, do I eat a child,
    Do I eat a child today?"

"Old Quibungo who swallowed children," came a chuckle from the door. Duarte lounged there, watching the busy women with patronizing approval. "Irene used to terrify me with that story."

Striding over to Rachel, he drew her to her feet and jerked her into a crushing embrace, covering her mouth with his. He reeked of rum and tobacco.

"I'm a hungry man, little bride," he laughed. "In two ways. So let's have food brought to our room and celebrate our reunion."

The two-day respite had healed the worst of Rachel's inflamed swelling. Though far from enjoying Duarte's eager assault, she found it less painful, and was able to listen with real interest while he grumbled about the difficulties of the council.

"Not only must we find money to pay part of the wages, rations and clothing of the garrison, but the guilds are pushing to have representatives. It won't be long till the council will be overrun with impudent tinkers, tailors, goldsmiths and what-have-you!''

''They might pay their taxes more cheerfully if they had something to say about how they're levied,'' Rachel observed. She knew she'd better tell him about her excursion to the *aldeia* before Luzia had a chance to make malicious insinuations, so she plunged in, saying that in order to better understand the records, she had thought it important to see something of the fields.

She was relieved that his response was amusement. ''It would seem God means to send me diversity in my wives.'' He lazily played with a lock of her hair. ''The first wore her knees out in the chapel but produced only one stillborn son after another. When I try to remember her, all that comes to mind is a big belly that never justified itself. Don' Thereza ordered the household well but plagued me with her jealousy. Poor little Caterina was just a child. It'll be good to have a wife who can both control the house and overlook Manoel's figures, which, I confess, confuse me worse the more he tries to explain.'' His small hand closed over her breast. ''With all of that, you've a pretty body. I chose well when your ship docked.''

This time he excited himself by watching her as he toyed with her, laughing at her embarrassed protests and attempts to shield herself. When he was teased to readiness, he muttered huskily, ''For all your nun's airs, I'm bound there's fire beneath your snow.''

He tried to use restraint, whispering endearments that made her blush and try to turn her face away. His hot, damp mouth roamed the exposed side of her throat.

''My small nun bride!'' he gasped. ''There, there, isn't that good? Ahhh, you're tight—nice—'' He groaned, pumped frenziedly back and forth till she chewed her lip to keep from begging.

I am not the pain, she kept repeating, and at last he cried out and sprawled half across her.

When his sleep seemed deep enough, she extricated herself, dressed quickly and left the room. Though she had not wanted what had happened, a primitive thrill of triumph shot through her when she saw Luzia watching from down the hall.

Felicia was beside Rachel in a moment, sending Luzia a look that sent the younger woman retreating toward the kitchen, though she sneered, tawny eyes smoldering.

"She's afraid," Felicia said. "The slaves are starting to say the master likes you best."

"I'm just new."

"You're the sinhá, too," Felicia reminded. "You'd be that even if the master didn't want you. A slave woman— all she's got is the master's fancy. He stops liking her, she's nothing."

"She's welcome to the master's—attentions."

"Better you don't think like that." They had entered the small bedroom, where Felicia helped Rachel into the waiting bath. "Since the master seems to care about you, she'll be afraid to do anything open to hurt you, but if you make him angry—well, she'd think she could do something very bad."

"I thought she was afraid of your *mandingas,*" Rachel joked.

Felicia frowned. "She is. But the master sought you out when he returned today, not her. She knows the slaves are laughing and hope she'll be sent back to the *senzala.*" Felicia laved Rachel's shoulders and admonished, "What you ought to do is please the master till he'd let you sell that woman away."

Rachel flushed hotly. "I—I don't want to be with him a bit more than I have to!"

"Best not let him know that. Luzia, she's going to do her best to make you big trouble."

"I'll be careful," Rachel promised. In spite of detesting Duarte's embraces, they did give her a certain confidence, a feeling that Luzia didn't necessarily have the advantage in their struggle, a contest Rachel didn't want but one that seemed inevitable.

All the slaves attended Sunday mass and had the rest of the day free except for those needed for essential household tasks. Duarte surprised Rachel with his devout behavior at the service, though he and Tomé played cards through what was left of the afternoon after rising from the midday rest.

Glad that her husband seemed content in that pastime,

Rachel went to the library. She intended to read some works of piety, as would be fitting on Sunday, but as she hesitated between *Varias Rimas Ao Bom Jesus* and a book of Padre Vieira's sermons, her gaze wandered.

What a feast of books! The convent's half-dozen volumes had all been religious except for Camões' *Os Lusíadas,* which she had read and reread, swept up in the pageant of Portuguese history. Here were poetry, histories and books she'd heard the nuns roundly condemn—*Don Quixote* and *Amadís de Gaula.*

Almost as stealthily as if the Mother Superior might suddenly appear and rap her on the fingers, Rachel took down *Amadís.* Drawing a chair over by the window, she was soon lost in the adventures of the Child of the Sea, able to guess from their contexts the meanings of most of the Spanish words she couldn't decipher.

She had left the door open to encourage the cooling draft. A slight motion caught her eye and she glanced up. Luzia stood where she could look in. Rachel repressed a smile at the disappointment in the woman's face.

"You wish to ask me something, Luzia?"

"No. I'm going to the chapel."

"I didn't know you were so religious."

Luzia's teeth showed. "It is a vow. I burn a candle each Sunday for Don' Caterina."

"You were fond of her?"

"That one?" Luzia's mouth curved scornfully. "She still played with dolls. But she died young. I don't want her spirit mad at me because I'm alive." The beautiful slave eyed Rachel appraisingly. "Doesn't it worry you that the master's wives have not been lucky? Three buried, and he's still a young man!"

"I have a strong constitution," Rachel said, laughing. "But should you die unseasonably, I'll have masses said for you."

The mocking boldness left Luzia's face. "You—you threaten me!"

"Not at all. I meant it as a comforting promise."

Luzia paled. "If that witch Felicia—"

"Felicia will take an interest in you only if I begin to

sicken.'' Meeting the yellow eyes calmly for a long, tense moment, Rachel went back to her reading.

Trinity Sunday was the eighth week after Easter, and Duarte took Rachel to Bahia to celebrate the Feast of Corpus Christi and meet some of his relations. Tomé chose not to go, saying he couldn't trust himself not to berate the governor-general for his failure to expel the acursed Dutch.

''The truth is,'' said Felicia to Rachel while packing her trunk, ''that Don' Consuelo chided him roundly last year for molesting a young slave girl. Things are managed very differently at that house than here.'' She attended Rachel and Bento rode behind Duarte's litter.

The townhouse of Venancio Álvares Cabral was on a hill near the double-cloistered Convento do Carmo. Two stories high and a broad single room wide, the house formed a rectangle enclosing a large courtyard garden with fountains and shady trees. The side of the building opening on the street contained stables and slave quarters.

Venancio Álvares, a jovial, graying man with penetrating green eyes, embraced Duarte, patting him on the shoulder, and bowed over Rachel's hand. ''At your feet, senhora. Ah, Duarte, you rogue, you were rewarded for hanging about the docks till her ship came in!''

Duarte grinned. ''You won't believe this, cousin, but she can read. And do sums in her head faster than Manoel. He admits it.''

''My good cousin, I hope she can sew and run the household.''

''She can. And she can keep an eye on Manoel's accounts and free me of pretending to go over them.''

They might have been speaking of the acquisition of a clever horse. Or slave. *That's all I am.* Bitterness tainted Rachel's honest pride in her month's accomplishments at Seraphim. *A body at the master's disposal. If I have a brain, too, that's extra in the bargain.*

Dona Consuelo, only a few silver hairs in the black mass piled regally high, took Rachel in her arms and kissed her on both cheeks. ''Come, dear, you must be tired after that hot journey. I'll show you your room. After you're refreshed, Rozane wants to meet you. She's our only daughter, close to your age.'' Rachel murmured something to acknowledge her hostess' kindliness and was glad, once she and Felicia were alone in a big room, to be helped out of her perspiration-soaked garments, sponged off and made to lie down while Felicia put her clothes up before going to look for her friends among the servants.

Rachel had planned to rise as soon as she'd rested a few minutes, but the high-ceilinged room was so cool and quiet that she drowsed. She woke at a sound, hastily pulled the coverlet over her nakedness and sat up to face the girl who had frozen by the door.

''I—I'm sorry. I didn't mean to wake you.''

Great dark eyes would have melted Rachel if the voice had not. ''You are Rozane?''

''Yes.'' Closing the door behind her, the girl came forward. There was a glow to her ivory skin and glossy black hair waved over her shoulders. Staring at Rachel, she sighed. ''You're even more beautiful than Mama said, senhora.''

''You must call me Rachel, cousin. And if you have a looking glass, you must know that you're beautiful yourself.''

Scarlet stained Rozane's pale cheeks. ''My cousin Santiago thinks so.''

In truth Rozane was striking rather than pretty. Wonderful eyes dominated a long face with a determined jaw that belied an appealing mouth. And Rozane was thin and tall. From Tomé and Duarte's talk, Rachel knew most Brazilian men preferred plump women, especially those with ample posteriors. This was fortunate, since the habits of plantation gentry almost ensured that the women would grow heavy.

''This Cousin Santiago, you like him?''

Rozane poured out a story of devotion that had begun when the two were children. ''But when the Dutch took Bahia ten years ago, Santiago's family moved to their *fazenda* in the backlands. We stayed there, too, till the Crown's Armada drove the Dutch away. Mama and Senhor Pai don't want me to marry him because they'd almost never see me and they're afraid the Dutch heretics will overrun the whole captaincy beyond the city.''

"Couldn't Santiago move to the city?"

Rozane shook her head disconsolately. "No. He loves the *sertão*. And for his sake, so will I." She brightened a little. "Santiago's parents like me. They have persuaded Senhor Pai to agree to the wedding next year if I haven't accepted one of his cronies before that. And I won't. I'd rather die!"

"Then all you have to do is wait."

"But I'm getting old," wailed Rozane. "I'll be sixteen next month. All my friends are married. Most have at least one baby. What if I get scrawnier, really ugly, and Santiago doesn't love me anymore?"

Rachel had to chuckle. Though she was less than a year older than this girl, she felt a lifetime older. "A man who loves the wilderness, cousin, is not likely to forsake his sweetheart. Anyway, I'm almost seventeen and my teeth haven't fallen out or my skin withered."

Rozane scanned her. "That's so," she admitted with such relief that Rachel burst into laughter. The dinner bell sounded. Felicia hurried in to help Rachel dress and Rozane slipped away with a soft farewell.

The master blessed the table and the wine of Madeira before putting food on his plate in the form of a cross. There was fish stewed in coconut milk and spices, exceedingly tough beef, and the luxury of bread made with wheat flour imported from Portugal.

Every place at the long table was taken. Besides Rozane's brother, Paulo, a handsome bachelor-lawyer who made a point of letting Rachel know that he had studied in Lisbon, Senhor Venancio's heir, Raimundo, oldest son by a first wife, occupied his chair as if it were a throne. Probably in his thirties, he was swarthy and heavyset with piercing green eyes. Three children from perhaps eight to twelve sat between him and his wife, Maria, big with their fourth child, sallow-skinned with dark hollows under eyes that were the last vestige of her former beauty. Then there was the master's spidery-frail mother, Dona Consuelo's widowed sister, and an orphaned nephew and niece.

Breaking a piece of crusty bread, Duarte chewed it appreciatively. "You city folks are always complaining of food shortages, cousin, but on my soul, your table gives the lie to such croaking.''

"No croaking," retorted the master. "We got flour from the last Portuguese ship, but we have no rice or beans or even manioc. It seems to me that you planters could grow enough staples to feed the city instead of devoting all the land to sugarcane.''

"Let those farmers on the poor land south of this captaincy grow food,'' shrugged Duarte. "The Reconcavo's duty is to produce sugar.''

"Duty!" hooted Venancio. "Profit, you mean.''

Unruffled, Duarte helped himself to more bread. "Brazil is valuable to the Crown only as long as we send thousands of arrobas of sugar to Portugal. If it weren't for that, we'd be abandoned to the Dutch.''

"If you ask me, we've almost been abandoned,'' growled Raimundo. "Where are the reinforcements we're supposed to get? Where are the supplies? The king of Spain has his battles in Europe to worry about. If the council in Lisbon won't help us, why should he?''

"They claim Portugal's bled dry to pay for Spain's wars,'' interjected Paulo as if to end a discussion he found boringly familiar. "Cousin Duarte, did you know I'm to be Saint George in the procession?''

That turned conversation to the festival. Wine and a bewildering array of pastries and confections were brought in.

"Rosalia's a marvel with cakes and candies,'' boasted Álvares. "The only trouble is that she earns so much by selling them in the street in her time off that she'll be able to buy her freedom in a few more years.''

"She gives us half of what she earns,'' reminded Dona Consuelo. "Besides, senhor, we can buy her sweetmeats after she is free.'' Though the mistress of the house addressed her husband formally, the comfortable affection between them mellowed the atmosphere in spite of Raimundo's stolid surliness and Paulo's condescension.

It was midafternoon by the time the family rose from the table. Rozane plucked Rachel's sleeve. "Are you going to lie down, cousin?''

Rachel replied that she'd had her rest, so while the rest

of the household retired to beds or hammocks, the two young women sat in the shady courtyard by a sparkling fountain and stitched on clothes for Maria's expected baby as Rozane plied Rachel with questions about Portugal.

"A convent just isn't very exciting," Rachel apologized at Rozane's obvious disappointment. "If it hadn't been so deadly dull, I'd never have dared to come here—though I suppose they would have sent me anyway."

"But the voyage! That must have been exciting."

"Except for another orphan from a convent, the cabin was stuffed with Lisbon streetwalkers. It was stinking, the food was rotten and wormy, the water was foul, and if I tried to get a breath of air, some sailor would breathe garlic in my face and try to paw me."

Rozane digested this, tried again. "But you fell in love with Cousin Duarte the moment that you saw him, didn't you? There he was, waiting when the ship docked, and at first sight—"

Rachel lacked the heart to shatter such illusions and changed the subject. "My friend Elena was terribly frightened. I hope she got a good husband."

"Elena?" Rozane puckered her smooth brow before she laughed. "Why, it must be she that Uncle Tadeu married! He took a wife off the same ship and she's an orphan, too. I've seen her at church, and Mama and I called on her one day, but she was indisposed. If you like, I'll ask Mama if we could visit her tomorrow." Rachel noticed that Rozane spoke of Dona Consuelo as Mama but called her father "Senhor Pai" or "Senhor Father."

"That would be nice," Rachel said, but her heart sank for Elena. It sounded as if she'd been chosen by an old man. Rachel hoped that at least he was kind.

Indeed, Elena was blissful. After the entire household gathered in the chapel before breakfast, kneeling as Venancio led in prayers, Dona Consuelo sent a messenger to announce their visit. As soon as they had breakfasted, Dona Consuelo called for sedan chairs.

The silk-gowned young matron who met them in the reception hall of her balconied mansion was scarcely recognizable as the shrinking, fragile orphan girl of little over a month ago. Embracing Rachel, she whispered ecstatically, "Tadeu is so good to me! He buys me anything I want and goes with me to mass. He—he even thinks I'm pretty!"

"Well, so you are," laughed Rachel.

They sat down on handsome Persian carpets, making sure their slippered feet were decently covered by their skirts, and spent an hour in pleasant conversation over pastries served from a beaten silver tray by a stately mulatta.

Tadeu proved to be the red-cheeked, white-haired man Rachel had noticed at the dock, the one who had said a bath would do wonders for the bedraggled brides-to-be. If he remembered his prurient examination of Rachel, he gave no sign of it as he came forward to greet his sister, Dona Consuelo, his niece Rozane, and Rachel, now circuitously related by marriage.

He beamed upon Elena the whole time he inquired after Dona Consuelo's health and that of her family, cleared his throat and puffed out his chest. "I trust, sister, that by the grace of the Virgin of the Conception it will not be long before I can ask you and your good husband to stand godparents for my heir."

"Tadeu!" cried Elena, blushing.

Dona Consuelo patted her hand. "What grand tidings, my dear! I had despaired of being aunt to any children of Tadeu's."

He said dramatically, "In spite of all my prayers and those of my excellent departed wives, may all four rest in peace, it had seemed I must go childless to the grave." He tweaked a lock of Elena's hair. "But now we have great hopes."

Elena blushed again but looked so happy that Rachel felt a stir of envy and wonder. Perhaps, being old, Tadeu behaved gently in bed. Yet, asking herself if she would have preferred him, Rachel had to admit she would not. Whatever his virtues, it would feel obscene to be handled by a man old enough to be her grandfather. The envy faded, but she was glad Elena was content.

Both Duarte and Venancio Álvares were municipal councilors and would march with them. Raimundo would walk with the Brothers of the Misericordia, and Paulo, ar-

mored as Saint George, would ride his white Arabian. The
women had been invited to watch from the balcony of a
Cabral cousin.

First came Moorish dancers, spinning in diaphanous garments; then an enormous sea serpent, undulating with the
movements of the dozen men bearing the cloth-covered
frame. Each group of craftsmen had a banner and carried
its patron saint or the emblems of the trade. Ferrymen paraded the image of Saint Christopher on their shoulders,
followed by dancing gypsies. Saint John was escorted by
shoemakers. Stonemasons bore toy castles. Saint George
rode proudly between a dragon and a host of devils.

Shepherds, soldiers and fishermen. Rachel gasped as Sa-
lome, almost naked, danced sensuously, holding the gory
head of John the Baptist on a platter. The apostles, angels,
Abraham and King David marched before Joseph leading
the donkey that carried the Virgin, whose real baby cried
at the commotion. There was Saint Sebastian, threatened
by archers, and then the municipal councilors, the knightly
orders and the governor-general.

Singing hymns and bearing upraised crosses came Jesuits, Dominicans and Carmelites, and then the bishop of
Bahia, bearing a pyx that held the sacred host as he walked
beneath a canopy. The crowds below and people on bal-
conies knelt with bowed heads till the sacrament passed.
Rachel had seen more splendid processions in Lisbon, but
never one carried out with such spirit and such cheering
from the onlookers. Knowing a few of the people in the
parade had made it more intimate, while the hospitality of
the Álvareses and seeing Elena had lessened her sense of
isolation. For the first time Rachel began to hope that she
might someday feel at home in this country.

Next morning the Álvareses accompanied Duarte and
Rachel to early mass in the little chapel raised on the remains of the one built by Caramuru's widow, a baptized
Tupi princess. Not far from the fort of San Diogo, the
chapel looked out upon green-blue sea and white surf
crashing against the rocks.

Glancing at the ships in the tremendous crescent harbor,
Rachel wondered if the fort could repel a Dutch fleet should

another attack. There would never be peace of mind in Bahia so long as the Dutch were poised above them, ready to swoop down as soon as they had the strength. Though skirmishing continued in the north, major forays by either side had to wait on supplies and reinforcements from the home countries. It was the kind of seesaw war that could drag on for years.

"I hope next spring you can come to my wedding," Rozane whispered as she hugged Rachel in farewell.

"So do I." Rachel smiled.

She was sad to take leave of the Álvareses. Venancio did rule this household, but in a kindly, fatherly fashion, and Dona Consuelo had made her feel like a daughter. She sighed as Duarte closed the curtains of her litter.

Back to Seraphim. Thank heaven for Felicia.

As months passed that would have been summer in Portugal but were here the coolest time of the year, Rachel acquired skill and sureness in managing the big house. She coaxed Damião into serving the vegetables he despised as slaves' food and persuaded him to send a tray of fresh fruit to the table along with the sugary desserts.

Rivalry between Rosa and Eva kept upstairs and downstairs burnished. The heap of long-neglected mending had dwindled enough to permit the seamstresses to start working on new garments for the slaves. Every few days Rachel visited the *senzala* to see if anyone was sick, take tempting delicacies to the aged and admire the babies. As she offered a finger to be gripped by brown or dark ivory fingers, and laughed softly at dimples and sparkling eyes, she ached to know that these infants were Duarte's property, doomed from birth to slavery. Sometimes she bit her lip to keep from asking a mother why she conceived children for the master's profit. *Senzala* families loved and delighted in children. Duarte, unlike some owners, followed his forebear's example in not breaking up families and in keeping the elders in comfort till their deaths. Seraphim slaves were better fed and housed than many impoverished free workers, but it still seemed wrong to Rachel for a man to own another one.

Wrong, but that was how it was. Duarte owned her as surely as he did the slaves.

He didn't possess her every night now as he had at first, but these reprieves kept Rachel on edge, since she would start praying early in the evening that this would be one of those nights when he only fondled her a few minutes before turning over or rising to go down the hall, saying he was going to play cards for a while with Tomé.

Rachel suspected that he went to Luzia rather than to his father-in-law. She didn't care. The golden woman was welcome to him so long as she didn't try to challenge Rachel's place as mistress of the house.

The happiest hours Rachel spent were in the library. There were other romantic works besides *Amadís*, and she devoured them along with poetry, history and books of travel. For a few hours, she was swept into faraway places, enjoyed adventures, and wept or smiled over the fate of lovers.

Without talking about it, she and Manoel used the library at different times. She read in the afternoon when the household dozed. Manoel did his accounts in the hour or so before dinner. Each Monday, with Felicia present and the office door open, he went over the records with Rachel, answering her questions and giving her an understanding of the plantation's expenses and profits.

Duarte had come to the first of these sessions, began fidgeting within ten minutes and shortly thereafter got to his feet, yawning. "Rachel seems to know what your columns and figures mean, Manoel. Make your reports to her and don't bother me unless the tax collector tries to cheat us or we can't borrow what we need."

"Senhor, there is no need to borrow." Manoel's tone was modest, but his eyes had a prideful light. "If this cane crop is as good as the last, the remaining creditors can be paid and there'll be money enough to last till next season."

Duarte stared at him. "What are you saying?"

"That next year Seraphim will earn more than it spends."

Duarte sat down as if his legs had weakened. "But that's never happened! My father was always in debt. So was his father. So is everyone I know."

"Senhor, you employed me to manage your plantation and reduce the debts. I have done so."

"Don't take offense," Duarte said hastily. "If this is so, you've wrought miracles." Thinking back, he rubbed his chin and frowned. "That thoroughbred you wouldn't let me buy last winter! That cloth of gold you said didn't suit my physique! That luscious Fulah girl you swore had some wasting disease—ah, senhor manager, I begin to comprehend."

A smile twitched Manoel's lips. "Senhor, you had forgotten all those fancies within a week. Anyway, isn't it worth some restraint to be solvent?"

"I don't know. It never happened." Duarte looked tragic. "Most things, I can ask myself what Father or Grandfather would do. But to live without creditors! My dear young friend, no one in my family has been confronted with this!"

"Don't worry about it," advised Manoel. "And it might be as well not to mention it to your fellow planters and friends."

Duarte's eyes rolled. "If they knew I wasn't mortgaged up to the eyebrows, they'd be on me like chiggers on a bare ass. Never fear, I'll learn to live with prosperity." He added sternly, "Let's hear no more of your urgings against my buying what takes my eye."

"Not everything," implored Manoel. "A little discretion, senhor, or you'll wreck my efforts of the last six years."

Chuckling, Duarte let his fingers caress Rachel's cheek and throat. "Now that I'm so well married, extravagance has lost much of its charm. I'm amazed at how content I am to stay here and be a proper *senhor de engenho.*"

He sauntered out. As his careless hand left Rachel's flesh, she caught distress in Manoel's eyes, an anger she prayed Duarte wouldn't notice. When he was gone, embarrassed silence grew between them. With a muffled sound, Manoel shut the ledger.

"Your pardon, senhora, but I must meet with a planter who wants to send his cane to this mill for grinding."

He strode out, hands knotted into fists at his sides. A tide of small memories, the way his tone softened for her, the time she had found him holding the book she'd been reading, the manner in which his dark eyes sometimes lingered on her, his gifts of flowers—Rachel put them all together and burned with self-reproach.

Manoel loved her. She had enjoyed his worship without a thought. Since they were both New Christians, she had felt kinship with him. Apart from Felicia, he was her only friend at Seraphim, but she could never love him. Even if she weren't married.

And married she was, to a *fidalgo* of the kind who feared above all things to be cuckolded. Rachel got up slowly.

Sure enough, Luzia was just vanishing down the hall. Rachel's lips curved in bitter amusement. With that woman around, it would be lunacy to have a lover. Duarte wasn't cruel, but he was violent. If he even suspected her of infidelity, the results would be decidedly unpleasant. Manoel might not think so, but it was fortunate she didn't love him.

After breakfast Duarte usually rode about the fields for a few hours, was shaved by Bento, and retired to his hammock till dinner, which was served about two o'clock. After that, he played cards with Tomé and sometimes Bento until supper at eight. Of course he stayed overnight in Bahia two nights a week in order to attend to his council duties, which meant he was blessedly absent half of the time. Otherwise the routine was occasionally broken by the visit of another plantation owner.

On the first such visit, Rachel innocently appeared at the table. The guest, a portly neighbor, was extremely gallant, but Duarte's brow was thunderous, Tomé looked spitefully pleased, and Father Paulo and Manoel distressed. Rachel retired early, but was roused from sleep by the angry grasp of her husband's hands.

"Decent women don't parade themselves before strangers! Do you want the whole Reconcavo to buzz with tales of my shameless wife?"

Amazed, fuddled with sleep, Rachel tried to pull away. "But, senhor, I supposed—I didn't know—"

He took a deep breath. "Perhaps you didn't. Well, let me make it clear. Unless the guest is a close relation of mine, you must not expose yourself to his eyes. Otherwise, wagging tongues will have it that I wed an exported harlot, not a convent-reared gentlewoman.''

Rachel stiffened. That was enough to bring Duarte's mouth and weight down on her. "You are mine!" He thrust aside her thin garment, finding her shrinking body. "Mine, and don't you forget it!"

He was so brutally punishing that Rachel's bones ached for several days. Felicia, who'd been tending a sick baby and hadn't been present to warn her, looked furious when she heard what had happened and made Rachel soak in a tub of astringent herbs that stung her lacerations but made them less painful afterwards.

Rachel was too angrily humiliated to talk about it, but Felicia expressed her feelings, and more pungently than Rachel could ever have. "Fine for him to have a mistress right in the house and the good God knows what wenches in town. Only decent thing those small gentleman's hands of his ever curve around is his rosary! Otherwise, his fingers don't fit anything except cards, snuffbox and *mucamas'* breasts.'' She grinned wickedly. "You know what slaves say, sinhá? That every master has two left hands, so his slaves need two right ones to light his cigars, draw on his trousers and hunt his lice. Some senhores even have slaves wipe their behinds.''

That ludicrous thought shocked Rachel into laughter. Collapsing in Felicia's arms, she laughed until she cried and then, tight knots of outrage melted, felt much better.

The great many-trunked cashew trees were in flower as the cane matured in September. Preparations were made for the feast that was given on the day of the first grinding. Venancio Álvares brought his wife and daughter to the celebration, for he had grown up on a plantation, though it had since passed to an older brother, and he still felt nostalgia for country customs.

Dona Consuelo complimented Rachel on the appearance of the house, but her lips thinned at the sight of Luzia, resplendent with gold ornaments, playing with her son in the courtyard.

"You are not yet with child?" The motherly woman

frowned. "Well, I will offer candles for you to the Virgin of Conception, and you'd better do so yourself. It would be shameful for a fine old place like Seraphim to fall into a bastard's hands."

Flushing, Rachel murmured something and sent for refreshments. The first moment she was alone with Rozane, the girl gave her an ecstatic hug. "Cousin, Senhor Pai has finally agreed that I shall marry Santiago!"

The twinge of envy Rachel felt didn't prevent her from warmly returning the embrace. "And when is this to be?"

"Next spring, soon after Easter. It's *ages,* but I'm too happy to mind that. You'll come in for the wedding, of course. And you must be godmother to our first child! Say you will!"

"I'll be delighted." Rachel laughed.

"Dona Elena sends you her love," went on Rozane. "Uncle Tadeu is so proud that he's to be a father that he's given a huge silver candlestick to the church. Should he get a son, he's promised a gold monstrance."

Rachel winced. If old Tadeu had sired an heir almost at once, Duarte's grumbles were bound to increase.

Family, guests and slaves heard mass and then proceeded to the mill, the younger slaves cheering and dancing. Father Paulo sprinkled the mill wheel with holy water and generously bedewed those who pushed forward to share the benediction. Next came a sermon about how lucky the slaves were to be owned by a Christian master rather than some heretic Dutchman under whom they would have no feast days. The priest adjured them to work diligently and deserve their good fortune.

Ceremoniously Duarte helped place the first bundle of ripened cane, tied about with red ribbons, into the mill. The oxen were urged forward and the cane, crushed and oozing juice, squeezed out between the vertical cylinders.

As soon as the token grinding was done, Duarte and Father Paulo led the whole procession back to the big house, where the slaves' banquet was spread in the reception hall: whole roast pigs, turkeys and chickens, codfish stew, rice, beans, manioc served half a dozen ways, and platters of caramel pudding, sugar-coconut, milk-rice, stewed fruits and jugs of the fiery rum called *cachaça.*

Upstairs, the master's table had the same foods with re-
finements like marmalade from São Paulo and wine from
the Canary Islands. Long before the leisurely meal was
finished, music floated from the courtyard, with gay shouts,
singing and clapping.

"They'll dance till daylight," Duarte chuckled. "I don't
grudge them that so long as they work with a will tomorrow."

"Cane grinding's heavy work," nodded Venancio.
"Your mill runs on Sundays, too, I believe."

"You have the right of it, cousin." Duarte looked bel-
ligerent. "The cane must all be crushed before the rainy
season or the moisture ruins it. Even the holy orders own-
ing great plantations, Carmelites and Benedictines, work
their slaves on Sundays during grinding season."

"I know," sighed Venancio. "It's a marvel more slaves
don't drop from the toil. They'll be at it till April."

"My slaves eat well," Duarte said defensively. "I have
the bishop's dispensation for them to have meat on Fridays
and holy days except Christmas Eve, Ash Wednesday,
Holy Week and the Vigil of the Ascension. I am not as
pious as you, cousin, but I endeavor to make a profit while
remaining a faithful son of the Holy Church."

"There's not an unbaptized slave on the place," said
Tomé loyally. "And the men and women marry properly,
senhor. No loose fornicating of the sort you'll find on many
plantations."

Rachel swallowed a gasp at his hypocrisy. Duarte, mol-
lified at the praise, sent a serving girl to summon Damião.
Beaming, white lace smock immaculate, Damião graciously acknowledged compliments and the toast Duarte
proposed to him. By then it was late. The company sought
their beds and Duarte, to Rachel's relief, went to sleep at
once.

The mill wheel creaked incessantly for what seemed
endless months, broken only at Christmas and Epiphany,
when the Three Kings' gifts to Jesus were remembered by
festivities and the bestowing of presents. Every woman in
the *senzala* got a bright new dress, and the men received
coarse cotton shirts and nankeen trousers. Every child over

five got a dress or trousers and all the little ones had sweets and a toy.

Rachel had sewn fine linen into ruffled shirts for Duarte, and her women had stitched plainer ones for Tomé, Bento and Manoel. Duarte gave Father Paulo pious books and delighted his *mãe preta,* Irene, with lilac silk and more golden charms for the ''claw'' pinned at her waist. He touched Rachel by presenting her with a handsomely bound volume of *Cancionero Geral,* a collection of poetry, but he also gave her an evil-smelling packet of powdered leaves.

''I've consulted a physician in Bahia about your failure to conceive.'' His tone was half blustering, half shamed. ''He prescribes three pinches of this each evening in a goblet of heated wine.''

As Rachel stared at him, feeling the inevitable trap begin to close around her, he added gruffly, ''Every time I see Tadeu, he asks in front of the whole council if I'm expecting an heir and then he boasts about what a fine son that whey-faced little wisp is going to give him.''

As her nerveless fingers held the foul-odored packet, he fastened a wrought gold and emerald necklace about her throat, so heavy it dragged at the back of her neck. Its barbaric ostentation glittered as if it scorned the modestly cut gown of gray silk it lay against.

''I'm well pleased with my nun-bride except in this,'' he said more kindly and turned up her face to claim her lips with his moist ones. ''Let's call for wine, my pretty, and when you've drunk the potion, we'll give it a trial.''

She had no opportunity to evade the nasty stuff, for each night Duarte measured it into heated wine and made her drink to the dregs. The wine had the effect of relaxing her, making her languid in his fervid embraces. This excited him to prodigious feats, but Felicia's preventive thwarted any power the powder might have had.

On the Day of the Candles, the second of February, Elena was delivered of a lusty boy. Tadeu sent a messenger with the news and twisted the knife by reconfirming Elena's invitation for them to stand godparents.

They did, and Duarte made an admiring fuss over the

tiny pink creature with its silken tonsure of black hair, giving his godson a massive silver crucifix to hang above his bed, a silver cup and a ruby-encrusted coffer containing a knucklebone of Saint Anthony, one of the heavenly warriors who had helped Portuguese Christians drive out the Moors. Rachel had embroidered diminutive robes of soft white cotton and hand-quilted a silken coverlet sprinkled with blue flowers.

Elena's hollowed eyes brightened at the lovingly made gifts. "I'm glad the robes are white, Rachel, for I vowed to Our Lady of Childbirth that if I was safely delivered, the child would wear only white and blue till first communion, in homage to her, and would bear her name with his others."

So Christopher Duarte Maria Coelho Ribiera received his names and became a Christian, howling disapproval at being roused from slumber. Tadeu proudly feasted friends and relatives till late that night, so Rachel was weary when at last the godparents could congratulate the glowing couple a last time and slip off to the Álvareses'.

"If that wasn't an ugly brat!" grunted Duarte as Bento pulled off his boots, hung up the hot velvet doublet and left them. "Flat nose, head all over with bumps!"

"I think most babies—"

Bento returned with a goblet of warmed wine. Did this silent young red-haired man, brother in milk and probably in blood to Duarte, know what the wine was for? He almost certainly did. All the Seraphim slaves were doubtless whispering about the master's efforts to get a crop from his plowing.

Inexorably pushed toward the time when she must stop delaying pregnancy, Rachel faced a chilling thought. What if she truly couldn't conceive, either because of some natural defect or from continued use of Felicia's draught?

"At least," chuckled Duarte, handing her the treated wine, "I no longer suspect that Great-uncle Tadeu was cuckolded. The baby has his squinched-up eyes and weak chin." His heavy hand slid from Rachel's shoulder to greedily fondle her breast. "Our son will be well-favored and strong, not the paltry get of an old man's failing seed."

He made Rachel drain the goblet. The bitter taste that lingered in her mouth was not all from the wine.

Late that month a less fortunate child was born to peach-skinned Izabel, just turned thirteen. Going to the *senzala* to take milk-rice and fresh cane juice to the new mother, Rachel halted on the threshold, alarmed at the stony expression on Rosa's purple-black face.

"Izabel? She's all right?"

Usually cheerful Rosa had a grim set to her fleshy jaw. "The baby, he blind."

"Are you sure?"

"Pus running out. See this before. Not first baby born with pox since Senhor Tomé come to Seraphim. And Izabel she got no milk, breasts too little."

"Maybe one of the other women—"

Rosa shook her head. "Poxed babies give disease to wet nurse." She had made a cloth teat for the infant to suck watered milk from. It was doing this, weakly, as Rachel came to stand by Izabel's hammock.

Dark eyes looked up at her from the childish face. Izabel's father had been white, or mostly so. Duarte? Some visitor? There was no doubt in Rachel's mind about the procreator of the spindly pale-skinned mite whose eyes filmed with a sickly ooze. The long umbilical cord looked as substantial as the wizened arms and legs.

French pox, Spanish pox, the Portuguese sickness. However it was called, the ailment was rampant in Brazil. Duarte's father had been afflicted, and there was no guessing how widely he had spread the taint. Duarte seemed healthy, but Rachel felt cold as she turned from the pathetic newborn. What if she had a child like this? A frail hand touched hers.

"Sinhá," the girl whispered, "my little boy, you help him?"

"We'll do whatever we can." Rachel smoothed back Izabel's sweat-damp hair. Nothing but a child herself, defenseless, and that loathsome Tomé—

Rachel controlled her outrage long enough to talk cheeringly with the girl a few minutes and lift her spirits by promising to be the infant's godmother. Then she asked if she might take him to the big house.

"I want to show him to Felicia. Maybe she knows some medicine."

Hope dawned in the big eyes, but Rosa said flatly, "Felicia have strong *mandingas* and medicine, but nothing for this." All the same, she wrapped the baby in a clean white cloth and handed him to Rachel.

She would ask Felicia's help, but Rachel's real purpose was to confront Tomé with this pitiful mite and shock Duarte into checking the predations of his in-law-by-marriage.

The men's voices came from the smaller parlor. She found them reclining in hammocks, playing cards on a small table placed between them while handsome yellow Gaspar fanned Duarte and Valeria did the same for her florid, balding master.

They all glanced up in surprise at Rachel's approach. Tomé tugged at his calico dressing gown in a vain attempt to make it close over his bulging hairy belly.

"What have you got there, little wife?" asked Duarte.

She drew the cotton away from the baby's face. Duarte recoiled. Tomé made a disgusted face. "Faugh, senhora! You shouldn't be carrying that wretched morsel about. And why you brought it here—"

"I thought you should see your child, senhor."

"My child!"

"Izabel was already showing this babe, senhor, when I told her to stop cleaning your room."

Tomé's red face seemed to swell around his blue-veined nose. "Just because that little slut threw herself at me doesn't mean I sired that bit of ulcerous flesh!"

"The boy is almost white," Rachel pointed out, displaying the skeletal body.

"Cover it up!" Duarte thundered.

Rachel did, but she said relentlessly, "Husband, your manager has spoken to you before about blind and diseased slaves. If the *senzala* produces many children like this, you had best save up to buy a whole new generation of healthy slaves from Africa."

She left him chewing his lip and went to find Felicia.

* * *

Felicia anointed the mattering eyes. The pupils showed dead white. "This is how my sister's baby looked," said the tall black woman. "And too many others born since. Usually they die young or the *senzala* would overflow with cripples and idiots."

"There's nothing you can do?"

Felicia shrugged. "This salve should heal the sores on the eyes, but the child was born rotted from within." She placed her long black hand on the baby, almost covering its entire trunk. She seemed to stop breathing. Rachel could feel the power of her intense concentration passing through the diseased body to her own tingling arms.

"He must die." With a heavy sigh Felicia stepped back and folded the cloth over the sad little form as if it were a shroud. "But Yemanjá, she has promised to take his spirit."

"Yemanjá?"

"She rules seas and rivers. Helps mothers and babies."

A cold chill shot up Rachel's spine. "You—you don't pray to some heathen goddess?"

Something flickered in Felicia's impenetrable eyes. "Yemanjá is Virgin Mary. There are stars on her crown and the crescent moon is under her feet. However you call her, she will take this little blind one to her breast. He will drink her milk."

All the same, Rachel wept as she carried the small body back to place it in Rosa's sturdy arms. She left the salve and said she'd come again in the morning.

The baby died that night. When Rachel and Father Paulo walked down to comfort Rosa and Izabel, the mother seemed almost joyful.

"That baby an angel now, isn't he, Father? Little soul go straight to heaven?"

The priest assured the sobbing mother that it was so, that her son was among God's angels. But Rachel preferred to hope that Mary-Yemanjá held him in her arms.

Rachel saw to it that there was a sky-blue coffin for the child and a funeral in the chapel. She walked with Izabel to the slaves' graveyard on a slope beyond the mill, which had not ceased grinding because a slave child had died. The small mound was covered with palm leaves and flowers and Felicia and Rosa joined in a chant.

At least this one won't be a slave, Rachel thought. If I were a slave, I'd never have a child, never give the master one more body. I'd—

Then she remembered the potion Duarte made her drink each night and curled her lips in self-mockery.

Her daughter would be subject to Duarte till a husband took his place. The only hope was for a kind master. A son? If a son grew up under the influence of Duarte and Tomé, he would be a slave to indolence, unrestrained sexual use of slave women, sadistic impulses, the casual acceptance of staggering debt to finance luxurious display. Brought up among slaves on plantations where the master ruled absolutely, the wonder was that any owner's son retained a shred of decency or kindness. Religion, so far as Rachel could see, consisted in ceremonial observances with the master's face directed toward God and the saints rather than toward fellowmen and daily conduct.

All were enslaved, masters, workers—even the earth itself—in producing sugar, that single crop desired by Europe and the Crown.

Duarte, appalled at beholding the result of his father-in-law's license, now fully supported Rachel's order that no young women were to wait on Tomé. That didn't change what had happened to Izabel, though, and Rachel was still brooding about it when she went to the library later that week, attended by Felicia, to go over accounts with Manoel.

Several smallholders who leased land from Duarte were sending their cane for grinding. "These leased *partidos* produce about forty *tarefas* a year," Manoel explained. "These smallholders get two-fifths of the sugar, Seraphim three-fifths, and the Crown's sugar tithe collector takes a hefty amount from both."

He flipped to another page. "Yesterday we ground thirty-five cartloads for Senhor Avilos, so I credit that here, and in this column I debit—"

"How will you debit Izabel's baby?" Rachel demanded.

She felt she would suffocate if she couldn't talk about her feelings to someone. Duarte dismissed them as those of an unexperienced girl from a convent, and Father Paulo murmured some piety about there being no slaves in heaven.

Manoel's dark eyes met hers in a kind of shock. For a few minutes he seemed to consider before he turned to the black woman. "Felicia, you can forget anything it might harm your mistress for you to remember."

She inclined her head.

Again, Manoel's gaze searched Rachel. He touched another ledger. "The child's death is here, along with records of buying and selling slaves, their births, disablements and deaths. But within my heart, Dona Rachel, I bring such things to God who brought our people out of slavery in the land of Egypt and abides with us still, though we are scattered throughout the world."

He spoke of the Jews. Long-forgotten memories stirred in Rachel, painful, bittersweet. Her heart pounded, for to voice such words or hear them was to risk the Inquisition, always suspicious of New Christians.

" 'The Lord is my strength and song.' " Manoel's voice deepened. " 'He is become my salvation: He is my God, and I will prepare for Him a habitation; my father's God, and I will exalt Him.' "

Rachel trembled, trying to remember. A table and candles; her tall father, face veiled by time, blessing wine; the dear, comforting presence of her mother. Longing swelled in her throat.

"Have you heard Moses' song before, Dona Rachel?" Manoel probed gently. "That was his rejoicing when God saved Israel from the pursuit of Pharaoh's soldiers. Did you know that Jesus, whom we call a prophet, was in Jerusalem celebrating the Passover when he was arrested and condemned?"

She hadn't known that. Only that Jews were hated and called Christ-killers. How strange, when she thought about it, for surely Jesus was a Jew and so had been his mother, adored now by all Christians except heretics like the Dutch.

Rachel felt as if the ground were moving beneath her,

that she might drop into an abyss. "Senhor," she whispered, "this is dangerous."

He shrugged. "I left Amsterdam in order to bring relatives of mine back to their true religion. I succeeded. Most of them now live in Recife or Olinda, where the Dutch do not persecute them. But there are secret Jews in Bahia. I have stayed to instruct them and strengthen their faith."

"That's what you do when you leave Seraphim." Rachel had wondered, for he didn't seem the sort to visit waterfront dives or tumble harlots, yet before harvest began, he had usually been gone Fridays and Saturdays.

He nodded. Felicia said angrily, "Why do you tell the sinhá these things?"

"That she may be restored, at least in secret, to God and her people."

"But—"

"Felicia," he said softly, "why do you remember Yemanjá?"

He didn't press Rachel, but in the brief periods they met now that he was occupied with the grinding, she found herself asking questions, eager to know more about this forbidden faith her parents had lived by and for which her grandparents had gone into exile. They spoke in lowered tones, eyes on the door, for both knew that though the Inquisition had no headquarters in Brazil, it sent occasional investigators to ferret out Jews who conformed outwardly to Christianity but practiced Judaism in secret. Suspected heretics were sent to Lisbon for trial.

"The nuns once took us to an auto-da-fé," she told Manoel with a shudder. "Most of the convicted recanted and were granted their lives, though condemned to imprisonment. Some recanted at the stake and were garroted with an iron collar tightened by a screw before their bodies were fed to the flames. But one man—" She swallowed hard, remembering black, greasy smoke and the sickening odor. "He called out words I did not understand and the nun that made me watch was angry. She said some of the words were those Jesus cried out as he hung on the cross."

"*Eli, Sabahot?* Why should not Jesus call on the Lord of Hosts? I know Christians do not agree, but I have thought he died reciting the Sh'ma: 'Hear, Oh Israel, the Lord our God, the Lord is One.' ''

Rachel was still trembling. "That burning—it was an awful death!"

Manoel's usually calm eyes blazed. "To die glorifying the name of God is a blessed end."

It might be, but Rachel remembered the flames.

The harvest was almost over, which was good, for soon the rains would start. Venancio Álvares rode out to announce Rozane's marriage in two weeks. The date had been set after the grinding so that all of the Alvareses' friends and relatives who owned mills or plantations would be able to attend the several days of merrymaking.

"I don't like to think of my little Rozane living out in the wilds," Venancio admitted. "Especially when there's no telling when those Dutch heretics may overrun the south. I've always regretted that Virgilio was set on pushing back into the *sertão.*"

"My father always said it was because his mother was half Tupi," Duarte suggested.

"So? You and I and all Bahians whose families have been here from the earliest have Indian blood."

Duarte laughed at Venancio and lowered one eyelid in a wink. "Well, cousin, just as the finest old Brazilian families count Indians among their ancestors, in another hundred years I vow it'll be impossible to say with certainty that one hasn't a trace of African blood."

"God forbid," frowned the graying patriarch.

Duarte slapped his shoulder. "Come now! Even a strait-laced husband like you must have noticed some of our most tempting women are mulattas."

"Temptation's one thing, yielding another."

Jaw dropping, Duarte scoffed, "Do you mean to say you've never bought yourself a piece of dark cake?"

Reddening, Venancio looked apologetically at Rachel. "This is no fitting conversation to hold before your wife, cousin, but I have had neither concubines nor bastards."

"Then you're a prodigy! Except for the Jesuits, who, I'll admit, generally honor their vows, there's scarce a priest in Brazil who could swear the same."

"That's between them and God." Venancio turned to Rachel before Duarte could pursue the subject. "I called on Uncle Tadeu and Dona Elena yesterday. They send greetings and look forward to seeing you at the wedding."

"How's my godson?" asked Duarte. "Does he still look like a skinned monkey?"

Venancio grinned. "He's vastly improved. The bumps on his head are rounding over, and he's guzzled so much of his *mãe preta*'s milk that he's fleshing out. He's going to be spoiled rotten, of course. Tadeu dotes on him even more than the women do."

Duarte scowled. His eyes touched Rachel fleetingly before they traveled to Gilberto, lording it among his darker little companions. A chill edged up Rachel's spine. Even if Duarte wasn't getting impatient, she couldn't evade the problem much longer. She must either bear her husband a son or see Luzia's temporarily diminished influence increase till it would be intolerable to be under the same roof. She was sure, moreover, that should Luzia triumph, she'd find a way to get rid of her rival.

Rachel knew all this, yet she could not quite bring herself to abandon Felicia's herbs and try to conceive a child.

Rozane's wedding festivities lasted for a week. The big house overflowed with guests; many stayed with other relatives but assembled each day for feasting and dancing. Tadeu had loaned his group of skillful black acrobats who performed dizzying feats. Besides wrestlers and musicians, there were contests and demonstrations of *capoeira*, a swift, graceful dance of mock fighting, feigned butts with the head, chopping with hands, tripping and kicking. Bento was a master at eluding and attack. Under his breath Duarte boasted to Rachel, "Bento's tumbled many an armed ruffian in the streets. *Capoeira*'s more than a dance."

Rachel had never seen such a display of finery and jewels, though some of the silk, satin and velvet garments reeked of old sweat beneath cloying perfumes. Rozane was breathtaking, her dark beauty set off by snowy lace and satin, black hair crowned with a wreath of white roses. Watching her with Santiago, a tall, smooth-skinned young man with frank gray eyes and auburn hair, Rachel forced back memories of her own marriage and prayed for their happiness.

She thought they would find it. There was something different in the way Santiago, his brothers and his father moved, an energy that set them apart from city folk and planters of the Reconcavo. None of the family, including the women, had an extra bit of fat, and all had clear, healthy complexions.

Rachel had helped the other matrons prepare the bridal bed, smoothing embroidered sheets and counterpane, pumping up the big pillows. Lucky Rozane, to lie in the arms of the one she loved. That was a grace found by few women. Nor would Rozane go alone to the wilderness *fazenda* of her husband's family.

Along with a thoroughbred for Santiago, there was a gilded blue sedan chair for Rozane, chests of embroidered linens, a massive silver service, and four slaves, two young women well trained by Dona Consuelo and two husky young men.

A grown son and daughter of Rozane's *mãe preta* were freed as a sign of rejoicing, and the beaming nurse was granted her liberty, too, though she chose to remain with her mistress.

"The way Venancio frees his servants it's a wonder he has any left," muttered Duarte. "I may free a couple in my will, but as long as I can use them, they're staying slaves."

He had business in the city, so he and Rachel stayed on at the Álvareses' after the newlywed pair and Santiago's family had been escorted some miles beyond the city and last farewells were said. Santiago had ridden alongside his bride's sedan chair, silver stirrups and saddle mountings gleaming. He, like the other men of his family, had changed velvet and silk for supple leather trousers and vest. Even their hats were hard leather, narrow-brimmed, with crowns shaped like a soldier's metal helmet.

Only the women rode in litters or chairs. Santiago's mother, flame-haired Dona Firmina, had laughingly said that on the *fazenda* she and her daughters rode horseback and much preferred it to being joggled about in a stifling litter. Still, one had to make concessions to ease Venancio and Consuelo's fears that their child was going to dwell among uncivilized backwoodsmen.

After that the escort turned back to the city. But Rachel, peering from between the litter's curtains, envied Rozane that wilder, freer life, and, most especially, the incredible joy of living with the man she loved.

The Dutch attacked that day. The boom of cannons and sound of firearms carried up from the forts an hour before the alarm swept the mansions, convents and government buildings on the heights.

Count Johan Maurits of Nassau, a seasoned commander and cultured nobleman, had been sent last year by the Dutch West India Company to be governor-general of Netherlands Brazil. It didn't take him long to win back such regions of Pernambuco that Brazilian forces had painfully taken in the eleven-year struggle with the Dutch. It was he who had now landed thirty ships—thousands of soldiers and Tapuya allies—and was already in possession of the outlying forts.

Venancio and Raimundo had on baldricks and swords and were thrusting pistols in their belts when Paulo ran in to arm himself. "I expect Duarte's already below," Venancio said. "Dona Rachel, in case those heretics surround the city, it would be well to send now for supplies from Seraphim." He embraced his wife. "We should have troops enough to hold them even with that dawdling Italian, Count Bagnuoli, in command. Those Neapolitans he brought with him aren't worth much and he let Maurits drive our soldiers out of Pernambuco last year, but most of our garrison are stout fellows."

"Senhor," pleaded his wife, "you've fought often enough! Let the soldiers and younger men do their duty."

"Better fight now while there's a chance of stopping Maurits. I've no wish to hide in the country as we did twelve years ago. Besides, from all I know of the count, if he takes Bahia, he'll keep it."

Father and son hurried out, followed by all the able-bodied male slaves, who carried knives, staves, clubs—anything to serve as a weapon.

There were no Seraphim slaves left at the house except

Felicia and Rachel didn't trust the frightened young boys remaining at the Álvareses' to ride to Seraphim or spread word of the invasion to the other plantations so they could arm themselves and send supplies to the city.

"I'll go to Seraphim," Rachel said. "I'll be back tomorrow with all the food we can collect."

"But your litter-bearers went with my husband—"

"I can get there a lot faster on a horse."

Dona Consuelo looked shocked, but after a moment she nodded.

Rachel sat sideways on the saddle till they were beyond the city, but then she gingerly swung one leg over the pommel and, astride, urged the ancient mare Venancio kept out of sentiment into a faster pace. Felicia did the same, though her long legs almost reached the ground, for she rode a small donkey that was the pet of Raimundo's children.

In spite of her fear and the mare's shambling gait, which jarred her very teeth, Rachel felt as if her lungs were drawing in a new kind of air and marveled that anyone would prefer a litter to being out in the air and light.

Duarte would think her shameless, but perhaps he wouldn't have to know. Anyway, compared to the Dutch threat, such considerations seemed trifling. Honesty compelled her to admit that she'd be more grieved should Venancio be killed or wounded than if Duarte were.

She tried to squeeze up some wifely concern, but the lack of it, and even more damningly, a repressed but insistent thought that his death would free her from that hot drugged wine, greedy mouth and punishing body, forced her to admit that, sinful or not, she hated her husband.

Manoel sent messengers to neighboring plantations, the *aldeia* and cattle-raising outposts, instructing the last to drive beef animals as swiftly as possible to Bahia. As he and Rachel were supervising the loading of manioc, dried meat and such food as Seraphim could spare, Tomé waddled up, panting from the unusual exertion. "Of course you'll be joining the fight, senhor," he gabbled to Manoel. "Every strong young arm will be needed! Terrible fighters, those Dutch, and their ranks full of ferocious heretics from

England, France and Germany who got a taste for blood in the Thirty Years War. If that's not bad enough, those cannibal Tapuya fight for the Hollanders, who turn their prisoners over to them—"

Manoel said calmly, "It's well known that Brazilian commanders have refused quarter to the Dutch and have Indian allies who still savor a roast human haunch. I daresay that being a prisoner of either side is unenviable." He turned back to his task.

Tomé caught his arm. "Diniz can attend to this! You should be on your horse and riding!"

"You forget that I was born in Amsterdam." Manoel shrugged. "When Senhor Duarte employed me, we specifically discussed such a situation. I said that while I would not bear arms against my country, I would not aid her against Brazil. This was agreeable to Senhor Duarte."

"A convenient way to get out of risking your neck!" sneered Tomé.

Manoel ignored him. Rachel spoke sweetly to the quivering Pernambucan. "Age need be no barrier to your patriotism, senhor. Venancio Álvares is much your senior, but he had on baldric and pistols while Raimundo was still thinking about it."

"Much as I'd give to raise my sword against those buggers, my health would make me a burden," said Tomé in haughty reproach. "However, since the *fazenda*'s manager clearly can't be relied on, I shall organize Seraphim's defense. You may assure my dear brother and son-in-law that I will expire protecting his property."

From beneath a bed, Rachel thought. Diniz had already departed with all male slaves willing to fight for the city. That left women, old men and boys. Though Father Paulo and Manoel would have to assume leadership if Seraphim were attacked, for Tomé's uselessness was all too evident, Rachel entrusted Rosa and Eva with getting everyone inside the big house should it become necessary, and provisioning it for a siege.

Luzia listened to these plans with a superior smile. Rachel suspected that should the *fazenda* fall, the beautiful mulatta would manage to become some Dutch leader's mistress.

Father Paulo urged Rachel to stay at Seraphim. "It's not fitting that you should gallop about the countryside like a man, my daughter. I'm sure your noble husband would order you to wait where you're comparatively safe."

"I want to help Dona Consuelo. There are sure to be wounded."

"It's not fitting—"

Rachel put a selection of medicines and old sheets for bandages into a saddlebag. "There's nothing fitting or decorous about a war, Father."

Elena had come to stay at the Álvareses', for in spite of his age, Tadeu had belted on his sword and hurried to the battle. She was so upset that it was a good thing little Christopher had a wet nurse. Dona Consuelo had turned most of the ground floor into a hospital, and though she barred Rachel and Elena from dressing wounds and tending the men's intimate needs, they spooned porridge and broth and held water or diluted cane wine to the lips of men unable to feed themselves, sponged fevered skin and talked soothingly to those who babbled in delirium or whose eyes showed agony.

Black, mulatto, garrison soldier or volunteer, Dona Consuelo moved among them with medicines and kind words. Slaves helped the men to chamber pots, or "tigers," and bathed bodies, but the mistress performed these services, too, and it was she who held the younger ones in her arms as they died, she to whose hands the roughest mercenaries clung after the priest had given them the last rites.

Venancio, Duarte, Tadeu, Raimundo and Paulo came to the house when they were exhausted and slept as if drugged for eight or ten hours; then they would drag themselves up and return to guarding the defenses.

"Bagnuoli and our governor-general have made up their quarrels and are giving those damned heretics more than they counted on." Venancio grinned, though he still looked bone-weary after a night in his own bed and a hearty breakfast. "The Dutch haven't been able to keep food and volunteers from coming in, and they must be running low on supplies themselves. Maurits has close to five thousand men to feed."

Tadeu cackled. He had shed weight and looked younger and fitter from his exertions. "Yes, he's learned that Bahia's not the sort of cat to be taken without gloves. His troops can't get past ours to forage, and when the food he brought on those ships is gone, he'll have no choice but to run back to Recife with his tail between his legs."

"The Count of Nassau didn't win his reputation by giving up," warned Duarte. "Mark my words, Bahia's going to have to stand up to more than a month's siege before those buggers sail away."

He was right. On May 17, word fanned through the town like wildfire. A deserter from the Dutch side had bought his safety by informing the commanders that Maurits was staking everything on an all-out assault. Both Tadeu and Raimundo were recovering from slight wounds, but they brushed away their wives and hurried to the lower city.

Night darkened. The besieged city was filled with prayers, with dread and hope. The women in the Álvares house didn't go to bed that night but readied more pallets and bandages for the wounded who were sure to come, and knelt in the chapel between ministrations to the disabled men. These had heard the rumor, and the few who could rise up and keep their legs did so and went to fight.

The doors of the house were bolted with the heaviest furniture close by to barricade them and the windows should the attackers penetrate into the city. Except for young children, every member of the household had some kind of weapon either tucked into clothing or placed near at hand.

"You must decide," Dona Consuelo told Rachel and Elena. "But if the Dutch break in, I'll cut my throat before they can dishonor my beloved husband through me." Her usually sweet face was stern as she glanced at whimpering Maria, her daughter-in-law, so heavy with child that she could scarcely move. "Don't worry, my dear, I'll take care of you first."

"But my children!"

"I've already told their nurses to hide with them and Christopher behind the stables. After the looting, perhaps they can get away into the country. As for the babe you carry, better it dies within you than carved out by some soldier's blade."

Rachel had a kitchen knife thrust into an improvised sash. She thought she would die fighting rather than kill herself. As for Duarte's honor, that was the last reason she'd draw a blade across her throat. Elena plucked at her sleeve.

"Rachel, if—please, will you kill me? I—I'd bungle it. I've always been afraid of blood."

"I don't like it myself," Rachel said, trying to joke. She gave the girl who had crossed the sea with her a bracing hug. "We're scaring ourselves for nothing, I'll wager! Don't we have more soldiers than the Dutch, and cover to fight from as well?"

"They took Bahia before," Elena shivered.

"Only because everyone ran away. This time no one's running."

Dona Consuelo rose. "Let's go to the chapel and pray. Then we'd better be sure the men in the hospital have everything they need before new ones start coming in." She crossed herself as cannon boomed. A bedlam of shouts, firing and shrieks rose up from the beach. "Merciful mother, pity the dying."

Men died in Rachel's arms that night. The wounded were brought in too unceasingly for Dona Consuelo's prohibitions to be observed.

"The Dutch!" gasped a young man as Rachel probed for the ball that had lodged in his shoulder. "Wave on wave of them—like the sea. Giants they are—"

In the faintest light of dawn, Duarte limped in, supported by Raimundo and Bento, who were followed by Paulo, Tadeu and Venancio.

A pistol ball had torn a groove through the side of Duarte's thigh and Venancio's arm was soaked with blood from a sword cut, but they were so elated that they scarcely seemed to mind the sting of wine on their hurts.

"It was hot and hand to hand for hours," growled Venancio. "We had all we could do to keep them out of the city. But they finally fell back, and just as we were leaving, Maurits proposed an armistice so both sides can bury their dead."

"He may want more than an armistice," Tadeu crowed. "We killed a lot of his bravest officers and men."

"We should have counterattacked," scowled Duarte. "Chased them right into the sea!"

"We were too tired to do anything but praise God they were going," Venancio said wryly. Wincing, he got to his feet. "We'd better sleep while we can."

"You can't fight with your arm cut to the bone!" Dona Consuelo protested.

"I could if the Dutch were coming up our street," Venancio assured her. "Don't worry, dear wife, we'll leave the fighting to the garrison now unless we're really needed."

Duarte was carried upstairs. Rachel helped him undress, washed him and brought him a glass of Madeira before she started back down to help with the battle's heavy toll.

"I don't like your working among those common soldiers," Duarte grumbled.

"They were defending us, too," Rachel said. "Dona Consuelo's ready to drop. Surely you want me to help her."

It was clear that he didn't, but to protest would be a reproach to his cousin and hostess. "Well, if Dona Consuelo's there— Put a pillow under my leg, will you, so the wound won't be drawn so tight."

She did as he asked, moving the leg as gently as possible. He swore anyway. As she straightened, he ran a hand over her. "I can't sport with you for a while, but never fear, we'll make up for it."

She had no answer for that, could only wait stiffly till his fingers dropped from her. A wife in such circumstances should tell her husband how she rejoiced at his preservation, but she couldn't bring herself to say such words.

The city's defenders counted the dead they turned over to the Dutch for burial. Two hundred and thirty-seven men. "The flower of the Dutch soldiery—the finest-looking men who ever were seen," as Tadeu put it. "And no telling how many others were carried back as they withdrew."

Bahia, too, buried its dead and braced for whatever might happen next, but a week after the desperate onslaught, the city woke to find the Dutch ships gone. The besiegers had embarked in the night.

The entire household gathered in the chapel to give

thanks and offer prayers for those who had fallen. Two of
Venancio's slaves were given Christian burial in a plot he
owned beyond the city. Duarte had given careless orders
that a vaqueiro and plantation hand of his should have shallow graves along the beach or be thrown into the sea lashed
to boards, but Venancio had intervened.

"There's room in my plot for those who died loyally
defending us."

So after thanksgivings, burials and final prayers in the
chapel built on the site of the one raised by Caramuru's
wife, in some way or other the ancestress of many of the
city's highest and lowest, Duarte was impatient to be off
to Seraphim.

"Your wound might heal faster if you don't jolt it,"
argued his hostess.

"Don' Consuelo, only the Virgin is kinder than you,"
grinned Duarte. "But you know how country folk are. No
air is as sweet to us as that of our own acres."

An hour later, Duarte and Rachel set out for Seraphim.

Bento moved more proudly after their return, was in sub-
tly indefinable ways less Duarte's shadow. With the pride
of one relating the qualities of a favored mount or watch-
dog, Duarte boasted of how Bento, out of charges for his
pistol, sword knocked from his grasp, had employed *capoeira* against the amazed Dutch.

"Butted out the wind of a bugger coming at me from
behind, lifted another straight up in the air with a kick to
the balls, stove in a cannibal's painted face with his knee—
I tell you, this *capoeirista* can do more than dance!"
Duarte's small, effeminately well-kept hand dropped on his
milk-brother's shoulder. "I can't free you, since my father
already did, but when you decide on which wench you
want to marry instead of sampling the whole *senzala*, tell
me, and I'll free her for a wedding gift."

Bento thanked his master, but he no longer laughed every
time Duarte did or hunched over so he wouldn't be tallest.

One of Damião's kitchen helpers was staying home with
her new baby and the cook complained of being short-
handed, scornfully dismissing new apprentices from the
senzala after brief trials. Duarte, prevented from attending

council meetings by his still-painful wound, sent Diniz to
Bahia to purchase a young slave fresh from Africa.

"You'll have the whole training of her yourself," Duarte told his temperamental cook in some exasperation. "So
you can't blame her failings on the *senzala*."

Damião muttered something about dirty savages under
his breath but seemed to realize that there were limits even
he couldn't safely exceed. His eyes, jaundiced where
women were concerned, rounded in admiration when Diniz
presented his purchase. Duarte's gaze roved appreciatively
over uptilted young breasts straining against a striped cotton shift, the clean line of long legs, still a trifle coltish.
Tomé ran his tongue over his lips. His sigh was audible.

In contrast to the ripeness of her body, the girl's thin
ebony face was a frightened child's, though the chin lifted
proudly and the fine nostrils swelled. Crisp black curls
framed the exotically beautiful face. She was magnificent—
with just that hint of dread, the rapidly rising and falling
bosom, to betray how she must feel.

What a moment it must be for a slave, Rachel thought,
*to meet her owners, learn where and how she must spend
the rest of her life.* She smiled reassuringly, but the slanting
dark eyes stared unseeingly straight ahead.

"About fourteen, still virgin," Diniz said. "All her
teeth, of course. She's from Dahomey, like Damião's baking assistant, so he can instruct her till she learns Portuguese."

Duarte made a gesture of dismissal. "Rosa, take her to
Father Paulo for baptism and then find her a place in the
senzala. See she's in the kitchen early tomorrow."

Rosa spoke soothingly as she led the new slave away by
the hand. "What happened to her family?" Rachel asked.

Diniz looked astonished. "I don't know, senhora. Perhaps they died on the slaver or weren't captured."

There were many slaves in Lisbon. Rachel had grown
up without much thinking how they got there. Seeing this
girl straight from the ship made her think of how it was for
those not born tame in the *senzala,* for those who were
snatched from an accustomed place, wrenched from friends
and family, packed into a vessel, sold into the hands of
strangers. Rachel got to her feet.

"If the girl's baptized, she needs a godmother."

"Rosa can serve," said Duarte negligently. "Diniz, you bought her. You'll stand godfather."

"Please, senhor," Rachel insisted. "She is so young— so far from home. I want to be her sponsor."

"Oh, go ahead." He shrugged. "We'd give her a new dress every year anyway."

So Rachel was godmother to the girl baptized as Hagar. Along with everything else, the child lost her African name. Slaves were often speedily baptized, not so much out of concern for their souls as from fear of having a pagan in the household, one who might invoke heathen gods and spirits to the harm of the masters.

Rosa kept Hagar in her quarters, perhaps hoping a companion of her own age would cheer Izabel, who since her baby's death had gone about her duties apathetically, staying inside after Sunday mass instead of joining in the leisure-day flirtations and skylarking of the *senzala*'s younger folk.

Finicky Damião admitted by the start of Hagar's second week that she never needed to be told anything twice and was clean, swift and painstaking. Too, she was quickly picking up Portuguese, but though she answered Rachel's questions, she didn't reveal what she was thinking or feeling.

When Rachel asked Father Paulo the church's stand on slavery, he quoted Paul's advice to slaves: "Be obedient to them that are your masters according to the flesh, with fear and trembling." Saint Augustine wrote that slavery was God's punishment for Adam's sin. "And," added Father Paulo, "since the Africans are heathen, slavery is a boon, since it makes them Christians and saves their souls."

Manoel's response to her questioning was that the patriarchs had owned servants and it was provided for in Mosaic law, though masters were enjoined to show justice and mercy, since they had been captives in Egypt.

"But when Israel was a country," the young man said dreamily, "every fiftieth year was one of Jubilee, to observe the freeing of our people from the Egyptians. In that year, lands were restored to those who had lost them and those in bondage were given their liberty.''

"There's no Jubilee in Brazil,'' Rachel said. However Jews and Christians justified the trade in human beings, her heart cried out that it was wrong. But what could she do about it, she, who was as much a captive as anyone in the *senzala?*

A few days later, she came upon Tomé trying to lure Hagar into his room with a strand of bright beads. The girl was trying to get past him, but he kept interposing his bulk between her and the way to the kitchen.

"Senhor!'' Rachel cried.

He sheepishly thrust the beads into his dressing gown. Hagar darted past. Rachel was left confronting the potbellied brother-in-law of her husband.

"Senhor, I am amazed,'' she said grimly. "After Izabel's baby, you should understand the necessity of restraint.''

"What does a convent mouse know about a man's needs?'' he blustered.

Duarte emerged yawning from his private chamber. He smelled of Luzia's musky perfume. "Bickering so early?''

Rachel tried to speak calmly, though she was seething. "Senhor, after Izabel's baby was born blind and diseased, you asked Senhor Tomé to confine his attentions to his servant. It seems he has forgotten.''

Duarte scowled at them both. He obviously hated being in a position where he must side with a woman against a man, but if Tomé's rutting was going to lessen the quality or number of Seraphim slaves—well, that was a sin against hospitality and kinship.

Tomé shifted small, fat white feet. "You know what they say about black virgins, son-in-law,'' he wheedled. "If I could use the wench at her first bleeding, I might be rid of this affliction—''

Duarte's mouth hardened. "My father, may he rest in peace, must have tupped a dozen coal-black virgins. He passed the pox to some of them, all right, but kept it himself. What finally burned it out of him was malaria. He almost died, but it left him clean as a whistle.''

"But—"

"Leave my slaves alone. If you're so anxious for a cure, stay down at the swamp for a few weeks. All the *caboclos* who live around here have malaria. No doubt you could get it, too."

Out of temper with both of them, the master of Seraphim turned on his heel and padded back to whatever he had left, presumably Luzia's arms.

Tomé's pale lashes blinked rapidly from the fatty circles around his buried eyes. "You sneaking little New Christian! Shaming me, carrying tales—I'll pay you off if it takes the rest of my life!"

"You will keep your hands off the girls, senhor."

He backed angrily into his room, slamming the door.

Relieved that Duarte had stood his ground but distressed by the clash and Tomé's malice, Rachel stayed in the kitchen only long enough to discuss the day's meals with Damião and say softly to Hagar, "Don't be afraid. The senhor won't hurt you."

She wasn't sure the girl understood till white teeth clamped over the full lower lip and a tear rolled down the smooth dark cheek. "You good, sinhá."

For keeping an aging lecher from defiling a helpless child? Rachel fled from the words as if from a reproach.

Duarte's thigh was healed enough that he resumed the nightly preparation of heated wine before retiring with Rachel to the great silken bed. His lust was tempered now with angry resolve.

"Why aren't you fruitful? Over a year now, and it's not because I've neglected you!"

"Senhor, I cannot order my womb to swell."

Caressing her in the candlelight, he said with a wry grin, "I don't know why not. You seem to order everything else around Seraphim—and on the whole, I confess to being much more comfortable. But well as you play the sinhá-dona, well as you please me with your beauty—for you are beautiful and blooming, little nun—the reason you are here is to give me sons." He drew her to him, watching her face. "Yes, you are sweet, my wife. Burn more candles to Our Lady of Conception."

Rachel grasped at a frail hope. "Senhor," she murmured when he lay sprawled with one arm pinioning her, "if I cannot conceive, isn't that grounds for an annulment?"

"There'll be no annulment with gossip and jokes about my potency," he growled. He didn't voice the threat, but it weighed on Rachel, heavy as his arm.

How long would he give her?

Each time she drank Felicia's draught, she gambled with her life. She was afraid. And still she was not able to try to bear the child that would be her safety.

III

The Man Whose Eyes Were the Sea

An unfortunate result of Tomé's hotness for the fresh black girl was that it called Duarte's attention to her. As far as Rachel knew, since she herself had come to Seraphim, he'd divided his attentions only between her and Luzia, but it was no secret that in his teens he had helped his father deflower *senzala* virgins and sample any new female flesh bought for the plantation.

He watched Hagar, savoring her. There was no hurry. When he was ready, he'd pluck her like just-ripe fruit.

Rachel saw this but knew appeal would only hasten the girl's fate. She also noticed that Bento sometimes stopped by the kitchen, and once she saw him talking to Hagar outside Rosa's door—at least, he talked. The young slave, usually proud-standing, had her head bowed and seemed ill-at-ease.

Duarte's milk-brother had cut almost as wide a swath as his master. It seemed the most Hagar could hope for was to escape being pox-ridden Tomé's prey. Thus Rachel was almost as taken aback as Duarte when one night after dinner Bento lingered to speak to him. "Senhor, you have said that when I wish to marry, you'll free the woman. I've chosen a wife."

"High time," laughed Duarte, clapping his hand affectionately on his milk-brother's shoulder. "So, you old red-headed lady-killer, who's the lucky wench?"

Knowing Duarte as well as he did, Bento must have seen his interest in the new slave. It took courage to look the master in the eye and say, "Senhor, give me Hagar."

Duarte gaped. "That little black beanpole?" He grinned and winked conspiratorially. "Come, Bentinho! When you can have a luscious little peach like Izabel, or Floria, who must be about ripe now, or a high yellow like Paulina? Choose something better. Weren't we fed from the same breasts?"

"Yes, and they were black." Bento didn't say anything else. He just waited.

"If you're ready to settle down," proposed Duarte, "I'll set you up in trade in town or give you a little land. But you need a woman who'll know how to do things, who can help you get ahead. Eva's smart and pretty, and you used to like her."

"Senhor, you told me, 'Pick any girl.' "

Their eyes locked. The bronze-haired mulatto's did not drop. Duarte's jaw closed with a snap. "All right. You can have her. We'll have the wedding on Saint John's Day. That ought to get you off to a good start."

Both men knew what would happen in the intervening two weeks. For a moment it seemed that Bento would argue. Something flickered in his hazel eyes, which then grew cold, though he bent to kiss Duarte's hand.

"Thank you, senhor."

"It's nothing," shrugged Duarte, gracious again now that he'd crushed any scruples about using Bento's bride before he passed her on.

Next morning Bento didn't come for breakfast and Rosa fearfully reported that Hagar was gone. "Must have slipped out in the night. Didn't even wake up Izabel, who was in the hammock beneath."

Questioned, Izabel claimed ignorance of Hagar's flight. No one in the house or *senzalas* had seen her or Bento. Gritting his teeth, Duarte sent out search parties and called for Diniz's brother, the *capitão-do-mato* whose living and pleasure was tracking down runaway slaves.

The bush-captain, Justo, who lived with his mother at the *aldeia* when he wasn't in the *sertão*, was a lean, sinewy man of indeterminate age with straight black hair and Diniz's green eyes. He nodded at the description of Hagar but frowned in surprise at the mention of Bento.

"Bento, he's free surely, senhor?"

"He's free, but he stole my property. I'll see him flogged for that and shipped to Angola."

Justo flicked a rawhide whip against his boot. "If he puts up a fight—"

"Kill him," said Duarte. "Just don't let Irene know about it." The bush-captain bowed and turned toward two other armed *caboclos* who waited for him. "The girl," called Duarte. "She'd better have her maidenhead."

"Senhor!" Justo threw up his hands. "When Bento's been with her all night?"

"He may have been too busy making tracks to dip in her honeypot." Duarte's tone granted that was unlikely, but he offered a just-in-case incentive. "We'll agree you get double for a virgin."

Justo swallowed a chuckle. So! Bento had grabbed that dish right out from under the master's sniffing nose. Well, Justo had always liked Bento, would give him a break if he could; just so he wasn't stubborn about this little black one, who must be something to get two such experienced studs in a tizzy. Too bad he couldn't sample it himself. He would if Bento had already been there. If not, there'd be double money, enough for a spree with Bahia's best. Justo grinned philosophically and started scouting for tracks.

Distressed by the hunt but knowing Duarte wouldn't listen to her protests, Rachel went to the chapel, offered candles and prayed. That the pair might escape, deep in the *sertão,* or might find refuge in one of the settlements, or *quilombos,* of runaway slaves that had sprung up in the wilderness during the interminable war with the Dutch. Some of the bravest fighters against the invaders were free blacks and mulattos, but hundreds of slaves had escaped while plantations were being ravaged by both sides and there were no soldiers to spare for expeditions against these growing villages.

Bento knew the country. He'd have started as soon as possible to win all the advantage he could before their flight was discovered. Rachel knew that she was praying against the policy of church and state, but in spite of all evidence Rachel had to believe that God was good; so she prayed.

* * *

Later, she walked. If only she could call for a horse and ride as she had during the siege! But she wasn't allowed to roam beyond the plantation buildings.

So she wandered through the orchards and courtyards and past the big vegetable garden and plots where ambitious slaves could grow crops to sell in Bahia. The money gained was theirs. In fact Manoel had told her that just before she came to Seraphim, an old slave couple bought their freedom with coins painfully accumulated over forty years. They now lived in Bahia, where the man was a barber and his wife made and sold sweetmeats.

It was outrageous that people had to pay to regain the liberty they should never have lost, but at least slaves could. And there was the hope they might be freed to celebrate some special event or upon a master's death. Rachel's mouth twisted.

Slaves had some chance, sometimes, of freedom. She had none.

She was passing the mill, abandoned now till the next harvest, when she heard something. She halted. The muffled sound came again, one of pain, though she couldn't guess whether it was human or animal.

It seemed to come from the shed where cane waste was stored. Moving past the distillery, Rachel opened the door.

Light spilled on fair hair, an outflung arm. Except for that hair, blended glow of sun and moon, the figure might have been a scarecrow. Bony shoulder blades protruded through the tatters of a grimy shirt. Bare feet were crusted with dried blood and filth. A stench rose from him, the smell of putrefying flesh.

Who could he be? Why had he crawled into this shed rather than to a habitation? "Senhor?" she whispered.

Jerking, the man tried to lift himself, fell panting to one side. Strong jaw and chin were covered with flaxen stubble. The eyes that stared at her, fever-bright, were the changing green-blue-gray of the sea. One scarred, nail-broken hand lifted toward her face, dropped weakly.

"*Moesje!*" Dark lashes fringed his gaunt cheeks as his eyes closed. Rachel knew that word. Manoel used it sometimes when speaking of his mother. She sucked in a deep breath.

This man was Dutch. From the look of him, he'd been lying out in the brush, dragging himself along when he could. He must have been wounded during the siege and overlooked by his comrades when they embarked.

Peering closer in the shadows, she saw a slight motion and located the wound, gagged at maggots gorging in a fist-sized jagged hole between right ribs and hip. Some of it had healed, but the center oozed pus.

She started to call for help, then checked herself. Presumably Duarte would allow the man to be nursed at Seraphim till he could stand the journey to Bahia, but then what? Rachel knew that prisoners were sometimes exchanged, but often they were slaughtered.

This man wasn't a soldier now. He was weak, starving. And somewhere he had a mother who might be mourning for her son. Rachel smoothed back the bright hair.

"I'll bring you food and water," she said. Even if he heard, she doubted if he could understand, but he smiled and sighed. Rachel got to her feet, looked both ways to make sure she was unobserved, and hurried to the house.

Within a week, Rolf Drouet could feed himself and sit up for a few minutes, but Rachel still tended his wound and washed him. She had brought him a razor, some of Duarte's discarded clothes, and sheets to cover the cane refuse. Held prisoner by the Spanish for some months during the bitter wars between Spain and Holland, he spoke considerable Spanish, which was close enough to Portuguese to make conversation possible. Even had there been no words, their eyes spoke. Rachel's pity was changing to something else, something impossible and frightening—yet something that made her feel she had not been alive till then.

He was master of his own ship, which was being outfitted in Recife when his good friend, Johan Maurits, had organized the attack on Bahia.

"I joined him," explained Rolf at Rachel's frown, "because I think he'll bring justice to this country, which sorely needs it." He added with a challenging grin, "Anyhow, I like a good fight. I'm a Zeelander, and our motto is 'A turd for trade if there's booty to be had.' "

Rachel remembered the dying and wounded she had nursed in Bahia. "What right do you have to attack Brazilian settlements?" she asked fiercely.

He regarded her with amusement. "Strangely enough, lady, I suspect that my roots in Brazil go further back than those of most Portuguese."

"How can that be?"

"From what you say about your husband being descended from Raya, the Sun Virgin, we're distant relations." As Rachel gasped, he continued. "My grandfather was Ansiet, taken to France by his father, Étienne. Cheated out of his French inheritance by half brothers, Ansiet married a girl in Zeeland, which is now one of the United Provinces. He died fighting the Spanish the same year my father was born, but I remember my grandmother. She told me stories—what Ansiet remembered of Brazil. It sounded like paradise. He'd always hoped to come back and settle here."

"You're Raya's great-grandson?" Rachel was still unable to believe it.

"Yes. Since the daughter she had by Étienne was fruitful, and her offspring more so, I suppose I've been battling with a lot of my kinsmen." His tone sobered. "Believe me, I take no joy in that. Maurits would have been content to leave Portugal with Bahia and the south, you know. That's why he stopped at the São Francisco River when he had Brazilian forces on the run last year."

His voice slowed with effort. Rachel frowned. "You'd better rest." She started to rise to her feet. He caught her hand. "Lady, don't go."

Trembling fire ran between them, turned her body strange. "If anyone misses me—"

"Your husband?" Long fingers tightened on hers. "What is he like?"

"He's a knight-commander of São Bento de Aviz, a member of the municipal council, *senhor de engenho* and—"

The silver-gold head, bright even in the dimness, gave an impatient shake. "I don't care what he is to the world. What is he to you?"

"Why—he is my husband."

"He stood with you before the priest. He shares your bed." The voice, though soft, stripped her like a lash. "What else?"

Helplessly, bitterly, Rachel said, "He is my master." Before Rolf could torment her further, she wrested herself free and hurried away.

All that day her flesh burned when, eyes closing involuntarily, she thrilled at the memory of Rolf's touch, saw his face with the slanting smile and eyes that could change to all shades of the sea.

She had never felt this way. How could she loathe Duarte's embrace yet long to feel Rolf's arms around her? How could she, shrinking from her husband's hands, be consumed as she remembered Rolf's?

Amazed as she was at this bewildering tumult, she was sure it had to be a sin. The sweet madness that kept her dreaming over Rolf's every word and look, each accidental brush of fingers, made it devastating to be possessed by Duarte.

Before, she had only wished not to be in Duarte's grasp. Now she dreamed of lying close to Rolf, no matter how she tried to banish the imagining. To her prayers that Hagar and Bento would never be caught, she added implorings that Rolf would not be found.

She could not ask for what duty thundered that she must, to be delivered of this fever that was torment, wonder and all things lovely.

The searchers had come back except for Justo and his *caboclos*. "He'll get that pair," gloated Duarte. "And when I get my hands on that little black slut, she'll learn who's her master!"

Rolf was better now each day, restless from being confined to the cane shed though he stretched and moved around and did all he could to build up his strength, for once he left shelter, he'd have to move as swiftly as possible through the wilderness till he reached the Dutch lines. Rachel wanted him safely gone. She lived in dread that he might be discovered, yet the time when there would no longer be those treasured stolen moments stretched like a wasteland of deserts and thorns.

She couldn't always slip away for even a few minutes, but when Duarte was attending the council or off visiting other plantation owners, she often went for an hour or more several times a day. She wouldn't let Felicia accompany her; she had never told Felicia about Rolf. In case he was found, Rachel didn't want anyone else punished.

"Why didn't you turn me over to your husband?" Rolf demanded one day. "It can't have taken you long to guess that I was an enemy."

Why?

Because he was helpless, had reached for her hand, called her "Mother"? Because she was angry at the way Duarte had that very day sent trackers after Bento and Hagar? Because her own captivity made her feel for those who might be imprisoned or abused?

She shook her head, but he persisted. "A rare villain I must have looked, filthy, starving, maggots tumbling out of my side. Why didn't you take to your heels and call the slaves?"

"I don't know. I just couldn't."

His eyes were the sea. She longed to sink into them, drown, be swept irrevocably away. Trembling spread from within her as her pounding heart turned her giddy. She rose, whirling blindly toward the door, but he was in front of her seizing her hands.

"Rachel, my valiant, frightened dove, you pitied an enemy." His voice dropped, but it reverberated within her. "Only I think it isn't pity that makes you flee me now."

"Please—"

"Tell me you love your husband and I'll ask no more questions."

Cheeks flaming, she cried, "You have no right to ask that!"

"I have no right," he agreed slowly. "I would rather die than offend you." He framed her face within his big hands, tilting it upward. "Rachel—lady, does it offend you that I love you?"

She could not speak. Molten honey stopped her voice, sweetened her mouth as he kissed her. His lips were cool and firm, yet they touched off a blaze in her that fanned through her being, pulsed in her blood. When at last he took his mouth away, pressing her head to his breast and stroking her hair, she would have fallen except for his arms.

"I'll come back for you," he said. "I don't know how, but I will."

"You can't! You'd be captured. Anyway, I'm married."

"To a man who picked you off the ship like a horse or heifer? To a man you don't love?"

"It would be a great sin—"

"Not as great as the sin of what's been done to you."

His mouth was hard this time, urgent, demanding. She couldn't struggle, didn't want to, moaned as his hand grazed her breast.

He broke away, gasping. "No! I won't have you, my sweetheart, till you're mine alone. If I tasted your sweetness, I couldn't send you back to your husband, and I can't take you with me now." He kissed her hands and held them against his heart as if he offered her his very life. "My love, I'm leaving tonight. The sooner I go, the sooner I can find some way to come back and carry you away."

She didn't doubt his love, but how could he return, how could he take her out of Duarte's house and bed?

The sweet flowering of her senses and body shriveled, numbed. She felt as if she were being sealed, as if she were dying. But every day he stayed increased the chance of discovery. She could not ask him to wait.

"Do you need anything?" she asked through stiff lips.

"You've supplied me so well that I've put back quite a trove," he said tenderly. "I have my knife and pistol. No, love, all I need's your blessing and your promise not to forget me."

As if she could! Pressing her lips to his fingers, she murmured brokenly, "God keep you. Have a care—" Her voice choked off.

They clung to each other. He took her soul through her kiss.

Her love was gone. Rachel went about her duties like one of the zombis whispered of in the *senzala*, a body with no heart or life of its own. What virtual imprisonment and Duarte's sensual brutality had not been able to destroy—Rachel's interest in life, a persistent dream that somehow she would one day lead a contented, if not happy, life—was now extinguished by her hopeless love.

For she dared not hope. It was impossible that Rolf should win through his enemies to take her away. She couldn't even pray that he would try, for it would mean his life. Weeping soundlessly into her pillow, she relived those moments when Rolf had touched her, kissed her, spoken of love.

It was all she had, besides visits to the cane shed, where she would lie on his pallet, touch her lips to the goblet from which he had drunk. If only she'd tempted him past restraint, if only she could at least treasure the knowledge of him deep within her, a glowing light in the darkness plundered by her lawful husband . . .

Felicia thought she was sick and dosed her with tonics. Even Duarte, far from perceptive, said, "You're almighty quiet these days. Maybe you're breeding."

The Feast of Saint John, with bonfires and dancing, had come and gone while Rolf lay recovering his strength. It was August now, the cane was growing fast in the daily rains, and in six to eight weeks Manoel said the grinding would start.

Before then, the mill would be put in readiness. Rachel knew she must remove Rolf's pallet, the empty wine jar and goblet, yet she hated to put away these tangible evidences of his presence.

Each time she pressed herself against the sheets where he had rested, kissed the goblet, and evoked his face, his voice, the sweet bitterness of their brief lovemaking, she would resolve, after the last time, to carry off the telltale signs; yet each time she would pause in the act of gathering up the sheets, bury her face against them, and think, *Another day won't hurt. Just one more* . . .

When Duarte was in Bahia, she allowed herself more time for dreamy remembering. She was lost in this poignant voluptuousness one morning after he had summoned his litter and departed when suddenly there was a grating sound, a flood of light.

She sat up. As her rudely dazzled eyes made out three forms by the door, Duarte in one stride was beside her. "So it's true! Here you are, lolling in the waste shed like the garbage you are."

He shook her till her head jerked like a doll's and her teeth bit blood from her tongue. "Well, bitch, he won't come to you today! He's under guard, and now that I see with my own eyes what Luzia and Tomé have sworn to—" He ground his teeth together. "I'd kill you both now, but it's my duty as a son of Mother Church to ship you to Lisbon for interrogation."

Had they caught Rolf? But he'd been gone ten days. She'd been telling herself that by now he was in Dutch territory. Beyond Duarte's livid face, the exultant ones of Luzia and Tomé swam before her.

"All the while you were so pious about keeping me from virgins, you were trolloping with that sneaking Judaizer," Tomé sneered. "Son-in-law, let's see if they put a crucifix beneath them so they could defile it!"

He yanked up the sheets. "Not there," he muttered. "But I'll be bound that somewhere there's an image of our Lord that they flog and spit upon."

Rachel's head whirled. Whatever else could be said of Rolf, he wasn't a Judaizer. "What are you talking about?" she choked. "What do you mean?"

Duarte's flat-handed slap would have felled her if the fingers of his other hand hadn't been dug into her shoulder. "As if you didn't know! Always so careful in the library, weren't you, to leave the door open and have your black woman there!"

"I told you from the start, master," Luzia purred triumphantly, yellow eyes agleam. "But you said they were doing accounts."

Tomé chortled. "Accounts? Oh, they were adding all right! The horns they put on you got bigger every time."

Merciful God! They spoke of Manoel. The nightmare changed to absolute horror. "Manoel Vargas hasn't done anything," Rachel cried desperately. "He's never touched me!"

Duarte sneered. "So you just lie here for the fun of it, legs spread wide? Then in my bed you act like a green virgin! Have you practiced your sacrilege all your life, or just since your seducer led you into it?''

''I am a Christian,'' Rachel said through trembling lips. ''Senhor Manoel has not seduced me into anything.''

Duarte set his hand at the top of her bodice, ripped dress and shift, baring her to Tomé's avid pig eyes. ''Look at that white skin, Father-in-law. Have you ever seen prettier breasts? I'll bet you could get the truth out of her in a hurry.''

''Anything to oblige you, dear son.'' Tomé was almost drooling.

''You're too good for her,'' gritted Duarte. ''A night in the bucks' quarters ought to make her confess, if there'd be a piece of her shameless hide left.''

Rachel almost fainted with terror, but her mind worked. Rolf couldn't be hurt now by the truth, and her own case would be no worse. With all her strength, she wrenched free, retreating to a corner.

''Listen, before you wrong a faithful servant! Manoel Vargas was never here with me. And I have not betrayed my marriage vows. The man who stayed here was a wounded Hollander.''

''A Hollander!'' Duarte roared with venomous laughter. ''What wild yarn will you spin next?''

''But he was,'' Rachel insisted. ''He—he dragged himself here. when I found him, he was near death. He'd fallen wounded in the brush and was left behind when the Dutch sailed.''

''That's not a tale to win you mercy,'' Duarte growled. ''To aid a heretic would be as sinful as frolicking with your fellow apostate. Cover your nakedness, hussy, and get to the house!''

Manoel limped in to the library, Diniz and a husky slave on either side of him. The white linen of his shirt hung in bloody ribbons from his back. One eye was swollen shut. Blood trickled from his mouth.

''Well, whoremongering Jew!'' rasped Duarte. ''Are you ready to admit your adultery?''

''There was none, senhor.'' Manoel did not look at Rachel.

Duarte leaped up and struck the slighter man so hard that he staggered against the overseer. "Confess!"

Manoel's tone was low but firm. "I have already said it. I am of the Nation. I have kept its laws as well as I was able among Gentiles."

"And this Jewess, with her you committed not only adultery but sacrilegious abominations?"

"Your wife, senhor, was brought up Christian. She has not departed from that faith."

"Don't deny infecting her with your heresies! It can't have been difficult, since she drew in the taint with her mother's milk."

"Dona Rachel is Christian."

Duarte sneered. "She can tell that to the Holy Office. I've a mind to travel to Lisbon to see you burn—if you have the courage. But what can happen to you here may make you joyful to see the Inquisition's prison. Admit your guilt with this woman and spare yourself more of Diniz's inventiveness."

"I will not damn myself with lies." For the first time Manoel's dark eyes came to Rachel. "But you are welcome to the confession I can make: This is my God, and I will praise him; my father's God, and I will exalt him."

Duarte knocked him down. "Give him the lash again," he told the overseer. "Then rub him well with salt. If he's not dead by the time you get to Bahia, put him on the first ship for Lisbon and see that he's well ironed. I'll attend to the formalities when I take this woman in to follow him."

As Diniz and the slave hauled the young man to his feet and half carried him away, Rachel cried, "Manoel, forgive me!"

The only answer was Duarte's blow across her face.

None of the slaves took her when she was spread-eagled on a crude table behind the lower *senzala* by wrists and ankles. After night fell, Izabel's old grandmother brought her a drink and Izabel struggled with the knots till she could loosen them, ease the torment. Rosa brought gruel and salve, which she applied to places where Duarte's rings or fingernails had opened Rachel's skin.

"Felicia? Where is she?"

"She—gone, sinhá," muttered Rosa.

"How?"

"She not answer master's questions."

"She didn't know anything!"

Rosa's tears fell on Rachel. "They pull her other teeth. Tongs break her jaw. She bleed to death." As Rachel froze in shock, Rosa covered her.

"Sleep if you can, sinhá. No man's goin' to touch you."

Rachel woke at the sheet being stripped from her. Duarte stared at her from some distance away as Diniz and a slave unbound her. "Are you ready to confess?"

"I have confessed what is true."

"Lying heretic!" He shuddered and crossed himself. "Thank heaven I never planted a child in your accursed womb! When I think of how you fooled me! You won't sail with your dog of a lover—he's already gone—but perhaps you'll share a prison. The Holy Office sometimes spends years in trying to bring you Judaizers back to the true faith."

He turned on his heel. That was the last she saw of the man who had been her husband.

Rosa brought her food and a clean, faded dress much too big for her. "Lord bless you, sinhá," she said softly, glancing around to be sure nobody heard. "All of us in the *senzala*, we're goin' to pray for you. Not just to Jesus but to our *orixás.*"

Diniz approached, not looking directly at Rachel. He permitted Rosa to finish combing her hair before telling her to get into the waiting litter. Before he closed the heavy curtains, he tied her hand and foot.

As she was carried through Bahia, unable to peer through the curtains, Rachel thought of generous Venancio Álvares and Dona Consuelo, of Elena and Tadeu. What would they think when they heard Duarte's accusations? Elena might shed a tear for her, though she knew it was sinful to pity a heretic, and devout Dona Consuelo would cross herself in horror and pray that Rozane hadn't been contaminated by knowing such a duplicitous renegade.

A stench proclaimed that they had reached the lower city

before the sea breeze cleansed the air, riffled the stifling draperies. There was a wait amid the hubbub of the docks. Then Rachel was borne up a creaking, dipping board, carried a short distance and set down.

Again not looking at her, Diniz untied the ropes, jerked his reddish head toward an open door. "In there." Beside him, a ship's officer said warningly, "Behave yourself and you won't be chained."

Rachel's legs throbbed as blood rushed painfully to where the ropes had blocked it. Reaching for the doorjamb, she leaned there till her feet felt alive and then moved into a small cell. Diniz tossed a cushion and shawl after her.

"Hello, dearie," cackled a big-nosed toothless crone. In green dress and red scarf, she resembled a large parrot. "What excuse have the fine gentlemen for shipping you to Angola? You're not gypsy like the three of us."

"I'm falsely accused—" Rachel began, only to be interrupted by shouts of laughter.

"Aren't we all now, and that's the truth! Lina, scoot over and let the poor thing sit down. Can't you see she's been roughed up?"

Lina moved over a trifle, grunting, but since her narrow bunk was already shared by a thin girl who seemed to be asleep, Rachel didn't attempt to perch on the scant inch or so won by the sacrifice.

"Sorry, lamb." The older woman shrugged. "My old bones give me such miseries that I can't abide anyone in bed with me." One wrinkled eyelid drooped in a wink. "A sad case for old Tonita, who was as lusty as any till a few years ago."

"That's all right." So long as her companions didn't abuse her, Rachel was inclined to think them miracles of kindness. Her legs wove under her. "Your pardon," she whispered. "I'm—tired."

Sinking down, she spread the shawl on the evil-smelling floor, put the pillow under her head and lapsed into slumber.

When she woke, it was to the remembered swaying of a ship under sail. She opened her eyes and thought she was dreaming.

Felicia was looking down at her.

Breathing her name, Rachel started up. The regal black face didn't vanish. Ghost, zombi or dream, Rachel embraced her, sobbing. The hands that stroked her hair were strong, the breast supporting her firm and warm.

"It's fine, sinhá." Felicia's words hissed more than usual but she sounded real. "Maybe we can sneak off this ship while it's anchored at Angola. We'll find some way."

"But how—they told me you were dead."

Felicia's bitter laugh revealed more gaps. Only a few white teeth showed in front. "I belong to Yemanjá. Through her, I made my blood and breath so slow no one could tell I lived. She held the earth of the grave out of my nostrils. After they left me, I rose up. I hid in a shed in the trees behind the *senzala* and prayed to Yemanjá to shield you."

"She or someone did. But you can't hide long on a ship. You'll be sent back as a runaway."

This time Felicia's mirth was wholehearted. "Sinhá, the slave died back at Seraphim. I'm a free woman with papers to prove it, and I paid my passage in gold after I followed your litter to the city and saw which ship they put you on."

"You paid in gold?" Rachel marveled.

"When the master was wild for me, he gave me more gold *balangadans* than ever Luzia wheedled." Felicia's mouth curved in a wry smile. "Sometimes I got coins for working *mandingas*. I kept everything because I hoped to buy my freedom someday." She chuckled. "The master killed him a slave and I saved my money."

Nodding toward straw pallets and a basket heaped with provisions, she said, "This is heaven compared to the slaver my parents came over on. When this ship docks in Angola, it'll trade sugar and rum for slaves and ivory to sell in Lisbon. Then it'll load up with dried codfish, olive oil, wheat flour and such things for Brazil. It's a golden triangle—for everyone but slaves."

The gypsies, shunted out of Portugal as undesirables and now being shipped from Brazil for the same reason, accepted Felicia with a tolerance that changed to gratitude when she shared the good things in the basket. A bit of guava paste vastly improved rancid cheese and ship's biscuit, red peppers and dried shrimp and beef gave substance to the watery stew brought twice a day by the scrawny cabin boy, and spindly little twelve-year-old Lela sucked rapturously on brown sugar pieces that Felicia hacked from the hard cones.

The child was recovering from a miscarriage. She had been impregnated by the same Bahian councilor and planter who frequented her mother, plump Lina. When Tonita had tried to persuade the *fidalgo* to pay something toward the maintenance of her granddaughter and the scrap growing in her, he had remedied the bulge with a kick to Lela's belly and had them deported.

"Maybe Angola will be better." The same woman pensively rubbed her beak. "It can't be worse."

The gypsies were too preoccupied with their own doubtful future to pry into Rachel's history, nor did they fear contamination from an accused heretic.

"Just one thing counts if you're a woman," grumped Tonita. "How heavy does the man with his foot on your neck bear down? If he loves you, he'll let you raise up enough to breathe, but mostly it's face in the dust and eat it, bitch!"

Rachel thought of gentle Manoel and of Rolf. "That might be just Portuguese men."

Lina stirred herself to say dreamily, "A whore from Recife said that Dutch women go to banquets. Imagine, they drink and eat with the men, and dance, too."

"I don't believe it," Tonita scoffed, but after a moment she sighed. "Too bad we're not headed for Recife. If there's any place on this earth where women are treated as well as a smart man treats a good mule, I'd like to see it before I die."

The gypsies went on deck now and then to escape the cramped cabin and fetid air and, Rachel suspected, to swing their hips at the sailors. It was during these moments of privacy that she told Felicia about Rolf.

"I thought if I didn't tell you I was hiding him, there was no way you'd be bothered in case it was found out," she mourned. "And the worst part is that I didn't get rid of the sheets and things once he was gone. I know I should have, but I kept putting it off. So you and Manoel suffered—and, Felicia, he'll burn before he recants!"

Felicia let her weep. At last she said, "Senhor Manoel was bound to be caught soon or late, sinhá. A lot of us guessed that he practiced Jewish ways, and word's spread from plantations with Jewish owners that after he'd visited them, slaves started getting Saturdays free as well as Sundays."

"It's still my fault. And you—you were always so good to me!"

"You didn't say yank out my teeth. The master did, and it was on account of him I lost the first ones years ago." Felicia's smile was chilling. "I made a magic. Just to help it along, I slipped into the house and mixed broth stewed from old Tomé's poxy drawers into the master's best Madeira. Poison's too fast. I want him to rot, and that yellow whore with him."

Rachel couldn't wish such a fate on anyone, but she suspected that if either spell or infected garments accomplished Felicia's revenge, rumor would transform her, Rachel, into a Jewish witch whose curse afflicted the worthy councilman, knight and *senhor de engenho* who had so generously taken an orphaned New Christian for a wife.

About half the voyage was finished. All the women in the stuffy cabin were more or less plagued with seasickness, and frail little Lela was prostrate much of the time. Trying to beguile her attention from the pitching roll of the ship, Rachel, though queasy herself, often sat by the girl and told her stories.

She was thus occupied one afternoon while Felicia slept and the older gypsies were strolling on deck. When a clamor arose, Rachel scarcely noticed, assuming the noise was due to one of the fights that often broke out between men in close quarters or one of the officers raising a flurry over something. But then the racket increased, the ship lurched about, and there was a boom of guns.

Lina and Tonita burst into the cabin. "It's the devil Dutch! One of their privateers is on us."

Lela wailed and burrowed in Rachel's arms. Rachel petted her and said to the huddling women, "The Dutch can't be any worse than the men you've known. Comb your hair and tidy yourselves. If they gain the ship and break in here, greet them like guests."

"Guests!" howled Lina.

Rachel shrugged. "If we hide in a corner like chickens waiting to have our necks wrung, they may take the suggestion. Act pleased to see them and they might be startled into treating us well."

"That's fine for you," quavered old Tonita. "Everyone knows the Dutch are hand in hand with Brazilian Jews." Blinking her tiny bright eyes, she said coaxingly, "If the Dutch break in here, dearie, you'll put in a word for your cabinmates?"

There was a rending crash. The ship seemed to convulse amid sounds of firing, the clash of steel, cries of triumph and screams of pain. Then loud cheering rose above the tumult.

In spite of her brave words, Rachel's heart was in her mouth. She remembered rumors that had swept Bahia during the siege, accounts of horrible atrocities committed by the Dutch. The only weapon the women had was their wits.

"Fasten your bodice, Lina," she said. "Felicia, help Tonita with her hair."

Rachel was working the tangles out of Lela's long black hair when a kick sent the cabin door open. A couple of burly men with butter-yellow hair peered in.

They whooped with delight as they saw the women. Felicia crossed majestically to stand in front of Rachel, who sat with her arm around the gypsy girl.

Rachel knew only one word of Dutch, the name called by her love in his fever. As the men surged forward, seeming like blond giants, she put Lela behind her and lifted her hands in pleading, rebuke, command.

"Moesje!"

The men stopped in their tracks. One asked a question Rachel couldn't answer, but at that very moment a tall figure ducked to enter, shoved the men back.

Rachel gave a cry of unbelieving joy. Sunlight turned Rolf's hair to spun gold-silver, limned him in a nimbus with his naked sword. She might have thought him an angel or warrior saint had it not been for the blaze in those sea-change eyes.

In one long stride he had her in his arms. Like a storm-ravaged craft coming to harbor, she pressed against his heart.

He didn't move Rachel to his long-waisted galleon with ten heavy guns on the lower deck and two tiers of lighter pieces on the upper deck and forecastle. Instead he ordered the captain's room cleaned and prepared for her and Felicia, transferring the defeated master to his ship and replacing him with his chief mate, who would take the prize ship to Recife.

At Rachel's intercession, Rolf ordered his crew not to molest the gypsies, but from the way Lina was casting appreciative glances at the sturdy blond sailors, not all of them would be denied female attention.

Outgunned, moving sluggishly because of her heavy cargo, the Portuguese vessel had put up little resistance. Both sides had a few wounded men, none critically injured, and two Brazilian sailors had died during the boarding. Even so, Rolf had much to attend to and Rachel alternated between watching impatiently from the small window for a glimpse of him and marveling to Felicia over their good fortune.

"Rolf said he was bound for Holland on important business for Johan Maurits, but when he saw this fat ship, he couldn't resist it. Of course it's nothing unusual for Dutch ships to capture those of Spain and Portugal. But for Rolf's to be the one that saved us!"

Felicia shook her head. "What was that name you called?"

Rachel frowned. "When the Dutch broke in? The only word of theirs I know—*moesje*, little mother."

"That's what I thought. It was Mother Yemanjá saved us, she who rules the sea. She sent your golden hair."

Rachel was not inclined to argue. Radiant, she embraced Felicia. "He came! That's what matters. Oh, Felicia! If only you hadn't been hurt—if Manoel were free—"

"Be glad for what is," advised Felicia. "No ifs, no buts." She pushed Rachel into a chair. "Sit still, sinhá, and let me get your hair fixed before your man comes."

* * *

When at last he entered the cabin, Rachel flew into his arms. His hard yet tender lips seemed to draw her life into him, unite them even while her body melted against his. She didn't know how long they stood like that. When they drew apart, Felicia had discreetly disappeared.

Hands on her shoulders, Rolf gave Rachel a long look and a brief kiss. "Let me wash, and then, my love, we have to do some talking."

He sounded grave, but nothing serious could lie between them now. She was no longer Duarte's wife. As for wedding an enemy of Portugal, she felt little loyalty to a country that had shipped her to Brazil like a brood heifer and that would very probably have put her to death. She admired Rolf lovingly as he stripped off his stained shirt and washed face, arms and torso clean of sweat and dried blood from a few inconsequential cuts.

Browned from the sun, in vital health, he was beautiful. No one could have guessed him for the fevered near skeleton she had found in the waste shed except for the puckered hollow that showed partially above his broad pistol belt.

He dried the crisp gold hair on his chest, thrust back ringlets that curled damp around his face, and took her in his arms, but this time, though she clung to him, he made a stifled sound after a moment, drew back, trembling, and seated her in the single chair while dropping to a stool at her feet.

Taking her hands, he said, "Rachel, I love you, only you. Will you remember that while I tell you something?"

Puzzled, beginning to be apprehensive, she nodded. He kissed her palms and her fingers, seeming to nerve himself. "I'm married."

She felt as if a pistol ball had slammed into her heart. "Married?" she echoed as if it were a strange word, one she had never known.

"Yes. But it's not the way you think." As she tried to free her hands, he held them and went on. "Ansje's a minister's daughter. She hates Brazil. I think she hates me. It was a mistake from the beginning—she would shrink from being any man's wife—but I had hoped that in a new country we could make a fresh start."

Mouth tasting of metal, Rachel found each word cut her throat like a flake of glass. "So in the shed, when you promised to come back, you knew you wouldn't."

His grip tightened. "No, Rachel, I meant to come, but before you left with me, I would have had to tell you what I'm saying now and hope that you still would love and trust me."

"For what?" Rachel demanded acidly. "If you have a wife—"

"My wife in name. You'd be my wife in fact."

Rachel thought of Luzia. "Your concubine? Whose children would be bastards?"

He winced. "Rachel, if you liked, I would marry you in the Catholic Church, for it holds Protestant rites void. Living in Netherlands Brazil, what will it harm you if a woman in Amsterdam bears my name till she goes to her pious grave? Your children would know me as their father, grow up with my name. What different does it make?"

"The difference that you *are* married."

With an exasperated sigh he took her shoulders and gave her a shake. "I wanted you to know the truth. Can't you understand that? I didn't want a secret between us."

"It was between us at Seraphim. When you kissed me. When you said—"

He closed her mouth with his, urgent, commanding. When she kept her lips tight, he drew away. "At least remember that I didn't do with you as I longed to—as I could have."

"I must thank you for that much conscience." Unable to endure his closeness, Rachel got to her feet. "I think we have nothing more to say."

Flushing, he blocked the way to the door. "Rachel, my legal wife is on my ship. She's glad to be returning to Amsterdam, her family and friends. I have secured property and income to make her comfortable the rest of her life. She doesn't care what I do. It was my intention, as soon as I had helped her settle, to come as Maurits's envoy to Bahia and one way or another get you back with me to Netherlands Brazil. I didn't tell you about Ansje before because—it was easier not to and besides, I feared that in the months I was away, you'd come to doubt me.'' When she couldn't reply, his voice took on an edge of bitterness, "I didn't expect you to be so squeamish about formalities. After all, you were married when we vowed our love.''

"That was different!''

"It always is, when the shoe pinches your own foot.''

Stung that he could compare her forced marriage with one willingly made, she said, "Duarte is having our marriage annulled. I never felt it was a true one.''

Rolf said wearily, "I can't deny that I loved Ansje—or thought I did. She seemed to me a perfect lily, and she was. What I didn't realize eight years ago, what she couldn't have known, either, was that an altar flower is not meant for handling. It's my fault more than Ansje's. What did she know of life and men? I'm releasing her from what should never have been.'' He recaptured Rachel's hands, made her look at him. "Did you save my life, love, only to make it bitter?''

His eyes robbed her of will. She longed to go soft in his hands, forget everything but the rapture of his kiss. Battling the almost overwhelming urge, she compelled herself to look into the future.

She loved Rolf, body, soul and being. Life without him stretched gray and cold. For herself, so long as he loved her, she would have endured the scorn of honest women like Dona Consuelo, accepted ostracism as the cost of loving Rolf. If he tired of her in a year or two or five or ten, she could bless what they'd had and go away, though it would tear her heart out. But the sticking point, what she couldn't bear, was having children who'd be known as bastards, barred as such from honors, prestigious occupations and desirable marriages.

That price would be paid by those who had no voice now in her decision. Her conscience had to be their pleader. But if there were no children? If she continued to take Felicia's draught?

Tempted, she wavered, but after a moment the core of her cried out against it. Even now she wanted Rolf's children.

For them, it was all or nothing.

Mouth tasting of ashes, she carried his hands to her lips. "I must not live with you, my love. I beg you, don't try to persuade me."

He stiffened and drew away. His eyes were like frozen waves. "I'm a privateer, not a pirate. I've never plundered an unwilling lass—nor begged one, either." Pulling on his shirt, he paused in the doorway. "This prize ship will take you to Recife. I'll instruct the mate to conduct you to the governor-general, who will assist you in whatever you choose to do. If you wish it, he can doubtless arrange for your return to Bahia."

Rachel took that for a cruel gibe. As an accused heretic, she could go neither to Portugal nor to Portuguese-dominated Brazil. She had no country, no husband. She could not have her love.

Wailing inwardly, she stood erect. "Thank you for saving me from the Inquisition. May you ever journey safe and well."

Anguish dissolved the coldness of his gaze. "Rachel—"

She stepped back as he reached toward her. "Good-bye. God keep you."

"You say that but send me to the devil." Green-gray eyes delved into her so that it was all she could do to keep from reaching out to him. "Sometime you might remember that when a man doesn't sleep with a woman he loves, it means more than if he does."

The door slammed behind him. Through the window, Rachel watched the sun make glory of his hair as he strode away. She sank her teeth into her lip to keep from calling him back.

IV

Queen of a Lonely Country

Johan Maurits, governor-captain and admiral-general of the West India Company's forces and possessions in Brazil, president of the High and Secret Council, colonel in the States-General's army, was the son of a princess and grandnephew of William the Silent. His education was cut short by service in the Thirty Years War, where he won a reputation for valor and military astuteness, but he delighted in the company of artists, poets and philosophers.

Not yet forty, he carried himself with grace, a splendidly built man with wavy brown hair and a precisely trimmed mustache. As his wisely humorous dark eyes rested now on Rachel, he pensively rubbed the side of his long nose.

"Dona Rachel, in the three years since you blessed me with your acquaintance, have I asked you a favor?"

Rachel concealed a smile. "No, my gracious lord." She was sure the Count of Nassau, when importuning a woman, thought he conferred a favor. To be fair, even after she'd repulsed him, he had graciously helped her in every way, sponsoring her in Recife society and letting it be known that an insult to her was one to him.

Most of all, he'd found Bom Jardim—"good garden"—for her. One of many plantations and mills abandoned by fleeing owners, Bom Jardim had been bought for a fraction of its worth by a speculator, who was glad to sell it for what Maurits not too laughingly called Rachel's dowry, Rolf's share of the prize ship, which in a letter the mate delivered to the count, Rolf had directed was to be used to establish Rachel in a new life.

At first, she had rejected the money, but regarding her with a twinkle, Maurits had challenged, "You say that you can work as an accountant or manage a household, Dona Rachel. Accept my friend's investment as a loan—I can draw up papers if you like—and with one good harvest you can pay him back with handsome interest and work for yourself instead of for others."

That appealed mightily to Rachel. She was afraid of failing, of staying in the ignominious position of being Rolf's debtor, but she was more afraid of being a penniless woman trying to exist without a protector in a man's world. And she had Felicia to think about, and Lela, Lina and old Tonita, for the gypsies had begged her to keep them with her.

She sighed now, remembering three years so short in crowded, busy days, so long in solitary nights when, exhausted though she often was, she tossed and turned between bittersweet memories of Rolf and hopeless longing.

Maurits had found a trustworthy overseer and a few freedmen, but that first season Rachel and the women had stood their turn at stoking fires, skimming boiling syrup, arranging wet clay to refine loaves of brown sugar. Because of the war, few dared labor beyond the protection of the soldiers, and Rachel refused to work slaves. Gradually, though, Bom Jardim acquired good help, a mixed crew of soldiers whose enlistments had expired, Dutch citizens eager to earn stakes for their own hoped-for farms, and former slaves, some runaways from the south, some left behind when their masters had precipitately fled. Each worker got food, shelter, a small basic wage, and when the sugar was sold, a percentage of the proceeds.

Between grinding seasons, workers found employment in Recife or Olinda or tended truck gardens and sold fruit and vegetables in the market. As some left, like the old soldier who found Lina to his fancy and took her, her mother and her daughter to the little farm he'd acquired, others took their place. Bom Jardim thrived, and Rachel had two years ago entrusted Maurits with the money to repay Rolf's loan with interest. She was now sole mistress of a rich property, and moreover, mistress of herself.

Except for nights when she ached for Rolf—

The count's amused voice was chiding. "You've refused to come to my balls and banquets, Dona Rachel, or be painted by the artists I've brought from Europe, or help me decorate Vrijburg, my countryseat. But I'll forgive all past refusals if you'll attend my tournament.''

"My lord, I know nothing of knightly skills."

"You can still enjoy spirited horses and daring riders. Come, Dona Rachel, the grinding's finished. Even the most duty-ridden *senhors de engenho* can come to Recife for a few days.''

She eyed him searchingly. "You swear that you won't try to foist me off on one of your guests?''

"I swear it." Gaily he bent to kiss her hand. "You've promised, then! I shall expect you day after tomorrow. You'll stay at Vrijburg, of course."

He was gone before she could argue. Half annoyed, but as always totally charmed by him, Rachel shrugged, laughed and called to the one she knew wouldn't be far away during a man's visit.

"Felicia! We're going to the governor-general's tournament."

"About time you had some fun." Felicia's smile showed a dazzling array of gold teeth fitted in between the remaining white ones. Maurits knew a skillful tooth-puller who also fashioned replacements, and Felicia had received her teeth even before Bom Jardim was purchased. The teeth were the envy of all who saw them and had led Bom Jardim's handsome manager, Francisco, to court Felicia, though she was some years older than he. Rachel had given a feast for their wedding and the count himself had attended, dancing with the bride.

He was loved by the blacks, for he freed those who escaped from the South or who were the property of owners who'd deserted their plantations to take refuge in Bahia. The Tapuyas were his staunch allies. Common soldiers adored him for mitigating the rigor of courts-martial, which sentenced a soldier to hang as easily as they would a hen, and for endeavoring to see that the West India Company paid them adequately and on time—though this was a feat, as he somewhat sacrilegiously remarked, that God himself couldn't have accomplished. He punished foraging on Portuguese plantations and allowed Catholics freedom of worship, often entertaining clergy in his home—this in spite of being a determined Calvinist himself, and being thundered at by Dutch ministers and officials for encouraging idolatry.

Most remarkable of all, in an age when all stern Dutch Calvinists and heretic-hating Portuguese Catholics had in common was their horror of Jews, Maurits protected their right to practice their religion. There were two synagogues in Recife, and in Olinda a refugee from Portugal's Inquisition, Branca Dias, had established a boarding school for girls, where they were taught cooking and sewing. Hoping to learn something about Manoel, Rachel had visited Dona Branca one Friday when the house was being cleaned and scrubbed to prepare for the Sabbath.

Dona Branca, a stately woman with graying hair and fine dark eyes, received Rachel hospitably, but when she heard her question, the older woman turned away for a moment in outraged grief.

"You knew Manoel Vargas? He died a martyr *al Kiddush ha-Shem*, to sanctify God's name. I saw him burn in the square before the royal palace. Others in that procession recanted and were garroted or remanded to prison, but Manoel died steadfast, calling on the Lord of Hosts: *Ely, Adonai, Sabahot.*"

Rachel had bowed her head. To whatever God might hear, she prayed for her gentle friend. These thoughts and memories crowded her head as she sat in the spacious reception hall of Bom Jardim. Felicia had to speak twice before Rachel really heard what she was saying. "You've got nothing decent to wear, Don' Rachel."

"My gray silk will be fine."

"That old thing!" Felicia snorted in disgust. "While you're young and pretty, sinhá, you ought to get some crimson silk and green satin, wear lace and jewelry! Nobody'd guess you own a plantation and mill that produced ten thousand arrobas of sugar this year."

"Better they don't." Rachel grimaced. "As it is, I have a hard time convincing penniless noblemen and ambitious former officers that I'm not eager to invest them with Bom Jardim in return for their name and favor."

"There have been some who'd marry you if you stood

up only in your shift," Felicia rebuked. "Even the governor-general—"

"Has done well at eluding marriage," Rachel said. "Didn't poor Margaret Soler, that minister's daughter, die of grief when Maurits abandoned her for the garrison-commander's daughter? The count is my valued friend, but I'm glad I don't love him."

"It's better to moon over that pirate?" scoffed Felicia. "I'll wager you'd care about your looks if he were buzzing around like the other honeybees."

Rachel evaded this ongoing argument. "The tournament starts day after tomorrow, so we must leave in the morning." She smiled coaxingly. "Just be sure the gray silk is clean."

"And mend the holes it's gotten from lying in the chest since the last blessing of the mill," grumped Felicia.

She went out, shaking her head. Rachel went into her adjoining office and library, where she had been working on accounts when the count had arrived. This was where she spent most of her waking hours and where she had indulged in luxury, for the other rooms, as Felicia dourly remarked, might have been in a nunnery.

The walls were lined with books except for where paintings hung, the count's gifts and the work of two of the half-dozen painters he'd brought from Europe, Frans Post and Gerbrand van den Eckhout, a pupil of Rembrandt. Persian carpets glowed like soft gem mosaics on the floor. A big chair, comfortably cushioned, shared the best window light with the polished brazilwood desk, and there were brass lamps for reading or working after dark.

Ordinarily soothed by this retreat, today Rachel found she had no interest in reckoning up profits or even in reading one of the last tempting books Maurits had brought. Rolf always haunted the back of her mind, and Felicia's scolding had provoked an overwhelming tide of recollections and longings.

So far as she knew, Rolf had never returned to Recife, but Maurits now and then gave her news, already stale by the time it had traveled from the North Sea, the Mediterranean, around the Horn of Africa or the reaches of the mighty Atlantic. Trader, privateer, Rolf's sails bore him along rich trade routes or to waters no one else had ventured into, but his favored prey were Brazilian sugar-laden vessels.

"Ten this year," Maurits had marveled some weeks ago. "He must be as rich as princes wish to be." He gave her a shrewd glance. "Is it for his sake you sleep cold and lonely, dearest lady? The letter that accompanied you said only that you had saved his life."

"And he saved mine. We are quits."

Maurits had laughed softly, shaking his comely head. "Accountant's words, Dona Rachel. Beneath them, in that heart I have not been able to touch, lives a woman." His gaze traveled over her with appreciative ruefulness. "I envy the man who'll one day rouse her."

She had been roused. She burned for one man, and he was forbidden.

She snapped a carefully sharpened quill in half, flung it away and slammed a ledger shut. Arrobas and profits were no solace in the long nights. She was only twenty, but she felt already old, already blighted and finished. No matter how she tried not to, she relived her moments with Rolf during her sleepless hours, moved desperately breathless to imagine his kiss, his hard body. Her tears were more bitter for the certainty that *he* wasn't celibate.

No, he would have taken women as he did prize ships, in whatever waters he seized them. And perhaps he had found one to love—

Running from the house and her thoughts, Rachel met Francisco near the stables and asked him to have her mare saddled. Francisco shouted an order and turned back to Rachel, smooth forehead knit. His straight dark hair came from his Tapuya mother, his thin nose from a Portuguese grandfather and his perfect teeth from an Angolan grandmother. All these bloods mixed to make his skin the dark gold of a rosy peach. He was an excellent manager, but what most endeared him to Rachel was the joy he brought Felicia. There was never any doubt about whose hammock he was in as night fell.

"Is something wrong, Don' Rachel?"

She forced a laugh. "No, I'm just tired of doing sums." By the time she had told of the count's tournament and he had delightedly agreed to accompany her and Felicia, Bonita, her chestnut mare, was brought up.

Rachel stroked the rippling muscles of her horse's neck, whispered admirations, and gave Bonita a piece of sugarcane Francisco provided. He helped Rachel mount, properly glancing away while she arranged her full skirts.

"I'd better come with you, Don' Rachel. There's no telling when Dutch soldiers may be prowling around."

"I won't go far," she said, and gave the mare her head, bending low to her mane as the thoroughbred swung into a canter.

Wind stinging in her face, loosing her hair, Rachel lost her gloom in exhilaration. No man could shut her up in litters, forbid her this pleasure! She ruled Bom Jardim. Here she was queen.

Queen of a lonely country.

It was noon next day when Rachel's party clattered over one of the wooden bridges connecting the mainland to the island on which the count was building his new town of Mauritsstad just south of Recife. After Rachel had refreshed herself and partaken of a sumptuous meal, the governor-general, proud as a boy with a new plaything, showed her his gardens.

Thousands of coconut trees were planted in long avenues leading through fruit trees of every kind that grew in Brazil and many from Africa, Asia and Europe. Among magnificent plantings of flowers were vegetables, which he exhibited just as proudly. Peacocks trailed their many-eyed feathers across grass while swans glided on a lake and snowy egrets, scarlet ibis, white-necked herons and smaller ones fished in shallow waters.

Pavilions were scattered about the grounds and there were benches shaded by trellised vine arbors, some heavy with grapes, others spangled with flowers of blue, scarlet, white or crimson.

"This isn't just for my pleasure," the count said. His Portuguese was fluent, though he laughingly vowed that he spoke any of his other languages better—French, German, Dutch and Latin. "It's to show the great variety of fruits, nuts and vegetables that will grow here. It's ridiculous that the city and garrison—why, even the plantations—have sometimes been near starving because supplies from Holland were delayed." He scowled. "If only all planters would follow your example, Dona Rachel! You grow plenty of manioc and other foods, but most of the owners want to plant every inch of cleared land to sugarcane."

"It was the same in Bahia," Rachel said. "People chewing on dried codfish from Europe instead of raising fresh food."

"I've passed laws that plantations must grow enough manioc to feed themselves and supply the towns, but such decrees are the devil to enforce." Maurits expelled a breath of disgust. "Dutch planters obey no better than the Portuguese. As you know, I've returned their weapons to the Portuguese so they can defend themselves from marauders, though they are excused from fighting guerrillas of their own people."

Rachel smiled. "Yes, they call my lord their Santo Antonio after their favorite saint."

"I've tried to be just. I dream of a country where landless farmers from Europe can dwell beside the Portuguese in harmony, leaving the Tapuya their forests and streams. But the Dutch have much to learn about sugarcane. Come now and let me show you my newest animals!"

Parrots and macaws flashed among trees beneath which strutted turkeys and pheasants. Ducks and chickens of many kinds occupied a fenced yard with several ponds. In a huge walled area with grass, thickets and trees roamed goats from Cape Verde, Angolan sheep, tapirs, coatimundis and armadillos. Beyond this were caged apes, monkeys, wild boar, tigers, jaguars, ocelots and other beasts.

Rachel had exclaimed over the creatures, but she fell silent. She pitied the monkeys, whose natural life was swinging through trees with others of their tribe; the big cats confined in so small a place. Maurits lifted an eyebrow.

"You don't like my animals, Dona Rachel?"

"My lord, I do not like to see anything caged."

He shot her a curious glance. "Is that why you work no slaves?"

"I work no slaves because I have been one."

"Ah! That's why you won't marry."

She thought of Rolf and her fierceness died. "It's one reason."

"Alas, most of these are gifts, many from other countries. I can't insult the givers by letting them go. But I'll release for your sake these swift little monkeys my servants have caught."

He opened five cages. Bright eyes peered at him out of near-human faces. One ventured out, sprang up on a neighbor's cage. In seconds they were chattering. Some bounded off across the grass. Others vanished into trees. At least one ingrate pelted them with seed pods.

Laughing, the count shielded her with his arms and hustled her away. "That's what comes of pitying the oppressed! Hurry, before they throw something worse!"

Guests streamed in the rest of that day. After a lavish banquet, there was dancing and drinking till those present, women as well as men, could scarcely keep to their feet. Many Dutch officers and officials had married Portuguese women, but none of the Portuguese planters had taken Dutch wives, nor had they brought their own women with them.

"I can't believe it," muttered a descendant of one of the oldest Pernambucan families who was seated a few places from Rachel. "That woman across from us has drunk more than her husband. See how she laughs and flirts with other men? If my wife so disgraced me, I'd kill her! Women who drink in public are no better than whores."

Rachel was almost as shocked as he at the behavior of the Dutch, French and English ladies, these last wed to officers of the garrisons, but at his words she provocatively sipped her wine.

"Is that indeed the senhor's opinion?" Smiling sweetly at his glare, she divided her attention between the men on either side, Maurits' young personal physician, Dr. Willem Piso, and the barely older German scientist Georg Marcgraf.

Besides extensive collecting of botanical and zoological specimens, Marcgraf was compiling a geography of Pernambuco, with daily records of the rainfall, and a study of local Indians.

"There could be no better patron than our noble count," the husky blond young man praised. "He's ordered all ships' captains to note down eclipses and other celestial phenomena. Best of all, he's made an observatory of one of the towers of Vrijburg. Perhaps, Dona Rachel, you'd find it interesting?"

Though Maurits was some persons removed, at the head of the table, and blaring trumpets made it difficult to hear even a neighbor, his gaze caught Rachel's. "You must by all means see the observatory, my lady. I'll accompany you and my good friend, for I myself have unending enthusiasm for heavenly bodies."

"It's ever an honor to discourse with my lord," bowed Marcgraf, but he looked a trifle disappointed as Maurits excused himself.

With servants to light the way, the three ascended the tower. The young German soon lost himself in explaining his methods. "So much has happened in less than the hundred years since Copernicus published his work concluding that the earth revolves around the sun! It's only forty years since the Dutch invented telescopes, thirty since Galileo improved magnification from three- to thirty-fold."

The count smiled, taking Rachel's arm and bringing her to the telescope mounted on the parapet. "Here, dear lady, let me show you some of the things Galileo demonstrated to the Doge of Venice."

Rachel gasped, stepped back in an awe approaching fear. The moon had filled the sky! And those faint markings on it enlarged into mountains and ravines, a mysterious world brought so close that it provoked questions. Were there plants there? Living creatures? She would never look at the luminous orb again in the same way.

After letting her gaze at other stars and planets, he lit candles and reverently exhibited the works of Copernicus, Galileo and the Prague astronomers Tycho Brahe and Kepler.

"The books and theories of Copernicus and Kepler have been banned by the Roman Catholic church," the scientist regretted. "Eight years ago Galileo was tried for heresy and forced to recant his beliefs."

The governor-general shrugged. "So much the worse for nations like Spain and Portugal where the church can dictate science. They'll be gripped in the dead fist of the Middle Ages, while freer-thinking countries forge ahead with inventions and discoveries."

When they went downstairs, Rachel begged leave to retire. "I'm sad to lose your company," Maurits said gallantly. "But the banquet is becoming—spirited. Very well, Dona Rachel, I'll escort you to your room."

"That's not necesssary, my lord. Felicia's waiting."

"She always is," the count retorted, gripping Rachel's arm more firmly.

They bade Marcgraf good night and continued, Felicia a few steps behind, to the luxurious chamber Rachel used when she was the governor's guest.

"Sleep well, sweet lady." The count kissed her hand, then turned it palm up and let his mouth linger. His voice deepened caressingly. "If there's aught I can do for your comfort or pleasure—"

"My lord is ever gracious," Rachel smiled, though his physical closeness was perturbing. "He has anticipated my every need."

He sighed reprovingly but chuckled. "If only you needed more! Till morning, then."

As the echo of his fashionably high heels faded, Felicia urged Rachel inside and barred the door. "Lord help us, sinhá, that gentleman never gives up!"

Rachel held up her arms to be undressed. "After all, Felicia, his motto is: 'As wide as the world's bounds.' "

"And he should add: 'With all the women in it,' " Felicia observed. Rachel laughed and went to bed with a light heart, a sense of glowing femininity evoked by the admiration of Marcgraf and the doctor, the count's courtly blandishments.

Was she to mourn after Rolf Drouet forever? It couldn't hurt to follow the example of the foreign ladies just a little. In a few days she'd go back to being the careful, sober mistress of Bom Jardim, perhaps the only woman in Brazil who ran a mill and plantation, but for this short time she was going to smile at men, taste the power, after knowing so much of its bitterness, of being a woman.

In spite of being carried about so much in litters, every Brazilian male of any pretensions had splendid horses and consummate skill in riding. In contests with French, Dutch and English gentlemen brought up where horsemanship was losing its importance, the Portuguese carried off prize after prize as they performed the feats with which they celebrated weddings and saint's days, riding at rings, bending low to pick up scarfs tossed on the ground, looping their mounts in caracoles so that they seemed almost to be dancing on their hind legs.

In crimson, green and blue velvet, with saddlecloths and guidons in matching colors, they made a gallant sight. Their swift Arabian horses outshone the heavier, less agile mounts of the Dutch as much as did the riders' easy grace.

Instead of cheering on their own men, the foreign ladies clapped and called admiringly to the Portuguese, who reveled in this acclaim, smacking as it did of a sort of cuckoldry. None of their wives had come, and even if they had, they'd never have dared applaud their husband's opponents, much less send rings and chains to them as these shameless women were doing.

The crowning event was duels on horseback, the aim being to score by touching the opponent with a wooden sword while eluding his strokes. At this, too, the Portuguese prevailed until a new Dutch contestant rode out on a rawboned jugheaded little sorrel that must have come straight from the *sertão*.

In armor, as were all the participants in this contest, the man charged in on his ungainly steed and tagged both Portuguese horseman and caparisoned mount before he rode away.

The next Portuguese champion had won more events than anyone. A Dutch lady's emerald necklace flashed from his helmet as he sent his curvetting black stallion forward.

It seemed the stallion would run right over the scrubby, thin-tailed backlands animal and its impudent rider. At the last possible instant the rider relaxed the reins. The sorrel veered out of the way of the oncoming stallion, spun behind him and swept by on the other side. As he passed, the rider swung his mock sword upward and knocked the emeralds into the dust, then flicked them up and caught them.

Furious at having his lady's favor tumbled to earth, the Portuguese shouted and swung after the victor, but Maurits called: "Enough, gentlemen! The touch was fair."

Wheeling in disgust, the Portuguese galloped from the field. "That Dutchman's got a cow pony!" muttered a *senhor de engenho* who was too corpulent for tourneys. "Nothing can dodge or turn as fast. Who'd have thought it?"

Certainly not the haughty cavaliers, seven or eight of them, who tried and failed to humble the preposterous challenger. When no one else cared to try, the winner jogged his beast to the pavilion erected for judges and spectators. Maurits rose, smiling.

"Our Portuguese friends cannot grudge us one triumph when they've garnered so many," he said. He turned to Rachel. "Dear lady, I'm sure this gentleman would rather receive his prize from your hands than mine."

Flustered but unable to think of a way to refuse, Rachel made her way to the count's dais and accepted a silver-sheathed dagger from him. Facing around to the winner, who had lifted his helm, she stifled a cry.

The eyes that watched her were the color of the sea beyond, green with gray-blue depths. He shoved sweat-dampened pale gold ringlets back from his tanned forehead. His mouth curved sardonically as he took the dagger from her paralyzed hands.

"Your servant, gracious lady."

Lifting her fingers to his lips, he kissed them, never taking his eyes from her blushing face. "Netherlands Brazil agrees with you," he said softly. "You must tell me all your news as soon as I've shucked off this load of steel."

Bowing again to the count, he presented the dusty emeralds to the bosomy Dutch lady to whom they belonged, and led his inglorious mount away. As the trumpets blared for him, Rachel turned reproachfully to Maurits. "My lord! You knew he'd be here!"

The governor chuckled. "I *hoped.*"

"You might have warned me."

"Why? So you'd find an excuse not to come?"

Rachel tried to pierce his jaunty unrepentance. "I'm bound you found that tricky horse for him!"

The count gave her a droll look. "Must I let the Portuguese win all the honors? However, I assure you that the horse is Rolf's, from a ranch he owns in the backlands."

"I didn't know he had property in Brazil."

Maurits' smile broadened. "Quite possibly, my dear, there are other things you don't know about our friend." He raised his voice and called gaily, "Fair ladies and brave gentlemen, let's go to the banquet!"

Again seated between Marcgraf and the doctor, Rachel's confused thoughts were so centered on Rolf that she scarcely heard what either man said and was constantly jolted by a repeated question and a puzzled look into murmuring apologies and entering briefly into the conversation before the buzzing queries in her head distracted her again.

Why had Rolf come? Had something happened to his wife? Perhaps he was just as surprised to see her as she'd been to face him. It had been three years, and since then he must have had many women in many lands. And behind and over the other perplexities drummed the insistent one: *Does he still love me?*

She was beginning to think he wasn't coming when his voice came from her side. He greeted Marcgraf and the doctor warmly. Obviously they were friends. They congratulated him on salvaging some credit for the Dutch that afternoon. He shrugged the praise aside.

"It was all Caboclo. A cow pony that's used to handling wild bulls and mean mother cows isn't much worried by show-off horses and wooden swords." His gaze traveled to Rachel. Her heart turned over, seemed to wedge in her throat. "Georg, Willem, will you forgive me if I rob you of this lady? We're old acquaintances and have much to discuss."

Both men looked flatteringly disappointed but rose to bid Rachel a courteous good night. She said desperately, "You haven't eaten, sir. Let's call for another plate—"

"The count has granted us use of a small drawing

room," Rolf said. "A meal's being brought to us there."
He nodded to his friends, swept a bow to the governor,
who beamed indulgently, and bore Rachel off.

"Wait!" She held back as soon as they were out of sight
of the merrymakers. "It—it's not seemly for us to go off
alone!"

"Felicia's with us." He slanted a grin at her. When she
flashed him a wider one, he said heartily, "Gold teeth!
You've got a fortune in your mouth, Felicia!"

"It's not fair, trying to get on her good side," Rachel
accused.

Rolf winked at Felicia. "Do you mind?"

Her smile was for him, her scowl for Rachel. "You've
been on my good side ever since you kept us from winding
up in the Inquisition's prisons, master. Shame some folks
have a short memory." She yawned and turned away.
"Since you have lots of talking to do, I'll go along to bed.
Wake me up, sinhá, if you need anything when you come
in."

"I need you now!"

Felicia didn't look back.

Betrayed, Rachel shouted after her, "If you were still a
slave, I'd have you whipped! Come back this minute!"

The tall woman moved on, but the motion of her hips
seemed to increase. "Of all the—" Rachel began.

Strong fingers forced up her face. Rolf's mouth found
hers. She tried to break away. He swept her close against
him, branding her body with his. Long-buried hunger
stirred, fanned higher, sent blood coursing through her like
honey-fire. He caught her up, laughing exultantly as he
strode down the sconce-lit corridor.

"You haven't forgotten!"

"Rolf, please! I—"

He muffled her words with another kiss, turned in an
open door and put her down on a velvet couch. A tray of
covered dishes waited on a low table with goblets and a
decanter of wine. Rolf shut the door. He had bathed off
the sweat and dust of the tournament and wore dark green
satin that made his hair shine even fairer. He pulled over
a graceful chair of jacaranda, poured her a goblet of wine
and drank down his own in a few swallows.

His eyes searched her. He gave a brief nod. "No, I haven't dreamed you different from what you are—a woman, not a girl. By now you should be wise enough to listen to sense."

"And what is sense?"

He said dryly, "Don't take that prissy tone with me when you've just been soft and eager in my arms." Taking one of the silver plates, he filled it and gave it to her before he helped himself. "We shall dine, my love, while you tell me about the tasks of a *senhora de engenho.*" He laughed, watching her in a manner that set the pulse hammering in her throat. "Then I want to know what she dreams."

Dangerous ground. She had no appetite but took a few bites of crisp fish as an excuse not to meet his gaze. "Did you receive my payments for your share of the prize ship?"

"Yes, with interest. I knew you wouldn't take it back, so I gave it to an orphanage."

"That was generous."

"I didn't want your money."

"Strange words, sir, for a trader and privateer."

He drained another goblet. "The count tells me that you don't use slaves. How have you managed to turn such profits?"

"My workers get a share of them. That's simple enough."

He considered. "That might work. They can't desert during the milling season or they'd lose their pay, and after that it hardly matters if they go on a rampage and stay drunk in brothels for a couple of weeks."

"I suppose some do that," Rachel admitted. "But seven or eight have saved enough to take up small holdings."

"Maurits told me about that. You almost gave them the land."

"It's to my advantage. They're close enough to work at Bom Jardim during the harvest, and it's good to have neighbors with looting soldiers roving the countryside."

"You shouldn't be out there," Rolf growled. "I'd never have given you a start if I'd guessed you might do anything so crazy!"

"Then isn't it fortunate that I've paid you back and have

clear title to Bom Jardim?'' She shifted subjects. "I didn't know you owned a ranch."

"I own two. One I've never seen. It's in the interior on the São Francisco River. The other's in the backlands a long day's ride from the nearest plantation. I bought it on my first visit to Brazil, shortly after Maurits arrived. I've spent enough time there to learn how vaqueiros ride."

"But you're a mariner. Why did you want land?"

He hunched a broad shoulder. "I'm a Zeelander and grew up on my father's ships. I'll always love the sea. But I have other blood, remember? Ever since my grandmother told me her husband Ansiet's wonderful stories of Brazil, I dreamed of seeing it for myself. And when I did—" He laughed, shaking his head. "I felt like Duarte Coelho, who gave Olinda its name by crying, 'Oh, beautiful,' when he stood on a hill and saw the sea. Or our count, who calls it the most beautiful country under the skies." He sighed. "My wife hated the ranch even more than Recife, but I still planned to live there when I tired of voyaging."

Rachel winced at mention of his wife. She must still be alive. "You'd really settle in Brazil?"

"That was my intention. After being here, Holland's too neat and crowded, and I've never meant to spend my whole life under sail." He regarded her somberly. "But you may drive me to that, Rachel. I could never live in the same land as you and not have you with me."

Her heart pounded. "But if the Dutch are vanquished—"

"How likely is that? Since last year, Portugal has her own king again and is solely responsible for Brazil. If with the aid of Spain, she couldn't oust the Dutch, what chance is there now?" When she had no answer, he added, "For Brazil's sake, I hope Maurits will eventually govern it all, but even if the Dutch lose, that wouldn't keep me from living at the São Francisco ranch or somewhere even deeper in the wilderness. Government has nothing to do with you in a place like that." He drew a deep breath. "Neither does a wife far over the water."

"It makes your children bastards."

His mouth twisted. "You think it'll matter to wild Indians and wilder vaqueiros?"

"I won't have children who could be shunted around and mocked if anything happened to us."

"Why do I want such a stubborn woman?"

Rising, he drew her up into his arms. His mouth plundered hers, her breasts ached against him. Fiery languor weighed her body. She moaned and clung to him.

His warm hand found a way to her flesh, caressed her nipples till they were engorged with pleasure near to pain. Sinking to the couch, he bared one breast, stroked it with his tongue, drew it against his teeth. She cried out with need.

"Oh, my love!" he groaned.

His fingers spread exquisite shocks along her thigh, curved down to that sweet, dark secret, opening her, making her bloom. She felt the smooth warm hardness of him between her legs. It was so long since she'd had a man that he entered slowly till the melting honeycomb inside her sucked him deeper.

She rose against him. "Fill me! Fill me!"

He plunged deep. She gasped in delight. He rested like that a moment, swelling, penetrating her depths. They moved together, wild rhythm building, till he lifted her out of herself into soft explosions like colored fountains spraying high within her, and drew her to his heart as he fell beside her.

She could have died happy. Indeed, close in his arms, she floated blissfully as if they had passed out of this life into one where man's laws and problems did not exist. His words shattered that blessedness.

"The priest Father Calado is the governor's guest. Shall we ask him to marry us?"

Misery as complete as her joy engulfed her. Black ice seemed to clog her veins. Drawing away from him, she got heavily to her feet, straightened her garments. "You are already married."

"What?" He sat up, eyes full of disbelief. "Can you say that?"

"It's true."

He sprang up, clenching his hands. "And what just happened—isn't that true?"

"I can't be sorry for it." For that she would have gone

to anybody's hell; it must warm her lonely bed all the years that stretched endlessly into the future. Her mouth tasted of bitter ash. "But it must never happen again."

He swore in languages she did not know, took her shoulders and shook her. "I've a mind to carry you off to my ship!"

"Like a pirate?" she taunted, though she almost wished he would.

Releasing her, he flung away, then swung around. "What if I've made you with child?"

What she said was hideous. It struck him like a twisting blade that pierced her, too. "Felicia has herbs."

The pupils of his eyes almost blotted out the irises. His mouth hardened. "You'd destroy the fruit of our loving?"

"Before I'd raise a bastard."

He towered over her. Rachel braced herself for the blow. It never came. He spun about and left her.

"Rolf sailed with the tide," Maurits told her next morning. As she flinched and paled, he raised a baffled shoulder. "I don't understand you, Dona Rachel."

She found no reply, Maurits' tone lightened. "There'll be a French comedy performed this afternoon. I think it will divert you."

"Thanks, my gracious lord, but—I am not well. I must return to Bom Jardim."

He was beginning to argue when her imploring look checked him. "Then farewell for this time, dear lady. Your complaint is nothing my good doctor can remedy."

He nor anyone, Rachel thought. She thanked the governor for his hospitable entertainment and went to find Felicia.

It was May 1644, one month and three years after the grand tournament. Johan Maurits was going home. Rachel was the only woman in the cavalcade of over a hundred that rode with him to Paraíba, where he would take ship, but the entire road was thronged with men, women and children, soldiers of many nationalities, Portuguese and Dutch from richest to poorest, slaves and freedmen. The more important spoke with the count and shook his hand;

the humble tried to touch his garment or horse. All mourned his going and many wept.

The West India Company, discouraged by the return on the money it had spent in Brazil, had economized by cutting the garrison to a risky level and recalling the governor, whose free spending on science, the arts and his country-seats had long irritated company directors as much as his tolerance for Catholics and Jews.

Only his great personal popularity and success in ruling such a divided populace had persuaded the cheeseparing Heeren XIX to keep him as long as they had. Since the United Provinces had signed a European truce with Portugal, though it was good only in Europe, not including colonies they were fighting over, the company felt it could risk replacing Maurits.

As trumpeters played lustily, the count kept reining in his mount and turning to gaze at Mauritsstad, the city he had built. Rachel's eyes kept filling with tears. He had been a good and chivalrous friend. Who now would make peace between Dutch and Portuguese, give even justice and keep a firm but understanding hand on the motley assemblage of soldiers?

They reached the shore, where the ship lay at anchor some distance from the bank. Riding next to Rachel, Maurits kissed her hand and then her cheek. "Fare you well, Dona Rachel. May you someday be as happy as you are beautiful." Her throat ached, but she managed to smile. "May God be with you, my gracious lord."

Suddenly hundreds of Indians, some in paint and feathers, others wearing articles of European make, pushed through the horsemen. Pressing about Maurits, their laments and pleading filled the air. The count spoke to them gently. Some cried out in broken Dutch, which Rachel understood well enough to know that they were begging to go with Maurits if he could not stay.

At first refusing, he finally said, "My good friends, I cannot take you all. But six may come, be my guests in Holland and return on another ship."

They shouted at that. Some raised him to their shoulders and carried him through the high surf to the small boat that would take him to the ship. That was the last Rachel saw of him, borne high by his Tapuyas.

Felicia and Francisco had escorted Rachel to join the count's cortege and had ridden some distance behind the procession. They rested their horses while sharing the lunch Felicia had packed, and then rode briskly for Bom Jardim.

Regretting not only the departure of her friend but the loss of her tenuous connection with Rolf, Rachel lapsed into saddened reverie. The month after the tournament Rolf had joined other of Maurits' ships in taking Angola from the Portuguese. Next he was at the Hudson River in North America, where the company had establishments, and then was heard of variously from Guiana, Ceylon, the Caribbean, a restless wind.

She might well never have news of him again. That thought was like a death, though she argued with herself that it was foolish to treasure these scraps. Rolf had left her in anger. He had never pretended to be celibate. Doubtless he had long ago forgotten her.

A cry from Felicia jarred her into the present. She stared toward where Felicia was pointing. Smoke rose from a multitude of points.

It was not the season for burning to prepare for planting. Far away came the sound of firing. Could the ill-paid soldiers already be scavenging, rebellious at losing the commander who had done his best to provision and supply them?

Or was it guerrillas? A Portuguese uprising?

There were perhaps a score of pistols at Bom Jardim, even a small cannon Maurits had insisted on leaving there. Some of the smallholders had weapons and there was no dearth of lethal farm implements—scythes, hoes, spades, the heavy broad-bladed knives used for cutting cane.

Rachel turned to Felicia. "Ride back to Recife! Ask the garrison commander to send help."

"You go for help, sinhá. Francisco and me, we'll get to Bom Jardim."

"It's my plantation," Rachel said. "I want to be there."

Felicia started to protest. "Hurry!" Rachel cried.

At a motion from Francisco, the black woman swung

her horse and rode east. Rachel and her manager urged their horses toward the smoke and firing.

Smoldering fields. Burned thatch huts. Vultures flopped up from the remains of a pig spitted to roast over a campfire. A slaughtered ox lay nearby, killed for the delicacy of its tongue Its eyes were pecked out and carrion-eaters had been tearing chunks from its slit throat.

At least there were no human dead. Francisco reined in as they neared the sounds of battle. "Best leave the horses, sinhá Maybe we can slip in through the orchards."

Rachel nodded, glad that she wore stout riding boots. When Francisco started to tether the animals, she said, "Let's unsaddle them and turn them loose. In case we can't get back to them soon."

This done, they hid saddles and bridles behind a fallen tree, mounding dead leaves over them. Francisco wore pistols and a sword. Rachel had a dagger Maurits had once given her with the admonition to carry it any time she left her home.

Leaving the road, which ran through cleared lands till it reached the great stand of cashew and jacaranda trees that surrounded Bom Jardim, the two moved stealthily through the forest.

A burnt-sugar smell began to carry in the smoke. Rachel and Francisco exchanged grim looks. Most of the year's yield of sugar was still stored at the plantation. Francisco's black eyes flashed.

"At least the attackers aren't having it all their own way," he muttered. "Some smallholders must have warned Bom Jardim. That'll be a tough nut to crack if most of our people were able to fort up in the big house."

"But it's strange, burning the sugar and fields," Rachel whispered. "You know the count and the Portuguese signed an agreement to grant quarter to women, children and all who surrender, but neither side would consent to that till both promised not to destroy cane or mills."

"Yes, it was the crop and production that worried officials more than murder of their subjects." Francisco nodded, a cynical curve to his lip. "But there are guerrillas on either side who don't care what their governments order."

That was true. And if these pillagers had burned the almost sacrosanct sugar, they would pay no heed to the agreement about sparing enemy lives. As they reached where virgin forest gave way to the big orchard, the smoke grew thicker, the shouts and firing louder. There were shrieks and the boom of the little cannon. Francisco caught Rachel's sleeve.

"Sinhá, don't go on. What can one woman do? Get back to your horse and ride to Recife. You know I'll defend Bom Jardim with my life."

"I know. So I must be there, too."

Unsheathing her dagger, she hurried through the trees. Apparently the besiegers were too busy in front to detach men for attacking the rear palisades. Defenders were on guard, though, for as Francisco ran in front of Rachel, a pistol ball whizzed past.

"It's Francisco, you idiots!" he shouted.

"And the sinhá!" cried Meme, a giant smallholder, a branded runaway who had found freedom under Maurits.

The gate was opened and barred. "Couple of us watching here in case some of that bunch try sneakin' around," said Meme. "I saw 'em comin' yesterday, sinhá, just a few hours after you went past on your way to Mauritsstad. My woman and me made for Bom Jardim and warned our neighbors on the way."

It was his farm where the ox and pig were slaughtered. If he was caught, a two-time runaway, he'd be better off quickly dead. "Do you know who the raiders are?"

"Portuguese." He shivered, looking frightened for the first time. "And a gang of cannibal Tupis."

It was what both sides feared most, being turned over to Dutch or Portuguese allies who consumed human flesh. The big man hesitated a moment. "Sinhá, the leader, when he saw Bom Jardim wasn't easy pickin's, he called out he wouldn't hurt the rest of us if we'd hand you over to him."

Rachel's heart stopped. "Was he told I was away?"

"Yes, Don' Rachel, but he didn't believe it. Anyway, none of us would do that, good as you've been." He swallowed. "Just thought you ought to know that man out there sure means *you* harm, he's not just some guerrilla hitting whatever he comes across."

Only one man would have that kind of hate for her. But that had been so long ago, so far away. She had managed to put Duarte out of her mind except now and then a nightmare evoked his cruel body, his hot, avid mouth.

"Did the leader say who he was?"

The branded smallholder shook his head. "No, Don' Rachel. He was heavy and dark—a big master, not just some jumped-up fellow." ·

"How many of them are there?"

"Can't be sure, sinhá. Three hundred, maybe four. Countin' women who can shoot, we've got about sixty, but we don't have enough powder and shot to hold 'em off much longer."

Rachel knew what the end would be. Guerrillas breaking in the gate, hand-to-hand fighting till Bom Jardim's overmatched defenders were killed or wounded, then the worst part of such battles—dashing babies against trees, wanton slaughter, raping of women.

"Maybe they'll give up," said Francisco. "Or maybe the garrison will get here before we're out of powder."

Grasping at that hope, Rachel turned to Meme. "How long can we fight?"

"With clubs and knives, till we're all dead," he said with a grim chuckle. "With pistols and the cannon—today, maybe tomorrow morning."

Even if the Recife garrison was ready and willing to march, it would still be several hours before Felicia could alert them, it would take time for them to prepare, and it was at least an eight-hour march to the plantation.

Rachel's knees turned to water along with her insides. She'd already tasted Duarte's vengeance; how much more terrible it would be now if he'd hated her enough to forsake his ease and lead an expedition the long tortuous way through the backlands. But she knew just as clearly that a bargain must be struck while Bom Jardim was capable of defense. If she encouraged her people to hold out till they were overrun, she condemned them to torture and death.

She said to Francisco, "Go around and make sure our people are positioned for the best effect."

"Don' Rachel—"

She wanted to send Felicia a message of love and gratitude, but if Francisco knew her intention, he'd try to stop her. She motioned him away and hurried through the back courtyard into the house.

Women were nursing the wounded, brought to lie on the long veranda. Containers of water and food were stowed against the walls, and hammocks and pallets crowded the reception hall and overflowed into the chapel. Good smells of spicy stew floated from the kitchen, and the squeals and laughter of playing children also came from upstairs. Apparently, at Meme's alarm, the workers had forted up in the big house and prepared for a siege.

Rachel smiled at the women, spoke to the wounded and reassured them all. Felicia had gone for help. It would be all right. Then she took part of a sheet that was being used for bandages and walked down the avenue of palms to the main gate. The cannon, mounted on a tower built in one corner for that purpose, belched out a load of chain, scrap metal. Screams and groans rose from beyond the wall, and renewed firing. Bom Jardim's men aimed pistols and harquebuses through small holes in the wall, one firing his weapon while another readied the next charge.

There was a walled sentry post on either side of the wide gate. Rachel climbed the ladder of the left one. Efram, another runaway, stared at her but obeyed reluctantly when she ordered him to step aside. Thrusting the sheet through the firing hole with her dagger till it blew upward like a long flag, she waited.

A trumpet sounded. The firing diminished as the attackers drew back. "Are you ready to yield up the heretic?" shouted Duarte.

After all these years, she recognized his voice. It struck her with brutal force. She held to the stones to keep erect, peered through a slot. Duarte's helmet was closed and he sat his stallion heavily, but she knew him.

With their foes out of range, Bom Jardim's defenders held their fire. Out of the corner of her eye, Rachel could see some of them pointing and gazing toward the truce banner.

Her mouth was dry. When she first tried to call out, she could find no voice, but she swallowed and filled her lungs with air. "Senhor, I will yield myself if you will withdraw your men."

His gloating laugh reverberated in her ears. "Come out then, woman."

"First order the retreat."

He signaled. The trumpeters blew and the men at the fringe of the forest vanished into it, bearing their wounded. Duarte waited alone except for a dozen sprawled bodies that would never move again.

Efram barred her way. "Sinhá, you must not—"

"I must. Let me pass, Efram, or I'll jump from the wall."

His eyes brimmed with tears, but he stepped aside. Rachel moved down the ladder. Below, Francisco and many others barred the way. "We will not let you go, sinhá."

"But your families—"

"We have a chance." Francisco grinned. "We'll take it together." Pushing up the ladder, he shouted, "You cannot have our sinhá! And you'd better run while you can! The Recife garrison is on the way."

Duarte's howl of outrage carried to the wall. He shouted to his men. In a moment the assault began. Turning to Rachel, Francisco said, "Will you help with the nursing, sinhá, or must I lock you in your room?"

Swept high in a tide of love for and pride in her people, Rachel pressed his hand. "I'll help. We'll take that chance together."

The fighting lasted till dusk. Rachel tended the wounded through the night, but drowsed off in the first graying of dawn. She was roused almost at once by firing and distant screams.

Someone sounded the plantation bell. Men rushed toward the walls with their weapons. Running to the veranda, Rachel heard the sounds of pitched battle, though Bom Jardim's cannon and firearms were silent.

The Recife garrison!

Heart swelling with joyous relief, she hurried to the wall just as Francisco swung open the gate.

Rolf Drouet rode through. He saw her, sprang down and gave her a kiss that joined them forever.

* * *

"The woman who bore my name died last winter," Rolf explained as she brought him food and drink. "At first I wasn't minded to come to you, since you'd denied me, but it was no use. I couldn't put you out of my heart." His eyes, those sea-change eyes, searched her. "Is it so with you?"

She nodded, unable to speak.

"I docked at Recife too late to bid my friend Maurits good-bye, but I was dining with the garrison commander when Felicia burst in. I left as soon as I could get several loads of powder and shot together, for Felicia knew there wasn't a great supply at the plantation."

"Duarte?"

"I killed the leader. We let those who fled escape."

She raised his hand to her lips, only now able to believe that she was safe, and with him—that her love had come and he was free. "Thank God you came."

"I've come," he laughed, drawing her to him. "And you'll never be rid of me again!"

They were married twice, by Father Calado and a Dutch minister, their only regret being Maurits' absence. For several weeks after their marriage they reveled in each other, indulging every tender whim and sensual fancy.

"Six years to make up for," Rolf would tease when she breathlessly protested that there were other things they should be doing. "Come here, woman!"

He admired the plantation as she showed him around it, complimented her on her management, but something seemed to be troubling him. "Is something wrong?" she asked one day when she'd been talking about planting some new fields to cane.

He took her hands, watching her closely. "My love, would it be too bitter to you to leave Bom Jardim?"

"Leave?" she echoed. "Why?"

"Things won't be the same without Maurits. No other governor will match his fairness and vision." He sighed. "The truth is, my darling, that without him I think the West India Company will lose Brazil."

If that happened, even with Duarte dead, the charges

against her might be revived; and even if the Portuguese didn't confiscate Dutch property, she couldn't imagine Rolf living under enemy rule.

"But your ship," she said. "Won't you be going to sea?"

"This six years that I've scoured the oceans without you have given me enough of seafaring."

"Your ranch here in the north?"

"If you agree, I'd sell it. You could dispose of Bom Jardim and we could settle on my other lands on the São Francisco. People are their own law on that frontier. In our lifetimes, at least, neither Dutch nor Portuguese will bother us."

The *sertão*. The wilderness.

Rachel crossed to the window and looked out over Bom Jardim: the mill, the fields, the workers busy at their own plots, children tumbling by the neat thatched cottages.

Her place. Her kingdom. But it had been lonely.

She turned to the man who for the first time in her life had made her feel that she was not alone, she was not an orphan. "I'll leave Bom Jardim to the workers and small-holders," she said. "They will love it and keep it fruitful. We can leave as soon as this year's crop is sold. That gold we'll carry with us."

He laughed and caught her to him. "Always the sinhá-dona!"

"No." She drew his head down so his mouth found hers. "Always your love."

"Always," he murmured, lips straying to her breast.

Sweeping her up in his arms, he carried her through the hall to their chamber. Felicia smiled as they passed by.

BOOK III
Yemanjá's Daughter

Ogun, who, having water, washes in blood,
Ogun, who cuts in big and little pieces whomsoever he will,
Terror of the forest, dread of the huntsman,
Who kills wife and husband, owner and thief,
the one who sells straw pallets and the one who buys—
Ogun, lord of warriors!
Come fight beside me!

Yemanjá, who sits proudly in front of kings,
Lady of rainbows, cascades, and rivers,
Queen who dwells in the deepest waters,
Who embraces the city, destroying bridges,
Owner of a gun of copper, mother of gods,
Mother of Ample Breasts,
Nourish your children!

Sire. For some years the Negroes from Angola who fled the rigors
of captivity and the sugar mills of this captaincy have established
numerous inland settlements between Palmares and the forests,
where difficult access and lack of roads leave them better fortified
by nature than they might be by human art. . . . Your Highness
may be sure that this State is in no less danger from the audacity
of these Negroes than it was from the Dutch.

—letter to the king from Governor Fernão de Sousa Coutinho
of Pernambuco, June 1, 1671

This man is one of the worst savages I have encountered. . . .
He is no different from the most barbaric Tapuya, to say nothing
of calling him a Christian. . . . Ever since he first had use of
reason (if indeed he ever possessed it; for if so, he has lost it and
I venture that he will not easily regain it), he has roamed the
forest hunting Indian men and women, the latter to satisfy his
depraved appetites and the former to work in the fields which he
possesses.

> —the Bishop of Pernambuco in a letter of May 18, 1697,
> speaking of Field Master Domingos Jorge Velho

I

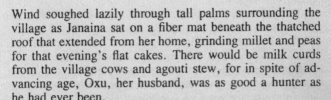

Wind soughed lazily through tall palms surrounding the village as Janaina sat on a fiber mat beneath the thatched roof that extended from her home, grinding millet and peas for that evening's flat cakes. There would be milk curds from the village cows and agouti stew, for in spite of advancing age, Oxu, her husband, was as good a hunter as he had ever been.

And as splendid a warrior. She glanced over to where he was hammering out a scythe blade on his forge. His muscles swelled and rippled. Tall and unbowed, he might have been Ogun, god of warriors and those who work in or use iron. When he was captured in the land of the Ifas almost a lifetime ago, he had already known the craft of smithing, and though there were four smithies in this village, it was to Oxu that men came for swords and daggers.

It had been some years now since Oxu had forged more weapons than implements to cultivate the many irrigated fields that supplied the *quilombo* with grain and vegetables, though many expeditions, Dutch and Portuguese, had marched on the settlements of runaway slaves stretching along the Ipanema River in dense palm forests about two hundred miles southwest of Recife.

A free kingdom of twenty-five thousand blacks, many of them born and reared in Palmares, was more than just an insult to slave owners; it was a danger. Not only did its presence encourage slaves to run away, but the warriors had raided numerous plantations, freeing slaves and carrying off women and plunder.

The Portuguese had failed as dismally as the Dutch in

putting down the slave confederacy. Palmares was well armed and provisioned. When enemies couldn't be routed, it was simple to abandon the stockaded villages and live in the forest, harassing soldiers from cover till they gave up and retreated.

Indians had also rebelled, angry at having their lands seized or at the constant slaving raids of *bandeirantes*. As the Dutch had done over thirty years earlier, the Indians, especially the Janduins, waged merciless and continuous wars that gave the Portuguese no time or energy to worry about Palmares.

The Janduins had finally made a solemn peace with the Portuguese, and the king of Portugal had directed that Indians captured should not be enslaved but should be sent to *aldeias* near Rio de Janeiro, a thousand miles south. Other Indians were still raiding and fighting, though. It should be a long time before soldiers or *bandeirantes* struggled through the roadless *sertão* to Palmares.

When they did, Zumbi, the great lord who ruled from Macoco, the most strongly fortified village, would defeat them as he had all those expeditions of the past—Dutch, Portuguese, soldiers, *bandeirantes*.

Under his rule, food was shared like labor, though the helpless were well provided for. Criminals were executed, and convicted sorcerers. Zumbi's wife, the stolen daughter of a haughty plantation owner, seemed well content with her powerful husband and his forest kingdom. Janaina had seen her at festivals and had a softness for her because she resembled Dona Rachel, though her dark hair lacked an auburn sheen.

Janaina sighed. The last time she'd seen Dona Rachel, that auburn hair was tinged with gray. That was, what— twenty years ago? Yemanjá's hand must have been in it— Yemanjá, who cared for orphans.

Who could have guessed that the white child Janaina had found crying in the woods near the ranch where her parents and relations had been slaughtered by Janduins was the daughter of Dona Rachel's friend Rozane, who had gone to live with her Santiago in the backlands? Janaina, with her children grown and married, had doted on the small white girl and reared her as her own, but when she learned that Dona Rachel was living with her new husband at his *fazenda* on the São Francisco, after an inner struggle, she thought it best to give the almost nubile girl into her former mistress's keeping.

Palmares should endure for Janaina's lifetime. The gods had already granted her seventy years. Her sons and daughters might even live out their spans in the confederacy. But sooner or later the Portuguese would push and not stop till they had destroyed the threat of Palmares, and even more dangerous, its dream.

For blacks it was better to die free. But young Rilia? Why tie her fate to a black husband and mulatto babies? Oxu was suspicious of all whites, even Dona Rachel, who was known not to have worked slaves while she was owner of a great *engenho* near Recife. Still, after much urging, he had escorted Janaina and Rilia on the long journey.

There were no slaves at Bom Jardim, so named after Dona Rachel's plantation. At first Felicia, of great age but still of queenly bearing, had not recognized the childish Hagar in the tall, mature woman who stood at the door with a pale, dark-haired child and a well-armed warrior, but when Janaina said who she was, Felicia flashed a mouth of dazzling gold teeth and embraced her.

"The sinhá will be joyous! She has always hoped you got away, though we knew Bento died."

So many surprises! First, as Janaina explained through Oxu's interpreting where and how she'd found the waif who had only known her name was Rilia, Dona Rachel had listened with amazement and at last burst out, "Why, this must be Marilia, Rozane and Santiago's youngest! We visited them when she was a baby."

Rolf Drouet, weathered but still handsome, still having a glint of gold in his silver hair, shook his head in wonder. "When we heard their ranch had been raided, I rode up to see if anyone had escaped." Even after eight years his face tightened. "All we could do was bury the bodies. But we never found Marilia's."

Marilia knew no Portuguese, but she was quickly absorbed by Drouet grandchildren and those of Felicia and Francisco, who were thrilled over this exotically reared "cousin." They bore her off to see their ponies, goats,

tame coatis and other pets. In order to make the change
less abrupt, Oxu and Janaina stayed for several days, and
through her husband, Janaina answered all of Rachel's
questions.

When the bush-captain and his trackers had caught up
with her and Bento, he had used his *capoeira* skills, kicking a pistol from one man's hand as he brought the flat of
his palm up so hard under another's chin that the neck
snapped. While battling the other three, he shouted at Hagar to run and keep going, he'd catch up with her if he
could.

She had watched the surviving manhunter pass beneath
the tree where she was hiding, and when he abandoned the
search she'd gone back to bury what was left of Bento.

Salvaging a broken knife and some of their scattered
provisions, she'd pressed on into deeper, virgin forest,
heading north as much as she could, for Bento had told her
of Palmares. At the first river, she bathed off his blood.

At every river, I bathed and prayed to Yemanjá. Janaina
didn't speak those memories aloud, nor had she ever told
anyone, even Oxu, how on the slaver, pressed between the
decomposing bodies of her father and mother, weeping because she'd been unable to bring them water or ease their
dying, she had been able to see through a chink in the hold
the play of starlight on the dark sea.

As she prayed for death, the waves swelled and took
form, and Yemanjá smiled, her hair full of stars. *"I will
be your mother,"* she had said in a voice like rippling
water. *"Have courage. You are Yemanjá's daughter."*

Each night during the rest of the voyage, Yemanjá appeared, her tenderness warding off madness, comforting
the orphan. At Seraphim, Dona Rachel's smile had been
kind as that of the goddess.

Returning to the story that could be told, Janaina thought
that Yemanjá had besought Ogun to send his son and warrior, Oxu, at just the moment that a roving gang of Dutch
deserters had cornered her along some cliffs.

"The six had firearms and swords, Oxu only a sword
he'd made himself, but he sprang out of the trees calling
on Ogun."

Oxu laughed at the memory. "I think they thought I was Ogun—or a devil."

"You took off two heads with one swoop and the others ran." Janaina smiled at her strong, unstooped husband.

Born in the *senzala* of a vast *fazenda*, he'd been almost beaten to death for defending his sister against an overseer. He'd run as soon as his wounds healed, and from Palmares led a raid, killing the overseer, rescuing his sister and many other slaves. Yes, he was Ogun's son.

He left the forge now and came over to sniff the stew appreciatively. "Fish is good, but agouti's better." He savored the gourd of palm wine she brought him. "When I finish these hoes and sickles that are needed, I'm going on a hunt. A fat tapir would be good."

Janaina patted out the cakes and placed them on the griddle-stone. Their sons, daughters and grandchildren lived in other villages and often visited, but this was one of the occasional days when no one shared their main meal.

Perhaps afterwards, as they rested in the shade of the hut— Janaina smiled as she ladled stew and handed it to her husband. She hoped the day would never come when they no longer found pleasure in each other. To the young it might seem bewildering, even indecent, but when Janaina lay in her husband's arms, it was sweet as in the days of their youth, only mellowed, more tender, less frenzied.

An age for all things, but some things had no age.

They were scooping up the last of the savory stew with flat cakes when two young warriors approached. A white woman was between them. A stranger, surely, though as she came nearer, there was something about her face, the way she held her head—

At the sight of Janaina, the young woman ran forward, embracing her. "Mama Janaina! Don't you know me?"

A white who spoke Yoruba? But Janaina had known as soon as those arms closed around her. Embracing her, Janaina cried, "Rilia! My little Rilia!" After the first rush of happiness, alarm chilled her and she drew back, scanning the other's face, finding there confirmation of disaster.

"What brings you, child? You haven't come all this way alone? Dona Rachel?"

"She's well and sends her love—she's the only one who understood that I must warn you."

"Warn us? Of what?" Janaina took the arm of this beautifully grown-up adopted daughter and made her sit down, bringing her coconut juice to drink. "Whatever it is can wait till you've eaten."

Marilia drank thirstily, but before she would partake of stew and flat cakes, she told them why she had made her way through the wilderness, accompanied only by a mulatto vaqueiro who was waiting for her with their horses on the other side of the river.

Domingos Jorge Velho, most cunning and brutal of all the *bandeirantes,* had left others to fight the sporadic Indian wars and collected a mighty force to march on Palmares. He would be aided by soldiers who would close in from other directions, cutting off escape.

This time, agreed the infamous *bandeirante* leader, the governor-general and the army commander, there would be no turning back. This time, aided by Indian trackers, they would root out the confederacy village by village, destroy the crops, pursue; they would not leave the field till Palmares was broken, till its people were dead or enslaved.

Oxu shrugged. "They have come before, my daughter."

"Yes, but with the Janduins at peace, even sworn to help the Portuguese in their battles, there'll be nothing to draw these forces away." She caught Janaina's hands. "Mama, please go! Tell your people and get away from here, perhaps to the Amazon or back so far they'll decide you're no longer a danger and give up the campaign."

"I'll take the messsage to Zumbi," Oxu promised, rising. "But we are many, we are armed, even with some pistols and shotguns taken from the whites. I do not think that we will run." He flashed a grin. "At least not so far that we can't pick off these would-be slavers."

He strode through the village, moving like a man half his age.

The two women embraced for a long time, silently expressing their love. It was unlikely they would ever meet again. "You were my sunbeam," Janaina said huskily. "I wish I could have rocked your babies."

"I have told them about you," Marilia said. "Oh, Mama

Janaina! Whatever the others do, please get your family to go where you'll be safe!''

"My daughter, bless you for your good heart and for making the hard journey. But many armies have failed to take us." She laughed. "I think Omolu, god of pestilence, aids us, too. Remember how yellow fever killed the governor-general who most hated us, and slew many soldiers six years ago? Yes, it was Omolu, for that sickness doesn't attack many blacks, mulattos or Indians."

Marilia sighed. "I will pray for you. Not only to the Virgin, for I am a Christian now, but to Oxossi, lord of the forests, as São Jorge, and to Ogun, lord of warriors, as Santo Antonio. They, and Yemanjá, will know for whom I offer candles."

"Beneath the names, they are the same powers," Janaina said. "May all gods bless you, daughter, in this world and forever."

The white woman bowed over the aged black hands that had tended so many children, planted so many crops, prepared so many feasts. "Good-bye, my mother. I owe you life. I will never forget that, nor will my children."

Janaina walked with her to the river, invoked Yemanjá to guard this white daughter and watched her out of sight.

Omolu sent pestilence, but it did not stop the invaders. Ogun fought beside the warriors, but they were driven out of village after village. Crops went up in thick smoky flame. Oxossi, god of hunters, was angry at the destruction of his peace. The animals fled or were hunted out by the *bandeirantes*. Yemanjá drowned some troops, but she could not finish them all. Towns burned, forges were broken, cattle and chickens slaughtered.

The people of the confederacy retreated to Macoco, Zumbi's stockaded town. For three weeks they fought off soldiers, Indian allies, *bandeirantes*, but they were cut off from hunting and gathering wild foods. When the granaries were emptied and there was no sign of slackening in the attack, Zumbi conferred with his headmen and captains.

No use to wait till they were weak and starving. Macoco must be abandoned. They would hide in the rugged Barriga Mountains, scatter in small bands that could live off the country. The fighting men of Palmares were valiant and well armed, but they had many women, children and infirm aged, while their enemies marched unencumbered.

The remaining food was divided. All persons capable of holding a weapon, be they children or near senile, were given a knife or hoe or sickle. Clothing, powder and shot were bundled onto backs along with babies, and that night, preceded and flanked by warriors, the people crept out of the stronghold that had so proudly, for so long, defied whatever forces Dutch or Portuguese could send.

Zumbi's scouts killed sentries and guided the people through the darkness. Mothers stifled their babies' crying. Sons and daughters supported their elders, sometimes carrying them, though the parents often begged to be left behind so they wouldn't slow the others.

Janaina carried her youngest grandchild when Dedi's short legs could trot no farther. Oxu and a friend held a wounded comrade between them. This man died slowly as blood drained from a sword thrust in his side. So did over a score who might have lived had they been able to lie quietly and heal.

As the dark hours passed, those burdened with others began to stumble and fall. When this had happened twice to the son who bore her on his shoulders, one old woman seized his knife and slashed her own throat, blessing him in her last choked breath.

During that night two women came early to labor. Janaina, the most skilled midwife, brought forth the infants, saving the mothers, though the tiny creatures died in the air their lungs could not draw in.

Two more children were born alive and the mothers walked onward, though one hemorrhaged and died, leaving her husband to carry the babe, the living new mother to nurse it.

So there was life that night, though more death, for the people of Palmares. They reached the mountains in the pallid dawn. There Zumbi, massive and ebony-skinned, addressed the assembled of Palmares, praising their valor, reminding them that they were the proudest legend the blacks had ever had—and their legend was true.

It would endure, should all of them perish. But it was

their duty to live if they could, to raise their children free. To that end, they must scatter. If the invaders gave up and returned to settled regions, Palmares might thrive again. But for now, small groups could better forage and elude the enemy. They could flee deeper into the wilderness, even to the Amazon, as some Tupi had done years ago.

It was his glory to have been their king. Whatever happened now, he thanked the gods for that. "You have lived free," he told them in his voice that carried like a drum. "We have all been free."

Many came to bow at his feet. Mothers held up their children for him to bless. Tears ran down the cheeks of even the most hardened warriors. Women wailed softly. But at last, in scores and dozens, they dispersed.

Oxu knelt to Zumbi. "Great Lord, we would stay with you."

The king's face showed emotion for the first time. "My friend, I will not run farther. I will stay in these mountains. Go to safety, you and your good woman."

"Lord," said Janaina, kneeling also, "we have lived good lives. We would end them with you."

He moved his head in assent, turned to his white wife. Janaina and Oxu embraced their children and grandchildren, blessed them and said farewell.

Last of all, Janaina cuddled Dedi, her favorite, and called on Yemanjá to protect her. "Never let the children forget," she told her children. "Never let them forget Palmares."

Then as the young and middle-aged faded into the jagged cliffs, the old woman and her warrior followed their king.

They followed for a year, with a few score others. Unable to plant and harvest, they lived on roots, fruit, nuts, wild greens and small animals they snared or killed with spears, for they dare not use firearms that might bring down on them the *bandeirantes*, who, living in the same fashion, were relentlessly pursuing their escaped quarry.

Sometimes the hunting went the other way—a ragged, single-file column attacked suddenly from all sides; stragglers pounced upon; squads murdered where they slept. As Zumbi's group ranged from one end to the other of the mountains, they came upon the vulture-picked bones of many who had fled from Palmares, identifiable by a shred of garment or the remains of a shriveled face. Several times they rescued old friends and neighbors who had been taken alive and were being marched back to slavery.

Always before, the enemy had given up after some weeks or months. Now, as harried days stretched from dry season to rainy and back again to dry, conviction grew within the little band that this time was different.

This time, that cruel slave taker Domingos Jorge Velho would not return till he had captured or wiped out the people of Palmares.

"I will die here," Zumbi said one night as they rested wearily, without a betraying fire, without that cheering warmth, light and hot food. "But the rest of you—go on while you can. Vanish into the forest of the River Sea where Velho will not follow."

There was silence. Janaina reached for Oxu's hand. He spoke into the darkness. "Great lord, it is our honor to share the end as we shared good days."

As assenting murmur ran through the others. After that night, there were no more quarrels, no more small jealousies. Brothers and sisters, they were given to death. All that remained was to fight as long as they could, run high the cost of crushing Palmares, leave behind a flame of courage, a beacon to burn for the enslaved.

One by one their numbers dwindled. The marauders had become a net, drawing closer and closer around them, limiting where they could find food. Powder and shot were gone, the firearms discarded.

At night, to inspire and comfort themselves, they told stories of the gods when they had been kings and queens of Ifa, Ketou, Ibara and other African cities, men and women who had passed the bounds of mortality and now watched over their descendants: Ogun, who taught them metalworking and whose name could be invoked in time of great peril to summon him to his votary's aid; Yansa, warrior woman whose magic sword had been a gift of Ogun, her first husband, before she became the wife of Xango, handsome Lord of Thunder; Oxossi, mighty hunter;

Oxalá, greatest of all, worshiped through Jesus; Yemanjá, queen of rivers and seas.

"We will make our gods strong," vowed Zumbi. "We will remember them, and as the years pass, they will feel at home here. They will protect our children's children, and their glory will grow."

Though this small band of aging faithful counted themselves a sacrifice, all had descendants who had escaped to other regions. Might they reap the good grain of their own fields. Might they take plenteous fish and game as these elders no longer could. Might they live unchained and forever remember Palmares.

At last there was no more food. At last the jeers and threats of their pursuers came from all sides. "Let us not risk being overwhelmed and captured," Zumbi said. His hair was white now. His wife was dead. His once splendid frame was bone hung with wrinkled leather. "Brothers, sisters, let us climb to the highest cliff, fight as long as we can, and then leap."

Under cover of darkness, the starving band crawled and stumbled to the promontory. As dawn broke, they could look across the sea of palms to the blackened patches that had been their fields and homes. They rested, gasping, emptying the last water from their drinking gourds. As they leaned against each other, almost drowsing in exhaustion, they heard the hunters coming.

They rose, closing ranks, some with spears and swords, all with knives. Indian bowmen let fly their arrows to cover the swordsmen who rushed in, some firing pistols and shotguns. Zumbi, an arrow in his throat, sprang forward, beheading one man, wounding another, in his dying gathering two foemen in his arms and dragging them with him over the precipice.

"Ogun!" shouted Oxu.

He picked up Zumbi's fallen sword, cleaved his way through Indians and *bandeirantes*. Janaina followed, swinging a sickle, hacking with her knife.

"Ogun!"

And then, without feeling anything, she lay on the earth,

one leg almost severed, in time to receive her husband's body, pierced by many arrows, slashed by many swords.

The shouting dimmed. The sun faded. She cradled her warrior in her arms.

Yemanjá smiled, rose high in a lulling wave that swept them into kindly peace, swept them into her arms. "Rest," she said. "Rest now, children."

She rocked them against her bosom in the fall of her starry hair.

BOOK IV
God Made Him a Leper

They go without God,
But they come back with slaves.

Barefooted, single file, following the tapir,
Following beasts' trails that turn into men's.
Mother's tongue lulls men, lures men, soothes men:
"Come take the red cloth, beads, knives and needles,
Follow where we lead you, there's better and more.
And if you won't come, soldiers will fetch you—
Come with us, brothers. Come to the shore."

Emeralds, Shining Mountains, Amazons, Lost Cities,
Golden Lake, Death River—up there on high,
There on the highest peak of the Martyr Mountains,
Don't you see the gold?
That is Christ's crown of thorns, nails, and the Roman spear.
Hurry, it beckons! Hurry! It calls.

Rib of the cow swords, tapir-hide daggers,
Salt in a tube and a pouch full of flour;
Push into Spanish lands, drive out the black priests,
Raft down the rivers, climb through the Andes,
Woodswise as Indians, fierce as white sires,

And when slaves are gone,
Still there are emeralds, still there is gold.
Always the far sky stretching to mystery.
Always the forests and never a home.

Therefore is condemned the criminal Joaquim José da Silva Xavier, known as Tiradentes, lieutenant in the colonial militia of Minas, that he be bound with rope and with proclamations be led through the public streets to the place of the gallows, and there die a lasting and natural death and after his death, his head shall be cut off and carried to Villa Rica, to the most public place where it shall be fixed on a high post until time consumes it; and his body shall be divided in four quarters and fixed to posts along the Minas road, in the locations of Varginha and of Cebolas where the criminal practiced his infamies, and at other places of his worst provocations, until time also consumes them. The criminal is declared infamous, and infamous his children and grandchildren.

—the death sentence of Tiradentes,
delivered by Chief Magistrate Francisco Luís Alves daRocha,
April 19, 1792

God loved him with an especial love; therefore
chastened him. At forty-five, God made him a leper.

—Frank Waldo on Aleijadinho

I

Blood and Diamonds

Plastered with yellow clay, the mud-and-wattle shelter blended with the sandstone cliff that formed its sides and back. Even its thatch was faded gold. Not that the sandstone was all yellow. It glittered with white quartz, was patched with green lichens and streaked with crimson. The dwelling was guarded from the fierce gales that howled from the bleak range to the east, especially at the new moon, but these winds had sculpted sandstone ridges into towering monuments, jagged walls, lurking monsters and giant skulls.

Scrub trees and squat bushes anchored tortuous roots about stones to hold against scouring onslaughts of wind and rain. Few grew as tall as the tree lilies spread along the ridges: some white blooms with blue and yellow stamens flaunting as high as the head of a tall man on horseback; another, smaller variety rich with purple flowers, sharing the ground with foot-high pink and white mimosas.

A river, dwindled by the dry season to a stream, dashed down from narrow, climbing plateaus to flow, now murmuring amiably, beneath the shelter. During the rains that lasted from October to April, it would swell out of its banks and carve away much more earth and a little rock as it swirled only a stone's throw beneath the shelter with its several orange and lime trees, straggly coffee plants, and little field of maize, beans and squash.

The winds blew cruelest at early morning. Inside the hut-cave, a dark-haired man whose blue eyes looked keenly out of a weathered face rose from one of the stiff cowhides that served as beds and seating, the only furnishings in the single room except for two leather chests. A crude hearth with a stone and clay chimney took up most of one side of the front wall, and an iron pot of aromatic coffee and an empty pan of mush sat on a large smooth stone. Niches built into the walls held a few dishes, a gourd of salt, cones of hard brown sugar, a rush-wicked lamp and a small wood image of the Virgin standing on a crescent moon, smiling at the baby in her arms.

Gabriel Avelar yawned, poured a stout drink of *cachaça* into a small glass and handed it to the muscular black man whose head almost scraped the ceiling. "Here's your *mata bicho*." He grinned, pouring himself a similar amount. "We've got to kill those bugs before they kill us."

Zé, clad only in a loincloth, patted his flat belly and chuckled. "I drank so much 'white girl' when I was a slave that it cooked my insides to where nothing can hurt them. But it does get a man's eyes open in the morning."

He tossed his down while Gabriel picked up a comb and sank to the other cowhide beside a girl of about five who popped the last section of an orange into her mouth and clasped her hands protectively over as much of her thick, honey-colored hair as she could reach.

"You'll pull, Papa!"

"No wonder, when you rub orange juice into your tangles! Zé, scrub her hands and face, will you? Why, child, you'd scare the headless she-mule herself if she met you!"

Renata had very dark blue eyes that she squinched shut as Zé washed her face and grubby hands and her father worked on knotted twists with his big, clumsily tender fingers before using the comb. She howled throughout the process, but Gabriel persisted. When he considered her fit for the day, he gave her a hug and kiss. She stopped in mid-shriek and burrowed against his neck, smiling through tears that glinted on thick, dark lashes.

"Now I get to comb your hair!"

He submitted, though he winced when she tugged too enthusiastically at the curls of his silky beard. Tilting a small triangular face, Renata approved her handiwork, kissed him moistly and scrambled down, heading for Zé.

"Oh no, zinha!" That was what he called her, short for *sinhazinha*, or little mistress. He warded her off with the arm on which he wore an iron bracelet. "You'd pull my hair out by the roots!"

"Then I get to wash your face!"

He stooped down and allowed her to make a thorough job of it before they gathered up gourds, pans and spoons and went to clean them in the river. Gabriel set smoked corn and jerky to cook for their noon meal, frowning at his daughter as she skipped back in and stowed away the dishes.

"It's time you had some real dresses." She was wearing one of his shirts with the sleeves cut off, gathered in against her wiry body with a handwoven sash, bought in Villa Rica de Ouro Prêto, that was her pride next to the silver medal she wore around her tanned throat. Gabriel sighed in the way that Renata knew meant that he was freshly bewildered at the problems of rearing a girl child. "I'd better take you with me next time I go to town."

He and Zé usually sold their diamonds to a man who came by the diggings, but once or twice a year one of the partners journeyed to Ouro Prêto to sell their better stones and get supplies.

"Will you let me carry some of the diamonds?" Renata begged. "You could fix me a knife like yours with the hollow handle—"

Zé roared. Gabriel cast her a glance of admiring dismay. "I'm a smuggler, a *garimpeiro*, and not ashamed of it, sweeting. The Crown drove my family off the ranch we'd had before anyone knew diamonds were more than pretty crystals good for playing backgammon. The Crown's greedy for its fifth of all our gold and diamonds so it's always made hard laws in Minas Gerais, but the Royal Intendant of the Diamond District is an absolute tyrant!"

Zé nodded his elaborately poufed head. He was one of the Mina tribesmen prized as slaves for their strength and endurance, whose homeland was on the West Coast of Africa. His hand strayed absently to the livid pink F on his shoulder. "A soul can't go or come without his permit, or run a business."

"Just because he tried to make a living by panning for gold on what had been our land, my father was sent to prison for life," Gabriel added bitterly. "I'm glad he soon died. He'd never have been able to endure cities." Shrugging, Gabriel opened the door and let Renata dart out. "I'm a smuggler," he finished, "but I don't mean for you to follow the life, live in fear of those damned dragoons that prowl the district. Even without finding any big stones, I'll have enough gold saved in a few more years to buy a ranch, maybe close to Bom Jardim, where my grandfather came from."

Renata touched her medal of the Virgin of Conception. It had been her mother's. She had died when Renata was an infant and was as shadowy to her as Trisavó Flor, her great-great-grandmother. Trisavó Flor had given her pendant to the son who in his wanderings had taken after his grandfather, the fabled Sertão. Renata's favorite stories were about these kinfolk, especially the women. Apart from men who bought diamonds or the rare *garimpeiro* who asked for food and shelter, she couldn't remember seeing human beings other than Zé and Gabriel. Women were particularly mysterious, though Renata knew she would grow into one someday.

Because of this mystery and because of something unnameable that she missed, Renata often imagined that her mother or Trisavó Flor or even remoter Rachel came to visit her while she washed gravel for diamonds, especially when Gabriel and Zé were some distance off, as they were this morning. After the rains started, they wouldn't be able to dig treasure-bearing *cascalho* from the riverbed or banks, so they were doing that now, heaping up piles of crusted rock and clay to be washed during the long season of rain.

Gabriel was working around the bend below the hut. Zé was on the other side of Renata, swinging his pick at the bank upstream from where she had perched on her favorite rock after filling her cone-shaped shallow basin, her *bateia*, with quartz-laden gravel from the big stone trough where it was soaked with water till it had softened to mud.

She had dipped in just enough water to cover the *cascalho* and moved the bowl in a gently circular motion that would gradually free any gold or rough diamonds and let them settle to the bottom of the cone. If no gold showed, certainly there would be no diamond, though there could be gold without stones.

Now and again she carefully tipped out some water and gravel and added more water as the profitless material was discarded. It took a long time to thoroughly wash a pan-load, and Renata was thorough. It was up to her to find any *pedra de dedo* Zé and her father might miss, tiny dia-monds called "stones of the fingers" because they could be picked up by pressing a fingertip on them. Washing for diamonds strained the eyes. The men admitted ruefully that anyone over twenty-five would throw away a lot of small stones along with the waste.

It was a demanding task, but Renata could stop any time, swim and splash in the river when it wasn't too cold, wan-der the slopes in search of flowers or thick, resinous tree-lily stalks to burn for fuel, or coax Zé or Gabriel into telling her stories as they worked.

She enjoyed working gold or diamonds out of the mud, though, and thrilled when she found one large enough to hold up to the light. The clear ones flashed rainbow fires, but she also loved the colored ones: yellow, though these decreased in value as the hue increased; rare blue and rose and green ones; and rarest of all, the black diamonds that glinted more the shade of the fine steel of her father's dagger.

Renata had found only one of these, but it had been large enough to run show her father. "A black!" Gabriel had breathed on it to bring out defects and then held it toward the sun, turning it slowly. "No fissures or specks. You've done well, little one. This is a real prize for your dowry."

"What's my dowry?"

He had grinned at her, wiping a smudge of mud off her nose. "It's what we'll have to pay some brave man to marry you."

She thought of the diamond buyers and *garimpeiros* she'd seen and announced decidedly, "I don't want to get mar-ried."

"You will someday."

"I won't."

"Then we'll have to give some convent a dowry to bribe them into taking you for a nun."

Her vague impression of nuns was that they lived behind high walls and prayed all the time. "I don't want to be a nun, either, Papa! I just want to live with you and Zé."

He knelt to hug her. "Don't fret, sweeting! When the time's ripe, I'll wager you'll love some scamp. I hope he won't have a waxed mustache and powdered wig! But whatever happens, we'll make sure you have your own special treasure, beginning with this."

He'd wrapped the black diamond in a bit of old cloth and put it in a pouch that he'd hid in a crevice in the sandstone wall. After that, when she found a diamond larger than half a small bean, her father would add it to what he teasingly called her dowry bag. Renata wasn't impressed with the stones' value, but she loved to get them out and hold them to the light, marveling at the tints, though her favorite was the stark black diamond.

As she rotated the pan now, she idly wondered if she'd ever find another and began to chat with the sandstone figure across the river that suggested the Virgin's image with the veiled head turned slightly away. Zé called her Yemanjá. He said she was the same as the Virgin and was Queen of the Waters, but Renata turned her into whichever kinswoman she wanted to imagine.

"It's like this, Grandma Rachel," she explained, picking up bits of rock crystal and quartz and displaying them to the veiled form before she tossed them away. "These are *'cativos,'* slaves, of the diamond and are always found with it. If I found some *cativo preto,'* some black slave, there'd be a chance of turning up a black diamond, and Papa would put it in my dowry."

She made a face at the word. "Did you have to pay Grandpapa Rolf to marry you? I bet you didn't! I don't want to get married anyway. I'd rather hunt diamonds than have babies. That's what wives do." She sighed. "But babies might be fun to play with. I don't know. I've never seen one."

"Babies are nice," Rachel assured her. Renata spoke for her, saying whatever came into her head. She got into some interesting conversations that way. "You were a sweet little one. I used to help your mother sing to you."

"You did?" Renata frowned. "I can't remember."

"You do when you're asleep."

"Is that why I wake up sometimes feeling like someone's been cuddling me?"

Rachel gave a delighted silvery laugh. "Of course. Your

mother and your Trisavò Flor and all of us. We sing to you in your dreams.''

"What do you sing?''

"You're not asleep now.''

Renata pouted. "It wouldn't hurt to let me hear you when I'm awake.''

"Well—maybe one song.'' Rachel paused and after some thought crooned softly.

" 'Shut the door, Rosa, do,
    Cabeleira is coming for you;
    The bandit snatches women
    And little children, too.' ''

"That's not a nice lullaby!'' Renata cried indignantly. "It's a song Zé sings when he wants to tease me, just like the one about Quibungo who likes to eat children!''

Rachel said dolefully, "I'm sorry, dear, but I can't sing the others except when you're asleep.''

Tears stung Renata's eyes. "That's because you're not real,'' she muttered. "You can't know anything I don't, so you don't know if babies are nice. And you don't sing to me at night, either!''

"Yes, I do.''

"You don't!''

Renata glared at the figure till it became just an odd-shaped sandstone knob, dashed away her tears and balanced the bowl among the rocks. Usually she enjoyed her imaginary visitors, but when they made her sad, she went to see Zé.

Rinsing her hands, she wiped them on her fraying garment and ran to where Zé was resting from digging out the bank by washing *cascalho*. He looked up with a grin as she approached.

"Here's one for your dowry, zinha, if you catch it.''

He flipped a tiny thing that dazzled in the sun. Renata opened her mouth and swerved to the side, stopping the stone with her tongue so it wouldn't slide down her throat. She took it in her fingers and eyed it warily as she turned it against the light.

"Zé! It's got a *falha!*''

That was a grave imperfection, two flaws joined as if glued together. She tossed it back at him in disgust. He caught it deftly in his mouth before he put it in the rock depression where he was saving his finds.

"When it comes to diamonds, don't trust anyone, zinha."

She sat down beside him. "How did you ever manage to swallow them?"

"The other washers taught me how when I was sold to the mines. We practiced with beans and grains of maize, not just how to swallow stones but to hide them between fingers or toes."

Rising, he maneuvered a small diamond between his big toe and the next one and walked off with it. When he let it go, he laughed and said, "See if you can do that."

She got it between her toes, but then it dropped when she took her first step, rolling to where she couldn't reach it with her foot.

"No hands," Zé warned when she lost patience.

Renata grimaced. "I don't see how you ever got enough diamonds to buy yourself."

"Didn't try at first. Traded what I hid for 'white girl.' The food was slop not fit for hogs, and my best friend died from *mal do bicho*. That's when dysentery gets so bad that the anus rots. I ran off first chance I had."

"Is that when you lived in a *quilombo?*"

"Yes. There must've been several hundred runaways in the village and it had been there ten or twelve years. But a bush-captain and his gang found us. Everyone was branded like me, except for those who'd run away before. They lost an ear. The ones who'd been caught for the third time were killed. And I was brought back to the mines." He sat down and picked up the pan, beginning to revolve it. "I was lucky. I found a diamond of nineteen carats." He chuckled, remembering. "Yes, my friends put a crown of flowers on my head, as is done to anyone who finds a stone over seventeen and a half carats, and they carried me on their shoulders to the administrator, who let me go free, but with a sour face, since he had to pay my master for me."

"And after that you turned *garimpeiro* and my father helped you get away from some dragoons."

"That's how it was, zinha."

"A long time ago." She frowned, trying to picture a world where she hadn't existed. "Before I was born."

"A mighty long time ago," he agreed solemnly.

She spied the twinkle in his eye. "I am not a *young* child," she said haughtily.

He studied her as he dumped out sludge. "I guess you're not." He squinted at the sun. "Maybe you ought to feed the fire so the stew'll finish cooking."

Renata had started away when her ears picked up a sound, a sort of faint drumming. "Zé! Listen!"

He already had his ear to the ground. "Horses! Lots of them."

Her stomach shriveled into a tight little ball like a spider dropped into the fire. Their visitors came alone or in twos or threes, never in numbers. "Dragoons?" she whispered.

These dread beings, till this moment, had seemed as legendary and improbable as Quibungo and Cabeleira. Zé snatched up his machete and the blunderbuss he kept at hand in case a deer came in range.

"Come, zinha!" Zé caught her hand.

She hung back. "What about Papa?"

"Zinha, your papa and me, a long time ago we agreed that if one of us was with you when trouble came, he was to get you away and help the other one later if he could."

"But I want to help Papa now!"

"Then hide! That's what he'd want." Zé hustled her along till she had to run to keep from being dragged. "Likely he heard the horses and is cutting through the hills. Hurry up or he may get hurt coming back for you!"

That made Renata run as fast as she could. Long as Zé's legs were, she skimmed the earth so swiftly that he barely limited his loping strides. Angling off at the first ridge, they left the river and zigzagged through white and yellow reefs till Renata's breath came in sobbing gasps and she whimpered at a fiery ache in her side.

A crashing sound echoed from the cliffs, followed by a volley, then scattered firing. Renata froze. Zé halted, shaking his head. "Ogun help him!"

"What?"

"I said Saint George help your daddy."

They listened. The sun-heavy air distorted the mountains as if Renata watched them through a big yellow diamond. One with many flaws.

There weren't any more shots.

Zé slowly clenched his fist, raised it high, so the F on his shoulder seemed to writhe. Then, without saying anything, he picked Renata up and carried her.

She was still weeping when, much later, he stooped and lowered her to a ledge. They were in a sandstone cave, the mouth nearly concealed by fallen boulders.

"You stay here, zinha."

She clung to him, terrified. Gently he disengaged himself. "Child, after all that shooting, your daddy must be dead, but if there's a way, I'll send some dragoons after him."

"What if—if they shoot you?"

"They won't have a chance." He smoothed back her hair. "But if I don't come back tonight, in the morning you go to the river. If anyone's at the house, I don't think even dragoons would hurt you. They'd take you to Tijuco and some nice couple would adopt you. If you don't find anyone, get your dowry bag—you can bet the chest of gold will be gone—and all the food you can carry. Then follow the river. There's a tavern several days journey away. The folks there'll look after you."

"Zé—"

He hugged her and left the cave.

The sun climbed to the center of the burnished sky. Renata had cried till her eyes were puffed nearly shut and her head throbbed. When she peered outside the cave, she saw strange country, though these weird battlements and creatures of white and yellow were splashed, like the familiar ones, with orange and green and a crimson that now seemed to her the color of blood.

Her father's. She shivered at the thought and prayed he might be all right. Her thirst grew. She hunted the surrounding region for a spring or seep but found nothing. She knew better than to get far from the cave. In this bewildering maze of pinnacles, giant walls and grotesque knobs, she could become hopelessly lost.

A pebble in her mouth made saliva flow and eased her thirst a bit, but she was also hungry. That made her think of the stew her father had put on to cook that morning. It was terrible to fear that he'd never eat again, or drink, or do anything. She buried her face against the ledge and sobbed till she fell into exhausted sleep.

It was late afternoon when she roused and gazed dully about, slowly remembering what had happened. What if Zé didn't come back? If there were more shots, could she hear them? She scrambled from the depression in the wall and shivered as she thought of spending the night there alone.

Would the headless she-mule get her or the dwarf with feet turned backward, or the toad-goblin or one of the *almas penadas,* souls in torment, who smeared children with ghost broth so they'd die unless they washed their faces first thing in the morning? All the scary stories Zé and Gabriel had swapped on rainy days churned through her head. She ran out of the cave and started hunting for old tree-lily stalks, though she had no way to start a fire. At least she could have fuel ready for Zé.

If he came. Panic overwhelmed her at the sudden realization that he might not. All her life either Zé or Gabriel had always been within hailing distance. If she had bad dreams, she could roll from her cowhide to her father's and be soothed by his warmth and steady breathing.

He wouldn't be there anymore. Never. A wave of hatred for the men who'd shot him washed over her fear, followed by grief so heavy she could scarcely move. Part of her mind warned that it would be cold tonight. Even if Zé returned with blankets, it would help to collect bedding to soften the ground.

A young moon, pale as a few wispy clouds, was well above the line of triangular rock mountains on the western horizon. As the sun's light died, the moon's would increase, so real dark wouldn't close in for a long time.

She went pillaging again for tree lilies, live ones this time. Most of the other shrubs and plants had spiky leaves or thorns, but these *canelas de ema,* "shankbones of the ostrich," were more hospitable. She twisted off younger, more pliable fibrous stalks and from plants as much as three times her height broke stems with their bunches of narrow leaves.

When there were withered flowers, she took them; they provided a bit more padding. She also pulled what tufts of grass she came upon. Her arms wouldn't hold much. It took frequent trips to make one big heap long enough for Zé and a smaller nest for herself. She made her bed on the ledge, which was closed in on three sides and would seem less vulnerable in case—oh, horrid thought!—Zé didn't return.

The setting sun turned white and yellow stone to rose and orange. The pebble had gone dry in her mouth, so she spat it out. Her stomach gave a hollow rumble.

She had to have at least a drink. It couldn't be more than ten or fifteen minutes to the river. She'd just have to make sure she could find her way back to this cavern, which was now the only home she had.

Searching till she found a reddish rock that would make marks, she started off in the direction Zé had taken. When she came to the first barrier, she turned around to fix the location and look of the cave firmly in her mind. The cliff above formed a gigantic swooping hawk, an easy landmark.

Even so, she rubbed the red stone on one of the pillars she squeezed between, and thereafter marked her route each time it might be confusing. It was reassuring to glimpse the guardian hawk from time to time. The slope began to descend. Gratefully she saw the shining river.

How cool, how beautiful! Placing the red stone in a niche where she could see it, Renata memorized that shape. A giant lizard with her rock for the pupil of its niche-eye! She ran to the water, lay on a rock and drank.

She had nothing but her stomach to carry water in, so after her thirst was quenched, she lay on the rock, which still held the sun's heat, until she could drink some more. Then she rinsed her face, laved her swollen eyes and washed her feet, which tough as they were, had cuts and bruises from that wild flight into the hills.

No sound came from the river. She couldn't see the soaking trough from here, or even the woman figure. Powerfully drawn to creep along the river till she could glimpse her home, she trembled at the thought of what might await her there.

Time enough to see tomorrow. Besides, Zé had told her

to stay at the cave. He'd worry if he came back and she was gone. Kneeling and cupping her hands for a last drink, Renata rested for a moment on the warm rock and then made her way up the slope toward the lizard-shaped monolith.

By the time she reached the hawk cave, the moon was a curve of glowing silver in a sky the color of her father's eyes. Her throat ached when she thought of him, but no more tears would come. The wind was rising, piercing her thin garment, but she was reluctant to enter the dark hollow.

The sandstone rocks in front of the cavern still retained a comforting warmth. She moved about till she found a place protected from the fiercest blast. Her stomach was full of water, if not food. The moon held off the blackness. She closed her fingers around Trisavó Flor's medal. Pretending that the hawk would scare off bogeys and that she lay in her mother's arms, Renata sank into slumber.

She was shuddering with cold and some woe her mind was too hazed to summon. Strong arms raised her, wrapped her in lulling softness, put her down on something much springier than cowhide that cracked and shifted with her weight.

"Papa?" she muttered drowsily.

A big hand patted her. "You go to sleep, zinha."

She couldn't think why she was so glad to hear Zé's voice. He always slept on the other side of her. Snuggling deeper into the blanket, she slipped back into rest.

That merciful haze was stripped away with the opening of her eyes in the morning. The sad odor of withered lilies filled her nostrils as she sat up. Zé was stretched in his blankets on the couch she'd made for him. A jumble of things, including water gourds, a bandolier and half a dozen oranges, were heaped by a leather pack at the entrance.

Renata hated to disturb Zé, but she had to know about her father. Though she slipped off the ledge almost soundlessly, the tall Mina's hand closed on the knife beside him before his eyes came guardedly open.

"Zinha!" He put down the knife.

She ran into his arms. "Oh, Zé, you came back! Did you—did you find Papa?"

"Buried him, zinha." Zé stroked her hair as if to calm himself. Hot tears dropped on her shoulder. "The ball that killed him did it fast. He can't have suffered more than an instant."

Through numbed lips she asked, "Was it dragoons?"

Zé nodded, swallowing. "Your father shot two. Zinha, he must have fired so we'd be warned and get away. By the time I sneaked back, the gang had set a fire inside the hut and let their horses eat our maize. They searched around the river for a while before all but four of them rode off."

Renata looked a frightened question. Zé's laugh didn't sound like his at all but had an ugly grating sound. "There were enough tracks and signs to make them guess your father wasn't alone. Good thing a bush-captain and his squad weren't along the way they usually are or they could've trailed us. The dragoons couldn't, so a few were left to see if anyone turned up."

"Are—are they still there?"

"You bet they are. And they won't be leaving till they fly off."

"Fly?"

"In a buzzard's belly."

Zé sat her down beside him and reached for one of the rawhide cases in which supplies were carried when one of the men went to town. It was charred on one end and Renata wrinkled her nose at the smell, but her mouth watered when Zé handed her some smoked fish and a flat cake.

"Chew it good and slow," he cautioned, following his own advice. "The dragoons took away the gold chest and your daddy's good boots and cloak, but they tossed just about everything else in the fire." He showed gleaming white teeth. "Lucky those four left behind saved the blankets and some food."

He reached deeper into the pack and brought out the little wooden madonna and a pouch that gave a soft clank as he put it in Renata's lap. "They got all our diamonds but these, zinha."

She had a terrible feeling that if she looked at them they would all, even the steely black diamond, be the color of blood. She shoved them away. "I don't want them!"

He shrugged and put them back in the case. "They'll come in handy where we're going."

"We—we have to leave?"

"Certain sure, zinha. When those dragoons don't join their bunch in three, four days, the others'll come back. What they find—" His eyes burned and his smile made her afraid of him for a minute. "We don't dare be in the Diamond District a minute longer than we have to."

She felt as if the earth were spinning under her, that she would be swept off by the first wind, whirled away from everything she had known. Then she thought about her father and the slain dragoons and knew she couldn't have stayed had it been possible.

"Where will we go?"

Zé considered. "I think to Ouro Prêto. In Bahia, before my master got greedy and sold me to the mines, I was a carpenter. I'd like to work at that again. Had a gutful of washing for gold or diamonds."

It was what she had done since she was big enough to hold a specially made little *bateia,* but diamonds to her now would always carry the hue of crimson.

"I want to see where you buried Papa."

Zé inclined his head. It didn't take long to stow most of their belongings into the pack. Renata carried a water gourd slung across her shoulder and the smallest blanket draped around her like a shawl. Zé had a knife under his loincloth and another sheathed at his neck, and carried a shotgun he'd taken off a dragoon.

"It's against the law for a mulatto, let alone a black, to carry any kind of weapons in Minas Gerais," he said as he slipped on the bandolier. "But if I'm caught in the Diamond District it won't make much difference. When we get to that tavern I told you about, we'll be almost out of the district and I'll sell the gun to the tavern folks."

"Will they tell the dragoons about us?"

"Lord love you, they've got rich buying from smugglers!"

"Then why don't the dragoons—?"

"Because the tavern keeper is a second cousin of a high official and he's godfather to another," snorted Zé.

That didn't mean much to Renata, but she soon had all she could do to keep up with Zé.

Two rock-covered heaps showed where the dragoons had buried the men Gabriel had killed. Vultures rose from a sprawled heap at the bend of the river, a pile that Renata didn't want to see from closer up. The door of the hut had been torn off and the framing was blackened. The smell of burned leather and other things hung thickly in the air.

"Your daddy's over here."

Renata couldn't remember the rock resting beneath the cliff. Then she saw the broken earth almost concealed by it and understood. "You dragged that rock over his grave so no one can find him."

Zé smoothed the last of the betraying surface. His tears fell on the stone. Renata knelt by it. *Mother, Trisavó Flor, he must be with you now. Take care of him.* Then loss drove out all reason. She dug at the rock with her hands, raging and weeping. "Papa! Papa! Come back! Don't be dead!"

Zé gathered her to him. "That's no use, zinha. You've got to be brave like your daddy. Tell him good-bye now."

"I don't want to leave him!"

"You've got to, child. He died for us."

She had a sudden idea. "Give me the Virgin out of the pack."

Zé frowned but rummaged for the little figure and gave it to her. She scratched away the white soil at the edge of the rock till the madonna would fit, wedged the image as far as it would go, and patted the ground flat with her hands before she kissed the stone.

"Good-bye, Papa," she said beneath her breath. Rising blindly, she followed Zé from what had been their home.

II

Tiradentes' Head

Two days hard travel brought them to the tavern. Dona Alisa, who actually ran the rambling thatched establishment because her husband, Senhor Jorge, seldom stirred from his card games, at once gathered Renata to her full, lavender-scented bosom, put her to soak in a tub of warm water, and soon scoured and rinsed her clean from hair to toenails.

"What a love!" she exclaimed to Zé. She gave Renata a piece of sugarcane. "Here, my lamb, chew on this while I comb your hair. Wavy and just the shade of honey from the comb! You didn't pack her clothes, Zé? If that's not like a man! Well, I'll put Sabina to sewing, and for now we'll wrap this towel around you and tie it in place."

The buxom brown-haired woman had a softness for Gabriel and shed a tear, murmured a prayer, when told he was dead. Zé only said it had been sudden and made no mention of the dragoons. Dona Alisa didn't pry. In the Diamond District there were many things it was safest not to know. Nearing middle age without a child, she yearned for one and began a campaign as soon as she'd set the travelers down to a sumptuous meal.

"Let the darling stay with us," she urged Zé. "What does a man know about raising a girl? It's not decent! And with all respect, how can a freedman find her a proper husband?"

Zé's jaw dropped. "She's only five, Dona Alisa!"

"None too soon to start remedying the wild way she's lived!" Dona Alisa sniffed. "That wonderful hair in witch-knots! Wearing a man's raggedy old shirt! I daresay she's never even been to church."

"Well . . ."—Zé scuffed an unhappy heel against the packed sod floor—"maybe you're right. But I was friends with her daddy before she was born. Feel like I ought to—"

"You ought to consider what's best for her," Dona Alisa cut in authoritatively. She beamed at Renata, whose bliss in discovering chicken stewed with rice, mint, pepper and laurel, manioc fritters and coconut pudding, had kept her from heeding the grown-ups' conversation. "Wouldn't you like to stay here with me, little one, and have pretty clothes and all the goodies you can eat?"

Renata blinked. She slowly finished chewing a bite of crispy fritter dipped in flavorful sauce. "Is Zé staying, too?"

His warning glance reminded her that he had to get out of the district before the dead soldiers were found. "Zinha. I'm for the city and a different kind of life. But Dona Alisa, she'll take good care of you." He gulped. "Might be best if you stay here."

Renata's breath squeezed tight in her chest. She slid down from beside their hostess and caught Zé's plum-colored arm. "Don't—don't you want me, Zé?"

He gave her shoulder an awkward pat. "Well, sure I do, but I've got to think of what's right for you, child."

"And you know what that is," put in Dona Alisa.

Renata glared at her, clinging to the big Mina. "Zé's my family! I'm going with him!"

Dona Alisa looked incredulous, but after a baffled moment, she raised a plump shoulder and addressed Zé over Renata's head. "What can you expect when she's been raised like a heathen? It's up to you, out of respect to her gentleman father, to do what's best for her. I'll wager you won't be an hour up the road before she'll be trying on my jewelry and eating honey cakes!"

Zé didn't speak but hung his head in a disconsolate fashion that roused protective fire in Renata. She braced clenched fists on her scrawny hips and said with soft violence, "If you try to keep me, I—I'll wet the bed!"

It was the most enormous threat she could think of. The only time her father had ever scolded her was when, the year before, a howling storm outside had kept her huddling in her blankets till it was too late.

Dona Alisa's brown eyes narrowed, then widened again as she laughed in a joyous bubbling way that almost made Renata wish she could live with her. "You would, would you? I want a daughter, not a smelly infant, so go in peace, for the love of God." She burst into chortles again, wiping away tears of merriment. "Come eat your pudding, my ferocious angel-demon. You shall even have cashew fruit cooked in sugar and cinnamon."

Renata's mouth watered, but she said suspiciously, "I won't stay here, mind!"

"Indeed you won't," agreed Dona Alisa. "But I hope you'll come visit me someday. I confess to great curiosity as to how you'll turn out."

That night she smiled a bit sadly at Renata's awed caressing of snowy linen sheets fragrant with lavender. "Sweet dreams, my love. I'm glad you at least wear the Blessed Mother's medal. May she watch over you."

Renata returned her hug, marveling at how soft and good-smelling a human could be. "So you're a woman," she said drowsily. "I'm glad. I like you."

Dona Alisa's voice was muffled. "I like you, too."

She kissed her, fluffed the feather pillow and was gone. Renata meant to lie awake and savor the luxury of this incredibly comfortable bed, but she was weary from the journey and sated with rich food. She said a prayer for her father and, hoping heaven was half as pleasant as this, drifted into sleep.

Though Dona Alisa tried to persuade them to rest at least a few days, Zé, right after breakfast, interrupted the corporal's game with the hostler and swapped the shotgun, bandolier and one knife for coarse cotton trousers and a shirt, jerky, smoked corn, coffee, a sugar loaf, and, after some haggling, a bit of gold dust.

"Don't know why you want to go where they can make you pay that damned head tax," growled the corporal, rubbing his heavily veined red nose. "They say the Crown's going to levy it again because the queen's advisors reckon she's being cheated on the royal fifths. No way they'll believe the easy gold's gone and what's left is little and hard to get.'' He tossed off his *cachaça* and poured more. "It's good you have a trade and won't waste your time washing for gold that's all gone. Keep an eye out on the road. You may see poor old Tiradentes' salted quarters nailed up. And his head must still be on a post in Ouro Prêto."

"Tiradentes?" echoed Zé. "Tooth-puller?"

"That was his nickname. Made teeth and pulled 'em as well as being a lieutenant of militia." The tavern owner shot Zé an astonished look. "You don't know about the conspiracy?"

"What conspiracy?"

"Lord, you have been stuck in the backlands! The trial dragged on for two years down in Rio de Janeiro before it ended in April. Merchant who stopped here said it was a shocker, the way the chief magistrate handled the sentencing. Took three hours to read it all. Twenty-one out of twenty-four found guilty, twelve condemned to dangle on extra high gallows, have their property confiscated and their sons and grandsons declared infamous. Seven of them were to be quartered and have their heads chopped off and exhibited. Another four would lose their heads, but these wouldn't be stuck up on posts for everybody to gawk at." The corporal paused for breath. "After keeping the poor devils in torment all that time, the magistrate commuted all the death sentences except Tiradentes' to banishment and confiscation."

Dona Alisa puffed out her rosy cheeks. "What would you expect? Except for the tooth-puller, they were all highborn and wealthy—clergy, poets, ranking officials, even a commander of dragoons!"

"That's true, my jewel," granted the corporal. "But Tiradentes is the one who spoke loud for freedom all during the trial and claimed that he was to blame for inciting the others."

"He, an out-at-the-elbows country doctor!"

"Well, he did whip out the United States' Constitution and read it to anyone who'd listen." Senhor Jorge shrugged.

"Yes, and didn't most of the others attend universities

in Portugal and France and have grand libraries full of all those French ideas about liberty?"

"They don't have them anymore. But it's Joaquim José da Silva Xavier who doesn't have a head."

"I'm sorrier for his wife and daughter than I am for him," said Dona Alisa. "What with the king and queen of France in prison, and who knows, maybe even that new-fangled guillotine waiting for them, you can't blame Queen Maria for being nervous!"

"Why?" demanded Zé, rubbing his ear. "What was this conspiracy all about?"

"It came down to the way the Crown kept squeezing Minas Gerais for more gold and diamonds, making laws that pinched the powerful folks who've always run the captaincy. Mix that in with highfalutin' notions borrowed from France and the United States and you've got treason."

"What notions?"

Senhor Jorge reflected. "Independence from Portugal. Abolition of slavery. A university right here in Brazil, and building of the factories Portugal won't let us have—"

"No more slaves?" Zé interrupted.

The corporal laughed. "Guess that sounds like a good idea to you," he said, not unkindly. "Brazil's tired of being milked dry, so who knows what'll happen one day? But not in our lifetime, I'll wager." He poured more *cachaça* and returned to his cards.

Dona Alisa tied Renata's hair back with a blue ribbon and tucked the comb into a small leather bag she'd filled with delicacies. "Work your tangles out every night and they won't get so bad," she admonished, kneeling to gather the child to her for a last warm embrace. "Be a good girl and come back to see me."

"I'll try," said Renata.

She was sorry to leave this kind woman, but Zé was all the family she had, and if awful things could happen to people out here in the world, like having their heads cut off and being cut in pieces, she didn't want to let him out of her sight. Giving Dona Alisa a resounding kiss, she hurried after Zé.

Though she was proud of her ribbon and the quickly sewn red dress Dona Alisa had given her, Renata, now that

they were finally on the road at the very edge of the Diamond District, kept glancing about in fear.

"What's the matter, zinha?" asked Zé. "We're as good
as out of the district."

"I—I don't want to see that poor tooth-puller's arms and
legs, or meet any dragoons."

Zé swallowed a startled laugh and patted her cheek. "No
reason we should run into trouble, *menina*. My knife's hid
and your little dowry bag's under your dress. If anyone
stops us, let me do the talking."

Their story was that he had served her parents, who had
recently died of yellow fever on a remote farm, and that
he was taking her to a great-aunt in Ouro Prêto.

No one stopped them that day. In fact they passed only
one merchant with his slaves and pack mules and two other
horsemen who gave the big Mina and the small blond girl
a puzzled glance but rode on as if they had secrets of their
own.

Though she still wept silently when she thought about
Gabriel, Renata was amazed at the trees, lush grass and
flowers that increased as they drew away from the forbid-
ding Serra do Frio. They slept that night in a deserted hovel
located in the middle of a grown-over manioc patch and
made a good supper of chopped manioc leaves stewed with
jerky cooked in one of the two pans salvaged from the hut-
cave.

"No more slaves," muttered Zé, munching the cashew
sweetmeat Renata made him share. "I'm going to save up
enough to pay for a sung mass for his soul even if the
priests do charge sixteen drams of gold for one."

"Let's buy it with the diamond from my bag."

"Let's not even talk about that bag," Zé said severely.
"Wrong person gets wind of that and I'll get jailed for life
or sent to Angola!"

"Isn't that where you came from?"

He said with pride, "I was born in Bahia while it was
still the capital instead of Rio de Janeiro."

"But I thought you were a Mina."

"White folks call anyone from the Ivory Coast a Mina,"
Zé said with indulgent contempt. "My father was a Yoruba
chief. There are lots of nations along the coast and more

inland. They're as different as I reckon France and England and Portugal and Spain are, but that makes no never-mind to the slavers. About all they've figured out is that some work better than others and Muhammadans who can read and write may give trouble.'' He got out the blankets. ''Get to sleep now, zinha. Still a long trudge to Villa Rica.''

She woke to the pungent smell of coffee. Zé shaved hard brown sugar into the drinking gourd and they took turns sipping the steaming thickened brew between bites of mush.

''What will the city be like, Zé?''

''Well, it's the capital of Minas Gerais, so there are lots of fine buildings, the royal mint and churches just about everywhere you look.''

''Trisavò Flor was there when it was just a mining camp.''

''Yes, several camps straggled uphill and down and ran into each other. They're all in the city but have kept their old neighborhood names. The Paulistas and Emboabas fought and lynched each other for a couple of years, but then most of the Paulistas tore off looking for new treasure—and that's when the diamonds were found. I guess what really helped the Paulistas and Emboabas sink their differences was when the French captured Rio de Janeiro.''

''The French? I thought they were across the ocean.''

''They are. But they sailed over here during one of those European wars that Portugal drags Brazil into. Rio fell, but Governor Albuquerque raised six thousand volunteers in Minas Gerais and São Paulo—*mamelucos* and Portuguese who'd been at each other's throats the year before.''

''And they whipped the French?''

''Well, not exactly. Rio's governor, a craven who was later exiled, had already agreed to ransom the city with gold, cattle and sugar. But the French got out in a hurry because Albuquerque's men were there.'' He added grudgingly, ''It's said the French were decent to the women and the wounded and the commander rescued some New Christians who were going to be sent to the Inquisitors in Lisbon.''

''Like Trisavò Flor's Avo Rachel?''

Zé nodded, stowing things in his pack. ''Is there still an

In-Inquisition?'' asked Renata, having trouble with the word.

"Yes, but Pombal pulled its teeth. He didn't have much use for priests, especially not the Jesuits, and after it looked like they might have had something to do with a plot against the king, Pombal forced them out of every land Portugal owns and took all their property. They owned lots of plantations and land in Brazil.''

"I've never seen a priest.''

"You will. And a mighty lot of other things.''

They stopped to rest every hour or so, but Renata was thankful for the longer pauses at noon, and even with a nap then, her legs felt ready to drop off by the time they stopped at night. Zé said Ouro Prêto was almost directly south of the tavern on the edge of the Diamond District, but the road twisted and turned to make the easiest traveling through the mountains. Zé carried her across most of the streams, but where the current was deep and swift, he paid in gold dust to be rafted across.

Occasionally they stopped overnight at some small farm and were freely given food and shelter, but more often night found them in an uninhabited stretch and they slept in the open. At first Renata was frightened of *bichos* like the fiery bull and headless she-mule, but she came to enjoy waking to the rush of bird song that welcomed the first hint of dawn.

She lost track of days. It seemed she had never done anything but trudge along the narrow road, trying to stretch her short legs to keep pace with Zé. The woods and meadows they passed through were so different from the fantastically shaped sandstone ridges of her homeland that she began to wonder if that had all been a dream.

Perhaps it had. Or maybe *this* was the dream and she'd wake up beside her father some morning. Then she'd remember the ruin of their home and the rock Gabriel lay under, and she would cry softly as she trotted along beside Zé.

Several times when Zé had glimpsed squads of dragoons or a bush-captain's gang on a distant rise of the track, he'd led Renata to hiding in the woods. "No use talking to those fellows if we don't have to," he said. "I've got the paper that says I'm free, but those *capitãos-do-mato* aren't always real careful about who they haul in for runaway slaves."

This day, though, by the time they heard horses, Zé and Renata had nowhere to hide. They were on a thin ribbon of road curling around a mountain with jagged cliffs on the other side plunging to a river below. Zé glanced over his shoulder.

"A litter's coming," he said hopefully. "Let's drop back close to it. Maybe if that's dragoons headed this way, they'll figure we're with the litter."

They slowed, but before the litter could catch up with them, blue-coated horsemen rode around the bend, braid and buttons glinting in the sunlight. Zé didn't have to tell Renata that these were the dragoons. Like those who'd killed her father.

She made a sound of fear and hatred. Zé spoke quietly. "They won't hurt you, zinha. Keep walking. Maybe they'll not bother with us."

Her knees seemed to have no bones. Her spine prickled as if some big spider was crawling up it and her bladder seemed suddenly about to burst. The horses were beautiful but frighteningly large. They filled the road farther ahead than she could see, hoofs kicking up spurts of white dust.

The man at the head of the riders held up his arm and shouted an order to halt before he stared coldly down at Zé, frowning as he glanced at Renata.

"What's in that pack?"

"Shall I show your honor?"

"Set it down." The leader signaled one of his men. "Feira, take out everything in the pack and then search this Negro."

Renata thought of the forbidden knife Zé had concealed in his loincloth. If the dragoons found it— The litter borne on the shoulders of four black men was drawing abreast, slowing because the horsemen barred the way.

"What's the matter?" came a deep, husky male voice from within the litter. The words were oddly slurred.

Through the partly drawn curtains, Renata glimpsed a hunched shape she took for that of an aged man. He must

be rich and important to travel in such style. Important
enough to overawe the soldiers?

The dragoon was shaking out the blankets, opening
packets of food, checking even the coffee beans. In a few
minutes he'd turn to Zé, and from the thoroughness with
which he was examining their possessions, there was no
way he could miss the knife.

"Have they taken you for a hardened smuggler, child?"
The tone, though amused, had a note of sympathy in it that
spurred Renata into taking a desperate chance.

"Grandfather!" she cried, running to the litter. "Can't
you make them stop putting our things on the ground?"

A moment's silence tormented her almost to the scream-
ing point. What if the man was angry, what if he told the
soldiers he'd never seen them before? Then he pulled the
curtain open and leaned out. "Lieutenant, is it really necessary to pillage my servant?"

Renata smothered a gasp. A wide-brimmed hat obscured
much of the man's face, but the rest was covered by a kind
of coarse sack. And there were no hands protruding from
the coat sleeves.

The dragoon leader stared. "Are you Senhor Antonio
Lisboa?" he asked, the annoyance in his tone and face
softened by respect. "All Minas Gerais knows your work.
I've admired your altars and carvings throughout the captaincy."

"The lieutenant is kind." The hooded man bowed.
"Will he be kinder yet and allow us to proceed?"

Frowning at Renata, the soldier said in some embarrass-
ment, "I knew you have a son, Senhor Antonio, but this
child—she's so fair-skinned—"

Senhor Antonio chuckled in genial fashion. "So was my
father, Lieutenant, and this small one is an orphaned relative from my Portuguese side, not actually my grandchild,
though it pleases us both to pretend she is."

"So that's the way it is. A pretty little lass." The soldier
smiled at her and straightened. "Feira! Put back the things
and let Minas Gerais' greatest sculptor be on his way."

"Thank you, Lieutenant." The man in the litter nodded.

The dragoon bowed. "Senhor Antonio is the one to be
thanked for beautifying our churches. I was born in this

captaincy and I'm proud to show your work to officers from
Portugal so that they must admit that we have great artists
in Brazil.''

"Indeed, you overwhelm me," said Senhor Antonio,
bowing again. "Farewell, Lieutenant, and God keep you."

The troop moved off.

Zé took the sculptor's sleeve and kissed it. "Senhor, you
got us out of a bad spot. If I can do anything to thank
you—''

"Why," said the rescuer, rich laughter in his voice, "I
think you'd better travel with us so I can get acquainted
with my granddaughter. It's fortunate the lieutenant not
only goes to church but notices what's there." In the dim
litter, the eyeholes in the sack-hood gaped emptily at Renata and the man's tone changed. "Now that you see me,
child, could you call me grandfather?"

The loose hood, the sleeves that crumpled emptily,
frightened Renata. Where were his hands? How could he
carve things without them? But he had responded to her
appeal and she liked the way his voice could deepen like
the velvet Dona Alisa had let her touch, or ripple with
amusement.

"I wish you were my grandfather, senhor," she said
quite truthfully.

"I am mulatto."

"What is that, senhor?"

He made an ejaculation. Zé said hastily, "Senhor Antonio, the *sinhazinha* hasn't lived among people, only with
her father and me."

"You're their slave?"

Zé drew himself up, eyes on a level with those of the
man in the litter. "No, senhor. I was partners with the
sinhazinha's father. We had a . . . business. But Senhor
Gabriel's dead and I thought I'd better bring the little mistress to town and hunt for work."

"What kind of work?"

"I was a carpenter, senhor, in Bahia. Made furniture and
coffins and chests for shipping sugar. I even carved saints
and angels for my master's chapel."

"Would you like to work for me? I have helpers, but

I'm offered more commissions than we can handle. If your work's good, you'd do well.''

Zé's face glowed. "That's mightily kind of you!"

"I have to look after my granddaughter," retorted the sculptor. "There's room for you in my house, and the women will love having a child to fuss over." He moved his sleeve to indicate his bearers. "I cannot walk, so my friends and helpers bear me on their shoulders. These are Januario, Maurício, Felix and Ezekhiel. Let's get around this steep hill and find a good place to have lunch."

The basket that Januario unpacked held tangy white cheese, guava paste, sausages, the first wheat bread Renata had ever tasted, thin-sliced ham, cinnamon-sprinkled coconut cakes, sweet oranges and genipap cordial.

Master Antonio, as he had asked Renata to call him, sat inside the litter, facing the side opposite the others. Januario, splendidly proportioned with a face that looked as if it might have been honed from dark wood, filled a plate and took it around the conveyance. Renata couldn't see him, but she guessed that he was helping his master eat.

Maurício was a squat, broad-faced dark yellow man with graying hair. He asked Zé a lot of questions about working in wood and how he'd do certain things, scowling at first, but by the time he'd finished the interrogation, nodding approval. "Work as clever as you talk and it'll be fine. But mind you, we don't want to be covering up mistakes."

"And I don't want to make more than I have to," said Zé tranquilly. "I'll ask Master Antonio to start me off with rough work till I get back in practice."

Maurício nodded and cast Zé a sly look. "Been washing for gold?"

"Tried it." Zé shrugged. "But you know how that is. Pan just enough to keep you hoping."

They went on talking while Ezekhiel and Felix, sturdy brown young men who looked as if they might be brothers, leaned back against a tree to rest.

Renata felt safe for the first time since that morning weeks ago when she'd heard the dragoons' firing. She took a last morsel of coconut cake, sighed, and curled up with her head against Zé's knee.

* * *

She woke in a shadowy place to a soothing, swaying motion. A sweet heavy odor seemed to have beneath it the hint of a smell not so pleasant. The pillow on which her head lay felt like the silk of Dona Alisa's shawl.

Where was she?

She sat up, memory flooding back as the heavy-torsoed man at the other end of the litter chuckled gently. "You've had a long sleep, little one. We're almost home."

She blinked and craned to look out through the slightly opened curtains. "Are we in the city?"

"Indeed we are." With his elbow, he hitched the curtain away so she could see. She stared in amazement. A great white building rose before her, a windowed tower on either side. Elaborate stone carving framed a tremendous door.

"Does the queen live here?" she whispered, unable to think of any other reason for such magnificence.

"Bless you, yes, if you mean the Queen of Heaven. Queen Maria, though, lives across the waters. This is the Church of Our Lady of the Conception. My father, who's buried here, planned it and did some of the altars and sculptures. I helped."

"You did?" Renata's mixed feelings of gratitude and pity for this strange masked personage were further confused with worshipful admiration. "Oh, Master Antonio, I want to see everything you've done!"

"That's gratifying, child, but would mean a tour of all Minas Gerais. By the time you've seen all my works in this city, I'm sure you'll be ready to cry quits. We can start at this church, though, because it's the one I attend and my house is just a bit further up the street."

Up was the proper word. Once at the church, the rock-paved street slanted sharply uphill, the walls of what Renata supposed must be dwellings rising high on either side. On the long high hill above were more buildings and gardens, and she glimpsed what looked like an even larger church.

They passed through a gate in the street wall into a neat little yard with a fountain and orange and quince trees. Herbs and flowers grew in pots attached to the sides of the walls and a long low building ran the length of the back wall, roofed like the two-story house with red-brown tiles.

As the bearers halted, Master Antonio asked them to lower the conveyance. "Stretch your legs, little Renata, while I tell Cleonice you're here."

"Is she your wife, Master Antonio?" Renata stepped gingerly out of the litter. The blue, white and yellow tiles of the courtyard were so clean that she was afraid of getting them dirty.

Januario smiled. Maurício's sour countenance twitched, while Felix and Ezekhiel sniggered. Renata flushed. Was her question stupid? Had she offended her new friend?

"Thank God she is not," he said, but the hint of laughter was good-natured. "She's tyrant enough as it is. Zé, you may put your things in the room you'll find on the right end of the workshop there, and then you might like to look at some of the things we're doing."

He signaled. The bearers raised the litter and entered the house. Renata ran after Zé to inspect his room. A cowhide bed was its only furnishing, but there wasn't room for much more. There was a wide shelf and pegs for clothes.

The workshop was fascinating, stacked with all kinds of wood and pieces of stone. Tools lay on tables of various lengths and heights or hung from the wall, and shelves held smaller tools and boxes, jars and brushes. The place smelled enticingly of sawdust, resin and things Renata couldn't guess at.

Several angels were emerging from blocks of wood, wings appearing to struggle from the mass. A Virgin's face was lovingly painted, but her robes were only partly done. What most enchanted Renata were several creatures the size of large dogs with hair carved in curlicues on heads and necks.

"What do you think these are, Zé?"

"They could be lions," he decided after critical study. "This is a good workshop, zinha. These pieces are as fine as any in the great churches of Bahia."

"Will you like it here?"

"I think so. Maurício may be a fault-finder, but I won't let him bother me provided you settle in nice and cozy."

"How do you suppose Master Antonio works?" Renata wondered. "I don't think he's got any fingers."

"He doesn't."

Renata whirled guiltily. Maurício stood scowling in the doorway. "Janu and I fasten chisels to his thumbs and stumps. He hasn't got any feet, either, so when he's not carried he has to crawl. He wears that hood because his face is ravaged and his teeth have fallen out." The mulatto raised a sarcastic eyebrow. "Is there anything else you want to know about the man who got you out of trouble with the dragoons?"

"I didn't mean—" began Renata in a small, shamed voice.

"Anybody would wonder," said Zé matter-of-factly. "No need to yowl like a cat with its tail in a crack."

"Don't mind Mauro." The woman who shooed him out of the door was massive, and a loose calico dress made her look more so. Her light brown skin looked soft and smooth. A gold tooth flashed when she smiled at Renata, and frizzy red hair escaped a spotless white turban knotted elaborately to one side. She appraised Zé in one shrewd glance before she bent down. Beautiful green eyes with brown shadowings seemed to reach to the bottom of Renata's soul.

"I'm Cleonice," said the woman, taking Renata's hand. "I'm glad you've come to live with us. The house needs a child." She straightened and her look included Zé. "Supper's ready and there's lots of *xin-xin* and *acarajé.*"

Zé gasped with delight. "Chicken with dried shrimp! Grated beans with onions! I haven't had either since I left Bahia. Do you cook them with *dêndé* oil?"

"How else?" Cleonice looked affronted. "You're not the only one from the Bay of All Saints." But as she looked at Zé, her annoyance seemed to fade. "There's rice with coconut, too, and of course there's a good sauce of *malaqueta* peppers."

"Master Antonio may have saved my back." Zé grinned. "But I can tell it's you, Sia Cleonice, who's going to save my stomach!"

The food was even more delectable than that Dona Alisa had served. Cleonice and her daughter, Chalita, a slim, pale, golden girl with tawny hair and eyes, brought in hot dishes and took away empty ones till Renata couldn't believe so many delicious things could come out of one kitchen. To soak up delectable sauces, there were spongy-moist tapioca cakes, and Chalita kept a small silver cup filled for Renata with sweet cane juice.

Master Antonio sat at one end of the table with his back to everyone except Januario, who fed him with the deftness of long practice. The household was joined late at the big rosewood table by a young white man whom Master Antonio introduced as his brother, Father Manoel. The pale dark-eyed priest nodded to Zé, spoke kindly to Renata, inquired after the works his brother had just completed for a chapel in a small town to the north, and launched into an account of what had happened during the sculptor's absence.

"I don't know how much longer we'll have this barbarity of exposing heads on posts till they rot away," he said. "Or nailing up some poor soul's bloody quarters in different towns as a warning. You had a kindness for Tiradentes, brother, so I'm glad you weren't here when the dragoons brought home his head. The windows were decked with tapestries and silks just as if for a celebration, and everybody had to watch and shout vivas for the queen as the head was thrust on a pole on the northeast corner of the Rua Direita at the main square. Tiradentes' brother, who's a priest, tried to turn away—the head had already started to decay, though it had been carried in a cask of salt—but he was forced to stand there and later, like everyone else, he had to attend services praising God for punishing treason and preserving the queen."

"There were such services all over Minas Gerais," Master Antonio said quietly. "All the same, I've heard that when he was hanged, the crowd gave 60,000 *reis* to buy masses for his soul." He gestured to Cleonice. "The little one's about to drowse off in her pudding. You'd best take her up to bed."

Renata slid off the high cane stool that had been found for her. Her father had taught her that it was mannerly not only to ask for his blessing at night but also to request that

of any of their rare visitors. She moved over to the sculptor
and knelt at his feet. "Your blessing, Master Antonio."

Too late, she realized her error. *He had no hands to
place upon her head.* But after a moment something rested
on her curls. "Bless you, child. May you be happy with
us."

A tear dropped from beneath the hood to her hand. She
swore then, in the depths of her being, never to leave him
so long as he might need her.

For a time when she went to market with Cleonice and
Chalita or to church with Master Antonio or the more distant church of Santa Efigenia with Zé, Renata felt pressed
in upon by walls and buildings and was afraid of getting
lost if the hustling crowds swept her away from her grown-
ups. Her heart leaped into her mouth anytime dragoons
trotted by, though Chalita flirted perkily with the handsomely uniformed horsemen.

When obliged to cross the main square, she averted her
eyes from the white-haired skull-mask to which bits of
leathery skin still clung. How could people do such things
to each other?

One day the head was gone. "The governor can't find
out who took it," Januario said. "They say he's furious
because someone may give it honorable burial."

Maurício's habitual scowl deepened. "You can't marvel
at that when the tooth-puller was the one who was supposed to kill the governor."

"Plenty would like to," said Cleonice. "They say he's
had the great hall of the palace divided into eighteen rooms
in which he eats or sleeps at random so that no one can
know where he's going to be found."

"God will find him," Master Antonio said. Renata
thought she saw his eyes flash in the shadowy hood. "And
may God give that poor head a fitting tomb and eternal
peace to that brave man's soul."

Even Maurício murmured amen.

III

Aleijadinho

Renata still cried for her father sometimes or would awake expecting to see him on the cowhide next to hers, but life in Master Antonio's house was so pleasant and busy that each day it became more and more the reality while the hut-cave and barren beauty of sandstone ranges became places roamed only in dreams. She no longer made up conversations with Trisavò Flor or Rachel. Cleonice had an endless store of songs and exciting tales of phantoms who haunted mines and roads, and true stories of Henrique Diaz, the black commander who'd helped drive out the Dutch, and of Zumbi, lord of Palmares.

Ouro Prêto had its own memories, and Master Antonio figured in many of them. He seemed to get deep satisfaction in pointing out to Renata his works that beautified all parts of the city.

"This is one of my early commissions," he said as she drank clear cool water from a three-spouted fountain from which a beautiful woman's upper body, shoulders and half-naked bosom curved softly. "I've always liked it. While we're this close, we might as well go up to Santa Efigenia."

It was a steep trudge up the hill, but from the top Master Antonio pointed out the charred ruins on the opposite Hill of the Burning where earlier conspirators had dreamed of liberty from Portugal.

The bearers set the litter down inside the church and went to pray while Master Antonio pointed out Saint Francis, whose gaunt lifelike features he had chiseled in soapstone, and an image of Our Lady of the Rosary.

"This is my favorite church," he said softly. "Chico

220

Rei engaged my father to design it, and I helped with the plans. Many's the feast day when I've come here to dance with Chico Rei and his people."

"Who was Chico Rei?" Renata whispered, admiring the black ink drawings in the chancel showing dancers and lovers, hunters and soldiers and musicians, all dressed in modern fashion.

"Cleonice hasn't told you? Oh, well, she's from Bahia. Chico Rei was an African king who was captured by slavers. His wife and all their children save a son died on the way to Brazil, but Chico was determined to be free again. So he worked on Sundays and holidays, saving his earnings as slaves are allowed to do, and bought his son free, then himself. The two of them saved the price of a fellow tribesman and then there were three of them to earn purchase prices till all Chico's people were free."

"What a good thing to do!"

"That wasn't all. Chico's band pooled their wages and bought a gold mine, the Encarndideira. From it, they got the gold to build Santa Efigenia. Chico was a handsome, stately man, and it was something to watch him with his second wife and their children dressed all in their finest for saints' days and dancing to the same instruments and chants they'd had in Africa."

"Do they still dance?"

"Yes, though Chico's gone. You'll have to get Cleonice to bring you to a celebration."

On another day they ascended the hill to the main square and visited the Church of Saint Francis of Assisi, for which Master Antonio had drawn the plans, sculpted the wondrous soapstone portal with its medallions of the Virgin, Saint Francis and Christ, the fountain for the sacristy, the images of the Holy Trinity of the high altars as well as the work on the pulpits and in the chancel.

"How could you do it all?" Renata marveled, making bold to touch the chubby knee of an angel. "If you worked every day for lots and lots of years, I still don't see how you got through with it and had time to do anything else."

"Ah, child, I began this in 1766. I was thirty-six, at the height of my powers." The sculptor sighed. "I loved my work, but I loved living, too. I have not always been as I am now. This evil came upon me when I was forty-five. Seventeen years ago. Now work is all I have. Work and a fire that eats like quicklime at my bones.''

It was the first time he had spoken of his affliction. Renata ached for him. She picked up the limp sleeve and pressed it to her face. ''You make such beauty, Master Antonio, and it's real. The saints and Virgins look just like people we meet on the street, and poor Jesus—I want to help him carry his cross.''

''Do you?'' asked the man who was known as the Aleijadinho, the Little Cripple. ''I am glad.''

He signaled the bearers who carried him past the municipal palace, which was far from finished, though the city council met here and the jail was on the ground floor.

''Did you know that one of my saints was imprisoned there?'' chuckled Master Antonio as Renata trotted beside the litter. ''The governor asked me to make a Saint George who could sit a horse for feast-day processions. This was simple enough, and I had the saint done for the Corpus Christi celebration. Unfortunately, the horse stumbled and the saint fell forward and drove his spear into the back of the slave who'd been leading the horse. So Saint George went to jail for the murder, though I think it was rather the fault of the horse.''

Had he told that story to divert Renata's attention from the place where Tiradentes' head had been displayed? They passed the governor's palace and descended the hill where they paused near a magnificent two-story building which Master Antonio said was the House of the Exchequer, the Casa dos Contos.

''This is where the poet-magistrate Claudio da Costa was imprisoned when the conspirators were arrested. It was put about that he committed suicide after opening a vein to write a verse on the wall with his own blood, but it seems sure that soldiers strangled him on the governor's orders and buried him hastily in unconsecrated ground. A brave priest exhumed the body and buried it in the High Chapel of Our Lady of the Pillar.''

Renata and the bearers drank from the magnificent fountain across from the Casa dos Contos, and they proceeded down the streets of shops and taverns which led into a section of impressive mansions, some with glass windows and all with shutters or intricate grillwork. They passed another fountain and approached a church.

"The Brotherhood of the Rosary of Our Lady of the Blacks built this church," said Master Antonio as they passed between the leering gargoyles on the front. "I did the head of Saint Helena there on the first altar to your right, and Maurício did the rest of the statue. A half-brother of mine carved black Saint Benedict and Saint Anthony. Don't you think it's amusing that a Portuguese should sculpt Negro saints while I, a mulatto, did the Emperor Constantine's mother?"

This church was not as lavishly adorned as the others Renata had seen in the city. Its altar columns were painted, not carved, and it lacked the dazzle of jewels and gilding, but it acquired glory for Renata when Januario said proudly, "Most of the brotherhood are slaves in the mines, little mistress. On Our Lady's feast day, they were allowed to fill their hair with gold dust and then wash it out in the fountain. That's how they raised money for the church."

"They'd never have had one otherwise," grunted his master. "The Crown collects tithes to build churches and keep them in repair, but the money's seldom used for that, though the clergy are paid stingily with a fraction of the collected sums. Most churches in Minas Gerais were built by brotherhoods and are maintained by them, too."

Later, as they descended into the gold-seekers' settlement which had begun the city, the old *bandeirante* camp of Antonio Dias, Renata gazed across tiled or thatched roofs stretching below and at houses built along the hills, and white gleam of churches and chapels against green slopes or blue skies. Vines wreathed arches leading into courtyards and violets sprang from mossy grass that grew in chinks of the stones that walled embankments.

"I think this must be the most beautiful city in the world!" She sighed happily. "Don't you love it, Master Antonio?"

The heavy shoulders seemed to tense. "Love it?" he said slowly. "I don't know, little one. But it is my city." He added under his breath, "Even if I am mulatto leper, born a slave of a slave mother!"

* * *

Cleonice explained that rancorous whisper when Renata timidly asked about it. "Master Antonio's mother, Izabel, was his father's slave, but he set her free, and Master Antonio was freed when he was baptized, so he certainly can't remember being a slave." Cleonice herself had been freed in the will of the elderly Bahian master to whom she'd borne Chalita. "Senhor Manoel Lisboa married a white lady, the mother of Father Manoel, when Master Antonio was eight years old. He loves his brother and even paid the cost of his becoming a priest, but the master's always felt cursed in his birth, which bars him from many honors."

"Does he have leprosy?"

"Some think so. Other doctors call it syphilis." At Renata's frown, she added bluntly, "That's a sickness got from sleeping with the wrong people. In Bahia the young masters usually had it by the time they took first communion. Poor little devils, they thought it proved them men."

Another adult mystery. Renata grated corn for the thin crisp cakes Cleonice was making. "Things are better for mulattos now," Cleonice went on thoughtfully. "Even though they're not supposed to hold government posts, some do, provided they're pale enough to and their fathers made them wealthy. Once they couldn't be clergy, but the first bishop of Mariana ordained many of them. I doubt if there's a single old family of Bahia and Pernambuco that doesn't have a good dash of Negro blood. Plenty of them have a dark, kinky-haired baby or two they keep out of sight, or aunts and uncles they'd rather no one met."

"Did Master Antonio's father teach him to make statues and things?"

"He surely did, Master Antonio studied with the finest artists and builders in Brazil and got to work on many of his father's commissions." She gave her immaculate turban an emphatic shake. "It's not been all bad, being Senhor Manoel's son. Master Antonio bears him a grudge, but he loves him too."

Renata liked to help with the cooking and enjoyed tending the pinks, roses, gladiolas, violets and heliotrope that grew in the court. It was exciting to go around the market stalls and watch Cleonice test mangoes, guavas, papayas, cashew fruit, quinces, genipap and breadfruit for ripeness, select plump green corn ears, onions, yams, okra, and peppers. There were the round white cheeses for which the captaincy was famous, piles of coconuts, baskets of peanuts, Brazil nuts and cashews. The mounds of different colors and shapes were as much a feast to the eye as the candied pumpkin, sugarcane rolls, spicy stews and *canjica* were a delight to the taste.

One trip to the butcher shop, even though it was handsomely designed by Master Antonio, put Renata off meat for weeks. Only gradually could she taste *xin-xin* without seeing a plucked hen dangling by the legs, or eat pork in the almost daily beans without envisioning a flayed pig's corpse. Cleonice, after that, left her home when buying meat or fish.

When Cleonice didn't need her, Renata went to the workshop. Master Antonio would be seated on a leather cushion or kneeling at his work, deftly manipulating the chisels strapped to his wrists, thumbs and stubs of forefingers. It was amazing to watch him refine the expression of a mouth or shape the retina of an eye.

Januario and Maurício roughed out the work and usually did the robes and less important figures in a panel or group. They also made fine furniture especially ordered by the wealthy, and Zé soon regained and improved his skills, though he ruefully admitted that in such company he'd never dare attempt to carve more than basic forms or simplest backgrounds.

It was particularly fascinating to watch the master chip and pare at the pearly sandstone, which came in all shadings of green to gray. "Is that rock as easy to cut as you make it look?" she asked one day as he traced in the curling locks of a young angel.

"Soapstone sculpts well, but it stands up to time and weather. Would you like to try it?"

She nodded shyly. He was always kind to her, but she dimly sensed that he was more than human, both in his genius and in his suffering. "This angel needs feathers. Take that smallest chisel and make some lines here on the wing. Sweepy ones that follow the curve."

Renata shrank. "Oh, I might ruin it!"

Master Antonio snorted. "Now wouldn't I be a fine craftsman if I couldn't blend your lines into feathers? Take courage, *filha!*" It was the first time he had called her "daughter." "Make the angel fly."

Holding her breath, she barely scratched at first, but with Master Antonio's encouragement she finally made several straggly lines in the softly lustrous stone.

"Very good." The sculptor edged his chisel, grooving over lines, going back to work in graceful feathering. In a short time her hesitant marks were transformed into a bold quill. From the sound of his voice, she was sure that, under his hood, the master was smiling. "Now, my Renata, when you see this angel in the Church of Saint Francis, you'll know you gave him his first feather. Is there anything you'd like to make?"

She thought of her father's grave, lonely beneath the cliffs. Someday she wanted to go back, put some kind of marker on the flat stone. Her mother was buried beneath the floor of a chapel near Tijuco, but Renata wished her parents could be together. If she made an image— It would look like a madonna to any passerby, but Renata would feel she had reunited her parents as much as she could on this earth.

So she said, "Master Antonio, I want to carve a lady."

It wasn't that easy, of course. Master Antonio and the others showed her how to work with the grain of the wood, but she labored many hours before she turned a scrap of myrtle into a dove that was faintly recognizable beside its model, one that Januario had resting on Noah's outstretched hand. She rubbed it to a mellow glow with an old cloth and shyly offered it to the master.

"Would you like it? It's not very good, the beak's too thick and I didn't make any legs and—"

He held it with his chisels, turning it for the blessing of the light. "It's a beautiful dove. I'll be proud to keep it." Next morning, when she was helping Chalita make beds, she saw the bird was in the niche close by the master's pillow where he kept the *cachaça* that helped him sleep.

She next carved a lamb like the one lying by the manger Zé was finishing; a plump whale inspired by one pursuing

Jonah on the panel Master Antonio was making; and a sort of tree on which Chalita could hang her chains and bracelets and keep them untangled.

By that time she was using the little knife with enough assurance to try shaping features at the top of pieces of wood that had the rough form of humans. "Noses are the hardest part," she lamented to Master Antonio after ruining several otherwise rather good faces. "When I try to get them the right size, they get sliced off or go crooked!"

He chuckled and said, "You must think ears are difficult, too, little one. None of your people have them."

She blushed. "Isn't it all right to cover them up with hair or veils?"

"Perfectly. Why don't you try this thinnest blade for the noses? Take care, though. Wood noses don't bleed, but your fingers can."

The smaller tool helped, but she decided that what with ears, noses and hands, after she'd made the figure for her father, she would stick to animals, birds and simple things.

The nose she did best was that of Marilia de Seixas, a slender, fair-skinned young woman with tragic dark eyes who also attended Our Lady of the Conception. She was beloved of Tomaz Gonzaga, a poet and justice who had been a leader in the conspiracy. His death sentence had been changed to exile.

"Poor Don' Marilia," Chalita whispered to Renata, gazing sympathetically at the black-clad girl. "She asked leave to follow her lover, but it wasn't granted, and now they do say that Senhor Gonzaga has married a rich lady who nursed him through a sickness he took when he first reached Mozambique." She sighed. "But the poetry he wrote for Don' Marilia! I heard Father Manoel read it once to Master Antonio. All about how seeing her made his blood run cold, changed the color of his cheeks and tied his tongue. Gave him shakes, too. Oh, it must be grand to have a fine gentleman that much in love with you!"

"It sounds more like he had a fever," Renata observed, but she thought Marilia as lovely as a flower, and it was her sweet, sad face that she envisioned as she tried to create her mother's image.

This was of soapstone, pale blue-gray the shade of mist

at twilight. She had practiced with scraps till she could shape the substance, enjoying the feel of the wonderfully smooth surface. When she told Master Antonio what she was making and why, he had been silent a long time before he selected the most beautiful piece of stone in the workshop and himself roughed it to human shape.

"Let your hands do with it the best they can," he said gruffly.

She knew what he meant. Her hands had learned things from wood and stone that she had no conscious control over. Sometimes when she intended to carve one thing, another shape would insist on coming out of the wood or rock, shaping itself along grain and shadings. The master's touch had seemed to send his spirit into the stone, guiding her knife now as it formed the gentle mouth, long throat, broad forehead; refined the graceful sweep of robe and veil Master Antonio had already indicated.

It took her many hours over many days, and she put it aside well before Christmas in order to carve *pau d'arco* into beads for Chalita and Cleonice and to help them sew fine shirts for each of the men. These gifts and others were bestowed on the Day of the Three Kings, twelve days after the household went together to hear Christ's mass.

Zé and Gabriel had always seen that the kings left Renata sweetmeats and a gift, but she was overcome at the array heaped on the windowsill of the upstairs room she shared with the women: a mirror from Zé in a frame of carved birds; a flame-red dress from Cleonice and Chalita; a doll of jointed wood from Januario, dressed by the women and pillowed in a cradle from Maurício. She wept with joy and gratitude, more for the loving revealed by them than for the gifts, but nothing could express her marvel at Master Antonio's present.

It was an oratory, but she had confided to the master once that crucifixes made her sad, so the central arched recess held not a cross, but a flowering tree with Jesus in his mother's arms, reaching for a blossom. In one of the hinged side panels was the stable. Cow, donkey, sheep, doves and a cock admired the baby, while from behind the manger peered a curious wolf, jaguar and deer. On the other side paraded haughty camels bearing the three kings and several shepherds carrying lambs in their arms.

She ran down to kneel with her head against Master Antonio's knee, thanking him in broken words. "It's too wonderful! The donkey looks ready to bray and the deer's so pretty and the camels are so proud they won't even look at the little lambs! And that kind, happy tree!"

He patted her shoulder with his stump. "I'm sure the Lord will be glad to let you play with his animals, dear one—and my best present is knowing how you like them. Janu and Maurício helped me, so you must thank them, too."

She did, and even Maurício smiled, and Cleonice brought in sponge cake, milk-rice, corn fritters with preserves and wild cherry cordial. Renata, cuddling her doll, savored each mouthful of the delicious repast. The ruby-red cordial warmed her stomach and turned her drowsy. Snuggled against the good cinnamon smell of Cleonice's soft bosom, her eyelids kept drooping. Her last thought was that if only her father were here, it would be better than heaven.

As seasons and holy days passed, it began to seem to Renata as if she never lived anywhere other than in the red-tiled house on Rua Antonio Dias in sight of the belfries of the church which must have stood near the chapel in which Trisavó Flor had prayed and met her own dear love.

Renata had learned the city in many ways, marketing with Cleonice and Chalita, stopping with them to visit with tailors, shoemakers and artisans who worked near the large open window-doors of their shops; accompanying Master Antonio as he was borne about in his litter, sometimes to the governor's palace to discuss some princely commission, sometimes to a poor thatched dwelling whose owner had somehow scraped together the price of a medallion of a name saint or memorial for a loved one; or going with Zé and Janu (for Janu also wore that iron armband that marked him a devotee of Ogun) to attend the dancing and feast at Santa Efigenia after standing between Cleonice and the master's litter to watch Saint George ride in procession to celebrate his day while a dragon gamboled before him and the important personages of the city followed, bearing candles.

The saint was the same as Ogun in Minas Gerais and the South, explained Zé, though in Bahia he was Saint Anthony. Just to make sure he didn't offend his patron, he also made offerings on Saint Anthony's feast day, wearing his green mantle, carrying a cock or goat to the old priestess who lived in a hut not far from Saint Efigenia's church. Renata did not go with her friend then, for he had told her the creatures would be sacrificed to feed the God of Warriors and Iron.

One Saint John's feast Chalita didn't come home till dawning, and a few weeks later she was married in church to a handsome young Portuguese muleteer who was fast acquiring his own string of pack mules. Cleonice prepared a feast, paid for by Master Antonio, that was long remembered, and before a year was out, he was godfather to a dark-eyed beautiful baby with skin of palest gold. Chalita lived only a few minutes away and brought her son almost daily to her old home. Renata loved to play with him, carry him about on her hip and sing to him. She would have a baby, too, someday—maybe a lot of them—and Master Antonio would be godfather to the first boy, who would also be named Gabriel for her father; and there must be at least one little girl to carry her mother's name and those of Trisavô Flor and Rachel.

She had finished the statue of her mother. The gentle color of mountain haze, it stood in a niche by Renata's bed. Zé, who knew what it was for, had offered to take it to the grave beneath the cliff, but Renata was afraid for him to enter the forbidden Diamond District.

Maybe someday she could send it by someone trustworthy or, when she was older, somehow contrive to take it herself. Meanwhile, it reminded her of the sandstone shape on the river that she had so often turned into one of the women of her family. She felt protected by it as she fell asleep.

IV

Congonhas

It was rare for Master Antonio to be excited about a commission. Sabara, Mariana, São João del Rei, all the gold-enriched cities of Minas Gerais, had paid handsomely for him to beautify their churches. In Brazil, in South America, possibly even in Europe, there was no one who equaled him as a sculptor. The pain that gnawed at his body and robbed him of former delights drove him to work hours that exhausted his strong helpers. He sent them to bed while he worked on by the light of a lamp or candle.

Renata was often the only one who could get him to stop long enough to eat. He would not let her see his whole face, but he allowed her to hold up his hood and put spoonfuls of mashed food or soup into his toothless mouth. And now, if the men were asleep when the master finally crept in from the workshop, Renata napped downstairs till she had unfastened the tools from his maimed hands that could still work miracles in wood and stone.

"You do not find me frightful, little one?" he had asked when she first desired to serve him. The dark eyes shadowed by the hood watched her closely as she undid the straps from what was left of his hands.

"How should I? You make the most beautiful things in all the world, and you have been my father."

After that, he never demurred but accepted her help as part of what enabled him to go on creating altars, images, medallions, work after marvelous work. It was in 1796, when Renata was nine years old, that he received an offer that challenged even his genius.

A deputation from the wealthy Brotherhood of the Good Jesus of Matosinhos in Congonhas do Campo came to ask him to undertake a task that would have been a lifetime's work for most artists. Vast sums had already been paid to famous sculptors and painters to ornament the interior. This work was splendid; but what would make the church unique among the magnificent ones built with the gold and diamonds of the province would be six chapels built on the slope of a terrace below the church, each one devoted to a station of the Way of the Cross.

"It is our brotherhood's fervent wish, Senhor Antonio, that you conceive and execute the figures for these chapels." Dário Carneiro Ferraz wore diamonds on his fingers, a fichu of finest lace spilling from his satin waistcoat and a dark green velvet coat with gold buttons. His elegant tricorne was held up on one side by a diamond pin, and the buckles of his shoes flashed more of the stones. Renata couldn't guess how old he was. The long face with its proud-arched nose was smooth olive, but unlike the three older men in the group, he didn't wear a periwig or powder. It was his own thick silver-white hair that was clubbed at the back of his head and tied with a dark green ribbon. Though his tone was courteous, almost deferential, the slightest curl of full lips and something in the dark-lashed eyes of a brilliant silver hue made Renata feel that he wondered how a crippled mulatto leper could have powers worth his seeking.

"Does the project interest you?" Senhor Dário concluded. "We are empowered by the brotherhood to negotiate a generous payment."

"Will I be free to plan and work without interference?"

"Indeed, Senhor Antonio, that is why we have come to you. We want sculpture as fine as that at the pilgrimage churches of Portugal."

"Ah. Like the Court of the Kings at Our Lady of the Remedies outside Lamego, where chapels are set on a granite staircase and the Israelite kings who were forebears of the Blessed Virgin stand in a courtyard. Or the religious gardens popular in the province of Minho?"

Ferraz had a charming smile. "You take my meaning precisely, senhor. Since many of us are from Minho, we wish for the majesty of, for instance, Bom Jesus do Monte, outside Braga. Yet we don't want a copy. The glory of the old must be transformed with Brazil's vigor.''

"And I, a mulatto, barred by law from most offices and honors, am, in the distinguished senhores' judgment, best qualified to achieve this fusion?''

"We would not have come here else," rapped out a portly red-cheeked member of the brotherhood. "God bestows his gifts as He will. If we don't question His choices, neither should you.''

"The noble senhor will pardon me." The sculptor used the obsequious tone that showed his contempt for someone. "I merely find it strange that God has less discrimination than earthly officials.''

"We acknowledge your talents and are prepared to pay for them," cut in Ferraz. "What say you, Senhor Antonio? Will you come to Congonhas?''

His crystalline eyes moved beyond Master Antonio's hunched form, widened and seemed to plunge into Renata. She felt stabbed by a slim glitter of ice. Her heart pounded. A cry almost broke from her lips.

He smiled at her.

Renata stumbled as she backed through the door and fled to the workshop. Nothing, not even the heap of dead dragoons or Tiradentes' bleaching head, had ever frightened her as much as whatever it was she had glimpsed in that smooth face and silver gaze.

Six weeks later, Master Antonio had finished his outstanding commissions, the house was rented, Cleonice and Renata had made tearful good-byes to Chalita, her little son and new baby, and the household prepared to journey to Congonhas do Campo, about forty miles away. Pack mules hired from Chalita's husband, Vaz Asturias, were loaded with tools, clothing and household items it was deemed cheaper to carry than replace.

Renata left her doll for Chalita's little daughter, but Zé carefully packed the oratory for her as well as the soapstone figure she must one day get to the Diamond District. Master Antonio had her dowry bag concealed in his clothing.

"I doubt if the most vigilant dragoon will care to investigate me," he said wryly. "But carrying rough diamonds is still against the law. Perhaps we should get these cut, little one, so that you will have a less dangerous treasure. I'll seek out a discreet merchant once we're settled in Congonhas.''

He also directed that a rosewood box be handed into the litter. It must, thought Renata, contain something precious. Perhaps his gold?

At last the small caravan was ready to go. Though the bearers and Zé were prohibited from carrying so much as a staff, the muleteers wore knives and carried staves while Vaz had pistols and a sword.

Cleonice rode sideways on a small mule she almost covered with her voluminous skirts. Renata walked beside Zé. It seemed unreal to be leaving Ouro Prêto, but it wasn't forever, and besides, the people she cared about were with her, except for Chalita and her children.

She was excited about Master Antonio's task at Matosinhos, glad that he was caught up in planning it. He was nearing seventy and was besides consumed by a relentless affliction. If he could not lose his pain in creating works into which he could throw his whole being, Renata feared he would die like a flame that had devoured wick and oil.

The winding hilly road was difficult. Master Antonio instructed Januario, Maurício and the other bearers to stop when they were tired for a rest. Even with such halts, Renata's feet were sore and her legs ached when they stopped at a farm for the night. The owner was a Paulista friend of Vaz's and spread a generous meal, though Master Antonio preferred to have broth and mush in the big storeroom that had been converted, with cowhide cots, into quarters for all the party except the muleteers, who slept in the stable.

They spent the next night in a deserted hut in a small mining settlement. "If we push," said Vaz, sipping coffee sweetened almost syrup-thick with sugar, "we should be at Congonhas by nightfall."

"Good," said Master Antonio. "I've done all the planning I can till I see the actual location."

The mules seemed to sense from the men that the trip would soon be over and moved faster. Renata's sore muscles loosened and she found herself enjoying vistas that showed through gaps or valleys in the nearer hills, distant peaks and ranges muted to a dreamy blue-green except where rock showed its bones. Sertão, Trisavò Flor's redoubtable father, might very well have marched this way, before there were ranches and farms and mines pitting the hillsides where the search for gold had been carried once the easy findings had been washed from the streams and banks.

They had met few travelers: *faiscadores,* roving prospectors with loaded mules; farmers bound for market; a few sedan chairs or litters carried by liveried slaves; an occasional horseman. It was late morning when a muffled sound of hoofs grew louder behind them.

Glancing back, Zé muttered, "Dragoons!"

Renata's heart began to pound. She tried to draw comfort from remembering the lieutenant who had deferred to Master Antonio when the sculptor had protected her and Zé, but she had never gotten over her dread of the mounted soldiers who had killed her father.

The dragoons dashed past, then spun their mounts in a whirl of yellow dust. The heavy-jawed commander threw up his arm. Sun spilled from the fringed epaulets of his red-piped blue coat. Even in her fear Renata noticed that a heavily armed bush-captain's group had halted some distance behind, fanned around a pack train.

Gold, perhaps, being taken to Rio de Janeiro for shipment to Portugal? Or the mules might carry the Crown's diamonds, which were once a year transported to the coast under heavy guard.

"Who are you and what's your business?" demanded the officer, flicking back the curtains of the litter with his quirt. "They told me at the settlement that a mulatto leper was being carried about like a lord."

"I am Antonio Francisco de Lisboa, Captain, and I am on my way to sculpt figures for the church of Matosinhos at Congonhas do Campo."

"Surely you've heard of Senhor Antonio," put in Vaz. "We're transporting his tools and belongings from Ouro Prêto, since the commission at Congonhas will take some years."

The officer sneered. "I have lately arrived from Portugal, and I beg leave to doubt that a mulatto can be much of an artist. I think we must have a look in those packs, which could conceal much gold or many diamonds."

Vaz turned and in a voice of smothered fury bade the men to take off the packs and open them. It took an hour for the dragoons to paw through Cleonice's snowy linens, carefully folded clothes and bedding, tools, paints, brushes, pots and dishes, leaving a careless jumble.

Angry at the fruitless search, the square-faced officer strode over to the litter. "Now why didn't I think of that! What better place to hide contraband but in a leper's chair? Come out of there, senhor sculptor! On your feet!"

"Captain, I cannot stand."

"Why can you not?"

"I have no feet."

"Crawl, then."

Hate for the sneering officer welled over Renata's fear. She ran from behind Cleonice and assailed the commander, kicking at the high boots, beating him with her fists. "Leave Master Antonio alone, you bully!" She added some other names she'd heard in street or market brawls.

"*Filha!*" cried the master.

She scarcely heard him. The dragoon grabbed her arms. She sank her teeth in his thumb. He let her go with a curse and slap that spun her into Zé.

"Stop it, zinha!" Zé hissed. "You'll make things worse."

"The brat needs a drubbing," growled the captain, shaking blood from his hand. "All right, *pardo!* Out of that litter!"

"The captain cannot mean that." The pleasant voice behind him came from a masked horseman, who nudged his big gray horse forward. "If he considers, I am sure he will find he respects the greatest artist of Brazil and Portugal. He will wish to apologize for inconveniencing him."

The officer's hand moved for his pistol, but the stranger's weapon was already pointing. So were the shotguns and pistols of a dozen or more of the bush-militia who had lounged up to watch the dragoons harass the travelers. Each one had a dragoon in point-blank range.

The dark black hair of the leader blew across the white silk mask. Through slits, eyes the color of the black diamond in Renata's bag fixed on the officer till the man paled and dropped his hand.

"What is this?" The captain faced toward the *capitão-do-mato*, a hulking *mameluco* who looked more ruffianly than any of his band of other mixed bloods, Indians and blacks. "I don't take kindly to jokes!"

"Oh, I don't joke with one who has no sense of humor, Captain," said the man on the gray horse. "As soon as you've begged Senhor Antonio's pardon, my friends and I will get to our business of relieving you of your onerous escort duties."

"The Crown's diamonds—"

"Are going for a change to people who need them—after of course, the worthy *capitão-do-mato* is paid for his work."

The officer glared at the sallow bush-captain. "You'll hang on a high gallows for this, Antonil!"

The *mameluco* grinned and spat tobacco at the dragoon's boot. "You'll have to catch us first, your honor, and we both know how much chance you have of doing that."

"I'll hire another gang of savages to track you!"

Antonil cocked a bushy eyebrow at the horseman. "Shall we just slice their throats, sir? Save a lot of trouble."

"Yes, but it'll be more interesting to see how the captain explains this to his superiors." The leader chuckled. "Truss up your fine dragoons, lads, and throw such of their weapons as you don't fancy into the gorge yonder." His tone hardened. "Captain, you have one last chance to apologize for abusing an honest citizen."

"An Alves de Castro humiliate himself before a yellow cripple? You can kill me, but—"

The sword flashed out of the highwayman's scabbard. "I won't kill you, my proud dragoon. I'll cut your hamstrings and you'll be a cripple, too."

He wheeled the gray and bent in the saddle, drawing back the sword. "Wait!" The captain moved sullenly toward the litter. "I regret what has happened, Senhor Antonio."

"I'm sure you do," returned the sculptor with a hint of amusement. He called to his rescuer, "May God protect you, senhor! With your recklessness, you will need it. Thank you for your succor.''

"Ah, Master Antonio, I must thank you for beautifying the churches of Minas Gerais. The treasure you create will last after diamonds and gold are gone.'' He laughed gaily. "You will excuse me, though, if today I make off with the Crown's diamonds rather than converse with you. Antonil! Don't forget the captain here, and be sure his wrists are tied snugly to his ankles.''

As these orders were obeyed, the horseman swooped Renata up before him on the saddle. "Give me a kiss, sweetheart! Such fierceness in one so pretty! Your lover will be lucky or in deep trouble. I wish I could know you when you're grown, but I'll be hanged by then.''

The steel-colored eyes danced. His arms were strong and he smelled like wild thyme. Renata threw her arms about his neck. "Don't be hanged!'' she pleaded. "I—I want to know you when I've grown up, too!''

His breath caught in with surprise before he chuckled. "Well then, my little love, give me that kiss!''

He lifted the edge of the mask. She glimpsed a strong clefted chin, lean high cheekbones, a smiling mouth. Lifting in the saddle, she kissed his lips. His arms tightened and he lifted her down.

"Go with God, *menina*. I won't forget your sweetness. Pray for me sometimes.''

He gave swift orders. In a few minutes the dragoons were piled like discarded baggage along the road. "Senhor Antonio,'' he called, "I must ask you to proceed. In case you are tempted to forgive your persecutors and release them, I'm posting a guard to make sure they stay as they are till we're safely away. I give you leave, though, to send help from Congonhas.''

"I'll see you hang!'' snarled the captain, rearing up as best he could from the ridiculous position in which he was bound.

The *capitão-do-mato* said to the masked man, "Was it up to me, sir, I'd cut their throats. No tales to tell that way.''

"I've never killed a man who didn't have a weapon in

his hand. Come, mount your men on these government horses and let's see how far we can get by sundown.''

As the litter moved off, Renata watched as the ambushers, on the dragoons' mounts, urged the pack animals off the road, striking off across a broad valley. The leader turned, rose in his stirrups and waved to her.

"Good-bye, my sweetheart.''

She waved back. Desolation closed over her as the caravan disappeared over a ridge. "They'll be caught, won't they? All those horses and the mules—''

Zé laughed and patted her shoulder. "They'll use the horses to get a distance swiftly, zinha, but then I'll bet you they sell the animals to someone who'll blot the brands, divide up the booty, split into small groups and fade into the backlands.''

"A bold stroke,'' said Master Antonio. "Our masked friend evidently arranged it with the *capitão-do-mato* who was supposed to help guard the diamonds. A wonder it doesn't happen oftener. One year's harvest of diamonds would enrich such a party far beyond what they collect in years of sniffing out runaways.''

"Some of the Vira-Saias are still robbing gold shipments,'' reminded Cleonice.

"Yes, but not as they did before the first leaders were killed,'' said Master Antonio. "In those days the organization hoped to sabotage the treasury by intercepting gold. One of the ringleaders was a Frenchman, formerly a Jesuit, who hated Portugal as an enemy of his country. He was the one who suggested the Latin texts carved on many of my works. He disappeared after the ring was shattered. The gang that robs a convoy now and then these days has no political aim. They just want money.''

What did the man on the gray horse want? His party came in sight again, distant figures threading into a narrow pass. Renata's heart squeezed with fear for him.

She remembered the strength of his arms, the clean fresh smell of him, the tender hardness of his mouth. *Oh, Blessed Mother, don't let him hang, don't waste all that in an ugly death!* If she saw his head on a pole, those black diamond eyes pecked out by birds, she'd want to die herself. She didn't know his name, she might never see him again, but she would bless and love him all her life.

In Congonhas, Zé was sent to report the diamond robbery and plight of the dragoons to a magistrate at the municipal palace and the rest of them, as arranged with the brotherhood, moved on to the house that had been rented for the sculptor at the bottom of the street that led to the magnificent church shining white on a high hill above the town.

"A smart climb, master," sighed Januario, gazing up the steeply winding road.

"Don't worry, Janu," said the master. "I've told Senhor Dário that I'll need a tent set up near the church and I'll stay there when weather allows. No use wasting time and energy in going back and forth."

"Master, you work too hard," admonished Janu. "I know you! If you're that close to your work, you'll be at it when you ought to sleep."

"But when I can't sleep, Janu?"

The helper had no answer for that but watched his beloved master with troubled eyes. Cleonice had told Renata how when Januario had first been bought, he was so horrified at the sculptor's decaying face and body that he'd plunged a knife into himself, preferring death to serving such an owner. But Master Antonio had taken the blade from the slave's body, nursed and healed him, and Januario, like ill-tempered Maurício, had long worshiped the artist whose legs and hands he had become.

For several days Renata helped Cleonice unpack and set the new house to order. Zé and Maurício slept there but went up early each morning to work in the thatched shed beside the tent at the back of the church where Master Antonio had already launched into this monumental undertaking. Janu slept at the site, too, and Renata brought up food at noon and again for supper. Janu made a pot of morning coffee and the mush that had become one of the sculptor's main foods.

Bom Jesus de Matosinhos was a beautiful church, ornamented bell towers guarding the cross above the main entrance, walls dazzling against the blue sky. It overlooked the several hundred tiled or thatched roofs of the city below, and valleys stretching off to hazy mountains.

Ceilings of nave and apse glowed with soft, luminous paintings, and the altars and carved saints and Holy Ones were the work of masters, though to Renata's eyes they lacked the gripping realism of Master Antonio's figures.

The first time she entered, she knelt and prayed for the highwayman. She had no money for candles and didn't want to beg of Master Antonio or Zé, but she felt impelled to make an offering for the black-haired leader's safety.

What did she have of value to leave at the Virgin's shrine? As she bowed her head in perplexity, the silver medal that she always wore shifted against her flesh.

Oh, but it was her dearest possession! All she had from her mother and Trisavó Flor, all she had of her family. Well then, understanding that Renata had offered her best treasure, wouldn't the Virgin preserve him if that were possible?

Renata drew off the chain, blinking back tears as she placed it at the Virgin's feet and dropped on her knees. *Lady, place your veil between him and his enemies.* She prayed till she had a feeling that her supplication had been heard.

Leaving the church then, Renata went to the tent beneath some great palms. A black horse with a jeweled saddle was there, so she knew Master Antonio had a visitor. When she saw it was Dário Ferraz, she started to slip back out, but he raised an inquiring black eyebrow. "One moment, *menina.* Aren't you going to ask my blessing?"

Reluctantly she knelt and muttered, "Your blessing, senhor."

His hand settled on her head, fingers curling deeply to compass her skull. It was a terrible feeling, as if he could crush out her mind and will. "Bless you, my child. Wait a minute and I'll give you a ride to your house."

"The senhor is gracious, but I—" She thought wildly. "I have to clean the tent and fetch water and—"

"Oh, never mind that today, *filha,*" said Master Antonio. "Janu just brought water and the tent can wait till tomorrow."

It might embarrass him with his powerful employer if

she argued. Unhappily, Renata made the cots and tidied things while Ferraz said authoritatively, "Very good, Senhor Antonio. The brotherhood approves your proposal for sixty-six figures of cedar that will occupy the Via Crucis chapels. As for your suggestion about rebuilding the terrace and designing a stairway with pedestals for the Twelve Prophets, I see much merit in it."

"Senhor, it would be like nothing else in the world, for surely the prophets foretold the coming of Our Lord. It is fitting that they herald the approach to the Way of the Cross."

Ferraz nodded his silver head before he reached for his tricorne. "I think I can convince my associates." He smiled. "I rejoice that the project has fired your imagination."

"How could it not, with such a setting?" Master Antonio's tone was fervent and rang with a passion Renata had never heard before. "If your brotherhood will allow me time and means, senhor, I will, with God's grace, create here a wonder that will awe folk to devotion as long as stone shall last."

"Well said, master! Be sure I'll make the case for your prophets as eloquently as I can." He turned to Renata and those ice-colored eyes made her shrink. "Now, *menina,* you shall have your ride."

It was no pleasure to Renata, handed up by the slave to sit behind Ferraz, having to hold to him to keep from sliding off. Since they were going down the hill and Ferraz was braced to balance weight for his horse, Renata's cheek pressed against the silk of the coat that covered the hard muscles of his back. The gold silk was smooth, but instead of enjoying the texture, she felt trapped against the cold, sleek skin of a serpent.

It was with great relief that she saw the little house at the foot of the mountain. When Ferraz didn't rein in, she cried, "Senhor, this is where I live!"

"Of course, and I'll bring you back." He glanced smilingly over his shoulder. "First we'll go to the market and buy you something good to eat and perhaps a trinket."

He laughed and she felt the vibration in his powerful

frame. "After you've had your treat. I have no daughters, *menina*. You won't deny me the enjoyment of pleasing you."

He was grown-up and rich and important. She didn't know how to argue further, but now they were on level ground, she held to the cantle of the saddle rather than to him and kept as much space between them as she could.

At the market he swung from the saddle and lifted her down himself. She hated the sensation of helplessness when he held her in the air for a moment but somehow knew protest or struggle would feed a nameless, frightening thing in him. She kept her lips set tight together. After what seemed an eternity, he put her down, frowning a trifle, studying her with curiosity.

"Well, child, let's see what you fancy."

Ordinarily, when offered such indulgence, she would have gone from the proprietor of one tray or brazier to another, sniffing strong black coffee, spicy stews, dishes like *roupas velhas,* "old clothes," mashed black beans fried with onions and shredded dried beef, or examining the sugar-dusted little cakes reposing on the snowiest of towels, set off by paper flowers and kept fresh by a covering of banana leaves. And she'd linger over a rainbow of quince and genipap and cashew candy and the crunchy *pés-de-muleque,* "black boy's feet," of manioc dough and peanuts.

Today she stood oddly shamed as the elegant gentleman selected several of the fanciest cakes while the slave bought coffee and fruit punch. Ferraz handed Renata the punch and an elongated sugary pink confection.

"I trust that eating one of these 'maiden's tongues' will loosen yours for me, my Renata," teased the silver-haired man. "How do you like Congonhas? Do you miss your playmates of Ouro Prêto?"

She gave him short answers and nibbled at the cake, which was surfeitingly sweet. A dog escaping a vendor's kick ran into her, and she let the sugary object slip from her fingers. In a trice the dog snatched it up and fled.

"A shame." The strange pale eyes flickered. "I'll have Marco get you another."

"Thank you, no, senhor," she said desperately. "Please, Cleonice will wonder where I am."

He finished his coffee and, watching her, slowly devoured the pink cake, apparently letting the bites almost dissolve in his mouth before he swallowed. Renata had the terrible feeling that he was savoring her, that those full, handsome lips roved along her body, tasting lightly here and there before broad white teeth drove into her flesh and she vanished like the cake.

But that was crazy! Lordly gentlemen didn't eat girls: only savages deep in the backlands did that. He wiped his fingers with a lace handkerchief and gave a slight lift of his wide shoulders. "I had hoped to show you the roses in my garden and some of the beautiful paintings in my house, but that had better wait till a day when you're less anxious to get home to your black mammy."

"Cleonice isn't black."

"The blood's there, which is all that matters. What of yours, child? With that honey-blond hair and your deep blue eyes, it's strange to find you guardianed by a mulatto."

Could he make trouble over that? Take her away from Master Antonio? Renata's mind raced, but she could scarcely lie about being related to the sculptor, since the master himself would deny it if questioned.

"My parents died," she said lamely. "Master Antonio took me in."

"Commendable." The fleshy lips pursed. "But now you're growing older, you should be with your own color. Otherwise you won't get a suitable husband."

"I don't want a husband, senhor."

"Not today, perhaps." His eyes touched the little hard nubs on her chest that had just lately begun to have the slight roundings she hoped would one day give her beautiful breasts like Chalita's. "But many girls marry at twelve."

She had no answer for that alarming thought, only a swift flashing memory of the highwayman, how safe and wonderful she had felt in his arms, how firm and sweet his mouth had been. She would probably never see him again, but he was the only one she would ever want to marry.

Instinctively aware that the less Ferraz knew about her the better, Renata said, "I'm going to stay with Master Antonio."

"He's an old man. An old, sick, crippled mulatto."

The epithets enraged her, though they were delivered in a tone as expressionless as those watchful eyes. "He has been my father! I love him, and as long as I can serve him, I will!"

The *fidalgo*'s gaze narrowed as she clenched her hands and glared at him, but after a moment he smiled. "I knew you were a lovely child," he murmured, almost to himself. "But there's more here than I expected—yes, enough to merit patience." His eyebrows lifted quizzically. "Shall we pick you out a necklace? Perhaps some sapphire earrings the color of your eyes? Or will you have a shawl of China silk or slippers from Córdoba?"

"I want to go home." Why did he say these frightening things, pay her so much attention, pry and probe? Helpless beside his strength and power, she was on the verge of tears.

He swept her a mocking bow. "Then you shall go, my prim little angel. But another time I shall hope to content you better."

This time, instead of riding with her behind him, he leaned over and swept her up, holding her in front of him as he sent the horse smartly pacing down the street. He hadn't the masked man's scent of fresh thyme but smelled of oppressively opulent perfume. His arms were as strong as those she remembered with such longing, but these made her feel trapped, not protected and cherished. The heavy pumping of his heart was menacing, penetrating her senses till she seemed to be unwillingly melded to his body, breathing with him, living by the same current of blood.

What was happening? If he didn't take her home, if he carried her somewhere else, could she get away? Or had he robbed her of will, of strength, could she even move without his permission?

"Why does your heart trip fast as a frightened little bird's?" he asked softly. "I want to make you happy, *menina*. You've no need to fear me."

She trembled and didn't speak, staring fixedly at the

white froth of his neckcloth. When they reached the house, he handed her to his slave. The moment she escaped him, her chilled blood coursed through her in a rush, freeing her tight lungs, her constricted breath. Cleonice was on the step. Renata fled to her.

Ferraz checked his descent from the saddle. "Good day to you, Sia Cleonice," he smiled, giving her a title of respect. "I hope you haven't worried about the child. I thought to spoil her a bit, having no young ones of my own."

"Perhaps," suggested Cleonice, face a pale yellow mask, "the noble senhor should take a wife if he desires children."

Curtsying, she put an arm around Renata and took her inside. Though she had seemed so calm, her breast was heaving. She went down on her knees, searching Renata's face. "Did he bother you, love? Touch you where he shouldn't?"

Renata had heard enough gossip between Cleonice, Chalita and other women as well as morsels picked up on the street or at feasts to know that something happened between men and women that brought the big bellies from which babies eventually came. Breasts had milk for babies, but men also liked to watch them and make remarks similar to those elicited by a well-curved bottom or swinging hips. But it was one thing to be curious about all this, to anticipate it with equal degrees of eagerness and trepidation, and another to learn that apparently these mysteries could be sampled now.

"Where shouldn't he touch me?" she asked Cleonice, deciding it was time she understood things better.

Cleonice sighed, obviously reaching the same conclusion. "Sit down here, honey. It's time we had a talk."

For several days after the explanation, Renata was uncomfortably aware that men were possessed of a potent instrument that many would want to put into her as soon as she was grown, and a few might try to do so now. She couldn't get a baby from being kissed or having a hand up her dress, but these preliminaries could lead swiftly to the

fateful act, so she had better keep herself to herself till she
was ripe to marry.

"Some men like green fruit," Cleonice had warned.
"The old master in Bahia sniffed around the *senzala* and
used to brag he'd had every maidenhead bred there barring
his own daughters'. But one of his sons was worse. He
could only take his pleasure with girls who hadn't bled.
Soon's they turned women, he didn't want them, but there
were a few caught his babies all the same—went straight
from being children to having them." Her tawny eyes
smoldered. "I was one of those. Young master freed me
and gave us a little money, but he did something to my
bones. Birthing Chalita almost killed me. I've had men
since then, God knows, but I never wanted them. I'm glad
to be in Master Antonio's house and have my bed in
peace."

Renata shuddered and put her arms around Cleonice.
"Do you think Senhor Dário might try to—well—you
know?"

"I don't know, child. A fine gentleman can buy little
slaves, and who knows what he does with them before he
sells them away, as Senhor Dário is said to do? He's had
some as pale as you. After what happened to me, I don't
trust any man who likes young girls too much." Rising,
Cleonice gave Renata a comforting hug. "Keep away from
him, *menina,* and I'll have a word with Master Antonio so
he won't send you with Senhor Dário again."

Renata mulled this information, fitting it with things that
had puzzled her before, till the shock of it faded and she
could again look at men and women as people rather than
wondering what they looked like unclothed and engaged in
motions that sounded awkward and ridiculous if not painful. The strange thing was that she shriveled when she
remembered being in Ferraz's arms. But when she thought
of the highwayman, she felt like an opening flower.

The chapel tableaux would begin with "The Last Supper" and proceed with "The Garden of Olives," "The
Arrest," "The Flagellation at the Column," "The Crowning with Thorns," "Christ Bearing His Cross," and "Cal-
vary." Working in cedar allowed clothing to flow in lighter

draperies than were possible in stone. Renata marveled at the realism of the face Master Antonio was carving for Jesus.

Flowing wavy hair and a tightly curled beard framed a sensitive long face with high cheekbones, wide-spaced eyes and a slightly cleft chin. The muscles of the throat ridged into the collarbone, and the tapering hands were perfect to the lines in the palms and the shaped fingernails.

Master Antonio would carve all the figures of Christ and do most of the other statues' heads and hands as well as add finishing touches. Renata, to her reverent delight, was permitted to work on the garments and other large expanses where any mistakes she might make could be corrected. The chapels would not be constructed till all the figures were ready. Meanwhile, the growing collection was turned over to master artists, who would paint in every eyelash with consummate skill.

Saint John's handsome features, Iscariot's hideous ones, brutal, jeering visages of Roman soldiers—all these took life from Master Antonio's crippled hands. The Saint Peter who hewed off a soldier's ear had the haughty look of an Iberian aristocrat. As Christ stumbled under a heavy cross, his agonized face that of a human in the extremes of fatigue and grief, the woman who wept for him had the sweet mouth and beautiful eyes of a young woman who came each morning to pray in the church and had several times stopped to marvel at the work in the tent.

It was endlessly fascinating to see how Master Antonio and his helpers could show the play of muscles in arms and legs, define the veins and bones that made feet and hands seem actual flesh. Members of the brotherhood frequently came to watch the progress of their commission, and none had anything but praise.

Dário Ferraz came several times a week, making the comments of a man trained to appreciate art. He never tried to carry Renata off again but occasionally brought her a gift, explaining in wistful tones to Master Antonio that he had no children of his own.

The master had been warned by Cleonice, but as time passed and the *fidalgo* made no effort to sequester her, even Renata began to wonder if she'd done him an injustice.

Even so, she didn't want the necklace of lapis lazuli he said matched her eyes, or an ivory fan, bracelets or earrings. She gave these all to beggars on the church steps, and gave to the men the candy, fruit and cakes she would have enjoyed if they'd come from anyone else.

Master Antonio had always thrown himself into his work, but now he was a man obsessed. He labored from first light to dark, grudging the times when Renata or one of the men insisted that he stop to eat. He used *cachaça* to dull the constant gnawing of his affliction at his body.

"I must make haste!" he burst out once at Januario who was begging him to rest. "How can I know how long I'll have even these stubs of thumbs and forefingers?" His helpers were in their prime and worked to the limit of their endurance, but the crippled old man was at work before and after them, and while they rested in the heat of the afternoon.

Several months had passed since their coming to Congonhas. Officials had questioned Master Antonio and the rest of them about their encounter with the dragoons and the robbery of Crown diamonds, but Ferraz and other influential members of the brotherhood made it clear that the sculptor was under their protection. Except for high connections, Captain Joaquim Alves de Castro would have been tried for negligence, if not conspiracy in the theft. As it was, he was reduced to the rank of lieutenant.

The diamonds, a veritable fortune, had vanished. The bush-captain's gang had scattered into the backlands. As for the deviser of the bold ambuscade, he was thought to be Juracy dos Santos Calvacanti, better known as Falcão, Hawk, for the swiftness of his descents and departures. His father, one of the Vira-Saias of Ouro Prêto, had been shot down by dragoons, who then tortured to death the slain man's wife and daughter to make them reveal the names of other members of the organization that had hoped to weaken Portugal by intercepting the fifths. Juracy had been abroad at the time, studying at the University of Coimbra, but after he returned to Brazil, it wasn't long till every dragoon who had helped kill his family was cornered in some lonely place, given a chance to defend himself, and skewered or shot.

That had been several years before Renata came to live with Master Antonio. Though the price on his head grew with each exploit, Juracy had never been caught. Instead of having a band, he recruited for each major swoop on the crown's gold or diamonds, divided the spoils, gave most of his share, converted to usable currency or gold dust, to the poor, and faded into the wilds to plan his next effrontery.

Juracy. A singing name. Renata treasured it, sometimes saying it aloud. *Juracy.* She made it an unformed prayer of which she dared shape only parts. *Let him come back. Let him be safe. Someday let him love me . . .*

V

Juracy

— ⸎⊙⊙⊙⊙⊙⊂ —

She was trudging up the hill with Master Antonio's supper basket when she heard a clatter of hoofs that slowed as they drew even. "You're heavy-laden, little one. Would you like a ride up the hill?"

She knew that voice! Halting, she almost dropped the basket as she cried, "Juracy! I—I mean, Senhor Juracy!"

He set a finger to his lips, those she had kissed beneath the mask. His eyes really had the transparent steel glimmer of the black diamond in her "dowry," and the cleft she remembered softened the determined chin.

"Since you know my name, sweetheart, can you forget it on the streets?"

"Yes, senhor, but—should you be here? Right in town?"

"Much safer than the hills, what with the dragoons searching for me." His eyes danced. "Anyway, I had to see what Senhor Antonio is making here. And make sure you don't forget me while you're growing up."

She blushed at his teasing and wished she had on her best indigo-dyed dress rather than this faded brown one. His laughter rippled like swift water over sun-dappled stone. "Here. Give me that basket. Then put your foot on mine. Up you come!"

He swung her to the pommel. Again, she smelled thyme and leather, the clean male scent of him. Her dream come true. She sighed with rapture as she put her arm around his neck.

"Where's your big gray horse?"

"Enjoying his pasture. I use him for my business trips. Mancha here is my town horse. One of them."

"Do you live here? Oh, I forgot! Don't tell me!"

251

He chuckled at her confusion, and the sound reverberated warmly through her, nothing like the frightening sensation she'd had of being possessed by Dário Ferraz's blood and breath. "I live where I am, sweeting. Never the same bed twice." As they reached the top of the hill and approached the tent, he said, "Unless Master Antonio and his helpers recognize me, let me be Julio Andrade, a traveling merchant."

"Are you?"

"Of course." When his smile broadened enough, a dimple showed in his cheek. "And a rancher, a *faiscador,* a gentleman of leisure. Sometimes I'm even a lawyer."

"I don't see how you keep track of who you are what with changing horses and names and beds. Do you change wives, too?"

"I'm waiting for you, remember?" His lips brushed her cheek before he sprang down and lifted her to the cobbles. He tethered the burnished chestnut and followed her into the tent.

After that, when business brought the merchant Julio Andrade to town, he stopped to watch the progress of the work, and often stayed to share a meal or coffee or *cachaça.* Renata thought that at least Zé and Master Antonio knew his identity, but they blandly called him Senhor Julio. So did she, but in her heart it was Juracy. Over and over, like a song.

He seemed to know everything that happened in the capital of Rio, and the tide of events in Europe since the king and queen of France lost their heads in 1793, the year after Tiradentes hung.

"After the Reign of Terror, Napoleon must seem a blessing to the French, but he certainly has all the rest of Europe nervous. Queen Maria's gone quite mad. She thinks the revolutionists are coming to murder her."

"She went mad the year Tiradentes was executed," said Master Antonio. "The regent doesn't seem of the stuff to defy French armies."

"João Banana?" Juracy laughed. "All that poor man wants is to chant plainsong with the monks and now and then wear the Abaeté diamond. That stone was found in the west of this captaincy by three convicts who won pardons by turning it over to the Crown. Think of it! Almost an ounce, a hundred and forty-four carats. The Braganza diamond is bigger, the size of a hen egg, but I think it's really a white topaz."

"You seem well acquainted with jewels, senhor," remarked Master Antonio.

"I deal in a little of everything."

"Do you know a discreet person who could cut some stones and hold his tongue about it?"

Juracy grinned. "My friend, everyone I deal with is discreet. I'd be happy to attend to such a matter for you."

And so Renata's trove was cut to best advantage and returned, except for the black diamond, already a double pyramid best set like that.

"You don't have any that cut to an *oitava*," said Juracy. That was the size which had won Zé's freedom. "But there are four of half that, at least sixteen vintens, or eight carats apiece, and two somewhat larger of wonderful fire. None of the other ten stones are under eight vintens."

Renata breathed on each stone, searching for imperfections, and held each up to the light. They dazzled all colors of the rainbow, flashed white brilliance. What was it Gabriel used to say? *"Each diamond has as many fires as it has facets."*

"Could you sell these?" she asked Juracy as a plan formed in her mind.

He frowned. "I'm sure I could. They should fetch a thousand English pounds in Bahia or Rio. But—"

"You've no need to sell your diamonds, *filha*," cut in Master Antonio.

Renata bowed her head. "I hoped that for some of the diamonds Senhor Julio would take that carving I made to my father's grave." Tears brimmed her eyes, though she managed to keep her voice steady.

Master Antonio looked out from his hood at Juracy. "I think the child needs to carry that gift to her father, needs to give him her love and farewell."

"But you need me here, Master Antonio!"

"We'll miss you, yes, and you must hurry, but if Senhor Julio is willing—"

"Oh, I can always do business in the Diamond District." Juracy shrugged. "I'll take you, *menina*, but not for your treasure. Zé, you'll give me directions?"

Cleonice liked Juracy, but not the idea of the prospective journey, and was only slightly reconciled when he appeared with boy's clothing. "It'll be easier for my nephew to ride astraddle," he said.

"But if you're stopped by dragoons—"

"They won't bother a boy, even if he's pretty." Juracy gave the anxious housekeeper a reassuring hug. "Don't worry, Sia Cleonice. I've roamed Minas Gerais for ten years now, and no one has ever stopped me unless I planned it that way."

She scowled. "Now, Senhor Julio, you aren't going to—"

"I'm not going to do anything but take Renata where she wants to go." Cleonice shook her head, but she sent them on their way with a pack of tasty food.

Renata had never ridden a horse before. She couldn't get enough of stroking the black pony's mane, patting his shoulder and telling him he was beautiful, clever and strong. Added to that was the miracle of being with Juracy on this pilgrimage she'd hoped for ever since she'd started the image of her mother. When she had given Juracy the figure to be stowed into one of the saddlebags, he'd turned it in his hands and whistled softly.

"You've caught some of Master Antonio's gift, *menina*. This is beautiful."

"Master Antonio picked out that pretty gray-blue stone. He helped me and so did Janu and Maurício and Zé."

"Your father will like it," said Juracy, and wrapped it in one of his fine white shirts before tucking it carefully where it could be undisturbed for the journey. In her own things, Renata had a rosary she'd carved, a gift for Dona Alisa, the kindly wife of the tavern keeper.

Juracy rode his chestnut and had powdered his black hair. As Julio Andrade, he had a passport signed by the administrator of the Diamond District allowing his entrance. He was also well armed. More than one set of rascally looking men eyed him hungrily but passed with a muttered greeting.

They never traveled after dusk and always stopped in time to eat and sleep at a ranch or settlement. Everyone knew Senhor Julio and gave him their best. If a few women were disappointed because the merchant's nephew shared his room, they still petted Renata—known for the trip as Pedrinho—and declared that such eyes and hair were wasted on a lad.

"Maybe I should cut my hair," Renata pondered. She wore it tucked up into a slouchy felt hat, but when she took this off inside a house, she always felt everyone must guess her secret.

"You'll not cut a strand of it," Juracy scolded. He twined his fingers through it. "By all the saints, though, you need untangling!"

In spite of her protests, he demanded her comb and performed the office Cleonice still did of every now and then getting out the matted snarls that hid at the back of her neck, deceptively hidden by the curling mass she could reach more easily.

The touch of the awkwardly gentle big hands reminded her of how Gabriel had used to comb her hair. So long ago. Five years now. He had been dead as many years as she had lived with him, but still that tightness ached in her throat when she realized she would never see him again. Never on this earth . . .

A tear trickled off her nose before she could dash it away. "Am I hurting you that much?" Contrition softened Juracy's voice. "Just one more bad patch, *menina,* and then we'll have that good *feijoada* and milk-rice our hostess has for us!"

To him she was a child, to be bribed with promises of good things to eat. Could she, to him, ever be anything else? Renata drew away from him, snatching the comb. "I can do my own hair!" she said, and retreated to a corner. "You—I don't go running my hands up the back of your neck to see if you have any tangles!"

His thunderstruck expression changed to amusement. "If you did, there might be a few," he admitted. "This damned powder! All right, Pedrinho, you're on your honor to keep the locks unsnarled.''

During studies at Coimbra, Juracy had met Pombal, powerful minister of the last king, who had stimulated new industries in Brazil and set up a trading company to encourage markets for raw materials. His laws had ended legal discrimination against New Christians and made it an offense to call them that.

"About time," said Juracy, "since the first donatory of Brazil, given the dyewood contract, was a New Christian.''

Pombal had also fostered intermarriage between Portuguese and Indians when earlier laws had forbidden it or barred public office to men married to Indian women. But after Pombal's fall from power, the affairs of Brazil fell to officials determined to keep the colony dependent on Portugal for manufactures and intent on wringing from it not only raw materials—hides, cotton, sugar, tobacco and indigo—but also its gold, diamonds and precious stones.

"Portugal takes from us and gives nothing but a plague of laws and officials," Juracy said. "Even so, some Brazilians have grown wealthy. Look at the Oliveiras, who had the diamond monopoly till Pombal abolished the system. The last contractor, Dr. João, so adored his mulatto mistress, Chica da Silva, that he made her hanging gardens, a great country house with furniture from Lisbon where he gave feasts, balls and theatricals for her amusement, and because Chica wished to see how ships could float on water, he designed a lake where a small ship with sails and a crew of ten could maneuver her about.''

"Really?" gasped Renata.

"Really.'' He laughed. "I knew Chica when she was still a slave, and I say 'Good for her!' The way Portuguese and Brazilians treat their women makes even Spaniards seem liberal.''

At noon they usually stopped in some shady place, removed saddles and bridles from the horses, and let them graze freely after a good rubdown, a watering and a handful of grain. "Always tend your horse before you worry about yourself," Juracy said. "Since you're a Paulista by blood, you could take one of their sayings as a motto:

'Ride slowly up the hill for the sake of your beast. Prick fast over the levels for the journey's sake, and ride gently downhill for your own sake.' "

He showed her how gold or diamonds could be concealed in whip handles or gun stocks, in false toes in boots or the stuffing of saddles. In return, she taught him tricks Zé had drilled her in, demonstrating how to secrete a small stone between her toes and walk with it or hide one in her fingers.

Juracy shook his head at this. "A fine rogue you are, with that angel face!"

During the noon rests, he read to her out of *O Caramuru,* an epic poem by José de Santa Rita Durão, which told the story of the shipwrecked sailor who was the ancestor of many living Brazilians. When he learned that Renata couldn't read beyond some Latin she had learned by rote from texts carved into Master Antonio's works, he began teaching her, scratching letters in the earth and showing her how they joined to make the words in the poem.

This was a new magic for Renata, as exciting in its way as the skill with which Master Antonio shaped form from a block of stone or wood. The other book Juracy had in his saddlebag was the poems Tomaz Gonzaga had written to his Marilia.

"I used to see Dona Marilia in church," Renata said. "I tried to make the face of my mother's statue look like hers, but of course it doesn't much, though Master Antonio fixed the nose and made the mouth better."

"Then you must have the poems," Juracy said. "And if you'll learn to read them, I'll bring you some books next time I go to Rio."

One night the only shelter they could find was under a tiled shed where muleteers already had their stew kettle hung over a tripod and the hide covers of their packs spread out for bedding. The pile of panniers, mule trappings and pack saddles gave Juracy and Renata privacy from the men, but not from the *carrapatos,* or ticks, *bichos do pé* and other attentive vermin. At the first stream they reached the next morning, they scrubbed off, washed their hair and smeared their bites and bumps with crushed leaves of wild tobacco.

Their night at a *venda* was pleasanter. Renata gazed in wonderment as she roamed amid salt bins, kegs of sugar, beans and maize, heaps of jerked meat, demijohns of rum, ropes of black tobacco curled around sticks, and an array of umbrellas, mirrors, belts, knives, clothing, guns, horseshoes, sewing needs, garlic, candles and prayer books. The storekeeper's wife gave them a meal of rice, fish and beans, which they ate while seated on boxes beside the counter, above which hung the weighing scales.

The small sleeping room was clean and the coarse cotton sheets on the cots were bleached white and soft, as were the towels on pegs above the washstand with a wood washbowl and coconut half filled with homemade soap.

Juracy's permit and a bribe got them past the customs inspector as they entered the Diamond District, and that night they stopped at the tavern of Dona Alisa and her husband, the corporal, who coaxed Juracy into a game of cards while Dona Alisa fussed over Renata as soon as she made herself known, and demanded a full accounting of all that had happened since the fugitives had stopped there.

"To think it's been five years since I waved you off in that little red dress you were so proud of!" sighed the brown-haired, rosy-cheeked woman. "And now you're the ward of Aleijadinho himself! But aren't you afraid, child, of catching his leprosy?"

"No one else has."

"Yes, but—"

"I owe him more than I can ever repay, senhora." Renata got the olivewood rosary out of her pack and put it around Dona Alisa'a plump throat, with a kiss. "And I owe you more than this."

The reunion brought back to Renata half-forgotten memories, and her sleep was nightmare-ridden. Instead of running with Zé from the dragoons, she fled with Juracy. They had almost reached the hawk-cave when Dário Ferraz stepped from behind a fallen pillar. A sword flashed in his hand, aimed at Juracy. She caught at the blade and begged. Ferraz's strange eyes glowed and became diamonds. He turned into stone. But he still lived and advanced on Juracy—

She tried to scream, could not, and woke dazedly. Juracy held her, and for a moment she thought the dream was real, tried to warn him, pointing. Ferraz's taunting granite features vanished.

"It's all right," Juracy comforted. "I'm here, *menina*. Nothing can get you." When she couldn't stop shuddering, he lay down beside her, pillowing her head on his shoulder, and told her stories until she went to sleep.

They camped that night near the river as the wind was rising, and late next evening rode up to the hut-cave, crumbled back into the soil except for the doorposts. Piles of rock had been raised over the dead dragoons, but the flat slab of white sandstone lay where Zé had placed it over Gabriel's grave.

A rush of longing for her father swept through Renata as they approached what had been her home. Tears blurred the glossy green leaves of the orange trees and the garden, where neglected maize and sugarcane still grew, raggedly harvested by birds and beasts.

Slipping down from the black pony, Renata hurried to the gravestone, pressed her cheek to it and sobbed. Along with her grief came the shock of having to struggle to recall Gabriel's face. If she forgot, who would there be to remember?

"He had blue eyes," she said to Juracy. "Sunny blue, like the fairest sky. His hair was light brown and wavy, and he was tall—as tall as you, I think."

"We'll write that all down," promised Juracy. It was as if he read her mind. "You can put down what you know about your mother, too, your Trisavò Flor and Sertão. You can give all of them to your children."

"I don't remember much."

"It's something." Half teasingly, he added, "You can write down your own adventures. After all, in time to come, you'll be an ancestress."

That was hard to imagine. But she felt less desolate as Juracy fetched the soft-colored madonna from his pack and they considered where to put it. "This is supposed to be my mother, you know," explained Renata. "She's buried in Tijuco, so I thought—" She swallowed and couldn't finish.

"I'm sure your parents both know what you're doing," Juracy said. "They're together now and happy, but your remembering must make them happier still." A catch in his voice made her remember how his family had died.

She put up her arms to him. For a long time they held each other and Renata thought she didn't weep alone.

There was a natural hollow in the side of the slab that faced the cliff. This seemed the safest place to put the figure, out of sight of any chance wanderer to that lonely place. It was a sort of burial and Juracy left Renata while she communed with unseen loving presences, drawing from them courage and a certainty that love did not end, that it lasted after death.

When she made her farewells, she found Juracy down the river and showed him the sandstone shape across the decaying trough where she had so often washed *cascalho* and made up conversations with imagined mothers and grandmothers. Then it was time to go.

The first rains fell on their journey to Congonhas, and they spent most of one day in a providential *venda* while the storm brought dead limbs crashing down and rain lashed the tiles. This *venda* had paper and ink powder, and with a sharpened goose quill Juracy showed Renata how to write her name. During the forced pause, he also wrote down most of what she could remember about her family, going back to Rachel and Raya. It gave her a good, proud feeling to see these stories written though she couldn't yet read them.

Knowing that Gabriel was in the words, that someone hundreds of years later could know by them how he had looked, the songs he sung, and where he was buried, gave her the solace of knowing he would be remembered after she was gone. She returned to Master Antonio's house with a sense of peace.

The rains came. Master Antonio moved back to his dwelling and was borne up the hill each day. On one occasion he carried with him the cedar box he had kept in the litter on the journey from Ouro Prêto. He had been working for an especially long time on the figure of Christ carrying the cross, and now, concealed by the fall of his robes, Master Antonio moved a panel that revealed a hollow. "Make sure that no one's prying," he told Renata. When she assured him that no one was near the work shed, he asked her to bring the cedar box. "Now, *filha*, take out what's inside and keep it wrapped. Place it in the hiding place."

She obeyed. The helpers, absorbed in their own tasks, seemed not to have noticed. With his chisel, the sculptor touched the covering back into place. It was indiscernible from the other folds in the draperies.

Master Antonio hunched lower. "Pray with me," he murmured to Renata. "Pray for the soul of Joaquim Xavier da Silva, Tiradentes, martyr. You wondered what happened to his skull. Zé took it down and I have hid it these years till I found for it a worthy resting place. That poor head will rest in the bosom of Christ, perhaps till the Day of Judgment."

Renata prayed. And Zé had seen, for he brushed away a tear, and for a moment, in salute to a brave man, clasped his hand on the iron band of Ogun.

VI

The Prophets

In December of 1799, Master Antonio finished the last of the chapel figures and received the impressive payment of 1,184 milreis, over 7,000 English pounds.

"Splendid, Senhor Antonio!" praised Dário Ferraz as he admired the Crucifixion, Christ's head strained back against the cross by the posture of the tortured arms and hands. "You have wrought beyond the brotherhood's fondest dreams. There is much here of Michelangelo and El Greco, but you have transformed all other influences with your especial vision."

"Thank you, Senhor Dário." The sculptor hesitated. "Has the brotherhood decided about the prophets?"

Ferraz sighed. "Delighted as we are with your work, Senhor Antonio, that would be a great expense."

"But consider!" In his eagerness, Master Antonio crawled to the edge of the work shed and pointed his fingerless hand at the church. "Can't the senhor imagine a broad divided staircase curving down the slope with the prophets outlined against white walls and blue sky? Each would have a separate character and carry a scroll with a passage from his book. And then, after passing among them, to follow the Way of the Cross! Senhor Dário, you must see how effective it would be."

"I do, but the brotherhood has just paid handsomely for the chapel figures. I think we must find a private donor. No doubt it can be done, but it may take some time."

Master Antonio's laugh was nearer a bark. "Time? That, senhor, is what a crippled man of seventy cannot count on."

Ferraz pondered, stroking his chin. His silver glance

touched Renata in that appraising manner with which he had watched her these past few years, a manner compounded of alert waiting and assurance.

"I'll see what I can do, Senhor Antonio."

"It's difficult for me to travel and transport my working materials back and forth. It would save trouble and expense, Senhor Dário, if I began at once on the prophets. This is a project of years. I haven't even days to waste."

Ferraz spread his hands. "Would you be willing to proceed on the understanding that it may take some years to raise the money?"

Master Antonio shrugged. "I can live on the payment just given for the cedar figures. But this may well be the last big commission I can undertake. The pay must sustain my final years."

"I'll do my best," Ferraz promised. "Don't strike your tent yet, Senhor Antonio!"

After he had gone, the master sat gazing toward the church. Renata was sure he was envisioning these majestic figures stationed along the stairs he would design to better set them off. She touched his shoulder.

"Master Antonio, we can sell my diamonds if the brotherhood doesn't have some money by the time you need it."

"Bless you, *menina*, but no. The diamonds are for you to take into your marriage, a little something to fall back on." He sounded bitter. "Senhor Dário could well afford the whole cost himself. I hear that he just paid a thousand milreis for a pretty mulatta. But he knows I yearn to do these prophets—have together in one place my finest work. And so he bargains."

"Does that change the way you feel about doing them?"

"Bless you, child, I need money and intend to have it, but that's nothing to do with my work." He chuckled softly. "That's between God, me, my tools and the stone."

With Janu drawing for him, the master planned a new terrace and approach with the twelve prophets commanding the two staircases and a graceful sweep of walls. "Daniel must have his lion," he mused. "And a whale for Jonah. Amos was a shepherd, so I'll dress him in trousers and a fleece-lined coat. Renata, you must help me find the right passage for each scroll. And I have already dreamed their faces: Jeremiah secretly gloating as he foretells doom; Hosea comparing God's love with his own for the harlot Gomer, whom he married and tried to save; Ezekiel beholding the four animals in flames by the ethereal throne and the fiery wheels turning—''

He broke off, pursuing his vision. Maurício cleared his throat. ''You want them eight feet high, master? Won't that be difficult?''

''We'll do them in top and bottom halves. The draperies and rich borders will almost hide the joinings.''

It was evident that even as he worked on the Passion, the concept of the prophets had been maturing in his artist's brain. As soon as mules labored up the hill with blocks of soapstone, he gave his helpers tasks and immediately set to work himself on Isaiah, who, with Jeremiah, would stand at the gate.

'' 'After the Seraphim had praised the Lord, one of them flew unto me with a live coal held in tongs, and laid it upon my mouth,' '' quoted Master Antonio, working away with mallet and chisel. As always, Renata marveled at how precisely he could manage the instruments. ''Isaiah saw swords beat into plowshares and the lion and lamb lie down together. He won't have a cap or turban, only his mantle falling like a monk's hood. His brow will furrow as he peers into the future: 'Unto us a child is born, unto us a son is given,' and calls him Wonderful, Counselor, and Prince of Peace.''

''Yes, master, but you must have some food,'' chided Renata. ''Cleonice made this corn porridge just the way you like it, with lots of peppers and onions.''

''I have so much to do and there's so little time—''

''You have to eat or you'll lose your strength. Here, it'll just take a few minutes. You won't even need to take off your tools.''

Grumbling, he settled on the thick rug and let her feed him *mingau* while the others devoured beans and dried meat. They all drank of the fresh-squeezed cane juice Renata had carried up. While his helpers stretched out for a rest, Master Antonio went back to his labor. Renata shook her head but knew it was useless to remonstrate.

If he could be given time and strength to finish! Pitted against eternity and his consuming illness, it seemed monstrous that he might be thwarted by men who squandered fortunes on their own pleasures. Renata gathered up the empty kettles and dishes and started down the hill.

She wished Juracy were here. He'd applaud Master Antonio's success in winning at least conditional backing for the enterprise and enthuse over its grandeur till the sculptor's mortification at being forced to haggle would seem nothing compared to what he might attain. But Juracy's visits had been few of late. In fact, since her figure had begun to curve and blossom a year ago, he'd come only on the Day of the Three Kings to bring her a book.

What was the matter? She thought with wistful yearning of the two years after their trip to the Diamond District, when Juracy had lodged in Congonhas for weeks at a time. He'd taught her to read and play backgammon, and even beguiled Master Antonio into conversing some nights rather then working on by lamplight.

Inexplicably, those happy times had ended. He no longer called her sweetheart in that careless laughing fashion, or kissed her even on the cheek. Perhaps he'd fallen in love. He might even be married.

These possibilities made her writhe inwardly but were welcome when she considered the dreadful chance that he might have been taken by the dragoons. He could be dead, imprisoned or exiled for life, and she might never know.

So sunk was she in this unhappy pondering that she didn't heed the sound of hoofs until a horseman reined in beside her. "Good day, my pretty," said Dário Ferraz. "Put down that load of pots and dishes. We need to have a talk."

Apart from watching her, which made her uncomfortable enough, he'd left her alone since the day he'd forced her to the market. Her hope that he'd decided her not worth his trouble was shattered now as he dismounted, tossing his reins to his slave. Renata shrank against the embankment, but his presence still overwhelmed her.

He took her burden from her nerveless fingers and put the things to one side so that even that shield was no longer between them. Hot, withering force radiated from him. She stared at her sandals.

"You've become quite a young lady, Renata," he said pleasantly. "Of an age to marry."

She glanced up in shock. His crystal eyes drilled into hers. She felt their intrusion like frosted blades. His next words startled her.

"You love Master Antonio?"

"Indeed, senhor. I owe him everything."

Ferraz nodded, silver hair contrasting strangely with the smooth dark face. "Then you wish for him to be commissioned to do his prophets?"

"Surely the senhor has already promised—"

He cut in silkily. "I said I would try."

"But he's already ordered the stone—begun Isaiah!"

"How rash of him."

She swallowed. "Senhor Dário, you can't mean the brotherhood won't let him do the work!"

"Oh, they'd be delighted if he chose to donate the labor as an act of piety. Otherwise—" Ferraz beamed at her. "Otherwise, the statues must be underwritten by someone willing to assume the cost." When she only stared, he spoke with patient distinctness. "I'll pay, Renata, if you will marry me."

"Marry you!" she echoed in disbelief.

"I must marry sometime for legitimate heirs. In fact I leave next week for Lisbon, where I shall be ennobled and carry out some delicate tasks for the regent, Dom João. I have delved into your origins enough to know you're of good family even if your father was a diamond smuggler, and I have money and power enough to marry as I will."

"But, senhor—"

"You'll give me sons of better mettle than I'll get from these simpering, pasty-faced *sinhazinhas* who've been shut up behind walls all their lives."

"I don't want to marry," she cried, but even in her distress she took care not to offend him more than necessary. "I—I must stay with Master Antonio, do what I can to repay his kindness."

"Even if it costs him the commission that will crown his life?"

Renata had no answer to that. Her mind darted like a trapped animal as she stared at the diamond pin in his lacy neckcloth. Long, beautifully kept fingers closed over hers. "I have always preferred tender buds, Renata, but a wife is another matter. Three years ago when you couldn't be blandished, I decided to save you for wedding. A little more time doesn't matter. If I married you now, I wouldn't take you to Europe. My duties there would be hindered by a wife, especially such a young one. So, if it will make you easier, give your promise now, but it needn't be kept till I return." He carried her hand, palm up, to his lips, which seemed to burn her flesh. "I think a few years will ripen you into welcoming the honor I would do you."

"You honor me too much, senhor. I'm not a fitting wife for one of your station."

"Whatever wife I choose is fitting," he said haughtily. "Well?"

"Perhaps the senhor will meet a fine lady in Lisbon."

"No doubt I will. Many of them. I've spent this past twenty years escaping their parents' nets."

Maybe he'd die. Maybe he'd never come back.

"I am riding up that hill," he said deliberately. "What shall I tell the master?" She could think of no way out.

"Tell him to do the prophets."

The block of soapstone gradually took on the aspect of Isaiah's head and shoulders. The rough mass of the beard was defined into matted locks, the mouth almost hidden by a flowing mustache. The hill swarmed with workmen laying terrace and wall, and Master Antonio kept a demanding eye on that, too, since for full effect, the setting and arrangement of the statues was vital.

While Janu did Isaiah's shoulders, the master worked on his hands and the elegant borders of the prophet's garments. The buskined feet and long scroll could be the task of Maurício.

Jeremiah's hooked nose, fastidious beard and tight-set lips were taking life from Master Antonio's chisel when Juracy rode up one afternoon. Apart from his delighted interest in the new project, he acted as if it hadn't been close to a year since he'd visited.

"I've got some books for you," he told Renata. "That *Fenix Renascida* anthology I've told you about and Padre Vieira's *Sermons*. They'll give you an idea about what it was like when it seemed the Dutch might take over the whole country."

Why did he speak to her as if he were a schoolmaster and she a student? Couldn't he see that she was almost fourteen? "Thank you," she said stiffly. "The senhor is kind."

"The senhor?" Dark eyebrows lifted and that gray-black gaze studied her, though his laugh was playful. "When did I stop being Juracy? Or at worst, Julio?"

Why tantalize herself with him when she was, however unwillingly, betrothed to Dário Ferraz? Fleetingly she wondered if there were some way out of her predicament, if Juracy might be able to help, but rejected the faint hope. Ferraz would be a dangerous enemy if Juracy thwarted him. Besides, it wasn't pity she wanted from this tall, black-haired man, and his long absences made it clear that he'd forgotten or felt uncomfortable with their earlier closeness.

"Young women," she said severely, "don't call gentlemen by their first names."

He blinked. Then his mouth quirked in a way that made her long to feel it against hers. Her eyes dropped to his hands. That was no better. If those strong brown fingers closed on her, caressed her cheek and throat as he had sometimes used to—oh, she couldn't bear it! Why, instead of Ferraz, couldn't *he* desire her?

"Then you're not my little one anymore?" His voice was teasing, but there was something different in the way he watched her.

She melted inwardly but straightened her spine. Since she was fated to marry that hateful Ferraz, it could only increase her misery to let Juracy carelessly charm himself back into her good graces. "I was little when you last were here," she said tartly. "But I'm quite grown now."

"Really?" he mocked.

Her eyes smarted with tears of frustration and loss. She hadn't told anyone of her forced promise to Dário, but stung into lashing out at Juracy, she gave a false, bright laugh. "I'm grown enough to be engaged."

Black diamonds could be no harder than his stare as, after widening, his eyes narrowed. "Engaged? May an old acquaintance inquire the name of this fortunate man?"

Zé had stopped working and turned toward her, jaw dropped. Even Maurício looked up, and Master Antonio's arms dropped to his sides. "Engaged, *menina?* How can this be?"

He had to know sometime, but certainly he must never guess why. Wishing that she had held her tongue, she avoided Juracy's probing regard as she sank down by her foster father.

"I said nothing to you yet, Master Antonio, because the wedding won't be till Senhor Dário returns from Europe."

"Senhor Dário!" gasped the master. "I thought—"

She interrupted quickly, "The senhor wanted my consent before he spoke to you, master. But since he'll be gone for several years, he thought it best to wait to ask for your permission."

Zé burst out angrily, "If all I hear about that one's true, it's a marvel he'd wait! You're old for him now as it is! I don't like this, zinha. How come you never told me about it?"

She had hurt her oldest, most faithful friend, but it was too late to call back her secret. And if Zé knew how Dário had extracted her promise, after that aristocrat's return, there would be another offering on Ogun's crossroads altar, or Zé would be caught and hanged for an attempt on Ferraz's life. She was properly trapped now.

Crossing to Zé, she laid a coaxing hand on his muscular arm. "Senhor Dário is rich and handsome. An orphan like me should be honored at his proposal."

Juracy had met Ferraz at the workshop but didn't know him well. Now he said harshly, "I've heard that Dom João is going to grant Senhor Dário a patent of nobility—or sell it. A dazzling prospect indeed, Don' Renata." He bowed. "Felicitations."

That formal naming stabbed like a knife. "Thank you, senhor."

Before her fought-back tears could spill, she snatched up the soiled laundry she'd collected and set off down the road. She was nearing the house when a chestnut horse danced in front of her and Juracy sprang down, looping his reins about a branch.

"You can't know what you're doing, Renata." He grasped her arm so forcefully that sheets and towels dropped to the cobbles. "You've grown up almost like a lad, helping Master Antonio, going back and forth to the workshop. Dário Ferraz will shut you up in his mansion. You'd as well be a slave!"

It took all her strength not to cry out the truth that would imperil him and her friends. Under Juracy's touch, her flesh tingled with sweet fiery shock and blood raced through her veins. "Any husband protects his wife," she retorted.

Juracy's lip curled. "Protects? That shows what you know!"

He caught her shoulders. "Do you know what he'll do to you?" he demanded in a shaking, furious voice. "If he's not impotent with any female past childhood?" As Renata tried to wrest free, Juracy sucked in his breath. "My God! He hasn't already—has he?"

"It's none of your business!" Renata kicked at him, struggled against relentless fingers. "You don't come around for almost a year, you act as if I don't exist, and then you think you can tell me what to do!"

She was crushed against him while firm, cool lips plundered hers, sought her throat, just grazed her breast before he groaned and straightened. "I'll not seduce a child, even a foolish one." His eyes blazed down at her. "I suppose he promised you gowns and jewels, perhaps a gilt sedan chair? What if I'd give you the same things not to marry him?"

Stricken that he'd think her so easily bought, Renata escaped his loosened grasp. Still trembling from the almost brutal kiss, she cried fiercely, "Don't think you have to save me from childish follies, Juracy–Julio Andrade–Calvacanti! I know what I want!"

"Do you?" he breathed. "Do you?"

Before, his mouth had assaulted hers, stormed her, but now his lips wooed with an intensity that robbed her of strength, sent a warm glow spreading through her that made her want to open, let him do what he would. Her young breasts ached against the hardness of him.

"Menina, menina," he murmured, cradling her.

In a moment her resolve would crumble. She'd tell him everything, sob out that she had loved him all her life, that she would love him always. And that would bring disaster.

Freeing herself, she gathered up the fallen laundry and said with a bitter laugh, "The senhor does honorably to lay hands on another man's betrothed!"

She thought he would seize her, but after a transfixed moment he swung away. "For a *vintem,* I'd give you the spanking you need!" Dragging loose the reins, he leaped into the saddle. "Somewhere beneath this nonsense there must be the brave little girl who rode with me to the Diamond District to honor her parents, the child who was growing into—" He checked himself. "Farewell for a time, Don' Renata. Remember my kiss—and consider well that Dário Ferraz will do more than that!"

He wheeled his horse down another street. Later in the day, an urchin brought his gift of books and a green silk shawl for Cleonice. Juracy did not come.

The company of prophets grew, Master Antonio's touch adding to or taking away from the work of his helpers on the handsome borders of the clothing, elaborate folds of drapery, scrolls and turban caps. Faces and hands were all the master's. Ezekiel's slanting eyes, gaunt cheeks and plaited beard contrasted with placid, smooth-shaven Baruch, who would stand opposite. Nahum's beard streamed down his neck like water, and the lines of his emaciated face repeated that modeling.

When unable to achieve what he wished with a face or figure, Master Antonio would go on to another work and return to the first when he had a fresher eye. "My hands know things that I don't," he told Renata. "And the stone has its messages."

"I love Jonah's whale," said Renata, stroking the graceful tail running up the prophet's back; the whale's mouth spouted water from beside his feet. Tail and fins were acanthus leaves that repeated the mantle's border. "But he looks more like a dolphin, don't you think? And he's not big enough to swallow a man."

Master Antonio laughed. "Oh ye of little faith! I suppose you'll think this lion of Daniel's isn't ferocious enough to rend anyone?''

Renata laughed into the animal's face as he seemed to smile up at the handsome young prophet, her favorite because he looked a lot like Juracy. "He seems to adore Daniel, master, but that's all right. The lions didn't eat him.''

She glanced out at where the chapels were being erected in this year of 1802. As artists finished painting the Passion figures, they were being arranged in the six shrines. It seemed a lifetime ago that Master Antonio had entombed Tiradentes' skull in the bosom of Christ, a happy, expectant time when she'd been free to dream a young girl's fancies. True, her devil's bargain with Dário Ferraz hadn't ended her thoughts of Juracy. How could it when her lips still felt as if they belonged to him, when slow flame curved along her bones and melted her thighs when she remembered how he'd held her?

As if reading her mind, Master Antonio said, "I wonder where Julio has got to? It's been two years since we've seen him. He seems to have dropped off the face of the earth.''

"I think he likes to worry us," she said dourly. "He must know we've no way of guessing whether he's been hung or shot or whether he's just dallying in Rio or Bahia.''

"You worry about him, then?"

Renata's cheeks grew hot. "Of course I do. He was our good friend till—''

She broke off. The master finished for her. "Till you dropped that thunderbolt about Senhor Dário." He shook his head. "I don't understand that, *filha*. I always thought that you and Julio—''

Renata scooped up bowls and kettles, banging them together. "I can't see what's strange about my agreeing to wed a rich, good-looking nobleman!''

Zé was frowning at her. Before he could join in the fray, she scowled back at him and flounced out of the workshop. She fretted about Juracy, yes, and inwardly writhed at what he must think of her, but she worried increasingly about Dário as the time approached for his return.

The administrator of the church often came to watch

Master Antonio work and gossip of this and that—how execution of the mulatto leaders of the Tailors' Conspiracy in Bahia should put an end to their kind's prating of equality; Napoleon's becoming First Consul for life; and how Senhor Dário, that man of talent and devotion to public service, had been created a baron and would soon be back in Brazil.

Swept with the rest of the household into Master Antonio's splendid vision, Renata had been able to push the day of reckoning out of her mind. Ferraz might marry in Portugal. He might die or decide he didn't want her. But the years had passed; so far as she knew, nothing had changed; and she was sixteen, considerably older than most brides.

Cleonice had gone to the market to look for new dress material, so the house was empty. Renata poured a little water into the pans and began to scrub them. It was one thing to promise to marry Ferraz with one's attention fixed on assuring that Master Antonio could do his prophets, quite another to approach the day of fulfillment.

Oh, Juracy!

As if her inner cry had summoned him, he came through the door from the small garden. She dropped a bowl. It clattered between them. Joy sang through her. She took a step toward him, arms outflung, before she remembered and turned the motion into a stoop for the dish.

The smile that had softened his face at her first reaction faded. He leaned against the wall, crossing his arms. Silence hung crushingly between them. She forced a smile and said with attempted cheeriness, "How good to see you, Senhor Julio! Only today Master Antonio was wondering where you've been."

"I've been exploring the country. I almost bought a *fazenda* on the Amazon, but decided the climate would keep me in a hammock. I stayed for a time in Cuiabá, but I've had enough of mining towns. After roaming the Mato Grosso with some Indians, I finally bought an old ranch on the São Francisco."

"You sound like a *bandeirante!*"

"I wasn't looking for gold. Or emeralds and diamonds. Just for a place to live."

"You're"—she searched for a word—"retiring?"

"More or less. At thirty-two, Don' Renata, don't you think a man should settle down and start a family?"

Her heart twisted painfully. "You found a wife, too?"

"I found her long ago."

"You—you mean you've been married all this time?"

"No." He didn't move, yet she felt as if he had advanced on her. His dark gray eyes searched her face. "I've been waiting."

"For what? Did she have a husband who had to die?"

"First there was waiting for her to grow up. And then to recover from a foolish notion." He was suddenly across the floor, taking her shoulders. "Have you recovered? Or are you still set on becoming a jewel-bedecked baroness?" Could he be saying that he'd waited for her? Joy blazed in Renata, then charred to ashes. That he returned her love only made what she was sworn to do more bitter. She had to swallow several times before the words would come. "Senhor, I am promised to Dário Ferraz. He will soon be back in Brazil."

"That's why I've come."

He gazed down at her. She trembled in his hands. If he'd kiss her once in spite of the contempt hardening in his face, she'd have that to remember through the bitter years. "So, Don' Renata, you intend to go through with that marriage?"

She nodded, unable to meet his gaze.

His tone changed. "Do you love him?"

"You have no right—"

"Say you love him and I'll leave you to your bliss."

She could not say it.

Juracy's breath came in a rush. "Get your things, Don' Renata. We're going on a trip."

"What?"

"I'm taking you where your bridegroom won't find you. In a few years if you still think a baron's crest is worth a lifetime's bondage, you may do as you will, but I've loved you too long not to try to save you from that."

"You—you love me?"

His fingers dug into her flesh. "Of course I love you! What have I been saying?"

"You didn't say that."

"I'll say it now if it gives you satisfaction," he grated. "I love you. But don't fear that I'll despoil your virginity. I'll deliver you to my ranch and take myself away."

"I can't go to your ranch."

"You've no choice about it. I've already talked with Master Antonio, Zé and Cleonice. They're glad I'm taking you to where Ferraz won't find you."

"But—"

"Get your things or I'll take you without them."

She cried imploringly, "But I can't go! Senhor Dário will stop the money for Master Antonio's prophets! He'll lose all the work he's already done and won't get to see them set up along the stair. It'll all be ruined!"

Juracy's eyebrows drew together. "What are you saying? What's Ferraz to do with the prophets?"

"Everything. He guaranteed payment so that Master Antonio could go on with them. And you know how much having them here with the Passion figures means to him."

"I know," said Juracy slowly. He laughed and caught her hands, eyes glowing. "Is that why you promised to marry Ferraz? To save the master's prophets?"

She nodded, a lump swelling in her throat. "I think it would kill Master Antonio not to finish his great plan. And it *will* be wonderful, Juracy."

He shook his head. "Why didn't you tell me? Little goose! Here I've thought—"

"I didn't want you dueling with Ferraz, getting yourself in trouble—"

He swept her against him. His mouth took hers. She clung to him, yearning, wanting only to melt in his arms, delight in his dear closeness. But nothing had changed, really. She was still bound to marry Ferraz. This would just make it harder.

She set her hands against Juracy's chest, but he was already drawing back, laughing at her exultantly. "I won't duel with Ferraz, but Master Antonio will go on with his sculptures. I'll simply go to the brotherhood and make a donation that will pay for the work." He gave her a little shake and added sternly, "That's what I would have done before if you'd told me instead of deciding you had to be a martyr."

"You have that much money?"

He grinned. "Sweetheart, besides redistributing the Crown's diamonds, I've inherited, quite honestly from an uncle, a rich gold claim and lucrative interests in some trading companies." Cupping her chin in his hands, he kissed her tenderly, then with growing hunger to which she responded so recklessly that he drew back, laughing breathlessly. "Gently, *menina.*" The old name was a caress. "If I don't marry you before I do all that I want, I'll feel that I've taken advantage of my playmate and companion, who has grown into a beautiful woman. Come. Let's go to Master Antonio and then I'll see the church administrator and call on the brotherhood."

They were married inside the church where most of the Passion figures still awaited their chapels. After a family feast, the newlyweds began their journey. Renata hated to leave Master Antonio and the others, but when the sculptor knew why Renata had promised to marry Ferraz, he agreed with Juracy that the nobleman would be furious at losing his long-desired prey and that the young couple had best disappear. Juracy's past didn't bear close examination even though he had retired Julio Andrade. The sooner they began a new life, the better. Zé had been torn between remaining with the work and crippled master that he loved and going with Renata, but she urged him to stay. "Please, Zé," she whispered, holding his hands, "I feel bad enough that I'm leaving. If you're here helping Master Antonio, I won't feel quite so much that I've deserted him."

"If you're sure," Zé said reluctantly. He pressed her hands to his forehead before he touched his iron armband. "But I will come if you send. I swear by Ogun."

She laughed through tears. "By Saint George, you mean! Oh, Zé, do you remember how you taught me to catch diamonds in my mouth?"

He chuckled. "A promising *garimpeira* you were, too!"

"Give me your blessing."

He did, and so, with tearful embraces, did Cleonice. Janu kissed her hand and Maurício croaked a wish for happiness. Renata knelt last before Antonio.

"You have my blessing," he told her. "Come back one day and see our prophets."

She embraced his knees, pressed her cheek against them and couldn't hold back tears. His sleeve-covered hands smoothed her hair as he murmured benediction in a breaking voice. Juracy raised her to her feet.

In the courtyard his chestnut waited, and the big gray horse on which she'd first seen him. "Smoke's retiring from robbery, too." Juracy laughed. "Time has quieted him. He'll be safe for you. And see, I've brought you one of those saddles with a horn on the side so that you can wear skirts and ride without making a scandal." He kissed her ear and whispered, "Feel free to create all the scandal you like whenever we're alone!"

With final good-byes, they passed through the gate Zé opened for them and rode toward their new life.

VII

Kingdom Come

Safely away from Congonhas, they stopped that night at the unused country home of a friend of Juracy's. It was staffed with servants and a beaming mulatta housekeeper-cook who knew Juracy and was delighted to fuss over him and his bride. "About time you had a wife, Senhor Julio! Now you just rest, sinhá, while I have a tub brought up." Paulina laughed knowingly. "Maybe you'd like supper sent to your room, Senhor Julio?"

"A good idea," he nodded. "And, Paulina—don't worry about regular meals these next few days. Simple food will do, and I'll let you know when we want it."

Paulina nodded understanding approval and went out, chuckling.

"Juracy!" Renata protested, blushing. "She'll think—"

"She'll be right!" His kiss made Renata lose any shame about what the servants might think. "I've waited for you a long time, my sweetheart." His eyes darkened and his hand moved from her throat to lightly pause at her breast. "You've entered this room a virgin, *menina*, but you'll leave it a woman, one who's learned to want me as I want you."

Putting her arms around his neck, she rose on tiptoe for his lips, moved softly against them, nibbling provocatively. "What makes you think I'll have to learn?"

"What?" He laughed. "Have I got a trollop?"

She nodded eagerly. "I think you have."

"We'll soon see," he vowed. "But first let's wash off our travel stains, and there's something I need to unpack."

Their saddlebags and packs had been carried to the adjoining room, where one bath was prepared for him while

Renata's was filled in the large chamber that was empty
except for an immense poster bed with a gold satin coverlet
and hangings, several jarcaranda chests and a chair.

Paulina's daughter, a pretty cinnamon-skinned girl of
perhaps thirteen, offered to help Renata undress and bathe,
but Renata smilingly thanked her and refused, though she
was glad to let Maria hang up her traveling dress and lay
out the white silk gown that Cleonice had embroidered as
a wedding gift.

Soaking out the stiffness of the ride, Renata scrubbed to
a fresh glow, tingling as she heard Juracy moving about
the next room. Would he be that warm honey-tan all over?
It seemed too wonderful, to be with him at last, loved as
she loved him. She stepped out on a mat and toweled carefully, anxiously examining her legs, thighs and waist.

Were her breasts too small? Would he mind that the
nipples were pink rather than large and brown like those
she'd glimpsed of nursing women's? She craned her neck
for a rueful glance at her bottom. Rounded but firm, nothing as softly opulent as swaying rumps she had heard admired in the market. Renata sighed and slipped on the
gown, then rang the bell as Maria had asked her to do for
a signal to remove the water.

Several boys seemed to be waiting outside. They entered
at once and carried out the tub. Paulina smiled over their
heads. "Would the sinhá like supper now?"

"Yes," called Juracy. "There's a table on the balcony
of this room. Will you have the food brought there?"

"Right away, Senhor Julio." Paulina's bare feet padded
off. Juracy came through the louvered inner door, a towel
kilted about him, startling white against the warm brown
of his lean waist. The muscles of his upper arm flexed with
the weight of what he carried.

It was the oratory with all the dear, familiar figures Master Antonio had made for her so long ago. It was her most
precious possession, but since they'd had no pack animal,
she hadn't wanted to ask if it could be taken with them.
She had just hoped that someday it could be transported to
her new home.

"Juracy!" she cried, tears of happiness at being so cherished coming to her eyes. "That's what you had in that biggest pack."

"Things are strange for a bride even without moving away from the others you love. I hoped this would make the ranch more like home." Setting it carefully on one of the chests, he closed the wings against the main panel and came toward her with a smile. "There, now, we won't shock the Holy Ones."

In sudden timidity, she raised her hands to cover her breasts. He dropped to his knees and kissed both guarding fingers and tremulous soft roundings. His breath sent quivering flame through her, made her nipples prickle against thin silk. She gasped and drew him close, caressing his wavy black hair, pressing his face to breasts now swollen with urgency. Sweet hot moistness seemed to spread meltingly from her belly to that place his fingers brushed gently through the cloth.

She moaned. He rose and swept her up in his arms, carrying her the few steps to that enormous bed. Laying her down, he kissed her, smoothing her body till she began to touch his, marveling at the flat hard stomach, the curve of neck into collarbone, the smooth ridged muscling of his back. She didn't dare venture beneath the kilt, but she drew a delicious power from the way he tautened when she stroked his navel, wonderingly explored slim, tough horseman's thighs. She trembled at the image of him astride her, that controlled force used to make them one.

"Please," she whispered. "Oh, Juracy—"

He was trembling, too. It was heady to know that she affected him as much as he did her. He rose up to toss away the kilt and in the same moment ran his hand up her thigh. She cried out as he touched her.

He sat up. Black pupils had spread over the gray of his eyes, but he was smiling.

"Darling, that's a pretty gown, but can we have it off?" He drew it slowly up her body, kissing her knees, her thighs, letting his tongue trace her navel before it traveled upward. With breath and lips and teeth, he visited each breast, and when she was gasping, moaning, writhing, offering herself, a tender hardness pressed into the moist flowering between her imploring thighs.

"Easy, *menina*. Easy, love. Just this time I'll hurt you, then never again."

She trusted him, bit her lips against an outcry. There was tearing pain, but she called his name in the shock and wonder of his filling her, entering that most secret place. He didn't move again except to slightly flex his hips until she felt a golden fountain spill within her, laving her darkness.

Still within her, he stretched out, cradling her head on his shoulder. "You'll have your pleasure soon, *menina.*" He kissed her forehead. "But we'll let you rest a little while, and then we're going to have our wedding supper!"

She had her pleasure many times in those next intoxicated days, and delighted in sometimes waking him with a kiss, a hand tantalizing him into awareness. After being a bit nervous of that amazing part of him that could grow so large and hard and then cuddle innocently, almost hidden, in the mass of springy black curls, she began to feel proud proprietorship, thrilling when it reared imperatively, waxing big for their enjoyment, feeling protective tenderness when, tamed, it left her.

Juracy was happily amazed at how quickly she lost her shyness. "You're the first virgin I ever had," he told her. "I thought it would take weeks or months to persuade you loving could be nice." He chuckled ruefully. "One of these days you may want more than I can manage."

She shook her head, tracing his lips with her fingertips. "Even when you're a hundred, you can hold me in your arms. I love that. Just being close to you."

After a week they journeyed on, and though Juracy wanted to leave a gold piece for Paulina, Renata insisted on leaving one of her diamonds. "They're my dowry," she pointed out. "Please let me."

"If it matters so much," he conceded. "But you put the rest of them away for our daughters."

"What about our sons?"

"They'll have the *fazenda* and our trading interests."

"Good. I thought for a moment that you meant to set them to waylaying the Crown's gold and diamonds."

"Falcão's disappeared." He laughed. "In fact, so can

Julio Andrade, except for when we visit his old haunts. I'll be dos Santos, that's all—use only my father's name.''

Five days after resting at Ouro Prêto, they followed the track along which cattle had long been driven to the mining towns around a bend of the river and Juracy pointed to a sprawling white house on a gentle slope, surrounded by smaller houses, fields, orchards, buildings and corrals.

"This is your home," he said. "The old name is Rosario, but you might want to change that."

"I do." She smiled, holding out her hand to him. "Let's call it Falcon's Rest, Descanso de Falcão."

To wake each morning in Juracy's arms, to go to sleep touching him; to help him gentle colts or inspect tobacco; drink fresh-squeezed cane juice with him, or tempt him into the kitchen with some new treat Brigida had taught her to make—how could she be so fortunate?

When Juracy scolded her gently for doing much of the housework, she left off polishing the tiles of the fireplace and threw her arms around him. "I love doing things here, Juracy! I never thought about it, but it's wonderful to have my own home."

She loved the feasts. Juracy not only gave one on Saint John's Eve, Saint George's Day and Saint Anthony's and Saint Peter's, but for the twin saints, Cosmé and Damian, Our Lady of the Conception and Saint Benedict, this last because a number of the *fazenda* folk were blacks and the dark saint was their patron. On the day of the Three Kings, Renata saw that every child at Descanso had a present. Some of these she carved, horses and cattle and jointed dolls that Brigida helped her dress.

Brigida, like most of the forty or so adults who had been born at Descanso, was of Indian blood with a mix of white, a *cabocla*. Tall and wiry with a seamed brown face, she had at first seemed wary of Renata, but this reserve had thawed. She kept the chattering young maids at their tasks and exerted herself to prepare delicious meals, especially after Renata conceived, for Brigida was convinced that her mistress was too thin, a view that Renata couldn't shake.

"You're skinny yourself, Brigida!"

"I'm not expecting any baby," retorted the copper-hued woman with a flash of white teeth that could have been either grimace or smile. "And I don't have a good-looking husband to keep interested. You ought to quit swimming, too. You want to birth a water colt, a *mãe d'agua?*"

"I have to do something," grumbled Renata. "Juracy says I can't ride anymore till the baby's four months old."

"You won't want to," Brigida predicted.

She was right about that, but by the time blue-eyed Antonieta, named for both Renata's mother and Master Antonio, was six months old, Renata had her swimming in a part of the river that was sheltered from the current by a sandbar, and Tieta was riding, stout little legs sticking almost straight out from her pony's back, when José Gabriel Antonio, named for both grandfathers and the sculptor, came squalling into the family in 1805.

Two-year-old Tieta's cherubic blond winsomeness had made her the pampered darling of the *fazenda,* but she wasn't jealous of her brother. She considered him an especially fascinating gift from her parents and loved to rock his cradle while crooning the lullabies she still liked to hear.

Zeques had been a big baby and the birth was difficult. Renata didn't regain her strength as quickly and miscarried when he was a year old. Something must have happened, for she didn't conceive again. When she fretted about this, Juracy loved her with all the exquisite amorousness of their wedding night, and when she lay with cheek against the hollow of his shoulder, he caressed her as if her body were fresh to him, never seen before.

"Don't look at me, Juracy," she pleaded. "I've got those stretch marks on my hips and breasts and—"

His mouth smothered her protest. When he had demonstrated to their exhausted pleasure that he found her as desirable as ever, he captured her chin and gazed deep into her eyes. "I don't want to hear any nonsense from you! Motherhood has made you curve even more delectably. I'd be a strange man not to adore the signs that prove that you've really borne my children."

"But I may not give you any more."

"So?" His eyebrows arched up wickedly and he nuzzled her breast. "Then that leaves this for me!"

"You truly don't mind?"

His lean face grew serious. "I want my sweetheart and companion, not a brood mare. We have the brightest, prettiest children in the world. I'm well content to stop with them." Neither mentioned what both knew too well, that few parents were fortunate enough to rear all their children. The small blue coffins of "angels" were all too common on the *fazenda*, though the food was good and plentiful and Juracy encouraged cleanliness.

Descanso was virtually self-sustaining, though Juracy seemed to find plenty to buy on his tobacco-selling trips to Bahia, or the cattle drives to Ouro Prêto. Tobacco took considerably more care than the cattle. After being cured and twisted into cords, it was dipped in a fragrant syrup of herbs, molasses, lard, ambergris and tobacco juice to keep it moist and increase its aroma. These cords were rolled to a weight of about eight arrobas, 264 pounds, and wrapped in damp hides for preservation. These traveled by boat to the city, being portaged around the most formidable rapids.

Renata had been content to stay home with the children when Juracy made these more or less annual trips, but when one of the travelers who occasionally stopped at Descanso for hospitality happened to remark he was from Congon-has, she'd learned that Master Antonio had finished his prophets and was returning to Ouro Prêto as soon as he'd carved a chandelier to harmonize with the organ case he'd already made for the church.

When the man had gone on his journey, Renata besieged Juracy with the reasons why she and the children should accompany him on his next trip. She longed to see Master Antonio, Zé and the others again, let the master see his namesakes, and have them baptized.

To her surprise, Juracy needed no persuading. "It's time you had a chance to do some shopping for yourself," he said. "But we won't wait for the cattle drive. It's too slow and tedious." He glanced over to where five-year-old Tieta was reading to black-haired skinny little Zeques, who had his father's gray eyes and dimpled cheeks. "Tieta can ride her pony, but I guess Zeques should ride behind you or me.''

Zeques set up a howl at that, and when they left a week later, he rode the placid mare he'd tumbled on and off of since he could walk. Brigida rode an easy-gaited mule and two of the men came along to help with camp chores when night found them a distance from some sheltering roof.

They traveled more slowly than on Renata's previous journey along the route. Zeques often wound up behind his mother or father. But the weather was perfect, and even Brigida enjoyed the outing, though they were all happy to stop and rest for several days at the big house where Juracy and Renata had passed their wedding night. Paulina exclaimed admiringly over the children, who had a good time playing with Maria's toddler, for of course the pretty young girl of six years ago now had her own family.

The party would overflow Master Antonio's house, so they found an inn in Ouro Prêto. Renata couldn't wait to see her foster father, so while Brigida put the children down for a nap, she and Juracy walked down the curving street to the familiar house just up the way from the belfried church she had used to attend.

Master Antonio was in the workshop. As Zé gave a cry of joy and hurried forward, the master hitched painfully around. "What? Can it be my Renazinha? And Senhor Julio!''

She knelt to embrace him, though his tools were still fastened to his stumps. "When I heard you were back, master, I had to see you! And bring your namesakes—two of them.''

"Ah, I had prayed to see you once more, though I didn't dare hope. Go in to Cleonice, child. I'll follow in a moment.''

She and Cleonice had a chance to hug each other and laugh and cry before the men came in. Janu and Maurício set down the master's litter and helped him to his chair. Cleonice brought genipap cordial and cashew sweetmeats and they caught up on each other's news.

"Yes, I'm still working,'' Master Antonio said. "Making two altars for Our Lady of Carmel and some other decorations, I'll work as long as God allows, but I breathe easy now. I've done the prophets and seen them placed along the stair and terrace. Till stone crumbles, they'll stand tall against the blue skies, heralding the Messiah.''

''When they're older, we'll take your namesakes there to see it,'' promised Juracy.

''Good.'' From behind the loose mask came a sighing laugh. ''I used to curse God for making me a mulatto bastard. Then I cursed him for making me a leper. I will not say that Congonhas was worth these afflictions—I had rather be whole than be the greatest artist the world has ever known—but if God has chastised me, at least He permitted a despised *pardo*, not a Portuguese trained in Europe, to create the most splendid art in all Brazil.''

Juracy went back to fetch the children and Renata helped Cleonice prepare a meal embellished with cheese, dried corn and preserved fruit from Descanso.

Renata had explained to the children that Master Antonio kept his face covered and had no fingers, but she was relieved when they went directly to him and asked his blessing. Juracy must have given them final instructions.

''Did you know my mama when she was little as me?'' Tieta asked.

''Indeed, she was just your size,'' Master Antonio assured her.

''If you hadn't pretended to be my grandfather, I don't know what the dragoons would have done to us,'' Renata said. She introduced the children to Zé, reminding them that he'd taken care of her after her father was killed in the Diamond District.

''Shall I show you how I carried zinha when her legs wore out?'' Zé grinned. He scooped the youngsters up and bore them off, one perched on each shoulder.

It was a joyful reunion, shadowed only by the master's obvious weakening. ''He's seventy-eight,'' Cleonice said resignedly. ''A miracle he goes on at all.''

''If he ever needs nursing—''

''He has a daughter-in-law, Joana, married to his natural son. She wants Master Antonio to live with her, but he'd rather stay in his own house as long as he can. Don't worry, Renazinha, we'll take care of him.''

Master Antonio attended the children's baptism as their

godfather, and Cleonice was overwhelmed at being asked, in preference to one of Juracy's highborn connections, to be godmother. It was a crowded week. Renata did little shopping, preferring to spend all the time she could with the people who had been her family and let Tieta and Zeques form a memory of them.

"Senhor Dário was in a fury when he learned you were gone," Cleonice said, shaking her head at the memory. "We told him you'd married Julio Andrade, a gentleman from Rio, so he went prowling off down there and then we heard he went to Portugal for a while, though he must be back in Congonhas by now."

"Has he married?"

"Not as far as I know." Cleonice's kindly face was troubled. "If you ever take the children to see the prophets, have a care that Senhor Dário doesn't find out about it. You must be the first thing he ever wanted that he didn't get."

Coldness prickled along Renata's spine, but she shrugged laughingly. "I'm an old married woman with two children, Cleonice. The baron likes young girls."

Cleonice said broodingly, "It was different with you."

When she embraced Master Antonio in farewell, Renata couldn't hold back tears. It was almost certain that she'd never see him again. But she was inexpressibly happy that her children had responded to him and that he'd been touched and pleased at their visit. Zé had asked privately if, after the master's death, there would be a place for him at Descanso, and Renata was glad that this friend and protector of her childhood would be again part of her life.

Master Antonio and the men had made the children a Noah's ark with pairs of animals and birds. The ark would have to be reassembled at Descanso, but their nightly stops on the way home were beguiled by jaguars battling with lions and wolves trying to capture sheep.

Brigida spoke for them all when Descanso came in view and she sighed mightily. "That was a mighty nice visit, but it's good to be home!"

Juracy didn't stay long. He needed to get the tobacco to the port before the rainy season made the river excessively dangerous, so they'd only a few nights to savor being back in their big familiar bed, catching up, as Juracy teased, on the lovemaking they'd missed at the inn where the children had shared the room.

"I'll make up for it when I get back," he whispered as he kissed her good-bye just before he sprang to the deck of the raft-like boat moored at the small wharf. It was heaped with hide-wrapped arrobas that exuded their aromatic smell, but there was an awning where he and the crew would take shelter from the sun and any early rains.

Zeques began to howl as the boat moved away, for he adored his father, but Tieta cuffed him and admonished, "Baby! Smile the way I am and wave real big or Daddy won't bring you any presents!"

Hiccuping at this threat, Zeques gulped and waved frantically.

Renata didn't cry, but her throat ached, and after the boat passed out of sight, she knelt to hug the children, drawing comfort from their warmth, their sweet flesh that was also Juracy's, till Tieta wiggled away, eager to race the other *fazenda* children who had come to watch the boat leave and were now shouting and playing their way back to the buildings.

In a moment Zeques had slipped away, too, and Renata walked on alone. Why should she feel deserted and suddenly, inexplicably, afraid?

The forlorn sensation wore off in the next few days as she supervised an orgy of cleaning, her proven antidote to the gloom that closed in when Juracy had to go away. But that vague fear haunted her, increasing powerfully at night in the big bed where she was used to knowing Juracy was with her.

Was it Cleonice's warning and seeing people who had known Dário Ferraz that had made him more real to her? Absorbed in Juracy and the children, the life at Descanso, she had almost ceased to think of her formidable suitor, but now she was gripped with dread that he would find her, that he would harm Juracy.

It did no good to argue that if he'd been able to trace her, he would have done it before. The premonition lingered disquietingly, but as that week passed, and the next, as the balance shifted from missing Juracy to looking forward with even more than a bride's eagerness to seeing him again—he was now more than a lover, he was her dearest companion and the father of her children—her anxiety faded.

The afternoons were hot, so she usually took Tieta and Zeques for a swim below the sandbar. Though she and Juracy shed their clothes when they swam alone, she wore a shift as she played and splashed with the children. They were making so much noise that she had no warning till a deep voice called from the bank.

"What a lovely *mãe d'agua!*"

She was standing waist-deep in the water. She turned slowly, unable to believe what her ears and eyes told her was true. Dário Ferraz watched from the bank. A short distance away, a servant held his horse.

"We have much to discuss, my dear." The baron's hair gleamed silver as he took off his plumed and jeweled hat. "Pray send your children to the house."

Numbly she obeyed. The farther her young were from this man, the better. As Tieta urged Zeques up the bank and dressed, frowning in puzzlement at the intruder, Renata moved back to where water covered her breasts, revealed by the clinging garment.

"Why are you here, senhor?" Odd that her tone was steady when she felt as if her bones had dissolved.

"You must know that."

"Senhor, I am married—"

"To a diamond thief," he said pleasantly. "Come out of the water."

He knew about Juracy. Her mind whirled. What should she do? What *could* she do? She moved toward the bank, shrinking as his coldly brilliant eyes ran over her before he smiled.

"Babies haven't ruined you, nor has time. I'm glad that what I undertook for pride's sake will be worth it for my pleasure."

"Have you done something to Juracy?"

He gave a negligent shrug. "Only informed friends of mine who are officials in Bahia know that a notorious smuggler would soon arrive to peddle his tobacco. If he's not in jail already, he will be as soon as he reaches port."

"What will happen to him?" Renata whispered.

"He'll hang."

The words pierced like a blunt sword, striking with a physical impact that made her fall back. "Can you—can you save him?"

The crystal eyes hardened before he smiled. "I might try if you pleased me enough. No promises, though. Diamond cases are of special concern to the Crown, and since it's highly possible that the court will be moving here, the regent will have a closer eye on such proceedings."

Even in her distress, the news startled her. "The court? In Brazil?"

Ferraz nodded. "The old queen's fears have finally come true. Napoleon's marching on Portugal—though I doubt he'd bother to lop off her addled head. When I left Lisbon, Dom João was already having government materials and supplies stored on ships in case it became necessary to evacuate. So yes, I expect the royal family in short order." He preened. "I have served Dom João well on some diplomatic missions. As a favor to me, he might grant your smuggler grace."

"How did you know? How did you find us?"

"When I found no trace of you in Rio, I had one of my slaves get Master Antonio's Maurício drunk. I didn't learn where you'd gone, but I did hear about Julio–Juracy and how he'd saved the sculptor from search and insult by dragoons. It was a simple matter to locate a certain Alves de Castro who was still smarting from ignominy. He was delighted to instruct his men to watch for you and your highwayman in Ouro Prêto and the area. I had a watch on Master Antonio's house in Congonhas." Ferraz spread his hands. "I had almost given up. But when Master Antonio moved back to Ouro Prêto, someone was always on vigil near his home. And you came at last to pay your respects. My man followed you here. He stopped at a vaqueiro's house to rest and learned dos Santos was going to Bahia. That simplified things."

Renata shuddered. It was her fault, then. She had led

Juracy into a trap. She stared into that mocking olive face. "What do you want me to do?"

"Come with me. If you make no fuss, you may bring your children. Don't think the *fazenda* workers can help you. I have a *capitão-do-mato* and his gang. If your *caboclos* try anything, they will be cut down like weeds." He caught her arm. "I have a whim to take my first taste of you in the bed of the man who robbed me of your first fruits. Time enough to leave in the morning." He laughed. "Your husband isn't coming back—at least not till long after you're gone!"

The heavily armed bush-captain and his men were lounging in the shade, flirting with the young women who were bringing them food. At Ferraz's order, Renata asked Brigida to prepare a meal and then take the children to one of the worker's houses for the night.

Holding the woman's astonished eyes, Renata said imperatively, "Master Juracy's in great trouble, Brigida. The only chance we have to help him is by doing as Senhor Dário commands."

"It's also the way to keep anyone from getting hurt," Ferraz added.

Brigida glared at him. With no change of expression, he moved his arm back and swung it against her face. She reeled against the wall, blood welling from her nose and mouth, but before Renata could run to her, she straightened and disappeared into the kitchen. Renata heard her telling the children that she'd bumped into the door and that they should run over to play with some friends.

"But we want Mama!" Zeques wailed.

"She's busy now, *menino*. Go along and later I'll bring you something nice."

Ferraz touched Renata's wet shift. "Charmingly as that displays your beauty, I think you'd better change. Don't be long, my sweet, or I might forget I haven't eaten for hours and satisfy another hunger."

It was twilight when he finished the cordial he had made her share and rose, drawing her along with him. From outside, she could hear music and laughter, almost as if it were a feast.

"Isn't that better than a slaughter?" Ferraz asked. "The *capitão-do-mato* was a little put out when I told him there'd be no murder and pillage unless your men gave trouble, but he's forgotten his disappointment in the hospitality your people are so wisely showing."

He closed the door. The musky scent of his perfume sickened her as he took her in his arms. "What?" he chided. "You'd better summon up a bit of animation, my love. I don't care for zombis."

She put her arms around his neck, trying not to flinch as this opened her body to his, brought them close from breast to thigh. His mouth took hers. The cold flame of his lips seared her, moved numbingly along her throat. He pulled her bodice open and flicked her nipples with his tongue before he covered her breasts with sharp small bites.

As if it excited him, he slowly took off her clothes, caressing her as he did so. He laughed huskily, guiding her hands to his shirt. "Now, my pretty, you must play valet."

Her hands fumbled clumsily, but all too soon his silks and linens and satin dropped to the rug. He drew her against him, and though his flesh was warm, to her it had the effect of chilling cold. She even had the sensation that the rigid phallus jutting against her loins was solid ice.

Now, as long ago, she felt as if his blood had replaced hers, thick, heavy, weighting her down. It seemed to freeze around her heart, pressing at it till it labored and she thought it must fail and stop. He lifted her to the bed. Oh, God, the bed where she had lain with Juracy . . .

Ferraz was moving on her, in her, whispering endearments and obscenities, but paralyzed by that strange cold, her body scarcely felt what he did. Like a distant spray of frigid particles, he spilled his seed. If they ever had a child, surely it would be a glittering, soulless creature of ice crystal.

He slept with an arm and leg thrown over her. In spite of that discomfort, the seeping ooze between her legs, she didn't move. If he would sleep till morning! A small mercy, only postponing the inevitable, but she implored any grace.

The sound of revelry outside continued. She heard it

with bitterness. The smell of roasting meat carried on the air and she remembered the many feasts Juracy had made on the *fazenda*, how many times he and she had been godparents. There were no slaves at Descanso, only free *caboclos*, blacks and mulattos. Juracy had manumitted the slaves he'd bought with the *fazenda* and given them a choice of staying or leaving. They must know that Ferraz had come to carry her off, but there they were, slaughtering Juracy's cattle to feed his enemies and, from the sound of it, drinking up all the *cachaça* in the storehouse.

Ferraz stirred. She held her breath. His hand moved over her. That limp object against her thigh quivered, swelled. This time he varied his rhythms, paused to fondle and toy with her. It was much worse than the driving urgency of his first assault. The blessed frozenness began to wear away. She felt his knowing hands, his bold and skillful tongue.

He knew it, laughed in soft triumph. "In a week, Renata, I'll have you as eager for me as I am for you! And why not? Why not enjoy what will be anyway?" He plunged into her, gripped her buttocks to lift her to his fuller entry, and rode her till he cried out and collapsed upon her.

In that position he fell asleep. Stifled, pinned by his weight, Renata tried to move, but he groped at her and she froze. Would the merrymaking go on all night? Many were surely drunken to insensibility by now, but the shouting and hilarity hadn't diminished. After what seemed hours, she drifted into half-dreaming stupor.

She was drowning. Thick warm fluid clogged her nostrils, poured into her mouth as she opened it to scream, flowed down her neck and shoulders. The weight that crushed her jerked, half lifted with a gurgling sound, crumpled on her, twitching, as she remembered who it was, all that had happened, struggled up to wipe her face.

There was a movement by the bed, a dark shadow, the faintest gleam as of a blade. Shocked past reason, Renata started to cry out. A hand gripped her shoulder.

"It's all right now, sinhá. That gang this silver devil bring, they're all dead. Just like him."

"But—"

Brigida chuckled grimly. "That bush-captain, he had his

men take all our weapons and lock them up, but he forgot a plain old kitchen knife can slice a throat. I talked around and got the men to have their women flirt and dance and drink with the trash, put on a big *festa*. When that gang passed out, or near it, it was easier than wringing chicken necks to take care of them.'' Satisfaction left her voice. ''I'm awfully sorry, sinhá, you had to go through this, but—''

Terror and realization flooded over Renata. She crawled out of bed, wiping at the blood with a sheet. ''Brigida!'' she wailed. ''You—you don't know! Juracy's going to be jailed in Bahia. This man might have been able to keep him from hanging!''

''I know all about that,'' Brigida snorted, leading Renata to the washstand. She sloshed water into the basin and began to clean off the blood. ''The *capitão-do-mato* was telling the men how the baron was having the master arrested for smuggling. But you don't really think, sinhá, that this one would have tried to get the master free? The first thing Master Juracy would do would be to kill him and get you back.''

Of course. It was plain enough if you didn't let frantic hopes blind you. Renata slumped to the floor and began to weep, but Brigida lit a lamp, finished washing her, and helped her dress, talking all the while.

''I studied on it, sinhá, but there just wasn't a way the baron could have had Master Juracy on the loose. And then I knew good and well that the master would a lot rather hang than have you go off with that white-haired *bicho*.'' Glancing at the limp body, she made a disgusted face. ''You're going to need a new mattress, but at least he didn't bleed on the floor. The men can cart him down to the river and toss him in like they're doing with the gang. We'll burn the clothes. Should we kill the baron's horse in case someone comes hunting for him?''

''No, just blot his brand and turn him loose. Are Tieta and Zeques—did they—''

''They don't know a thing. Sleeping down at my daughter's house. None of the youngsters saw what happened, and no one's going to tell them. Better that way if dragoons or travelers happen along.''

Renata nodded, grateful that her children need never know her shame. But that was a small thing beside Juracy's peril.

It was strange to pray for what she had always before hoped wouldn't happen—that the boat would overturn, or the boatmen fall sick, or something happen to delay his arrival in the port. Aside from grasping at such straws, what could she do?

A bribe?

Bribing magistrates was generally not difficult. But a diamond case, robbing the Crown, was far different from ordinary crimes. Provided the bribe outweighed the official's obligation to Ferraz, she could have bought Juracy out of murder and a host of other crimes, but she doubted that gold could get him out of this.

Still, she had to try. If not the judge, perhaps a jailer could be importuned.

"The little boat's left," Brigida said when Renata voiced her thoughts. "I'll go with you."

"But the children—"

"My daughter and others'll look after them. You know that, sinhá."

She did know. Brigida made her bed in the parlor while the bedroom was set to rights and Ferraz carried out to the river's myriad sharp teeth and avid gullets. It was almost dawn.

Renata slept heavily till the sun was well up. In spite of Brigida's cleaning, she still felt saturated with Ferraz's blood and semen. Going to the river, she scrubbed herself repeatedly and then took a swim as if the river could wash away all that had happened. She knew well that it couldn't but was determined not to think of it any more than she had to. The important thing was to reach Juracy. If she won his release, she knew that he would love away that one wretched night; if she couldn't free him, little else would matter.

Not a hint of the score or so bodies was to be seen. There were fish here almost as big as she was, and countless smaller ones. She was going to tell Descanso folk not to fish near here for a long time.

She filled a small chest with gold dust and coin, jewelry and her small hoard of diamonds, had breakfast with the children and explained to them that she had to go after their father, so they must behave like a *sinhazinha* and *sin-*

homoço. By then Brigida had packed clothes and food and the boat was waiting.

It was a wearing journey, but Renata would have enjoyed the songs and jokes of the men if she hadn't been so worried about Juracy. An awning gave some protection from the sun, and at night they camped along the bank or stayed at ranches or *fazendas.* One was the Bom Jardim where her several-times great-grandmother Rachel had lived, and Renata's distant cousins made her welcome indeed.

Though the water was low, at some rapids they had to disembark and the boat and its contents be carried by the men till the plunging falls were passed. All of this crew had been down the river, but only one, Basilio, a little mulatto, was as experienced as the men Juracy had taken, so Renata adjured them, when there was any doubt of negotiating a strait or gorge or waterfall, to pull to shore and portage.

At last they scrambled down the difficult, rocky path bypassing the tremendous thundering cataract called Paulo Affonso, King of the Rapids, and had a comparatively easy journey to where the river poured into the sea.

As they sailed along the coast, Renata thought she had never seen anything so magical as the turquoise waters. Beyond the pale sands and reefs rose high palms, while to the east, froth-capped waves undulated till they faded into the horizon. They stretched to the Azores, to the fabled Ivory Coast and Portugal, which seemed worlds away. Yet Juracy had told her that a person could journey from Lisbon in half the time it took to go from São Paulo to Cuiabá.

When they approached the vast crescent harbor of Bahia, it looked as if every ship in the world was anchored beyond the breakwater while smaller craft bobbed along the wharfs. As the crew jumped overboard to drag the boat up on the beach and secure it out of reach of the tide, Renata stood amazed at the teeming bustle in this lower city along the waterfront dominated by forts built to defend the city from the Dutch. A stream of people, horses, pack mules, litters and sedan chairs toiled up the steep ascents to the main city on the hills above. The governor's palace made a splendid show above a giant pulley that raised and lowered large baskets filled with food and other supplies. Belfries showed among trees and tiled roofs, but Renata was proudly sure that not even the cathedral could equal the glory of Ouro Prêto's churches.

The docks and shore were crowded with sedan chairs, well-mounted horsemen and people of every color with a predominance of all shades of black and brown. They were staring toward three ships, flying bright gonfalons, that were anchored near each other.

"Do you suppose the queen and Dom João will come ashore tomorrow?" one bewigged elegant in a gilt sedan chair called to an acquaintance astride a caparisoned horse.

"It may take longer." The other laughed. "In the confusion of departure, it seems the royal wardrobes were left on the docks. In fact everyone from stable lad to the queen has had to wear the same garments since they left Portugal. And since each ship was jammed with three to four times the number of passengers it had room for, they ran short of drinking water, much less any to bathe in." He lowered his voice, but Renata could still hear. "It's said the princess regent is furious because she had to shave her head to get rid of lice. I hope she and the court appreciate the clothing we've sent them so they'll be able to make a decent appearance."

"We ransacked our chests, too," said his friend. "I understand the governor sent Dom João his best ensemble, which may prove a little tight, and no doubt the courtiers will smirk at brocades and gold mesh our great-grandparents brought over, but it'll make a fine show for all that."

"If people, even royalty, leave home without their clothes, they have to be content with what they can get." The horseman nodded. "And perhaps we can get something, too. Wouldn't it be marvelous if the court was established in Bahia?"

"That would give us the laugh on Rio de Janeiro and those upstart *cariocas*," chuckled the man in the wig. "But failing that, perhaps the regent will open Brazil to world trade now rather than strangling it for Portugal's benefit. My friend José da Silva Lisboa, the eminent economist versed in the theories of Adam Smith, is giving one of the welcoming addresses. He proposes to expound to Dom João the ways Brazil is kept from developing and how permitting it to expand its economy and trade can only add to the glory and strength of the mother country.''

The horseman looked doubtful but shrugged. ''Perhaps there's a hope, since the court must stay in Brazil while Napoleon's running rampant. And those who've been out to meet him say the regent is vastly touched by the welcome he's received.''

''Well, I don't suppose the populace of Lisbon was thrilled to see the aristocrats sail off and leave them to the French.'' The man in the chair yawned. ''*Adeus*, my friend, I'll see you at the procession.''

His slaves bore him toward the upper city, and Renata's party followed in the wake thus created past warehouses, shops, taverns and buildings where multihued women, mostly dark to yellow, looked out of windows or enticed sailors from the doors.

Basilio knew where Juracy lodged in the city, a decent place away from the licentious taverns and bordellos around the wharves, and he and another crewman escorted the women there, carrying their baggage and the money chest. The mulatto couple who ran the inn must have been curious about Renata, but they gave her a small, clean room and slung a hammock for Brigida.

Renata was in a fever to learn where Juracy was. The innkeeper hadn't seen him, which confirmed her fear that he'd been arrested soon upon his arrival. Should she go to the prison or try to find the magistrate?

''You must let the men hang around the taverns and see what they can pick up,'' Brigida advised. ''Best thing you can do now is ask for a tub and get yourself looking like a lady, then have a good sound night's sleep. Basilio's got a cousin who works on the docks. He ought to know if a diamond smuggler was arrested.''

Renata knew it was good advice, but she was so anxious to find Juracy that she couldn't have eaten if Brigida hadn't forced her to. Brigida also washed the salt out of her hair and scrubbed her back as she sat, knees bunched up, in the copper tub. That was relaxing, but when Renata started pacing and staring out of the one tiny window, Brigida went out and returned with a glass of clear liquid into which she squeezed several big limes.

"Cachaça?" sniffed Renata suspiciously. "You know I don't drink it."

"Tonight you will. You need a good rest if you're going to do all you must."

By the time Renata had sipped a quarter of the fiery cane spirits, melting warmth softened her taut nerves, began to dizzy her. A bit more and she grew drowsy. The lamp wavered before her and she swayed as she got to her feet.

"Brigida, you've got me drunk!"

Brigida laughed and supported her. "Just a little, sinhá." She helped her into bed. Renata slipped gratefully into slumber.

It was well she had that sleep, for the next day was cruel. Basilio had learned from his cousin that Juracy had indeed been accosted by officials while unloading his cargo and hustled off to prison in the fort of São Marcelo. The tobacco had been impounded. The crew, not knowing what to do, had hung around the docks till they lost hope for their master's release. Only last week they had dispiritedly started overland to reach the São Francisco trail. "The magistrate," finished Basilio, "would usually be lenient in return for gifts. But a matter of diamonds and Dom João himself in port—"

"I'll have to try," Renata said.

Rather than have the gold chest carried through the streets, she took out the diamonds and some coins and left two of the men guarding the room. Her rapid calculations as she had packed all Descanso's portable wealth into the chest had been that it totaled about three thousand milreis, more than Master Antônio had been paid for the seven years of masterworks at Congonhas. A very sizable amount. But would it buy Juracy's life?

Basilio knew the way to the municipal palace. He undertook a judicious distribution of coins that eventually brought Renata before the *ouvidor,* or royal judge. She had no idea of how to offer such a respectable, stern person a bribe but when she stammered out her plea and added that perhaps a fine would expiate her husband's offense, the judge icily informed her that Juracy couldn't buy himself out with all the gold of Minas Gerais, and Renata had better take herself off before he had her charged with attempting to subvert justice.

At São Marcelo, built in the harbor facing the market the jailer had orders not to let anyone talk to Juracy. It was clear that Dário Ferraz's wishes were being followed even after he was dead.

Basilio said encouragingly, "Let me come back tonight, sinhá, and see if the night warder might not think it worth leaving Bahia if he got what's in that chest to turn his back and lend me the key."

There didn't seem to be much other choice, but as they walked past the cathedral, a wild hope formed in her heart. The *ouvidor* feared the Crown. The Crown was what Juracy had robbed. And the Crown in the form of the mad queen and the regent was not in Lisbon, but a short row from shore.

"Basilio," she said, "after night falls, can you get me aboard the regent's ship?"

There was light from the young moon as Basilio and another man rowed out to the breakwater toward the *Principe Real*, which was occupied by Dom João, his sons, and his principal courtiers. The princess regent and the princesses were on the *Affonso*, and the queen was in a barred cabin aboard *A Rainha*.

Brigida had wanted to come after arguing herself breathless against the idea, but Renata had said, "If things go terribly wrong, you must go back to Descanso and look after the children."

As the boat approached the looming frigate, Renata heard a splash. Something bobbed above the water, a hand flailed out. The head disappeared again, and the start of a cry was drowned. Renata had learned on the river trip that she was a much better swimmer than any of the men. She shucked off garments to her shift and slipped into the sea, making for the place where the hand had vanished.

The head broke surface again. She glimpsed a pale little face in the dim light, called, "Let me help you! Don't fight me!" But the child was past reason. He caught at Renata and, desperately trying to climb to safety, sent her under. He must have let go as soon as he went back beneath the waves.

Renata came up, sputtering, caught a breath and managed to grip him from behind, fixing her hand beneath his chin.

"Be still, *menino!* Just keep still!"

There was a clamor on deck, lanterns bobbing, frantic shouts. Basilio reached down and hauled the boy into the boat, cradling him over his knees so the water drained out of his gasping mouth. Boats were being lowered from the side. A lantern glanced on them.

"Is that the prince?" someone shouted. "You there, did you save the prince?"

Dom João, prince regent and ruler in all but name of Portugal and Brazil, was a much less frightening person than the royal judge. In periwig, with luxuriant side whiskers, this melancholy-eyed, rosebud-lipped prince of the Braganza line was pudgy and his thin hose showed that he had some distressing ailment that afflicted his legs with angry sores.

He kept his arm around his heir, nine-year-old Pedro, who hadn't taken his dark eyes off Renata. The lad was wonderfully handsome with black hair clustered in damp ringlets about his thin face. His younger brother, Miguel, sulking in a corner of the not very fragrant-smelling cabin, had pushed the heir overboard. He had whined that it was an accident, but Dom Pedro's tutor, who had happened along as the incident took place, maintained emphatically that it was not.

However that might be, Renata had been urged to name a reward, and she had.

Dom João gazed at her a long time, she thought a bit wistfully. Then he looked down at his son. "What do you think, Pedrinho? Is your rascally hide worth that of a diamond smuggler's?"

His son's wide eyes held just the hint of a laugh. "What do you think, lord father?"

Next day Juracy and Renata watched plumed, streamer-bedecked carriages labor up the hill to the governor's palace, where the *beija-mão* or ceremonial kissing of the royal hands, would take place before a solemn mass in the cathedral.

Thinner and paler from his time in jail, but with eyes that laughed as merrily as ever, Juracy kept his arm around

Renata as if he'd never let her go. People knelt as the carriages rolled by, but Queen Maria, who had ordered Tiradentes' death, screamed pitifully so that all could hear, "I'm in hell! I'm in hell!"

The Bahians looked at each other in astounded dismay, but at the palace, as the prince regent stepped out and smiled graciously at his people, it was little Dom Pedro, bowing and waving, who caused the wildest shouts.

"The prince of Brazil. Our prince!"

"So here they are," murmured Juracy. "Things will never be the same again."

"But don't you think the court will move back when it's safe in Lisbon?" Renata asked.

"Dom João may. But that Pedro, he'll grow up here. He'll care about Brazil. We're a kingdom now, not a colony."

The governor, commanders, rich planters, knights and officials, all pressed forward to kiss the royal hands. But Juracy kissed Renata. And she kissed him.

BOOK V
Pretty Mary

Tree that weeps,
Lament for the men who slash you, who drain your milk.
For thousands of years you gave them balls for playing,
A waterproofed quiver, a basket of daub.
Small tears; small weepings.

Another kind of man has come.
Another world requires your *cahout-chou*.
Like you, cupped endlessly,
The Indian works, trots his rounds,
Dips layer after layer of your milk
to smoke into the lumps that he must take to his master.
His life, bled like yours, scarred, soon ended.
Weep, tree.

There is drought, you are dying?
Messiah will come.
Sebastião will come.
Our knightly young king who died
Fighting the Moors,
With his court and his glory,
Sebastião will come.

He sleeps in the rock.
Show your faith with your blood.
Offer your babies.
When blood breaks the spell,

Sebastião will come.
His kingdom will come.

She was a flower, she was a song,
She was a bloom in the gray *caatinga*.
She was a flame in the harsh *sertão:*
the beauty of tortured thorns,
the toughness of drought-parched trees,
perfume and shade of the *joaz.*
And then she came out of cacao slime,
from gold fruit watered by blood.
She was Lampião's little sister.
Oh, brave police, to show her head!
But her spirit rides the *sertão,*
Her spirit rides, you cannot stop it.
Her spirit sings to the children:
Be free! Be free!

I

God Is an Absentee Landlord

The cowhunt was over, the branding done, and the bare ground in front of the bough-decked vaqueiros' houses thoroughly swept for the dance. Women and older men sat on stools, logs and stumps while children played in the light of the fire, on which an ox roasted, or slept wherever they could find a hammock or cowhide bed.

Most of the men squatted on their heels, weight on their toes, rolling *cigarros* or taking the edge off the day with shared jugs of *cachaça*. It was the Feast of Saint John, and though the *patrão*, Colonel Teófanes, lived on his cacao plantation near Ilheus, never in living memory having visited these backlands holdings, he permitted the vaqueiros who tended his herds to eat one of his oxen on this happiest celebration of the year.

He could be sure they would use only one. After all, year in, year out, didn't he trust them to put his brand on three out of four calves and put their own marks only on the fourth? This, though Colonel Teófanes didn't allow them to keep their calves so they might eventually have their own herds and become small ranchers as was sometimes done, though not so often in these new days.

Zeques dos Santos Avila had been born in 1889, the year Dom Pedro II, old, ailing and bewildered, had been told by the Army that he must abdicate. People who remembered his long reign thought of the Second Empire as a golden time, except for those who'd been ruined by abolition of slavery in 1888. The coffee planters of the South had long recruited free European laborers and were little affected, but many old sugar-plantation families suffered losses they never recouped. By 1912 rubber-tree seeds

305

smuggled out of Brazil, sprouted in England's Kew Gardens and established in Malaysian plantations, ended the Amazon monopoly and profiteers decamped. Some *seringueiros*, many driven from the *sertão* by cyclic droughts, eked out a living, but more *flagelados*, "beaten ones," sought work in seaboard cities or on burgeoning cacao plantations.

In the backlands, though, little had changed since *bandeirantes* started ranching there after the destruction of Palmares. Along with earlier *poderosos do sertão* they wiped out resisting Indians and fathered on the women a race of hardy *caboclos* with an admixture of blood from the few slaves and many runaways who reached the interior.

Since then, except when droughts starved them or forced them to flee, backlanders, *sertanejos*, tended cattle, drove them, with soothing songs, to market in Recife and Bahia or, during the gold rush, to Minas Gerais. Threatened always with catastrophe, the region produced a succession of gaunt mystics who promised their followers a Messiah. At Pedra Bonita almost a century ago, fifty people had spilled their blood to bring back Sebastião, Portugal's young king who had died on crusades against the Moors in 1578.

He did not come. Antonio the Counselor, not far from here, had set up his Kingdom of Heaven on Earth with eight thousand followers. He had preached against the Antichrist republic, and it had taken the army four expeditions and ten thousand men to wipe out Canudos, to the last defender, in 1897.

Antichrist or not, the republic and the succeeding government of Getulio Vargas, which had taken over after the Revolution of 1930, had not brought law to the backlands, though the power of formerly supreme *patrãos* had been divided. The humble had once been protected by allegiance to their landlord, but now these landlords vied for political leadership and fought private wars. Their tenants might be pillaged by their rivals' armed bands, and since the eighties there had been *cangaceiros*, bandits, lots of them.

Perhaps, as Zeques said philosophically, it was better to have an absentee landlord than one who stayed on his holdings and got into feuds with other important families.

At forty-three Zeques was as tough and weathered as the

leather he wore, a short, gray-haired, sinewy man who was still incomparable with his nine-foot-long cattle prod, the *guiada*. He could cure worms in cattle by a charm, was an expert maker of saddles and bridles, and was the best singer for miles around, though his voice was husky from years of crooning *aboiadas* to the cattle.

Zeques never boasted of it, but he was keenly aware that his great-grandfather, for whom he was named, had owned a fine ranch on the São Francisco that had been gambled away by his heir, and this great-grandfather's sister had been a love of the first Dom Pedro. It was Zeques' dream to hoard enough calf money to start his own little ranch someday, but the drought years, when not a coin was added to the little leather chest beneath the family altar, constantly frustrated his hope. He wanted this independence not for himself so much as for his daughter, Maria, most beautiful of the dozen women who were moving slowly, making no sound with their feet, as his guitar lured them to dance.

Maria had his gray eyes, startling in the amber skin inherited from her *caboclo* mother, dead years ago of childbed fever. Her lips were red and soft as the scarlet flower tucked into her black hair that hung straight and shining as satin, swirling now as tambourines clicked and spurred *vaqueiros*, jingling, revolved about the women.

Like Zeques, the men wore tight leather leggings and jackets. Several had vests of puma skin with the spots turned out, and young Sabino Ribeiro, circling Maria like a brown moth drawn to a flame, had thrust a red bromelia in his leather hat. As the music kindled into a stamping, fast *sapateado*, he clicked his fingers as they swept around each other and bent to speak in her ear.

"Maria, I branded for myself this year instead of for my father. Ten good calves. And I'm building a house."

"Are you, Sabino?" The rangy youth had a wide boyish face, the nose still stubby, the full mouth sensitive. His tightly curling mass of black hair bespoke a Negro forebear, but his face looked Indian. They had played together as children and she was fond of him in a sisterly way, so she smiled at him now and teased, "Who's going to live in your house, Sabino?"

"Will you?" he blurted.

She stopped in amazement. He moved her out of the dance to stand by a sweet-smelling *joaz* tree. "I've always loved you," he said, gulping the words, grasping her hand in his big callused one. "I know for a while you liked Roque Valente, but he's gone with the *cangaceiros*. Please, Maria—"

"I'm very fond of you, Sabino." Distressed to hurt this friend, she tried to soften her refusal. "But it wouldn't feel right. You're like family."

"I can change that."

She shook her head. "I love someone else."

Dark brows rushed together. "Roque? You can't marry a bandit!"

"No. All the same— Come, Sabino, they're starting a samba! Filomena's smiling at you."

"Let her smile at the devil!"

Stiff-backed, he stalked off to a knot of men who were more interested in *cachaça* than dancing. Maria, regretful but annoyed with him for blighting the evening, determined not to let him ruin this rare time of merrymaking and moved into the vibrant samba, smiling, though tears prickled at her eyes.

Last year at this feast Roque had finally realized that she was growing up, fifteen, an age when most girls were married. He'd stolen a kiss and whispered something about riding over soon from the neighboring ranch where he worked, but a few days later, the *patrão*'s son had raped his sister.

Roque killed him and fled. Word drifted back that he'd joined the famed Lampião's gang of bandits who operated throughout the interior. Maria supposed she'd never see him again, but it was his lean, smiling face she dreamed of. So long as that was true she wanted no other man.

When the first dancing ended, Marcolino, a squat, pock-marked vaqueiro with dangling arms, moved into the center of the clearing and made his *desafio,* a challenge to some other singer to match his improvised quatrains by picking

up his last line and composing a verse to be built on in its
turn.

Striking a rousing chord on his banjo, Marcolino began:

"In God's good time, amen!
 I am not jesting, no!
 I defy the entire world
 In singing at this show!"

Marcolino's skill at rhyming was so well known that for
a moment no one stepped out. Then a merry laugh sounded
from the shadows. Into the flickering yellow light strode a
tall young man.

He wore vaqueiro garb, but there was a green silk scarf
around his neck and the brim of his leather hat was pinned
up in front with silver medals; ruby, emerald and diamond
fires flashed from rings on his fingers, and he wore crossed
cartridge belts, a pistol and a sword-like *parnahyba* as well
as the broad-bladed "alligator knife" most vaqueiros carried. Crossing his arms, Roque Valente grinned down at
the shorter man.

"In singing at this show,
 You'd be wise not tarry.
 I've come here to play, friend,
 And dance with pretty Mary."

Mingled gasps and applause went up from the crowd.
Maria, holding a neighbor's fretful baby, blushed hotly and
then felt cold. Mother of God, how handsome he looked—
lithe as a wildcat, tawny eyes, hair and skin. Eyes that,
resting on her, shone with golden flame.

Marcolino was not to be thrown off by the shock. He
played an insulting little trill and echoed:

"And dance with pretty Mary?
 A *donzella* in bloom?
 Cangaceiros use hair oil
 And reek with perfume!"

"You win," Roque laughed, handing the banjo to its

owner. "But I've ridden a long way to dance. Let's have a good tune!"

People moved aside as he came to Maria. "I'd be worried if I couldn't see that the little one's too old for you to have had since I left these parts," he teased. The baby's mother took the child. Unshielded, Maria couldn't meet his caressing gaze.

"I—I'm glad to see you alive and well."

"Are you? Then quit looking at your toes and give me a smile."

She did, timidly, heart swelling with joy. He was only twenty, but he'd become a man. His face had thinned, the set of his mouth was harder, and he carried himself with assurance. As he watched her, his merriment faded. Without a word he led her to the clearing.

They stamped and whirled and clapped, danced to quick tunes and slow ones. Maria felt enchanted, as if Saint John, protector of lovers, had brought her sweetheart for this night.

It seemed forever; it seemed but a moment when a samba ended and he carried her hands to his lips. "Good night and good-bye, Maria bonita."

She clung to his hard brown hands. "Good-bye? You—you'll come again, won't you?"

"No. I had to have this last sweet time, Maria, but I love you too well to ask you to be a *cangaceiro*'s woman."

"Leave the *cangaço!*"

"Even if anyone dared hire me, my old *patrão* would have me killed." His voice roughened. "Marry a decent fellow like Sabino."

"I'll go with you. There are *cangaceiras,* I know."

"Do you know how they live, always on the dodge? No home, having to turn their babies over to someone else to raise because a child's a hindrance on a raid or in flight?"

She had no answer to that. He managed a laugh and nodded toward Zeques, who was watching them with a furrowed brow. "Anyhow, you don't think for a second your father would let you ride into such a life? I honor him too much to steal you."

He took a ring from his little finger, tested till he found a finger of hers it would fit. "I bought this," he said as the topaz winked. "Think of me sometimes, pray for me. But marry someone else."

His lips brushed hers. She cried out his name. But he had picked up his rifle and a worshipful boy brought up his horse. Maria followed him as far as the corral, leaned against the gate and sobbed.

Why had he come if it was to leave again?

She raged silently against him for a moment; then when her father came to take her in his arms, patting her hair as he had when comforting some childish heartbreak, she wept again.

Roque had come to tell her not to wait. Not to hope.

The cluster of vaqueiros' huts was situated above a large pond fed by dammed waters of a creek. From the growth beside it sang the mournful gray-necked rail and a harsher-toned horned screamer, a big, long-legged crested bird. Rolling tablelands, roamed by ostrich-like emus, stretched to dark hills that had been eroded to rock layers glittering with quartz. Bordering a "dead lake," a marshy area that showed green in the sere scrub thicket, rose *urucuri* palms, fronds swaying in the breeze. *Joaz* trees, evergreen, scattering their golden flowers on the earth, refreshed the eye, and the *umbú*, beloved tree of the backlands, lifted its interlacing boughs in a rounded shape. Cattle relished its leaves and its fruit made a delicious drink called *umbusada*. Dwarf cashews might spread their glossy green leaves only a yard above the ground, but beneath, the roots spread to an amazing depth.

Mandacarús reared above the thorny growth, at twenty feet high a cereus taller than most trees. Prickly pear found shallow rooting along spills of rock that sometimes looked like barricades or towers laid by human hands. There were many kinds of cactus, some rising like candelabra, others spread on the earth like spiny matting.

Wild pigs scavenged through the brush. Short-tailed little rock cavies scurried out of the way of pumas hoping for a deer or a weak and isolated cow. It was a struggle to stay alive in this harsh country, but Maria loved it, especially after rains that made leaves sprout on bare branches, covered the *umbu* with sweet-smelling white blossoms and made the *caatinga* flower scarlet, white and yellow.

This year, though, it began to seem there might be no flowering, no freshening of the silk-grass and browsing growth. The fitful *chuvas do cajú* in October could be seen falling, but heated air evaporated them before they reached the earth. Zeques' labor in cleaning out water holes, strengthening dams and plowing their small field to be ready to catch the rains seemed more of a mockery with each unrelenting day.

Thickets began to show skeletons of withered trees. Water in the pond sank day by day, and some of the water holes on the farther range were already dried up. Cracks split the tortured earth. Nights grew so cold that Maria shivered after she and Zeques had shared all their blankets, though the days stayed blastingly hot. Zeques' leather clothing stiffened and dried, though she rubbed tallow into it every night to try to keep it supple.

Fear of drought overshadowed Maria's longing for Roque. At night when she and her father knelt at the little altar niche lighted by tallow candles, they added prayers for rain to the usual ones for the souls of dead family members, especially Maria's mother, Caterina.

Caterina was buried beside the road to town so that she wouldn't be lonely but would have the prayers of those who passed by. Maria walked there with Zeques at least each Sunday, and the weathered cross above the mound of rocks had always been decked with boughs or flowers different from those of the week before. Everyone prayed at such graves, whether the dead were strangers or not, even if they had been enemies. Sometimes Maria went alone to sit by the cross and talk to the mother she had never known. It helped to pour out her heart. She loved Zeques, but there was much a man couldn't understand, more that would worry him. Like her love for Roque.

Not that Zeques could pay much attention to anything except the threatening drought.

On a short afternoon in November, he came in to sink dispiritedly into a leather chair. Their hut of wooden stakes and boughs covered by a foot of clay was like the other dwellings, but thanks to Zeques' skill, had better furnishings.

In this room that served every purpose except sleeping were a rawhide-topped table, two stools and handsomely carved leather chests to hold bedding and clothing. From pole rafters hung the hammock-like food container with dried meat, bags of *urucuri* fruit Maria had gathered, hard chunks of *rapadura,* leather containers of farinha, and *passoca,* a mixture of farinha, ground nuts, salt and sugar. There were leather water pails, baskets Maria had woven of ipecacuanha fiber, and hunting bags of tough cactus fiber. During the verdant season, from December to April, Zeques milked the cows, Maria made cheese and they enjoyed plentiful curds and milk, with *jerimum,* an edible gourd, but for over half the year the cows had all they could do to stay alive without producing milk.

At night Zeques slung his bamboo hammock in this room while Maria occupied the tiny sleeping chamber. A thatched roof extended in front of the house, with a long low bench opposite a stake-supported pole where Zeques' saddle, halters, bridle and other gear hung.

Cattle, the vegetation on which they lived, and the people who depended on both survived each year the formidable dry season of seven months, but if no rain fell after that, there was no store of moisture in creeks, ponds or plants to sustain humans or animals for long.

"Remember old Temêro, the brindle who followed me like a dog because I hand-raised him when his mama died?" Zeques asked.

Like the change from intense heat to chill, day passed at this season immediately into night, and it was so dark in the hut that Maria, busy stewing *jerimum* and beef, didn't notice her father's expression.

"Of course I know Temêro." She laughed. "Everyone calls him your *compadre* and jokes that he'll die of old age, since you'll never sell or eat him."

"He died, but not of old age." Zeques sounded so sad that Maria ran to him and pressed his work-hardened hands to her face. "I dug out a well in the far pasture last week. I thought it would keep that herd going for a while. But when I walked out there today, poor Temêro lay dead in the mud along with two others. I dug another well in the creek bed, but it won't last long."

"You walked those miles, Papa? In this scorching heat?"

"I can't ride Mancha, child. I bring him *joaz* branches, but he's bonier each day."

Fear clutched at her. Old people still spoke of that worst drought in 1877–78, when hundreds of thousands of people died, when *flagelados* jammed the cities looking for work while out in the perishing *sertão* people clinging miserably to life ate those who had died. This familiar little world, hard but built from their efforts, had always seemed safe, but Maria, cold to the heart, knew that unless it rained, all the cattle would die, this world would end. And what would become of them?

Maria made a silent prayer and tried to cheer Zeques. "It'll soon be Saint Lucy's Day, Papa. Perhaps she'll show us lots of rain."

As night fell like a black shroud on December 12, Zeques set six lumps of salt in a row on a stump near the house where dew would reach them. From left to right, each lump represented a month from January to June.

At daybreak Maria went out with him and felt sick as she saw that not a single lump had dissolved. She had prayed for moisture to have melted the lumps into a damp mass that would signify rain for the whole season, but if this old augury was right, no month would bring even light showers.

She put her hand on her father's arm. He took a deep breath and straightened his sagging shoulders. "Well, Saint Joseph may be kinder. Meanwhile I'll dig more wells."

He and the other vaqueiros did this. They hacked cereus into bits and lopped off boughs of the *joaz*, the only tree that still had leaves, and fed these to the famished cattle who huddled in the dead lakes, heads hanging, sometimes lowing pitifully as they tried to smell out some water.

Maria tried to conserve the dwindling farinha by making bread from the scraped roots of the *urucuri* and cooking the roots of the *umbu*, suffering tree that was slowly losing its life to nourish cattle and people. She gathered small coconuts and the tender inner stalks of bromeliads.

Parakeets and the other birds had long since flown to

kinder lands, but bats multiplied, swooping to feed on the scraggly cattle. Pumas, driven by hunger, came to the doors of the huts.

An image of Saint Benedict, patron of the blacks who was once himself a farmer, in the town where the weekly fairs were held, had brought rain before. Zeques, Maria and the other ranch people, as well as most of the surrounding countrymen, trudged to the small town with heavy rocks carried on their heads and shoulders, bore the saint in a procession, chanting prayers, walked the long way carrying tapers, but all they had to show for it was bruised feet.

On Saint Joseph's Day, March 19, not a cloud softened the blinding glare of the sun. It rose and sank without a hint to presage rain in the following year.

Zeques' despair was so great that he said nothing, nor did he pray aloud as he and Maria knelt that night at the altar. God and the saints had forsaken the *sertão,* but one might still pray to the Mother who had suffered as a mortal.

The vaqueiros dug, but the water had sunk far beneath layers of rock. By excavating the creek bed that watered the main pond, they managed to produce a seep that meagerly supplied water for the households, but it was only a matter of days till that would be gone, too. The other vaqueiros left on foot, carrying little bundles. All their life's toil in a few rags, an old musket, a few hoarded coins. If there was no work on the seaboard, at least they could fish. And there was water for drinking. It had come to that.

In this extremity, Sabino came to see them. He led his starving horse. "I'm going to my uncle in Fortaleza. He has a carpenter shop and I can help. Maria, will you come with me?"

"I must stay with Papa."

Zeques rolled a *cigarro,* handed it to their guest. "Go with him if you wish, daughter. I can't stand to watch these animals die. I'm going to drive those in my charge to market and take the money to Colonel Teófanes, ask him for work in the cacao groves."

"But, Papa, this is our home, you're a vaqueiro—"

"Child, we must get out while we can still walk."

"Then I'll go with you." She pressed Sabino's hand. "God be with you, dear friend. Good luck in Fortaleza."

He stared at her, ducked his head, muttered inaudibly and shambled away, he and his horse both pathetic caricatures of what they had been.

"Why don't the *patrãos* do something to help?" Maria cried, turning to her father. It hurt to see her childhood playmate, robbed of his dreams and labor, become a *flagelado,* though, having an uncle with a business, he was luckier than most.

"The *patrãos* can't make it rain."

"No, but they could decide to sell the cattle instead of letting all of us battle to keep them alive. They don't have to see the cows stagger around till they fall or hear them low as if they were weeping!"

"Soon we won't, either," Zeques said wearily. "Get what we can carry together, lass. I'm setting fire to the *macambira* to burn off enough thorns so the cattle can have something to eat before we start them to town."

The searing northeast wind carried the blaze through the impenetrable thickets, singeing off enough thorns so the animals could each get a few acrid mouthfuls. Since each hour's delay sapped both their energy and the cattle's, they set off that evening. The leather furniture Zeques had made with such artistry had to be left behind. Maria folded their extra clothing into blankets and stowed into leather bags the few remaining handfuls of farinha and dried meat.

At least, since Zeques, saving for his little ranch, had been so frugal, they had money enough, once they'd made their way to the nearest railroad, to take a train to the coast and then passage on a boat to Ilheus.

"Colonel Teófanes, he'll give me work," said Zeques, leading his horse. He would give this faithful comrade to a friend in town rather than leave him to die at the dry pond. "I'll give him the money for his cattle and he'll know I did all I could."

Maria bit her tongue. Be grateful to the *patrão* for giving her father a chance to die slaving in the cacao groves? When the colonel spent most of his time in Paris and Bahia, sustained by so many holdings that he could shrug at the starving of his serfs and animals?

In her brooding, as half the cattle fell on that march and could not be urged to their feet, Maria coupled God and the colonel, remote indifferent powers who judged but did not help. She hated both.

When she knelt with her father in farewell at her mother's grave, it was to Mary the afflicted woman she prayed, not to God the Father, who had shown no mercy to hers.

Or to the animals.

It was like a walk through hell after dawn came. Cattle lay dead, their hides so baked that even buzzards' beaks couldn't tear through them. Horses looked as if they'd been stuffed, legs and bodies hard and shriveled, necks long and thin. A puma had died clawing at a dry watercourse, its emaciated body frozen in a last paroxysm.

The sun's rays seemed to reflect, dazzlingly multiplied, from the barren earth. Silica and quartz gleamed like sparks from rents in hillocks and the very air, shimmering incandescently as if coming from a furnace, seared eyes, throat and nostrils. When a cow dropped for good, Zeques ended its woe by slicing its throat. The blood was so thick it scarcely flowed. Now and then Zeques handed Maria the leather bag and they shared the last slimy water from the pond.

If they died along the road, Maria wondered how long it would be before someone passed with the strength to bury them. After the first assault on Canudos, the bodies of dead soldiers and their horses had been preserved by dry, hot air so that they seemed to be resting all along this road.

But the people had been beaten at last. At the end a boy and three men had died defending their holy city and the grave of Antonio the Counselor as five thousand troops swarmed in.

The people always lost.

There were other *flagelados* on the boat, sleeping on the deck, eating whatever food they had. "You think you're going to get rich, save enough to go back to the *sertão* when the drought ends and start over?" jeered one cacao worker, a wizened *caboclo* who was returning from a trip he'd made to Aracajú to bury his mother. "By the time they charge you for your tools, your hut and food, you'll be in debt to the colonel—and you'll never pay him off.

Year after year, what you need at his store will come to more than what you've earned."

The other men shuffled their feet uneasily, but Zeques, smoothing his long cattle prod with which he had been unwilling to part, said confidently, "My *patrão*, Colonel Teófanes, he won't be like that. I've worked for him all my life and he's never questioned my accountings."

"He likely never saw them," said the other. He grinned, proffered his bottle of *cachaça,* suddenly becoming a friend. "But I hope you're right, comrade. I hope your boss is better than most. Of course if you're good at killing, you can earn real money. A colonel always needs *jagunços,* though not as bad as when they were fighting over land, bushwhacking each other and driving out small-holders who'd managed to get a little piece of ground." He spat. "The cacao grows well. It's mulched with flesh and blood."

"I'm not a *jagunço,*" Zeques said. That came out with conviction, though since they'd left the market town, the limit of his previous existence, he'd seemed dazed, so bewildered and lost that Maria had shifted for them, asking directions, getting them on trains and later on the boat.

The monkey-like brown man shrugged. "So much the worse for you, friend. Here, have another drink."

In Ilheus, some idlers at the dock stopped smirking at Zeques' worn leather clothes and cattle prod long enough to answer that, sure, Colonel Teófanes was in town, you didn't catch him at his plantation more than he had to be. His house was just off the square, anyone there could show them.

A turbaned mulatta stood scornfully in the door, but when she heard that Zeques had some money for the colonel, she told them to come in. After a moment, she reappeared and motioned them down the corridor.

"Leave that thing by the door," she said, nodding at Zeques' *guiada.*

Colonel Teófanes had ruddy cheeks, white hair and piercing dark eyes. As he put down his newspaper, Maria was fascinated by his smooth hands, the beautifully shaped pink fingernails. She had never seen such hands. He was in spotless white, which made her acutely aware of her crumpled dirty clothing. When there was water, she liked to bathe every other day, but she couldn't remember when she'd had her last full bath. The colonel's nostrils wrinkled and she burned with shame, which was quickly drowned by fury.

"So you're José dos Santos?" he said in a pleasant, mildly interested way. "Let's see, you're from Boa Agua. I've heard the drought's severe."

Zeques told him how bad in a few halting sentences, produced a small bag which he placed in those astounding hands, finer than a lady's, each finger glittering with rings. "I'm sorry I couldn't get more for the cattle, Colonel Teófanes, but they were skin and bones and everyone's selling so the beasts won't be a complete loss."

"I believe you did the best you could," said the colonel. "Fortunately, there's been enough rain for the cacao and my sugarcane's doing well." He picked up his paper. "Tell Otilia to give you a meal."

Zeques stood as if stunned. He gave a nervous cough. "Colonel, *patrão,* I need work. I thought you might use me in the cacao."

The colonel's eyes shifted to Maria. Not for long, but when he spoke to her father, she felt as if the colonel had seen through her clothes.

"Your daughter will work, too?"

"Yes, Colonel Teófanes," she said with a glimmer of hope.

If they both earned, if they saved—maybe in a few years they could go back, buy a few cows and start a herd. She was already homesick, and for Zeques it must be worse.

The colonel stroked his pink chin. He wasn't fleshy, but very solid, very heavy in his motions. "I suppose I can give you a place. Three milreis a day for you, two for your daughter. Your house is free, but you pay for your tools and food."

Zeques hadn't wept when he killed the dying cattle on that awful trip to town, or when he gave his horse away, but he did now, stammering as he bent to kiss the colonel's beautiful hand. "God preserve you, *patrão.* I'll—we'll work hard!"

"I'm sure you will." The edge of the colonel's smile

lingered on Maria, but joyous at the promised wages, she barely noticed.

They'd save every milreis they could; maybe she could grow some of their food and save on that. Her heart swelled with gratitude. The colonel was a good man after all, giving them a new start.

She was less sure of that after they'd been to the plantation store. Of course, seeing so much food after near starvation, they went a little wild, bought coffee, *rapadura*, farinha, beef, salt, rice and beans, a slab of salt pork, soap, *cachaça*. The storekeeper told Zeques he'd need a scythe, ax and pick for clearing forest to plant more cacao.

"Your cattle prod won't do you any good here, vaqueiro." The plump balding man chuckled. "You've got a knife, but if your daughter's to harvest, she'll need one. And you can't work in that leather. You need cotton pants and a shirt."

Zeques stared at the figures "A hundred and twenty milreis for the tools, senhor? Seventy for the clothes?"

"Of course they're cheaper in town." The clerk shrugged. "But it costs to bring them here and give you credit. You can't pay cash, can you?"

The journey had exhausted their little hoard. Zeques swallowed and made his cross on the bill. The food came to another twenty-five. It was a staggering sum, but Maria cooked them a good meal, for it was evening by then, and she scraped plenty of *rapadura* into the fragrant coffee.

That and the hot tasty food revived their spirits. "Between us we'll earn thirty milreis a week," Maria calculated. "If we're careful, we can eat on twenty, less if we can raise a little garden. So we can pay off the bill at ten milreis a week, Papa."

He finished the mental arithmetic first because he was used to counting cattle. "That's seventeen weeks, say four months, *filha.*" He smiled sadly. "But you need a dress. And my clothes will wear out. We may need medicine. It'll be a long time before we pay that bill off."

"I'll make our clothes." Maria got him more coffee and kissed his weathered cheek. "We'll save, Papa, and after the drought we'll go home. We'll buy a few good cows and you can work for someone who'll let you keep the ones you earn. Why, in a few years we'll have our own place and every widow in the country will be crazy to marry you!''

He laughed at that and had a *cigarro* while she washed out the spoons, gourd bowls and iron kettle they'd carried with them. Moving into the one-room hut had been simple, slinging hammocks, hanging their few extra garments from pegs, since they now had no storage chest, placing their Madonna in a corner niche, storing food in some of the fiber bags she'd brought along.

The last occupant had left the hard earth floor swept clean, and beneath the extended front roof thatch were a couple of stumps and a log for sitting, convenient slabs of wood close to the fire pit that served as tables for preparing meals. Maria was sorry Zeques didn't have his comfortable leather chair, but he could make new furniture when they went back to the Northeast, back where you could see for miles to the familiar dark mountains with their diamond gleamings.

They knelt before the Madonna and her child, prayed for the dead, for steadfastness and patience, and at the last, Zeques said, "Bless and protect our good *patrão*. Have in your keeping Colonel Teófanes."

At first the green after the blighted *caatinga* had seemed wondrous, and Maria's first glimpses of the golden cacao pods growing amidst glossy leaves made her catch her breath. Long ago some visitor had told her a story about magic golden apples, and she thought now that cacao must be as beautiful.

That was at dawn. In a few hours she had come to hate the fruits she and the other women and children picked up from the ground after the men had detached them from the tree with sickles mounted on long poles. Each pod had to be held in one hand while she split it open with the broad-bladed knife. It would be easy to lose a finger. She saw that some of the workers had, but an overseer rode through the grove, scolding at those who were slow or left pods on the tree, and she cut herself several times, though not seriously.

The cream-colored pulp was sweet and refreshing. When her mouth got dry, she took a few segments and crushed them slowly with her teeth, enjoying the small trickle of juice that tasted like pineapple, only milder.

Zeques soon got the hang of severing even the highest pods. He wore his shirt, unlike the other men, partly because his torso had no protective tan but more, Maria suspected, because he'd be embarrassed around the women. They stopped at noon just long enough for farinha, dried beef and a delicious jack fruit. They worked till dusk. Maria's shoulders and wrists ached and she was so bone-weary she could barely make farinha mush with beef. Zeques, who'd had to reach and cut for thirteen hours, must have been even tireder. She began to understand why the workers didn't have gardens.

They went to bed right after prayers, and their prayers that night were short.

The people sang while they worked. Soon Maria could join in the melancholy chants of the women:

> "My life's a hard one,
>   Hard as hard can be,
>   Where is my sweetheart,
>   Where wanders he?"

And the men would answer:

> "I harvest the cacao
>   In the cacao groves—"

The split pods were put in wicker baskets and carried by donkeys to the fermenting trough. Here other workers trod out the pulp, separating the kernels, which then went into the big drying trays for more treading before they were roasted in the oven.

"I don't mind harvesting," said Zeques the first day the overseer assigned him to the troughs. "But that rotting cacao slime, it's all I can smell now even though you've made us these good beans." He looked ruefully at his feet, still stained though he'd scrubbed them. "They say you get a rind on your feet after a while. They say once you get in the cacao slime, you never get out of it."

"We will," Maria said. But by now her aims had dropped to paying off the store and saving enough for the journey home.

At least they were eating; at least they weren't having to watch the suffering of animals they couldn't help. But when she sang mournful songs with the women, she wondered where Roque was, if she would ever see him again, and she sometimes thought her heart must break.

Usually the big plantation house was empty, but one night it glowed with lights and next morning the colonel rode with the husky mulatto overseer. He called out genial remarks to the workers. To Zeques, he said, "Well, vaqueiro, I see you've learned to handle a sickle instead of your cattle prod."

Coming even with Maria, the colonel reined in and again she had that naked feeling, as if he were seeing exactly how she looked beneath the cheap cotton dress that clung sweatily to her breasts and body.

"How would you like to work in the house?" he asked.

His lips looked red beneath his trim white mustache. Pausing uneasily, Maria stammered, "Oh, I like working outdoors, Colonel."

He frowned. "You'd get three milreis a day, and the work's much easier."

"Please, senhor—"

Zeques was in earshot and called to her with a note of rebuke, "You ought to appreciate the colonel giving you such a good job. Of course you'll work in the house!"

The colonel smiled. "That's settled. Take a bath and come right up."

Full of nameless misgivings, she bathed in the stream, put on a clean dress, and went reluctantly to the house, entering from the side, as she'd seen the servants do. A black woman who was polishing a satiny rosewood table gave her an appraising look. "The colonel wants to see you in his library. Just go up the stairs, and it's the first room on the right."

Maria felt sick with apprehension, as if she hadn't eaten for days yet was gorged with some unhealthy substance. She crept up the stairs, too frightened to pay attention to the splendid furnishings apart from seeing that there were great crystal chandeliers and many-hued carpets.

The door stood open. Maria knocked timidly. "Come in, my dear," called the *patrão*. He was sitting in a throne-like wicker chair with an attached footrest. A clove-skinned girl whose little breasts thrust like hard green fruit against her coarse shift knelt and massaged scented ointment into the colonel's pink toes, which were as exquisitely tended as his hands.

"That'll do for now, Lita." He gave the girl a dismissing pat on the flank.

She passed Maria, and as she did, shot her a sullenly venomous look. The colonel wore a white silk robe so thin that the color of his flesh and the contour of almost feminine breasts and mauve nipples showed through. He sat down a glass of juice and offered Maria a silver dish of round dark brown things.

"Take one, child. This is what happens to lots of the cacao you harvest. These chocolates are from Switzerland, the best to be had."

She nibbled, forgetting some of her uneasiness as she reached a nut-crunchy center that melted deliciously with the chocolate. It had the smell of the roasted kernels or she wouldn't have believed him.

"Have another," he encouraged. His tone had thickened.

Maria stepped back. "Thank you, Colonel Teófanes, but I won't be greedy."

"Why not?" He chuckled. "You can have all the chocolates you want if you'll be nice to me. A pretty dress, too." He reached in a pocket of the robe and extracted a necklace of multicolored brilliants, prettier than any Maria had ever seen at a fair. "Do you like this?"

Invisible weights seemed to press in on her from all sides, holding her where she was. She couldn't believe what her instincts were telling her, not about the *patrão* whom her father blessed each night.

She said desperately, "If the colonel would tell me where to work—"

"I'll do the work, my sweet little flower. All you have to do is enjoy it." His hand was soft but surprisingly powerful as he pulled her down beside him. He cupped her breast in his palm, ran his fingers down her body and up her skirt.

"*Patrão!* Please—"

She twisted wildly, tried to wrest free, but he laughed, sucked in his breath as his fingers moved between her legs. "Don't be scared, pretty. We'll play such nice games—"

She fastened her teeth in his wrist. He yelped. In the instant that he cuffed her, there was a sound of speeding feet and a smothered cry. A cattle prod transfixed the colonel, tearing through his throat to protrude on the other side of the chair.

Blood foamed from his mouth. He grappled with the prod, gurgling. Half a dozen *jagunços* shot Zeques at such close range that parts of him were blasted away.

II

The Bandits

~~~~~~~~~~~~~~~~~

Maria was imprisoned at Riacho, the nearest town to the plantation. The jailer raped her. None of it seemed real. Surely she'd wake up, find Zeques smiling at her in his calm, steady way.

How wicked she'd been to think they worked too hard for a wage that fed and kept them! The God who neglected his tenants had changed to one who punished. Guilt tormented her, though a part of her mind knew that the colonel would have had her whatever she did. If she'd made no fuss—

Zeques would have defended her anyway. From her cell she heard the jailer talking to the soldiers who were stationed in the town.

"Gal would never have stayed virgin to her age if she'd lived under the colonel's nose. The old goat took every girl on the plantation as soon as she bled. But you can't have wild men from the backlands spearing important people."

"Didn't the *jagunços* say this one made up to the colonel so her father could kill and rob him?"

The jailer chortled. "Sure, they said it, and they'll swear to it to the judge and the wench will spend her days in prison. But my brother-in-law's the overseer, and he says after she went up to the big house like the colonel told her, some of the workers started telling this José dos Santos that he ought to eat high off the hog as long as the colonel fancied his girl. When he heard how the colonel tups all the young ones, he went crazy."

"Those hillbillies are touchy about their women," a soldier said. "Ought to stay out in the *sertão*. Well, I think I'll go back there and try to cheer her up."

Maria cringed against the wall, but when he stepped in-side the cell, she met him with her claws.

They were struggling when the jailer opened the cell. Someone caught the soldier's hair, dragged back his neck. There was the sound of steel on cartilage and the body fell away.

Roque caught Maria up in his arms. He stepped over the soldier and down the corridor to the anteroom, where long-haired men in bright scarfs and turned-back leather hats held pistols on the other three soldiers.

For the first time Roque spoke. "Did these men molest you, Maria?"

"No," she said, and fainted in his arms.

Thirty *cangaceiros* had ridden into Riacho. They can-tered out again, tossing coins to the children, flirting with the girls. This was a lightning raid to rescue Roque's sweetheart. News of the colonel's slaying and her arrest had spread all over the country. The moment Roque heard of it, he'd asked for volunteers willing to risk a journey south of their usual range, one where there'd be no loot.

He'd wanted to kill the mayor, police chief and leading citizens of the town for allowing Maria to be jailed, but Lampião had forbidden it. The Bahia police and soldiery were more zealous than those of neighboring states, and he didn't want them on his trail unnecessarily.

It took three days to reach the ranch where Lampião was encamped. Scattered throughout his region of domination in northeastern Brazil were numerous *coiteros*, protectors, who sheltered and helped him, some from real friendship, others because they had no choice if they cared to live. Police and soldiers preserved a certain order in large towns, but in rural areas, in villages and on ranches, the power of the *cangaceiros* was greater than the government's. *Vo-lantes*, the "flying squads" that were supposed to pursue the bandits, scarcely lived up to their name.

"They come three days after I'm gone," Lampião liked to joke.

Virgulino Ferreira da Silva got his nickname, Lantern, because he could fire a lever-action rifle fast enough to make a continuous glow in the darkness. He was in his mid-thirties, and the mildness of his aspect was increased by the gold-rimmed spectacles. He wore his hair long and kept it doused with brilliantine, a style most of his followers adopted. Pictures of Padre Cicero, a backlands mystic and miracle worker, were pinned to his clothing, and he wore scapulars on neck and back. As much as possible he fasted on Fridays and prayed, carried out no banditry during Holy Week and refrained from meat.

"I don't like this life, little sister." He had taken a fancy to Maria and called her that. His woman, a handsome backlander also named Maria, wasn't jealous. Lampião took other women who caught his eye when he went to town or visited a ranch, but within the "family," faithfulness was strictly enforced to avoid quarrels. "I've been a farmer, a muleteer, and a vaqueiro—hard lives, but a bandit's is worse."

Corisco, a blond young man whose cruelties belied his angel face, slapped his leg and guffawed. "You'd make a good governor, boss. You're certainly expert in collecting taxes."

Life in the *cangaço* wasn't what Maria had expected. She had supposed the band raided continuously, but she had been three months with them and the wildest thing they'd done was go to a dance on a neighboring ranch.

With his reputation long made, Lampião seldom had to resort to armed robbery. Powerful politicians and ranchers were glad to pay him to leave their properties alone. When he moved into a new area, he'd ride into town and tell the mayor how much money he'd accept to depart without doing damage. Then he'd toss coins to street urchins and his men would spend freely in bars and whorehouses before they skylarked out of town singing "Mulher Rendeira," a song they'd composed themselves that had become their anthem:

"The girls of Villa Bela,
They're poor but full of action . . ."

Another surprise was that the bandits, like the *volantes* who pursued them, walked more often than they rode. When striking out across the *caatinga,* the thorny growth

was often too dense for a horse and rider to get through.
The bandits rode when they could, of course, and when
sojourning in regions with good roads sometimes hired au-
tomobiles and drivers.

But these were rare occasions. Usually, as now, Lampião preferred to live in the remote country where he was
lord, popularly called "the governor of the backlands,"
where he issued "passports" to those under his protection
so that no one would molest them. In spite of this power,
he couldn't settle long in a place. Soldiers had killed many
of his men over the years, and he often gave a new recruit
the name of a dead comrade in order to confuse his enemies
about his strength.

So though the bandits fastened their silk scarves with a
diamond ring and wore more on their fingers, though the
women had gold and jewels, there wasn't much the bandits
could do with their plentiful money. They lived in brush
shelters, cooked in the open, and ate the backlander's diet
of dried beef, farinha and *rapadura*.

Roque had tried to give Maria necklaces and bracelets,
ruby and emerald and diamond rings, but she'd refused
everything except a small gold band that had been his
mother's.

"Why won't you have them?" His smooth mouth wrinkled. "I want my Maria Bonita to look like a queen."

She didn't like to hurt his feelings, but he persisted till
she had to say, "Roque, these don't belong to me."

He stared. "I took them off rich women—the kind who
don't care if a girl like you starves or rots in jail."

"They're still not mine."

"Holy saints, Maria, what a fool you are!"

The dark center of his gold-brown eyes expanded. He
grasped her shoulders, gave her a small shake. "You're a
cangaceira now! You have to forget that nonsense."

Tears filled her eyes. She adored Roque since he'd saved
her from jail and hated to make him angry, especially since
the way she went rigid in his arms when he wanted to love
her must have made him wish he'd never risked his life to
get her. She couldn't help it, though, even after all these
weeks. It was the sweetest thing on earth to kiss him, rest
in his embrace, but the moment he started to touch her

where the jailer had—then he wasn't Roque anymore, her beloved.

He wouldn't take her when she lay frozen, though she did nothing to prevent him, had even sobbed once, "If you go ahead—if you keep talking to me, I'll try to know it's you."

"Hush, silly." Turning on his back, he cradled her head on his shoulder, stroked her hair with his big rough hand. "Some of the men like to rape women, especially those of soldiers or police, but I never have. Do you think I'd start with you? We'll wait till you want me."

So good to her. So patient. As he watched her in angry hurt, holding the rejected jewelry, she started to say she'd wear his gift of one thing, but her father's face rose before her.

Zeques, who'd care for a strayed cow whose owner was unknown till it died of old age rather than eat it or drive it to market. Zeques, who had shared out choice and scrub calves with absolute fairness between him and his *patrão*, not marking the best ones for himself.

So that *patrão* had betrayed his trust. So God didn't care what happened to people. That made it all the more necessary to have honor.

She brought Roque's brown hand to her face, kissed it supplicatingly. "My father wouldn't like it, Roque. If the dead know what we do, I don't want him to feel bad." She hadn't really cried about her father yet. The numbness that followed his death hadn't worn off in the jail, exposed as she was to brutal attacks. The horror had been so overwhelming that the healing of grief had been denied her.

Now that vision of Zeques released something. She began to weep, sobs wracked her, and she poured out to Roque how at first she and Zeques had hoped to save enough milreis to go back home, how he'd always prayed for the colonel. And her guilty wonderings, could she have kept her father from dying?

"But I never smiled at the colonel, Roque. I can't think of a single thing I did—"

Holding her close, he kissed her tears. "You were young and pretty and in his reach. I wish the old stoat were still alive so I could geld him. Cry for your good father, sweetheart, but don't think about the colonel. No one will ever hurt you again as long as I'm alive.''

He caressed her. His tears mingled with hers. At last Maria was purged, wept clean and free of poisons. When Roque's hands moved lightly from her shoulders to her breasts, brushing them light as the touch of butterflies, she stiffened for a moment, but this was Roque, this was her love. They were new together, this was different.

As if taking away every trace of the past he touched and kissed her all over. When he entered her gently, warm honey welled within her, welcoming, drawing him to her depths, clasping him there in pulsing, throbbing sweetness. His cry came with hers. A fountain sprayed thick gold glowing to her darkest parts, laving and lighting them.

Roque's tawny head rested on her breast. Strange, but when he'd become her man, her lover, he'd also become her child. She ached with tenderness for him. Perfect joy, perfect peace. Except for her father's death, this was worth everything that had happened to her.

Corisco and some of the more restless bandits sometimes went off for days and returned boasting that they'd taken over a ranch or village and made the owner or leading people ransom their peace. Maria avoided Corisco as much as she could after learning that he had once tracked down a man who had offended him and flayed him alive.

Maria also turned away from the speculative glance of tall black José Bahiano. It outraged Lampião to see women with short skirts and short hair. He used to whip them, but José now enforced the bandit's standards of modesty. A number of backlands women wore his brand, JB, on their faces or thighs, buttocks or more private places. José sang beautifully, but Maria never liked to hear him.

Still, in daily life most of the bandits were good-natured and behaved like brothers, with Lampião the respected eldest. A card game was always in process and there was much singing, swapping of stories, and dancing at night to the music of guitars and banjos. Lampião often read aloud, from newspapers and the small ''cordel'' books sold in markets, so called because they hung over a cord. Many of these books had been written about the bandit. His favorite was one in which he went to hell and made the devil glad to have a truce with him.

There were ballads about his exploits, and some mentioned his "sealed body" no bullet or knife could penetrate. This protection came from several handwritten prayers he always carried. He had copied off one of these for Roque, who told Maria the words, though he couldn't read them. ". . . *With the love of the Virgin Mary I am covered and with the blood of my Father Jesus Christ I am bound. . . . If they shoot at me, water will run from the barrels of their guns. . . . Delivered I was, delivered I am, and delivered I shall be."*

The brush shelters were scattered widely enough for privacy. A number of bandits had women. They had all been taught to shoot in case they had to defend themselves, but seldom went on raids. The saddest part of their life was having to give their babies almost at once into the keeping of a friend or relative. At least they could occasionally visit the children and spent much time in sewing for them as they sat together and chatted.

Dona Maria had a sewing machine and ran up new clothing for members of the band, which the other women handfinished. The captain's woman also made many dainty little garments for their small daughter, Expedita, who was being kept by a vaqueiro and his wife in Sergipe.

"When she's school age, she'll go to live with the captain's brother," said Dona Maria, carefully stitching lace to a little pink dress. "At least there's one, thank the good God, that didn't enter the *cangaço*. The other three who did are all dead, and my man's heart has been torn out of him each time, especially when Ezekiel, his kid brother, was killed last year." She gave Maria a shrewd glance. "Aren't you expecting a little one?"

Maria blushed. "Yes, in the autumn. Oh, Don' Maria, I'd give anything to keep the baby!"

The chieftain's woman shook her head. "I know, but a child's in the way when we have to move in a hurry, and imagine bringing up your baby in a bandit camp. The best thing is to find a good home and turn the baby over before you can get too attached to it." She added kindly, "If you and Roque don't know anyone trustworthy, the captain will find somebody.''

"Thank you, Don' Maria, but Don' Irici, the foreman's wife, has already offered.''

Maria nodded. "She's a fine woman. We surely won't be here that long, but you can get the baby back to her. And don't worry about a midwife. The captain helps most of our women. He's skillful and very gentle.''

Such assurances didn't ease Maria's fierce need to keep Roque's child. Though she'd accepted bandit life because there'd been no choice, she'd harbored a dream that someday Roque would leave the *cangaço,* that they'd be able to have a little farm or ranch in some remote corner. He quickly blasted this hope when she voiced it. "Have you forgotten I killed my *patrão?* His important friends and relatives would be on me in a flash if I left the *cangaço.* Besides, a poor man in Brazil is just dirt. As if it's not enough to contend with land and weather, he's pushed around by everyone, the colonels, soldiers and bandits. I couldn't put up with that, Maria.''

"But our baby—''

Muscles tightened in his jaw. He took her in his arms. "Sweetheart, Don' Irici and her husband will take care of our little one, and we can pay for anything he needs. When he's old enough for school, we'll give him a good education. He can be a doctor or lawyer or engineer. He won't live as we have. But think! Even if we managed to hide someplace and grub out a living, what could we do for the child?''

"We could love him—or *her.*''

He shrugged. "Our parents loved you and me, Maria, but did that protect us?''

He was right. Though it broke her heart, she talked to Don' Irici the next time they were both washing clothes down at the river.

The foreman's wife was a plump middle-aged woman whose greatest grief was that she was barren. Her skin was pale, but she had Indian features and straight black hair. She gathered Maria to her soft bosom and patted her shoulder.

"It's sad for your, dear, no getting around it. But I'll

love your baby like my own, and if you're ever able to take the child back, we'll not give you an argument."

"You're very kind. It's a lot to ask, even of a relation."

Dona Irici cocked her head. "Isn't your name dos Santos?"

"Yes. My great-great-grandfather, for whom my father was named, had a big *fazenda* on the São Francisco."

"So did mine." The older woman laughed. "His son had a beautiful *caboclo* mistress who stayed with him even after he gambled everything away. The *caboclo* gave him eight children. One was my grandmother."

"Then we are related!" Maria cried, kissing her friend.

"Yes," grinned Irici, dark eyes sparkling. "To half Brazil, we must be!"

Doubtless that was true, but it comforted Maria to know that kinfolk would rear her baby.

Lampião gave her his hands to hold during the two days she struggled to bring forth her baby, and it was he who cut the cord and slapped breath into the child, who was baptized a few days later by a friendly priest as Caterina Renata Valente dos Santos, for the parents took this opportunity to be married in church.

Caterina was beautiful. Never red and wrinkled or misshapen of skull, her tiny perfect fingers curled with tenacious strength on whatever came within their grasp. It was impossible to tell what color her eyes would be. They had that dark blue opacity that might change, and her fine hair was reddish-brown.

The baby was left with Dona Irici as the band was moving to a sheltering camp in Alagoas. The hardest thing Maria had ever done was to kiss Caterina and give her into another woman's arms.

A young Syrian filmmaker sought out Lampião and made a realistic movie of bandit life, in contrast to the sensational 1930 film *Lampião, Beast of the Northeast*. Captain Carlos Chevalier, a daredevil aviator who thrilled the capital's *cariocas* with parachute jumps, was to fly over the *cangaceiros'* field of operations and direct a force of a thousand men that would overwhelm them. *The New York Times* carried stories about Lampião. *Cangaceiro* hats were fashionable in the cities and a popular musical group wore bandit attire and billed themselves as Lampião and his Band.

Maria missed Caterina. All the time. As if her heart were gone. She tried to be cheerful in front of Roque, but she often went out in the brush and cried her eyes dry. Though the milk Caterina had not sucked had dried up painfully long ago, Maria's breasts still ached.

It would have been easier if the baby were dead. Maria couldn't have tormented herself then with wondering if her hair was still curly, if she was walking yet, what was her first word. Did she call Dona Irici "Mama"? Maria writhed in anguished envy, yet she couldn't have borne it had Caterina been with someone who wouldn't cherish her and deserve that tender name.

Caterina's first birthday was approaching. "Can't we go see her?" Maria asked Roque. "It's been six months, and that was such a little time! She didn't even get used enough to me to let me hold her."

Roque sighed, drawing her head against his chest. "Sweetheart, I love her, too, but the less we go there, the better. If the police learn we have a child there, they'll watch more closely. We might even bring trouble to Dona Irici."

Maria's yearning overwhelmed her. Not see the baby on her first birthday! She began to cry. Roque tried vainly to comfort her. At last he said, "All right, darling, we'll go. Just for her birthday." He laughed and kissed her tear-wet lashes. "We'll need a pack mule to carry all the things you've made for her since we were there last."

Not only her lovingly stitched little garments and a doll Roque had bought at a fair, but a leather stool Lampião himself had tooled. He'd been known as an excellent furniture maker and saddler before the police killed his father and he turned bandit. Dona Maria sent a hand-knit little sweater and the rest of the band contributed money. Maria didn't want that of Corisco and José Bahiano, but Roque was firm about not offending his companions.

It was a three-day ride to the ranch. They passed raw graves along the road leading to the big house, stopped with dread clutching their hearts, looking for a small one, one to hold a little girl, just one year old.

There were several like that. As they rode up the lane, there were mounds of all sizes, and the last weren't heaped with stones and had no crosses. These had been dug by animals. Bones, cloth, hair lay about like human refuse.

"Plague," said Roque.

Maria felt as if her entrails were dissolving. So many contagions could kill. Typhus, typhoid, yellow fever, smallpox. Milkpox, the mild variety, killed some children but not many adults, though it pitted many faces and left others blind. There was a vaccination for the deadly black smallpox, but like most backlanders, Maria and Roque had never had it. In fact neither had ever visited a doctor.

No one was stirring among the vaqueiro huts, the out-buildings or corrals. The rawhide door of the foreman's house hung ajar. "Stay back," Roque warned, but Maria slid from the saddle and ran forward. The place was deserted.

"Someone's in the big house," Roque said, catching her hand. "Hear that moaning?"

It carried on the faint breeze. They ran to the rancher's dwelling, stopped in the door as a wave of putrid smells assaulted them. The main room had been turned into a hospital. Men, women and children lay on beds of banana leaves. Dona Irici and a pockmarked old vaqueiro looked up from where they were tending the sick.

And it was smallpox. Bodies and faces were covered with bloated pustules, oozing or drying ones.

"Caterina?" Maria begged.

Dona Irici got to her feet. "She's all right. The children who are I've sent to a hut close to your old camp with two women who haven't had the pox. It was the safest thing, but now you've come, you can take her away."

As Dona Irici spoke, Maria saw the blisters inside her friend's mouth. She said to Roque, "You take the baby. Take her to the priest who married us and ask him to keep her till Dona Irici can send for her."

"Maria, you're coming, too!" Then his eyes widened as he saw Dona Irici's stigmata. The old man looked ready to drop and fifteen people lay on the floor.

Drawing Roque from the door, Maria threw her arms around him and kissed him. "Hurry, love. Get Caterina away from here. Give her a kiss for me."

"I can't leave you."

"You must, for her sake. When this is over, I'll come to you."

He saw she would not go, kissed her a long time and ran to the horses.

By nightfall Dona Irici was covered with blisters. As she had learned to do that afternoon, Maria punctured the pustules with a thorn, wiped away pus, wiped the sores with *cachaça*. The banana leaves didn't stick to the blisters as sheets would have done, rupturing them, making paths for frightful tunnel pox to spread great weeping abscesses down body and face.

These leaves had to be gently changed and broth and water given to those who could be coaxed to sip, for the fever parched them quickly. Maria and the vaqueiro, Cristovão, a black man, gnarled as a stump, were too busy to talk much, but as he brought in a load of dung and set it burning to purify the pestilential air, he croaked hoarsely, "God sent you, *menina*. When Don' Irici had to lie down, if you hadn't been here, I'd have given up."

He slept a few hours that night in one of the hammocks slung in the rancher's bedroom. The rancher's family had fled at the first sign of the plague to another holding, though a guest of theirs from the town had brought the disease, which Cristovão said was scourging this part of the São Francisco region. "There's only a few doctors and nurses and they're too busy vaccinating and working in the towns to worry about people like us."

Maria prayed that the plague wouldn't catch up with Roque and Caterina, that it would stop here where heaven knew it had devoured enough. An old woman died that night, and a strong young vaqueiro.

"Can't dig more graves," Cristovão grunted. "They'll have to go in the old caved-in well."

Next morning Dona Irici's eyes were closed with pus, her mouth so puffy that fluids had to be trickled down her throat with a spoon. Sometimes in her delirium she sang lullabies to Caterina, cuddling an imagined form, calling her "my baby." Maria's flesh crawled then. *Blessed Mother, don't let my baby die! If she or Roque or I must have the pox, let it be me.*

The condition of all the victims was so dreadful that Maria grew inured to stink and corruption. The wonder seemed to be that her own flesh hadn't erupted in those clear raised bumps that so swiftly became ulcers.

Night came again. Cristovão made her lie down. She slept at once and heavily till he woke her, as he had promised to do, so he could get a little rest.

Another woman died. But the fever dropped in several. The foreman, Dona Irici's husband, started scabbing over and was able to eat a little mush. Next day there were no bodies for Cristovão to scoop into a sack and carry to the pit. A frail old man passed away that night, but then slowly the rest got better, though it seemed to Maria that she and Cristovão fought the plague over every inch of a person's healing body, redeeming it one flaking bit at a time.

Maria kept waiting for the itching to start in her body, for the telltale sores in the mouth, but her skin stayed fresh and wholesome. She had lost all track of time, but she thought she must have been at the ranch at least ten days. In spite of her urgings, she had half expected Roque to come back once he'd got Caterina to the priest. She shuddered at the possibility that even his brief speaking with Dona Irici had conveyed the disease, or that Caterina had been affected in spite of the quarantine.

These thoughts tormented her. When several of the convalescents were able to look after the others, when Dona Irici was rational and regaining her strength, Maria knelt by her and said, "I'm going now, Don' Irici. In a little while I'll get Caterina back to you."

Tears squeezed from Dona Irici's eyes. "You—know I'll take care of her—love her."

"I know," said Maria.

Cristovão brought up her horse. She and the old black man embraced each other in farewell like survivors of a battle.

The priest's motherly housekeeper put Caterina into Maria's arms and smiled. "It's clear you're mother and daughter, except she's going to be a redhead." She said wistfully, "Are you taking her back to the ranch?"

"Everyone who's not dead is getting well," Maria said. "But Don' Irici's still very weak. If it's no trouble, could you keep Caterina another few weeks?"

"I'd gladly keep her forever!" The dark woman's laugh turned into a frown. "Didn't your husband turn up?"

Maria's heart stopped. Holding the baby close, like a shield from unspoken horror, she wet her dry lips. "My husband rode back toward the ranch?"

"As soon as he talked to the padre."

"He didn't get there," Maria said.

The other woman laid a sympathetic hand on her arm. "Maybe he ran into soldiers and headed the other way. They've been thick in the countryside of late. Guess they want to stay clear of towns where the plague's been at its worst."

"Maybe."

"Why don't you ride to the captain, senhora? Your husband's probably there."

Maria roused herself. "First I'll go back." She kissed Caterina again, held the warm sweet body close, and took the way to the ranch.

This time she rode slowly, following side trails till they ended, watching intently for any signs. She was several hours from the priest's when she saw where the brush had been trampled along a dry watercourse, found blurred tracks in the silt, a confusion of vaqueiro-type sandal prints and now and then a hoofmark. She knew, even before she found Roque's horse. She rode on in numbed stillness.

She was on her knees by his body when soldiers came out of the scrub.

BOOK VI
The Mother of the Waterfall

"The guard gave me a watch and told me I could come out at a certain time. He locked the door. I looked at the watch, and I realized I did not know how to tell time. There was a wind and a strange smell."

—Dream of a Mehinaku Indian from "Dark Dreams about the White Man" by Thomas Gregor, *Natural History,* January 1983

The lands inhabited by forest dwellers are inalienable as determined by federal law; permanent possession belonging to them; the exclusive use of the natural resources and of all the advantages therein contained being recognized as their rights.

—Constitution of Brazil, October 17, 1969, Article 198, Title V

The hope for the underdeveloped world lies in the transformation of the developed world.

—Dom Helder Câmara, Archbishop of Olinda and Recife

I

The Hunter Loves His Prey

"In those days," Caterina finished, "it was the practice to put the heads of bandits and their women on display in public places along the way till they reached the Nina Rodriques Institute in Bahia. My parents' heads were exhibited there as part of the Northeast's 'cultural patrimony' till I finally managed to get them buried in 1967."

Marilia, though free of fever and pain for several days, was still very weak. She turned her face away as tears began.

"You never told me."

"I thought it was too terrible to tell. But if you're going to fight it out with Janos, maybe you need to know."

Pretty Mary. Zeques, who prayed for his *patrão*. How many others? And today, so many villagers trying for the third or fourth time to scratch their living.

"How could you do it, Mother?" she burst out. "How could you have lovers of the class who drove your parents to desperation? Who put up their heads for everyone to gawk at?"

"It's not my whoring you blame, but whom I whored with?" Caterina asked, and Marilia flinched. For the first time in Marilia's memory, her mother's golden eyes were cold. Her voice was colder. "I could ask how you, who never had a day's hardship in your life that you didn't go hunting for, have the nerve to question me. If you don't know how the world works, you'd better learn. If I had gone back to open a shop or restaurant with my Free Town savings, I'd never have gotten my parents' poor heads to bury. Also, I couldn't have endowed several orphanages or sent a number of bright young men and women through the university. Over the years, I've been able to help a lot of people, people of our station.''

"You—you never explained it to me."

"It had nothing to do with you. I wasn't doing it to buy your favor."

Caterina's scornful tone stung. "I suppose it eased your conscience."

"Conscience, hell! I enjoy my house and luxuries, and by God I've earned them!''

Shamed, Marilia glanced away from the hurt, angry, beautiful face. "I'm sorry."

After a moment, Caterina said a little more softly, "Some of us survived. We had to put most of our energy into that. But you can do more, Marilia. All the women in our family would have been proud of you."

Marilia was better, but Caterina insisted she stay till she could be up for her normal stretch of working time without being exhausted. They were talking quietly on the terrace one day when Bela, the mulatta housekeeper, announced Trace Kendall.

Marilia gasped. Illness and the unfolding pageant of her ancestresses had dimmed her memory of him, but full awareness rushed back as he paused in the French doors and searched her with those dark gray eyes.

"You're looking well, Marilia. I tried to come before now, but this was the first I could get away."

"How's your study going?"

"Janos terminated it and sent me back to surveying for the Carajas Project."

"He didn't like what you told the minister about defoliants," said Caterina.

Trace sighed. "At least he hasn't started spraying." He smiled from mother to daughter. "I've brought you something that by rights should be in your family—all the way from Montana. Mother sent it with me because she felt it belonged in Brazil, and she wanted me to find someone to appreciate it. Both of you will."

Caterina got up and gave him a playful shake. "Stop tantalizing us! What is it?"

He moved inside and returned with a velvet-wrapped

object that he set on a table and uncovered, revealing a small, ornately carved and painted wall cabinet. He opened the doors, spreading them at angles. At sight of the interior, the women cried out and knelt to admire what could only be the oratorio Aleijadinho had carved two hundred years ago, in this very city, for his ward, Renata. Animals of all kinds had come to see the baby in his mother's arms. There was no cross or tortured corpse, but a flowering tree above them and bright birds flying against a blue sky.

"You can't give this away!" Caterina said. "It's too precious. And you're Renata's descendant, just as we are."

"Not in the same way. This belongs to the country as well as to the blood line."

Caterina reverently caressed the wood. To an orphan who had paid a fortune to learn about her family, the oratorio was inexpressibly marvelous.

"We can't thank you enough," she said to Trace, and Marilia nodded, awestruck.

"Dona Caterina, your daughter made me climb the slope to Santa Efigenia," Trace complained at dinner. "This town has more hills than Rome!"

Caterina smiled and asked, as she must have asked so many men so many times, "Your work is fascinating. Tell me about it."

The result of their exploring the city was that Marilia pled weariness and went to her room while Caterina was still asking shrewd questions about minimum critical-size plots and biomass. Marilia was tired, yes, but the underlying truth was that she simply hadn't been able to sit there and watch Caterina enchant this man as she had enchanted countless others.

She turned off the light and the moon spilled through the balcony doors. Slipping on a robe, for Minas nights were cool even in this hot, dry season, she stepped onto the balcony and breathed in the courtyard roses. A fountain splashed below, its waters gleaming. She leaned on the iron railing.

Street lights traced the Street of Aleijadinho running past the church where he was buried among his magnificent works. She looked past its towers and thought she could make out the dim shape of Efigenia on the high slope opposite the Hill of the Burning.

"You must love the town," he said beside her. Marilia whirled. The balcony ran along one whole side of the house, but she hadn't thought Trace might be there. She hugged her robe tightly, conscious of her nakedness beneath.

"Growing up here, I took it for granted," she admitted. "But since I left, it seems a fairy-tale place."

"You look like something out of a fairy tale."

He drew her up into his arms, mouth taking hers, pressing her thinly clad body to him. It was dreamlike, utterly still. He led her inside and sank down with her on the bed, lean strong fingers exploring her, lingering on her breasts before trailing lightly, burning, to her flanks and thighs.

When his mouth left hers, savoring her throat, she whispered his name, needing some word from him, but he only teased her tautening nipples with his tongue before closing his lips around them sensuously, gently using his teeth to make her writhe with desire.

"Trace!" she cried out in entreaty.

He laughed softly. She arched against him. He began to ease into her, but she thrust upwards to take him more deeply. He gasped and shuddered with the effort of control. They possessed each other in a storm, lightning, wild winds, and at last, release that laved her parched being like rain.

Cradled in his arms, she was too blissful to mind the silence. They'd talk later, or in the morning. She was drowsing when he disengaged himself, got up, and began to dress.

A wave of fear swept over her. "Trace?" It was the third time she had called his name and he had not answered her except by doing what he'd come for.

He bent over to kiss her. She averted her face. "Are you a zombi?" she demanded. "For heaven's sake, say something!"

"All right," he said agreeably. "What do you want me to say?"

That he loved her? That would be a lie. That he'd de-

sired her? That she already knew. Yet she longed for some
words of tenderness, something from him.

He waited, head to one side in what she took as conde-
scending patience. She could find no words to express the
needs that she thought he'd scorn. *Grow up*, she told herself. *Sex, especially for men, is often only that.*

Into that watchful silence, she could say nothing except
"Good night."

He didn't go. "Marilia, I wanted you. You wanted me.
I paid you the compliment of thinking you wouldn't want
lies or sales talk."

"I don't." Hurt slashed through her like a jagged knife.
If that was all he wanted to give her, she would take nothing.

Three days later, Marilia insisted she was fit to travel
and Caterina drove her to Belo.

"Thank you, Mother, for taking care of me," she said
as they started for her luggage. "And for telling me the
stories. When I feel discouraged I'll remember Rachel and
Janaina—all of them—especially Pretty Mary—and I'll keep
going."

Caterina smiled at her. "I can give you a little more
support than that, dear. You've told me how much time
the settlers lose in waiting for bank loans for planting crops,
and that the banks won't advance money except for certain
things that are often hard to grow. I've sent my banker
instructions to finance any loans that you okay."

Marilia was staggered. Caterina then opened the car
trunk. Beside Marilia's small duffel bag was a carton with
a carrying handle. "The oratorio. You need it more than I
do."

"But, Mother . . ." Marilia was speechless, knowing
how much the treasure meant to Caterina. "You keep it.
It might get damaged. Or lost."

"No. It belongs with you. And there's one more thing."

Caterina couldn't restrain a glow of triumph. "The defoliation's blocked."

Marilia blinked. "I—I can't believe it!"

"You can."

They embraced a last time. As the plane lifted, Marilia could still see Caterina waving.

She hadn't expected to teach when the foundation selected this place for her, or to serve as nurse-doctor, but for both needs, she was the best possibility. For the most part, people treated themselves with herbal cures picked up from the native *caboclo* families that lived in the area. The children came to Marilia because they loved to be painted with Merthiolate or adorned with Band-Aids, and the seriously ill went to Altamira in the battered old pickup Chiquino Domingos used to supply his store and hire out for hauling.

The village still lacked unity and leadership. Sinho had organized the protest to Grandeza, Adrien was the best hunter, Chiquino owned the store and truck, but so far there were no ties of family or godparentage that could mesh comparative strangers into neighbors. The village hadn't yet celebrated even Saint John's Day.

Marilia went to the nearest of the four shower sheds, lathered her hair twice to get rid of red dust caked on her scalp, and scrubbed her skin till the pores felt unclogged. Dressing in soft old jeans and shirt, she was so tired from the day's journey that she longed to go straight to bed, but she knew the villagers would want to know what news she had for them. It had taken great self-control for them not to descend on her the moment she arrived.

The men, sitting on barrels and boxes and a couple of benches, got up as Marilia entered the store. Chiquino, a massive dark man with kinky graying hair, rose from his stool behind ropes of tobacco and jars of candy.

"It's good to have you back, Don' Marilia. Are you well again?"

"Very well," she smiled, and delivered her news. If Caterina could have seen their elation! When Marilia told them that Grandeza would not be allowed to use poison spray, a cheer went up.

Adrien laughed. "While you were sick, you accomplished much, Don' Marilia."

"Not I, my mother. But Grandeza will still try to build the dam. We'll have a long fight and we may lose."

Chiquino escorted her ponderously to the door. After she was outside, a dozen voices exploded at once.

As she approached the office the next day, a small plane hummed over, angled and descended. Marilia suddenly was sick and weak. Janos?

It was. She gripped her hands tightly beneath her desk as Janos strode in. She smelled the faint spice of his lotions, a scent that, while she'd loved him, had turned her weak with desire. It brought a qualm of nausea.

"Marilia," he said, "you haven't forgotten any more than I have."

Marilia's breath lodged suffocatingly in her lungs. It was the first time she'd been alone with Janos since before their divorce. Oddly, in spite of the flood of hostile attraction between them, she felt as if they were separated from their bodies, dueling as spirits of air and flame.

"I haven't forgotten anything."

"You can't still be upset because I slept with your mother while you were a schoolgirl."

In her mind's eye, the flame that was her spirit contracted, a hurt creature turning in on itself. "If you'll remember, I'd asked for the divorce before I knew that."

"Why should you care that I evicted a bunch of dragtails who couldn't live on that land?"

"With fishing, too, they fed their families."

"They got new land in the Transamazon."

"Do you know how they fared?"

He shrugged impatiently.

"When I got back to Brazil, I tried to find out. Of the twenty families you threw off the *fazenda* so you could put in irrigated crops, only two are on the homesteads they took along the Belém–Brasilia highway. The others went deep in debt planting that disastrous type of rice that was the only crop the bank would loan them money to grow. They lost their land, went to the cities, and scattered like dust."

He stared at her. "What's it all to you, Marilia?"

"I tried to explain once." Her throat swelled at the memory. How she had pleaded, convinced that if he understood he couldn't be so ruthless. She had believed that!

"Those chronically sick, malnourished scum are sub-human. If thousands of them died, it'd benefit the country."

"It'd benefit more if the few like you who control the land and wealth were blotted out."

Janos' voice hooked into her flesh. "What's the matter, darling? Have you caught Cousin Saint Paul's brand of underdog rabies?"

She was afraid to turn her back on him and too weak to stand. "Why have you come?"

His eyes had the glint of frozen water in moonlight. "Thanks to your mother, Grandeza's been forbidden to defoliate the dam site. Our lawyers and lobbyists are on that, of course. But meanwhile I'm going to get some crews busy clearing land for our cattle and pulpwood operations."

"You—not on the Zarina Reserve and the settlers' lands?"

"No. That's where the dam will be when all this nonsense is over. Your blessed savages and *flagelados* can squat where they're at till the day we flood them out, for all I care. But Grandeza's going on with the rest of the plan."

"You are, you mean."

"Same thing." He grinned, a hard grin. "If your misfits don't like Grandeza for a neighbor, they can save everybody trouble and get out."

"You've already heard their answer to that."

"It could change."

"If you hire *jagunços* to murder and trespass—"

"Darling! You know how many hunting accidents there are."

"That can happen both ways."

"Yes, but I have to keep hiring to keep up the work force. I doubt you can recruit anyone to fill your villagers' sandals." He crossed to her in a panther-like stride. "That's not all I have to say to you, Marilia. You're mine, whatever the judge said. I turned you from a child into a woman!" His wide nostrils quivered and he clenched his hands. "You've come home to your own country. Just as surely, you'll come back to me."

"I have no man." Why did she think of Trace?

"I was your first!"

"But not the last."

"Who?" His eyes flamed.

"There were men at the university."

"You whored with Americans?"

"I didn't charge."

As if he didn't trust himself, he moved to the other end of the room. An image flashed into her mind of the "waiting," when a hunter slung his hammock above a fruiting tree and waited for his prey. Like an animal drawn to the sweet fruit it knew, she'd returned and Janos was here, at the waiting ground.

"Victor's taking me to Takara and the elders," he said. "I'm going to tell them that though the dam's delayed, clearing will begin close to their reserve. Maybe enough beads and knives will persuade them to move."

The enticements used by white men for over four hundred years. In the dim light, Janos loomed, changing, mirroring his forebears—gold seekers, diamond hunters, *bandeirantes, fazendeiros*—and along the line, an occasional Indian girl, a slave run off to the backlands.

"Offer them rifles," she suggested.

He stepped in front of her. "Don't you think you should speak to your people, give them a choice?"

"You can talk to them all you want. Most of the older men sit around in the store after supper for an hour or so."

"You won't call a meeting?"

"I'm not the mayor."

"Are there Sunday services?"

"When Paul gets around."

"I may come."

"Do as you please."

II

The Naming Feast

Marilia breathed more freely when Janos' plane took off the next morning. She went back to filling in Sinho's revised crop plan while her pupils copied spelling words from the blackboard or read their readers. Janos would be back.

A jeep growled up to her house that evening. She caught a joyful breath at sight of Paul climbing from the truck, then froze as another man got out.

What was Trace doing here? Why was she so dizzily happy? He'd left without even a scrawled note. She must not make a fool of herself over a man who'd plainly shown that all he wanted was uncomplicated sex.

"Come on in," she called, voice dry. "You can sling your hammocks in the office."

Saint Roque's Day was approaching, so the baby was named for that farmer's patron. Marilia's throat tightened as she repeated her godmother's vows. The baby squirming under Paul's ministrations embodied the hope of all the people, and she loved them fiercely.

The service was held in an arbor adjoining the store with the oratorio proudly displayed on a table. Women loaded plank tables with food. Game roasted on poles over glowing coals, and someone said the largest carcass was that of a tapir Takara had fetched at dawn.

He and a dozen Zarina men, in their most festive plumes and paint, had observed the baptism from the back of the arbor. Marilia picked up her godson as he started to fret, and the Zarina chief strode over.

Reaching into a pouch, he put a necklace of brilliant

small blue feathers around the baby's neck, spoke at some length in his own tongue, then smiled and said to Marilia, "This one must learn our ways and our language. I will teach him how to hunt. I will call him my nephew."

Trace had been at the fringe. He moved over to examine the baby with comic puzzlement.

"Is that how they're supposed to look?"

"He's a lovely child!" Marilia snapped. "Some have blotched or lumpy heads for a month or two. This one's perfect."

"Mmm." Trace stared into hazily opaque eyes that seemed to be remembering another world. He pulled off a massive gold ring with a red-brown stone. "He can wear this someday. It's hematite from our ranch, set in Black Hills gold."

Marilia laughed. "This is beginning to remind me of the stories where all the fairies at a christening party come bearing gifts."

His eyes touched her mouth. "You know I'm no fairy."

Awareness of him, a rush of desire, pierced her like a broad blade. She bent her head over the baby. "It's too bad you won't be around to take him up to the canopy."

"Oh, I expect I'll be back. As long as there are canopies."

Why should that offhand remark make her feel ridiculously happy?

Silence grew between them, was broken by the crunch of boots. "Lucky boy with such a godmother," Janos said. He nodded to Trace amiably, but his gaze was like polished steel. "Do you find this part of the forest more interesting than your new region?"

"It helps to compare." Trace didn't move.

Janos took an envelope from his pocket, extended it to Marilia. "A present for your godson. Fifty shares in Grandeza."

She gasped. "You drive his family off with one hand and give shares in your damned company with the other?"

"Call it a stake in the future."

"You may not have the future all your own way."

"Be real, my dear. What happens in the Amazon depends on what foreign business powers decide."

"Our country's a colony not just to Portugal now, but to the whole industrialized world!"

"Especially the United States." Janos shot a cold smile at Trace.

Marilia looked at Trace. His face was closed. "I'm not proud of my country's gold-star record of supporting dictators. But if men like you cared about your own people—"

Janos' voice cracked with scornful indignation. *"My* people! *Caboclos* and savages?"

And for the first time, Marilia understood something. "You—you'd really like them to all be dead!" She held the baby closer. "Out of your way."

"They drag the whole country down. Are we supposed to leave iron and gold and uranium in the ground, do without the electrical power Brazil needs, because of a scattering of Stone Agers and ne'er-do-wells?"

"And you have the nerve to come to a baptismal feast!"

"It's a good time to tell them what's going to happen." He went to Adrien and thrust the envelope into the startled father's hand, calling out to the people. His voice slashed through chatter and laughter.

"Friends, I have given the baby a gift—shares in my company. That will buy him a good farm when he's old enough, or start him in a business. My company will make gifts to all of you, pay for your homesteads and crops, if you seek other land now rather than wait till you're evicted."

There was a hum, like the sound of giant wasps who have been disturbed. Farmers closed in around Janos. He faced them arrogantly.

"We're through moving, senhor," Sinho Tavas said.

Janos glanced around. "If any of you decide otherwise, leave a message for me at the FUNAI post. Any time this week. After this week there'll be no money."

Paul's voice was quiet but clear. "If you try to take over the homesteads, I may not be able to get it in the Brazilian news, but it'll hit newspapers all over the world."

"So what good will that do?"

"If enough U.S. citizens demanded that their government stopped supporting outfits like Grandeza, they'd have to pull out."

Janos laughed. "When Americans let oil and mining companies tear up their *own* country, do you expect them to care about ours?"

"It's a hope."

Janos laughed again.

Adrien tried to hand him the envelope. "Thank you, senhor, but we don't want this."

"You'd better keep the shares. They may save you from starving."

Adrien flipped the envelope into the nearest fire. It crackled and writhed.

Janos took a step forward, checked himself. "You have this week." He strode away.

The golden noon pressed down. Men glanced at each other and women held their babies tightly. Even the children were hushed. Then Sinho said loudly to Adrien, "You know, it's time we picked a patron saint for this village."

Adrien nodded. "And time the village had a name."

Excitement released the crowd from Janos' awful spell. "But can we afford a saint's day feast?" wondered Sinho's brother-in-law. "It's no use asking a saint to be our patron if we can't honor him on his day."

"No one can donate a cow," said Sinho. "But I'll give a goat."

"I'll bring a deer or the same weight of smaller game," Adrien promised. His brother added, "I'll get plenty of big fish."

Within minutes a pig and chickens were pledged. "I'll supply beer and soft drinks," Chiquino said expansively. "But what about a church? Our saint will need a home."

"All that takes is work," said Adrien.

"For thatch and walls, yes. But a saint needs an altar and decorations and a bit of show. Not to mention that we'll have to buy his image."

Sinho looked around. "Why don't we have an auction? Each family donate whatever it can. Proceeds will buy our saint and make the church pretty."

The suggestion was acclaimed and people began to argue over which saint would best watch over their village. "He should be a farmer," Sinho said. "Otherwise he won't understand about crops and blights and rain."

"There's nothing wrong with a fisherman like Saint Peter," suggested Adrien.

Marilia, who had yielded her godson to his mother, was standing near Adrien and heard Takara come up to speak softly in his ear. Adrien glanced at his wife and child and nodded, a smile lighting his features.

"Our patron doesn't have to be a man," he called above the bickering. "Our Lady loves all her children. Takara says she is the same as the Mother of the Waterfall who takes care of babies taken from their mother's arms, and who helps those who want children. We want our fields and animals to be fruitful. Let's have for patroness Our Lady of Conception."

There was a murmur of agreement, the women looked pleased and a man from Bahia said, "Our Lady of Conception is the same as Yemanjá. A good choice."

"But her day is December 8," Chiquino objected. "That's when you'll be burning again and planting rice and corn—which can't be put off. And it's the other bad time for malaria."

"Maybe she'll protect us from malaria if we honor her," countered Sinho.

"It's a time of much fruit," Adrien pointed out.

Chiquino seized the moment to clarify the general will. He had apparently already decided to be the village's first mayor. "I propose Our Lady of Conception for our patroness," he boomed. "And that we call our village The Town of Our Lady of the Conception of the Waterfall."

"Catarata for short," whispered Adrien in the chorus of approving shouts.

Though the feast wouldn't be celebrated for months, this baptismal party of little Roque's was also Catarata's, since the people had defied Grandeza that day, taking a name and patroness, showing they were determined to survive as a settlement.

After everyone had eaten their fill, those with guitars, banjos or mouth organs brought them out. There was dancing, the *samba*, *choradinho* and *baiano* of the Northeast, and duels of making up verses on the spot, beginning with the opponent's last line.

Marilia held the baby while Adrien and Consuelo danced, so beautiful and tenderly in love that it made one's heart ache. Cuddling their child, Marilia implored: *Let life be good to them and this little one. Our Lady, Yemanjá or Zarina's Mother of the Waterfall, whoever you are, bless them.*

She didn't know Trace had come up till he said softly, "Quite some *festa*. I just hope the village isn't under water when the time comes to celebrate their patroness' day."

"They're tired of running."

He smiled grimly. "Aren't we all?"

She didn't know what to say. Consuelo took her son and Trace gave Marilia a mocking bow. "Can you teach me how to dance?"

"I'll try if you will." In spite of the humid warmth, a rush of sweet cool air seemed to fill her.

His eyes plunged to her depths. "Can you meet me tonight?"

No word of tenderness, no hint of love. But the urgency pulsing between them, the flame that fanned through her at his touch almost softened the bare words.

But the "almost" sent her back to the hurt of the morning he'd gone away without a word. In as spare a manner as his, she said, "No, I can't meet you."

His dark eyebrows rushed together. His hand tightened on her back. "Why?"

"Why should I?"

He brought her against his body. Hers wanted to cling, but she jerked away and he didn't stop her. "You damned well know why."

The dance had ended. "I'm not your unpaid whore, whatever you think." She drew free of him and marched off to her house.

Her room was dark. She leaned on the chest of drawers and wept with outrage and discouragement. As much as her starved body craved love, her heart needed it even more. But she hadn't expected wonderful things of the lovers she'd taken to forget Janos. Why was it different with Trace?

It must be that she loved him.

She cried till she was able to stop and splashed her face with water from the bucket. Instead of taking a vow of chastity, like Paul, Trace seemed to have taken a vow of sex without involvement. There was something to be said for that—though not much. Ordinarily she could have played that game. If she hadn't loved him.

It was then that she saw the object that glittered on her pillow. Picking up the silver chain, she turned its pendant to the light.

A black diamond. Renata's!

Another heirloom Trace's mother must have taken with her to Wyoming. How Caterina would love it! Though not as much as the Aleijadinho shrine, of course, which was beyond price.

Why did he give such gifts, yet withhold himself?

III

On the Floor of the Sky

Like spirits in the gray dawn, Marilia moved ahead of Trace down the trail that led to the fields. Brushing off her thanks for the diamond, he'd said he'd like to see the croplands that morning, then take her to his canopy station after the heat of the day.

The first plot they reached was Sinho's. The ring of an ax meant that he was clearing the forest at the end of the fields. Two of his sons were picking beans and breaking dried ears of corn off the stalks that had been left standing to support bean vines after the green corn harvest.

Chatting for a moment with Sinho's teenage sons, they passed the tobacco, which would be gathered next, and paused in a dense growth of manioc interspersed with bananas.

"Manioc's good cover for the soil and keeps it from leaching. The tubers can be harvested as needed, anywhere from six months after planting to two years later. Made into farinha, it stores well."

Trace cast a disgusted glance at Sinho, who was chopping at a tall tree. "And the soil's worn out in three years and more forest has to be cleared!"

"That depends on the soil. Around here about 8 percent, with rotation, can be continuously cultivated."

He stared at her as if she were an enemy. "You advocate villages like this scattered through the Transamazon?"

"No. I'm for breaking up vast ranches and *fazendas* so that common people can make a living. But your CIA pushed to discredit the peasant leagues who were working for land reform. Your government supports the generals' policy of throwing open the Amazon to huge multinationals.''

"Will you believe that I'm no prouder of my government's record here than you are of the generals'?''

"Yes, if you stop acting as if I want to level the jungle.''

They plodded on toward the new clearing.

The tree Sinho had been chopping at crashed as they approached, breaking limbs and shattering smaller trees. He took off his straw hat and wiped sweat from his face. "You're out early after such a party,'' he greeted, and pressed his hand to his head. "I can't drink the way I used to! But wasn't it a grand *festa?''*

Marilia glanced around at the thick layers of vines, bushes and small trees that had been cut a month or so before. "It looks as if you'll have a good burn.''

"May God grant it.'' He sighed with the fatalism of a farmer who knows that weather, blight and many other things are beyond his control. "There's plenty of underbrush for kindling. And I'll chop the biggest trees into sections so they'll burn better.''

Trace shook his head. "Hard work, senhor.''

"Yes, but easier than a *coivara.''*

"That's when the fire's not hot enough to do more than char the vegetation and leave big logs,'' Marilia said. "The leftover stuff has to be chopped up small and burned again with the help of kerosene.''

"Sounds like a dirty job.''

"It is, and takes more time than all the other clearing work put together. A bad burn leaves the soil more acid and prone to pests. A good burn kills parasites, insects and fungi, makes the soil less acid, and converts all the nutrients in the vegetation into ash except for nitrogen and sulfur.''

Trace nodded skeptically. "So now we get the sermon justifying slash and burn?''

Marilia smiled at him. "In just a minute, if you can restrain your enthusiasm.''

Sinho gave Trace a measuring look. "Don' Marilia knows what she's talking about. She's not like all those doctors the government sends who went to junior high school and took a short course in agriculture.''

"Some have taken the *curso tecnico,* senhor," Marilia teased, and explained to Trace, "That's a senior high program. And there are a few who're real agronomists."

"I never saw them," the farmer snorted. "Our *dotor* at my first *agrovila* never came to the fields because mosquitoes would bite where her halter didn't reach—and that was plenty! Also the mud would have ruined her high-heeled shoes. The government paid those spoiled brats a fortune and they didn't know anything, just talked snotty to us, hung around their social club and drove government cars if they were going a block away!"

"Never mind, senhor," Marilia soothed. "I don't think any of them will be coming to Catarata."

The village name made Sinho's dark eyes glow. "We're a real place now, Don' Marilia! With a patroness. What a feast we'll give her!" He glanced toward the sky. "If the good God grants it."

No one mentioned Grandeza.

Walking back around the fields, Marilia sent Trace a challenging look. "You may think slash and burn is a poor method, but even ecology institutes are using it now. Experiments in tropical places have proved that burned plots produce 30 to 60 percent more than land cleared by bulldozers and plowed. And machine clearing costs twice to twenty times what it does with machete and ax."

"There shouldn't be more clearing of any kind till we know the consequences."

"If you're going to say that half the world's yearly oxygen production comes from the Amazon—"

"I wasn't," he retorted. "I know as well as you do that only a trifling amount of the oxygen in the atmosphere is produced on earth each year. Nor am I much scared by predictions that destroying the Amazon will asphyxiate us with carbon monoxide. But we do know that where large clearings leave the ground unprotected, rains erode it and wash out the nutrients. This rapid runoff causes floods, but the bare earth soon bakes hard." He spread his arms to encompass the green forest and new fields. "This could be parched red desert in twenty years. Anything that involves two-thirds of the earth's river water and three-quarters of its rain forests must have drastic effects!"

"Better tell that to the foreign investors!"

Many trees had buttresses higher than their heads. Roots were near the surface, where fungi quickly broke up leaves and twigs, feeding them immediately back to the tree. The forest was a closed system, whole unto itself, unlike temperate-zone forests, where nutrients stayed in the ground after trees were felled.

Trace ascended the rope ladder first, swaying among vines and limbs till he disappeared above the layers of green. That was the jungle: many shades of green, countless shapes, never reached by direct sun. The only brilliant colors were long blooms of a crimson heliconia, the emerald flash of a jacamar. Disturbed owl-faced monkeys swung through the branches as Trace called, "Come on up. Orchids and hummingbirds await you!"

Telling herself that the ropes had supported him, she began climbing, not daring to look down. An iguana napped on a limb. Smooth pale strangler figs embraced the trees they were killing. Some branches were thick with ferns and air plants, aerial gardens speared with vivid red and purple flowers. Scarlet macaws screeched overhead with a loud "Raaah!" A sloth, green from algae, hung upside down from its strong claws.

When she emerged from the densest layer of leaves, those of trees up to forty feet high, she could see the more widely spaced trees of the next story. These were far enough apart to let sunlight reach the thick layer below.

Now she could see the sky, umbrella crowns of giants towering above the lower stories. She was inexpressibly relieved that Trace's station was a sturdy platform the size of a small room, with woven vine sides reaching waist-high.

"It's the most exclusive treehouse I've seen," she said breathlessly as he helped her clamber up. "But you may not get me on that ladder again!"

"You're shaking," he said, still grasping her hands.

He drew her close as if to comfort her. Her cheek rested against the pounding of his heart and her fear vanished. Then she was seized by another trembling.

His hand brought up her face. She looked into eyes

smoky as blue haze on the sea. The scent of flowers weighted the sunlight. His hands curved against her back, bringing her against him. She felt the lean, tough strength of his body and clung to him, buffeted by a storm.

His mouth came down on hers. She closed her hands at the back of his neck. He sank down with her, kissing the flesh he bared as he slowly took off her clothes, bringing her to feverish eagerness. He would have come gently into her, but she raised to meet him and they joined in struggle, joyful and fierce.

Resting in the greatest peace she had ever known, she opened her eyes to a lacy pattern of leaves diffusing the sunlight, savoring his salty male odor beneath a brisk shaving lotion, admiring the thick almost-wave of his black hair, long lashes resting above angular cheekbones, his mouth down-curved. Sun lines were etched at the corners of his eyes. She wanted to touch the faint cleft that forgave his chin some of its aggressiveness.

A man with the marks of life on him. But in rest, she saw the boy he had been, even the child. Overwhelmed with tenderness, she started to touch his face.

Warned, his eyes opened. He sat up. That youthful vulnerability left his face. He smiled, but the intimacy was gone. "Let me show you my world."

As they shared a canteen, she watched a keel-billed toucan, black with scarlet undertail and yellow face and breast, clamp his big hollow green-and-orange bill around some fruit. The purple masks of glossy blue cotingas hid stains of fruits they were gorging. Fork-tailed flycatchers snatched prey from the air. Morpho butterflies, incandescent azure, shimmered over the green expanse below. Hummingbirds whirred like large bees. Gazing across to other green trees, Marilia saw the hanging nests and the fibrous lodges of wasps and termites. A flight of red-crowned parrots flapped into a distant tree, settling like leaves after a wind.

The roots of a lush purple orchid hung free to catch moisture that it stored in the large bulb at its base. "This one has a trigger that shoots pollen and glue on any bee that brushes it. When the glue dries, the pollen sheds off on other flowers,'' Trace explained.

''Clever.''

''Yes. But some plants are only pollinated by certain moths or bats or whatever. A plant that seems useless may feed an insect that pollinates an extremely important fruit or nut tree. Plants, insects, birds, bats and rodents are so interwoven that a small break in the net can unravel whole sections. The Amazon is the world's greatest storehouse of potentially beneficial plants. That is why, for his own sake, man had better learn to walk humbly.''

She turned and caught her breath at a giant bromeliad, stripe-like purple flowers hanging from shocking-pink bracts, the pendant a foot long.

''Gorgeous!''

''Flowers can be too lovely for their own good. Did you know orchid gatherers sometimes cut down a whole tree to get one specimen that's too high to reach?''

''No!''

''Yes. One collector in Colombia cut down four thousand trees to get ten thousand of a particularly beautiful sort. Completely wiped out future orchids of that kind.''

''That's unbelievable.''

Gazing over this brilliant upper world of birds and flowers, Marilia understood Trace's anger at even subsistence slash and burn. ''You care about the forest the way I care about people.''

He drew a deep breath and tilted up her face, gave her a light kiss. ''Well, now you know what's up here. Ready to go down?''

''I don't think I'll ever be ready.''

His eyes darkened. He drew her close and they sank down together.

''Trace?''

''Mmmm?''

He touched her cheek. She turned to kiss the long brown fingers. ''I love you.''

His hand stiffened. He was so still that the hum of life around them seemed suddenly thunderous. Marilia sat up and began to dress, averting her face. ''I didn't mean that to trap you into saying something," she said tightly. "I'm sorry you find it such a terrible burden."

"Marilia—"

"Don't you dare feel sorry for me, damn you!"

He took her by the shoulders. "I don't. It's a good thing, being able to love."

She stared at him, heart sinking at the sadness in his tone. "What do you mean?"

"I care about you. When I see you, I want you till I ache."

Hope flashed across her face. "Well, that sounds as if . . ."

He shook his head. "I loved one woman. My wife."

"You—you're married?"

"I was."

She chewed at this for a long moment. "Maybe there's a special way to love each person. Do you think? I loved Janos—or my idea of him." Searching Trace's troubled eyes, she felt each word torn from her. "If you still . . . feel that deeply . . . maybe you can get her back. Why don't you try?"

"She's dead."

Ashamed of the tide of relief that flooded her, she pitied the woman who had lost her young life and this man. "Trace," she said gently, "you're mourning her?"

He released her and turned away, voice breaking. "I mourn Nguyet. Her people. My friends who died."

Slowly she understood. "Your wife—was Vietnamese?"

"Yes. So beautiful it hurt. So small I felt I held a bird I had to be careful not to crush. Our little girl, she would have looked exactly like Nguyet."

Dread built in Marilia. She didn't want to hear this.

"She was a year old. Just starting to walk." He buried his face in his hands. "She probably ran to the men who killed her. She loved everybody. And Nguyet—"

His breathing was husky. Marilia was afraid to touch him.

"They killed her, too. Because she was my woman."

He shuddered as if racked. "What they did—it makes me crazy to think of it. It makes me want to kill everybody in the world."

"She wouldn't want that of you."

"No." He gulped air. "No. If she could, she'd forgive them—and me."

"Can't you believe she has?"

The laughter that rocked out of him was more horrible than grief. "Playing psychiatrist? I've been to experts."

"You've got to forgive yourself."

He got up and began to dress. "Leave it, Marilia. It's time we got back to earth."

She didn't see him alone again. He left with Paul early the next morning.

IV

A Good Day for Burning

Chiquino hauled the last of the rice to market and each family gave a bit of cash toward the feast. The men who were through felling big trees on their new clearings started building the church, a thatched shelter on stilts with one end walled to protect the altar.

Chiquino could read and had a prayer book, so on the first Sunday the church was usable, the villagers held services. Aleijadinho's oratorio had the place of honor. Since there was no priest, they had no formal communion, but women brought manioc cakes and these were broken, with prayer, and shared.

It was October. The villagers grew nervous at each shower. The longer the clearings dried, the better they'd burn, but it would be disastrous if the heavy rains began before the plots were fired. After a space of six days without showers, they decided they'd better not wait any longer.

At noon the men went out with cans of kerosene and torches. It was a hot day with a slight breeze that would carry the blaze, a good day for burning. Smoke filled the sky, and Marilia was glad Trace wasn't there.

Adrien and his brother had clearings the farthest away.

When they came in that evening, grimy from the burning, they had ominous news. From their clearing, above the crackling of the fires, they'd heard heavy motors and rending crashes. Hurrying through the forest, they'd paused at its verge and watched, petrified, as two enormous tractors uprooted trees with immense angle plows.

"I've never seen anything like it," Adrien muttered. "Great trees wrenched out by their roots, the soil red and torn as if it were bleeding! Some birds and animals will get away, but many will perish.''

Everyone looked dazed. Consuelo hugged little Roque to her breast. The sight of her godchild strengthened Marilia even before she realized that the people had turned toward her.

"Did you see Senhor Janos?" she asked.

"He was in a jeep."

Her voice failed. Then she managed clearly, "There's no need to worry right now."

Ranged about Janos were a dozen tough-looking *jagunços* with pistols and rifles. As Marilia came down the road, she saw him lounging against the jeep. He waved to her.

She had always hated to see a tree come down, even when a man like Sinho did it to feed his family and attacked the trunk with only a single-headed ax, risking injury. That gave dignity to the death of the tree. There was a battle before it crashed.

This was no battle; it was carnage. A heavy chain was fastened between the tractors, weighted in the middle with a steel ball eight feet in diameter. As the machines ground forward, the chain caught trees and jerked them up by their dense, shallow roots, devastating the thin, fragile topsoil. When rains came, they'd batter the exposed earth, baking aluminum clays to an impenetrable surface.

"My American partners got us a good deal on these thirty-five-ton Caterpillar D-9s," Janos called to her. "Can you believe they clear two and a half kilometers of jungle in an hour?"

"Even you—"

His eyes glowed quicksilver. She fought her horror under control. "Janos, stop it! Please."

He laughed. "It's worth all this, bringing the Caterpillars out, to hear you ask a favor."

"I'm begging, if that's what you want."

Each moment ripped out the lives of a score of trees. She dreaded to think of small, secret creatures trapped in the heaps of wreckage, cut by giant plows, smashed by tree trunks. The canopy lay slaughtered, the floor of the sky, probably some of the trees she'd been able to see from Trace's station.

Tears streamed down her face. She caught Janos' arm. *"God damn you,* make them stop!"

"If I do, will you come back to me?"

She shrank away, mute.

Shrugging, he glanced at his platinum watch. "It'll only take a week to clear enough for the pulpwood plantation, then another week for the cattle pasture."

"Pasture! Do you think grass will grow after this?"

"Won't have to be much for Grandeza to get its tax breaks."

"Janos, I'll sleep with you a week or a month if you'll let the forest live."

"A week? A month?" His mouth curled in derision. "I can buy whores." He took her by the shoulders. Eyes of bright steel drove into her. "I want my woman."

"I'm not your woman."

"You are. You will be till one of us is dead."

She wrenched away. "Then I hope you die soon."

He laughed. She fled.

It seemed she could hear his voice even above the splintering, crashing forest.

Marilia ran to the FUNAI agency and eventually spoke with the foundation secretary, waited for her to phone Ouro Prêto, and learned that Caterina was in Rio, unreachable.

"But I'll see she gets your message," the woman promised. "Meanwhile, I'll be in touch with the foundation's friends in government." She hesitated before saying reluctantly, "I'm afraid there's not much we can do. Grandeza's within its rights and the government's desperate for investors to open up the Amazon."

"It's being butchered, not opened up! It's going to make a wasteland."

"I'll do what I can." The secretary spoke in the voice of one who had lived a long time in Brasilia.

Marilia made her way along the rocky trail to the waterfall and sat down there, burying her face in her hands. *Oh, Mother of the Falls, if you're really there, help us! Protect your forest. Protect your people.* She wept against a stony ledge. Even in her despair she seemed to hear that enchanted village beneath the falls, children laughing, crooned lullabies, faint sweet music. And then she felt a presence.

Sitting up, she glanced at the cascading froth, almost expecting to see a woman's form shimmering in the play of waters, but there was only the magnificent breaking plunge over the rocks as dark green river changed to glittering spray. Then she felt movement behind her. He heart stopped.

Janos?

She turned slowly, expelling her breath as Takara said, "What's wrong, Dona Marilia?"

In a few words, she told him. He made a hissing sound, patted his blowgun. "A few darts—"

"No. Police or the army would move in."

Takara grinned. "But we're heathen, wards of the government, Dona Marilia. Indians have never been officially punished for killing settlers."

"These aren't settlers. At the very least, you'd be moved. Nothing would be gained."

Takara pondered. "The drivers and gunmen. They're *caboclos?*"

"Looked to be."

"Then they'll have fears of the jungle. They'll believe in the spirits that take vengeance when animals or trees are wantonly destroyed."

"Takara, don't do anything that'll give anyone an excuse to shoot."

The butterfly wings painted around his eyes moved gently with his smile. "Don't worry, Dona Marilia. Can gunmen shoot the *mãe de seringa* who guards rubber trees? The *mãe de piassava* who punishes those who harvest piassava in a way that hurts the tree? The nymph who drowns greedy fishermen? Or Curupira who is guardian to all the forest, especially its creatures?"

If only these guardians existed! Rising, she shook Takara's hand. "I hope the spirits help us. We're going to need it."

That night the villagers gathered in the church, bringing candles if they had any, beseeching their patroness and name saints to halt Grandeza and preserve Catarata.

* * *

It had been a good burn. Families began to put in rice and corn and most were trying millet in poorer soils. There was no word from the foundation or Caterina. It was a time of waiting and dread. It took great courage for the villagers to plant with monster machines ripping out the forest's heart so close by they could hear it all.

One morning a motor roared to a halt outside the office. There were heavy steps on the porch—boots, not sandals or whispering bare feet. Marilia reached the door just as, from the outside, Janos did.

His eyes scalded her. "Did you or your *flagelados* poison my men?"

She stared. "I don't know what you're talking about."

"My drivers, most of the guards— I got back yesterday to find work stopped, my crews staggering around like zombis. The ones who recovered are scared and want to quit. They think the forest is after them." He crossed his arms and stared at her. "I say they were poisoned."

"How?"

"You tell me."

Takara was in Marilia's mind, but she said quickly, "Food spoils fast here, especially fish."

"This isn't ordinary food poisoning. It's more like a nerve toxin."

"You'd better get them to a doctor."

"If I take them to Altamira, they'll never come back."

"It doesn't sound as if they're much good to you now."

His jaw ridged. "I'm going to find out who caused this. If your village was in on it, I'll bulldoze it into the ground."

"That might be a good way to get shot."

He showed his teeth. "Oh, I'll bring in a crack detachment of jungle commandos if I have to. And you won't get help from the Zarina. FUNAI's sending Takara and the hotheads to a reeducation camp."

"To jail?"

"Let's just say they won't get out till they learn to be reasonable."

"I'll protest to FUNAI headquarters."

"Over Victor's radio?"

"Yes. And I'll get the foundation to bring pressure."

He laughed outright. "You mean you'll ask your mother to sleep with all her buddies in the government?"

"What do you mean by that?"

He mocked her surprise. "You don't know?"

"Know what?"

He raised a broad shoulder. "Caterina *is* the foundation. How did you think the foundation just happened to offer you a job when you got fed up with the government's bureau?"

So Caterina had been supporting the foundation and giving Marilia a job! Shame washed through her. Pushing it back to deal with later, Marilia met Janos' amused gaze.

"Where is Takara?"

"Do you think I'd tell you?"

Fear chilled her. "He—he's not dead?"

"Not even scratched. Soltas explained to him that if he and certain warriors didn't get peacefully into the truck for a vacation in another FUNAI compound, the army would be called in to move the whole village."

A soft voice came from the log steps. "Do you need anything, Dona Marilia?"

Adrien dropped the white-lipped peccary he had shot but kept his rifle. Janos strode toward the young *caboclo*, towering over him. "Maybe you know what the dona doesn't. Has someone sold tainted meat or fish to my men?"

"They are sick?" Adrien's sensitive features showed surprise followed by relief. "I've had nothing to do with them, senhor. As far as I know, none of us has."

"I suppose you'll say forest goblins did it!"

"Who knows?" shrugged Adrien. "Perhaps they ate puffer fish without preparing them correctly. My uncle died from that, paralyzed, glassy-eyed."

Janos' eyes narrowed. "Puffer fish?"

"There are several kinds. They're tasty. But they're deadly poison if they're not well cleaned."

Marilia said, "Before you start accusing everybody in sight, you'd better be sure your men didn't catch and eat the wrong kind of fish. Or something like that."

"I'll find out what happened. And I'll be back with another crew."

"Maybe not, if the men you try to hire find out what happened to this bunch."

"I'll bring in drivers and guards from Miami if I have to." He paused. "If my next crew has trouble—any kind of trouble—I'll see that there's not a stick left standing here, not a leaf in the fields."

In a tone of bewildered innocence, Adrien asked, "But, senhor, is that any different from drowning Catarata, as you intend?"

Janos looked as astonished as if an animal had spoken. "You'll get what you deserve. If that means you're buried under the rubble of your shanties, that's fine with me."

He gunned the engine, churning dust that settled some time after he had gone. Marilia probed Adrien's unreadable gaze. "Is that true, Adrien? About the fish?"

"Too true for my poor uncle."

"Then you think the poisoning was an accident?"

"God knows." He smiled. "Maybe it was a mother of the forest who made the *jagunços* sick."

His smile faded as she told him what had happened to Takara and his warriors.

"If the senhor brings bulldozers to Catarata, some of the men will die before we do."

"You're young. You can start over."

"And over and over, like Sinho?" Adrien shook his head. "If I die, Consuelo can tell our son his father was no coward."

"Yes, that'll put food in his mouth."

Adrien gave her a blank stare, then bent to sling the peccary over his shoulder.

V

The Waiting Ground

Caterina flew in next day and sent her pilot on to Manaus for Paul. Victor Soltas drove her from the agency in his jeep, abjectly dazzled by her beauty and importance. Marilia, embracing her mother, got wry amusement from Soltas' attempts to seem friendly. He had always been Janos' man.

"I am completely at your orders, senhora." He bowed, and Caterina smiled at him, a sinuous feline teasing a shabby, fascinated rodent. "You are kind, Senhor Victor. I'm glad you're disposed to be helpful because I have with me a letter from the chief of FUNAI instructing you to release immediately some Zarinas mistakenly taken into custody."

His jaw dropped. "But—but—Senhor Janos—"

"You don't have to do anything but cooperate," she said amiably. "The order was sent yesterday from Brasilia to your superiors in Manaus. They're instructed to return Takara and the other warriors by official vehicle."

Soltas scanned the letter. Sweating, he licked his lips. "I removed them for their own safety," he whimpered. "They poisoned a Grandeza crew! Does my chief know about that?"

"He knows that was an excuse to break Zarina resistance. He may or may not care about that, but I happen to know things he is most anxious to keep private." She beamed. "Don't fret, Senhor Victor. In this matter I can twist bigger tails than Senhor Janos."

Caterina visited the fields, chatted with the women. She wanted to see the oratorio. It was in the church. When she

373

rose from kneeling, her eyes were bright with tears. "That our branch of the family, *flagelados* and outcasts, should inherit this wonderful thing! Marilia, if you wanted a child for no other reason, you must have one to take care of the oratorio."

Thinking of Trace always brought a wave of grief and longing. "There's only one man I'd have children by, and his heart's in a grave."

"Trace?"

Marilia nodded, unable to speak. Caterina touched her shoulder. "Don't give up. He's a good man, I can tell that. And since he hasn't found a way to die, more of him wants to live than doesn't."

After a moment Marilia said, "Janos told me about the foundation."

"That bastard," Caterina said ruefully. "He finds out everything."

"It was stupid of me not to guess. Why didn't you tell me?"

"At first I didn't want you to think I was doing it to improve your opinion of me. Later, I was afraid you wouldn't work for something I supported." Caterina looked directly at her daughter. "Does it make a difference?"

"I don't know," Marilia said slowly. "I certainly won't quit during this fight with Grandeza. After that—I can't say."

Caterina braced as if against a blow. "You'll have to decide, of course." She turned back to the oratorio. "I wonder if the village would let me supply the *santa*. I'm nervous about what ants and humidity might do to our heirloom."

"The *santa* might mean more if Catarata paid for it."

"The money that's being raised could throw a glorious feast. Besides, I have a special devotion to Our Lady of Conception."

"I didn't know you believed in any of that."

Caterina put out the tip of her tongue. "There's lots you don't know about me. I've been a daughter of Yemanjá ever since I attended her feast in Bahia and she entered into me." Laughter pealed at Marilia's startled expression. "They say I danced gloriously."

"You must have had plenty to drink."

"Just a sip of *cachaça*, prim one." As was so often the case, Marilia couldn't guess if her mother was serious. "Let me ask the people. If I put it as a favor to me, a way to honor my special *santa*, they may agree."

"Have you ever failed to get what you wanted?" Marilia asked with grudging admiration.

"Many times," Caterina said soberly. "And I have to warn you that Grandeza stands to win this war. I could get the Zarina freed, no problem, but when it comes to building the dam or clearing forest, Janos can proceed with that so long as he doesn't use defoliants."

"There's no way of pressuring Grandeza?"

"American investors supply money and leave the rest to Janos. I've pulled every string I can, but there's no way the government will intervene. Even honest politicians are all for anything that looks like progress."

Paul flew in next morning, and Takara and his men arrived that afternoon. After letting his people see that he was alive, though one eye was shut and his lips were split and bruised, Takara came to hear mass, which was being held before dark.

After the service, Caterina winningly convinced the people that they would do her a great favor by letting her provide the Virgin's image. During the acclaim, a tall man moved swiftly to the altar and the applause died. Janos gave Caterina a mocking nod.

"Cousin Paul," he said to the priest, "I'm afraid you haven't taught your flock that poisoning is a sin."

"Poisoning?" Paul frowned.

"No one's confessed to you? Well, they'd better confess to me." His metallic eyes found Marilia. "My men had tetrodotoxin in their systems, the poison secreted by a kind of puffer fish. But they hadn't eaten fish for several days. Somebody sneaked puffer gonads and livers into the cook pot. The only men who didn't get sick were those who skipped beans because they were having diarrhea."

"Even if someone poisoned the food, you can't take it for granted it was a villager," said Marilia.

"At first I blamed Zarinas," Janos admitted. "But when

I learned how it was done, I knew an Indian couldn't have slipped into camp unnoticed. A *caboclo* could. To the guards, he'd look like a worker grabbing a bite to eat." He glanced around the church. "Any man here might have done it."

Silence.

"Whoever did it had better own up. I won't kill him, just turn him over to the police in Altamira."

Women glanced fearfully at their husbands. No one spoke.

"My men aren't going to die," Janos went on. "Chances are good they won't have any lasting damage. The guilty person won't be charged with murder. But if he doesn't surrender, this village is going to burn. Look outside."

The villagers peered from the unthatched part of the church, shrank as they saw men with rifles and revolvers ranged around them. Men with blazing torches were stationed throughout the village.

Adrien turned back and looked at Janos. "I did it."

Janos' eyes blazed in triumph. He clamped a hand on Adrien's shoulder. Takara came forward.

"My brother lies to save me," he said in his faultless Portuguese. "I dressed like a *civilizado* and dropped in the puffer parts." He grinned tauntingly at Janos. "Did your doctors tell you there was more than fish guts in your stew? I put in special toads that affect the heart and nerves."

"So you did do it, you heathen bastard!" Janos drew his revolver. Before anyone could move, he crashed the barrel down on Takara's head.

Blood welled from his scalp as the chief sank to the floor. Adrien and Paul knelt beside him. Marilia bent to stanch the flow of blood with the shawl Consuelo offered.

Caterina said to Janos in a matter-of-fact way, "Look, friend and son-in-law, you and I are realists. I know Grandeza can build its dam and clean out this village and the Zarina. But there'll be a stink and the bribes will have to get bigger. Why don't we see if there's not some way to compromise?"

"I tried," growled Janos. "If your daughter had listened—"

"I'll listen," Caterina promised. She linked her arm

through his. "Tell your men to put out those torches and let's talk this over. You could start by showing me what's going to happen to the waterfall. I hope there'll be a way to spare it, but . . ."

The torches were ground out and Janos and Caterina moved off together, like lovers.

A feeling of being betrayed by Caterina kept Marilia from catching up with them immediately. The pair paused on the rocks above the waterfall, and Marilia watched. Janos made gestures. Then Caterina put her arms around him. Her hands closed behind his neck, drawing his mouth down to hers.

Marilia stood transfixed. And then, Janos' hair pure silver, Caterina's a blaze of copper in the setting sun, they engaged in a curious dance that lifted them into the air, outlined against the crystal plunge of the water.

As they vanished, Marilia screamed. Shadows streaked by her, but she scarcely saw them. *Caterina! Mother! Don't die!* She ran. Someone caught at her, but she kicked off her shoes and dived for the deeper water beyond the thunder of the cascade.

Through green water she saw her mother's body. Setting a hand beneath Caterina's head, she fought to the surface, gasping, holding the pale face above the water. Blood trickled from a gash on Caterina's forehead, mixed in the wavelets.

"Mother!" Marilia cried above the crashing falls, but she couldn't hear herself. How long had Caterina been stunned from the impact of striking water from that distance?

Strong arms were lifting Caterina, helping Marilia up onto the rocks. Adrien and Sinho placed Caterina over a ledge, face down, and water poured from her nose and mouth. Marilia crept to her and pressed a limp hand to her cheek.

"She's all right," Paul said as Caterina moved feebly and spluttered.

An arm closed around Marilia. "How about you?"

Trace!

She wasn't dreaming. His hand went over her neck and

shoulders as if to make sure they weren't broken. "What a fool thing! Adrien and Sinho would have pulled your mother out. You might have split your head open!"

"It's my head," she said with hauteur. "What are you doing here?" She blinked. "Janos?"

"We can't find him, Dona Marilia," Sinho called out. "We dived under the falls and searched as far as we could. The Mother of the Falls has taken him."

Marilia cried to her mother, "Why did you do that? It was suicide!"

Caterina laughed. Bronze hair streaming in the last light, she might have been the guardian of the waterfall. "I believed Our Lady would save me. Instead it was you."

"What else could I do?" Marilia retorted. "You're the only mother I have." She added slowly, "The only one I want."

Then they were in each other's arms and it was as if everything but their love had washed away in the current.

On the eighth of December, the village of Our Lady of the Conception of the Waterfall celebrated its patroness' feast. The marriage of Marilia and Trace was blessed by Paul before the altar where a dark Madonna in white and aquamarine stood on a crescent moon with a waterfall behind her.

Zarinas added drumming and fluting to the guitars, and when Takara, hairline slightly puckered by a healing gash, danced with Caterina, everyone shouted approval. Returning the day before from Brasilia, Caterina had brought word that Grandeza's American investors had abandoned the project since their Brazilian front man was dead.

"We've won for a little while," Marilia said, so blissful in her husband's arms that she was floating. "I'll want to come back whenever we can. It's our village, Trace."

"We'll always come for this feast," Trace promised. "And try for your godchild's saint's day, too." He whirled in a wide circle. "I don't know whether to be mad or glad that you can work with Paul's Land Committee just down the road from where I'm clambering around in the canopy."

"Be glad," she said, lifting her mouth to his, her heart overflowing with love for him and hope for her people. "Oh my dear love, let's be glad!"

Caboclo, mazombo, cabra, jagunço,
Tupi, Guaraní, Tapuya, Caeté,
Flute names. Drum names.
Ashanti, Dahomey, Minas and Bantu.

English, Dutch, Frenchmen,
Swiss and Italian,
Japanese, German, all *caboerias,*
Mix in with Portuguese,
Moors and New Christians.

Ask the sun's blessing,
Dance for the fire bull,
Call the *orixás,*
Kneel to the saints.

All mothers' sons
For their fathers don't know them;
Yellow earth, red earth,
Black, white and chocolate,
When the seed's sprouted,
We'll guess the father.

Author's Note

First and deepest thanks for help with this book go to Dr. Don Worcester of Texas Christian University, Fort Worth. Don encouraged and advised me from the start, read the manuscript, and loaned me countless books from his Brazilian collection. His concise and flavorful *Brazil: From Colony to World Power* (Scribners, New York, NY, 1973) has been on my desk for reference throughout the writing of this novel. I very much appreciate the interest of his wife, Barbara, who loaned me her material on Aleijadinho and persuaded me to visit his masterwork at Congonhas do Campo.

Dona Eunice Ribeiro of Bom Jardim, Marajó Island, was a superb hostess and gave us a delicious introduction to Brazilian food and life on a *fazenda*. Much farther up the Amazon, our guide, Bader Chavez of Iquitos, Peru, was unfailingly eager to show and tell us all he could about the river, its plants, wildlife, and people. Juscelino and his lady shared with us the last night of Carnival in Bahia. My husband, Bob Morse, was a resilient companion whose knowledge of birds and natural history added immensely to our experience of Brazil. One bird excursion brought us into an open-air shrine dedicated to the African deities. I also appreciate the insights of Felice Loffredo, Lynda Miller, and Mary Jane Yaroch, all teachers in São Paulo, and the loan of a rare book from Lois Mamer of Tubac, Arizona. During long months of writing, the patience and support of my editor, Jan DeVries, and of my agent, Claire Smith, have been not only invaluable but necessary. Warm thanks also to Myrtle Kraft, and the staff of the Cochise County Library, who zealously solicited books for me through interlibrary loan.

The following sources are highly interesting, and I recommend them to anyone who has enjoyed this book:

The Amazon, John Man, ed. (Time-Life International, Amsterdam, Netherlands)

Amazon Jungle: Green Hell to Red Desert, R. J. A. Goodland and H. S. Irwin (Elsevier Scientific Publishing Company, New York, NY, 1975)

The Bandeirantes, Richard M. Morse, ed. (Knopf, New York, NY, 1965)

The Bandit King, Billy Jaynes Chandler (Texas A&M University Press, College Station, 1978)

"Colonization Lessons from a Tropical Rain Forest," Nigel J. H. Smith (*Science*, November 1981)

"Dam the Amazon, Full Speed Ahead," Catherine Caulfield (*Natural History*, July 1983)

Developing the Amazon, Emilio F. Moran (Indiana University Press, Bloomington, 1981)

The Dutch in Brazil, C. R. Boxer (Clarendon Press, Oxford, 1957)

Explorations in the Highlands of the Brazil, Richard R. Burton (London, England, 1869)

Food First, Frances Moore Lappé and Joseph Collins (Ballantine Books, New York, NY, 1981)

The Golden Age of Brazil, C. R. Boxer (University of California Press, Berkeley and Los Angeles, 1962)

The Heart of the Forest, Adrian Cowell (Knopf, New York, NY, 1961)

Lost Empires; Living Tribes, Ross S. Bennett, ed. (National Geographic Society, Washington, D.C., 1982)

The Mansions and the Shanties, Gilberto Freyre; Harriet de Onis, trans. (Knopf, New York, NY, 1968)

The Masters and the Slaves, Gilberto Freyre; Samuel Putnam, trans. (Knopf, New York, NY, 1956)

Rebellion in the Backlands, Euclides da Cunha; Samuel Putnam, trans. (University of Chicago Press, Chicago, IL, 1944)

Red Gold, John Hemming (Harvard University Press, Cambridge, MA, 1978)

Tereza Batista, Jorge Amado; Barbara Shelby, trans. (Avon Books, New York, NY, 1977)

"Tropical Rain Forests: Nature's Dwindling Treasures," Peter T. White (*National Geographic*, January 1983)

United States Penetration of Brazil, Jan Knippers Black (University of Pennsylvania Press, Philadelphia, 1977)

Victims of the Miracle, Shelton H. Davis (Cambridge University Press, Cambridge, MA)

The Violent Land, Jorge Amado; Samuel Putnam, trans. (Avon Books, New York, NY, 1979)

Jeanne Williams
Cave Creek Canyon, Arizona
January 21, 1986